"*A Rebel Heart* checks all the boxes on my wishlist for a satisfying novel. It brings a lesser-known slice of history to life and deals honestly with our national past. The characters are colorful and compelling, the setting richly painted, and the high-stakes plot carries the reader to the end without ever slowing down. Full of intrigue, grit, and grace, *A Rebel Heart* is Beth White at her finest. I can't wait to read the rest of the series."

Jocelyn Green, award-winning author
of *A Refuge Assured*

"With great skill, Beth White combines intriguing history with inspiring romance, and then adds a good measure of mystery and suspense to her newest novel, *A Rebel Heart*. From the first page to the last, readers will be wrapped up in Selah's quest to restore her family's stately Mississippi home and charmed by the touching romance. Levi's investigation to solve a series of robberies and find out who is behind the mysterious incidents that threaten Selah and her family will keep readers guessing and turning pages until the very end. Well done!"

Carrie Turansky, award-winning author
of *Shine Like the Dawn* and *Across the Blue*

"Pinkerton agent Levi Riggins stole my heart, beginning with his valiant rescue of Selah Daughtry after a train wreck in the opening scenes of *A Rebel Heart*. Selah couldn't help but lose her heart too, although she has more than one reason to be wary of the former Yankee officer. Beth White's careful historical research shines throughout this novel, as do her wonderful characters. Highly recommended."

Robin Lee Hatcher, Lifetime Achievement Award–winning
author of *You're Gonna Love Me*

Praise for *The Gulf Coast Chronicles*

"White's carefully researched story, set in what would become Mobile, Alabama, is filled with duplicity, danger, political intrigue, and adventure. This unique book will appeal to a wide range of readers."

Booklist

"A lush and highly detailed historical setting sets an atmospheric tone for this tale of love and life in New France. The well-researched story of the Pelican girls, so named for the ship that brought them, is an unembellished look at a slice of the human experience not often told. Recommended for fans of historical fiction."

Library Journal

"This book is a must-have for any historical fiction collection; few stories are written on this time period and area."

Congregational Libraries Today

REBEL HEART

Books by Beth White

GULF COAST CHRONICLES

The Pelican Bride
The Creole Princess
The Magnolia Duchess

DAUGHTRY HOUSE

A Rebel Heart

REBEL HEART

BETH WHITE

Revell

a division of Baker Publishing Group
Grand Rapids, Michigan

© 2018 by Elizabeth White

Published by Revell
a division of Baker Publishing Group
PO Box 6287, Grand Rapids, MI 49516-6287
www.revellbooks.com

Printed in the United States of America

Library of Congress Cataloging-in-Publication Data
Names: White, Beth, 1957– author.
Title: A rebel heart / Beth White.
Description: Grand Rapids, Michigan : Revell, [2018] | Series: The Daughtry house series | Includes bibliographical references and index.
Identifiers: LCCN 2017057414 | ISBN 9780800726898 (pbk. : alk. paper)
Subjects: LCSH: Man-woman relationships—Fiction. | GSAFD: Christian fiction. | Love stories.
Classification: LCC PS3623.H5723 R43 2018 | DDC 813/.6—dc23
LC record available at https://lccn.loc.gov/2017057414

ISBN 978-0-8007-3515-9 (casebound)

Scripture used in this book, whether quoted or paraphrased by the characters, is taken from the King James Version of the Bible.

This book is a work of historical fiction; the appearances of certain historical figures are therefore inevitable. All other characters, however, are products of the author's imagination, and any resemblance to actual persons, living or dead, is coincidental.

The author is represented by MacGregor Literary, Inc.

18 19 20 21 22 23 24   7 6 5 4 3 2 1

For Jan Johnson, who listens
and makes me laugh and think harder.

PROLOGUE

April 20, 1863
Ithaca Plantation

Selah could hear the horses thundering closer, oncoming hell and destruction. Cowering in the darkness under the porch with her arms around Joelle, she felt her sister's body heave with great, gulping, silent sobs. She had no idea how Mama had known they were coming, but thank God they'd had time to hide.

"Get under the porch, girls!" Mama had screamed, cloak billowing as she ran up the path from the gate.

Mama, who never ran, never raised her voice.

Dropping their books and sewing, Selah and Joelle ran down the steps and scuttled backward into the hidey-hole they'd loved as children. Their full skirts took up most of the space, and the thought of mice and spiders made Selah's scalp crawl.

"Mama, aren't you coming in too?" Joelle asked as their mother replaced the latticework and pushed at it to make sure it was secure.

"I have to warn the servants, make sure they get somewhere safe. Now back up out of sight, pray hard, and don't make a sound no matter what you hear. If something happens to me, I want you to go to Grandmama and Grandpapa in Memphis."

"Mama!" Selah burst out. "What—"

"Do what I say!" Mama's eyes blazed. "Promise me, Selah!"

"Of course." Selah wasn't going to cry. She was nineteen years old—a grown woman, for mercy's sake. But she wasn't going to Memphis like her little sister Aurora had either. Papa had left her in charge of Ithaca, made her promise to watch out for Mama and Joelle.

Mama's mouth relaxed a bit. "This will be over soon, and we'll have a silly story to tell over tea this afternoon." She stood, and her skirts had whisked out of sight.

Now the horses galloped closer until they pulled up at the hitching rail near the porch, snorting and blowing in the cold air. The riders dismounted, hooting and hollering, and Selah knew they must be drunk.

"We're free, boys," one man said, chortling. "Let's see what we can find to juice a celebration."

Through the lattice Selah saw butternut uniform legs and leather boots, heard the jingle of spurs and clank of sabers. If they were Confederate soldiers, why had Mama made her and Joelle hide? They'd entertained Rebel officers here before—two Christmases ago, in fact. Why would they hurt the women of this house, whose master had sacrificed everything to fight the Yankees up in Tennessee?

Maybe Mama was confused—

"These big plantations always have good whiskey."

That was a different soldier, and Selah noticed something

funny about his accent. He didn't sound Southern at all. Come to think of it, the first one hadn't either. Northerners in butternut? She'd heard about the spies riding with that devil Grierson. Tricking Confederate outposts into delivering false messages, and taking over rail depots and tearing up track.

Joelle whimpered, and Selah clamped a hand over her mouth. "Shhh!" They sat rigid, until Selah heard boots clomping across the porch overhead. She thought she counted four sets of boots going up the steps, then got confused. How many were there? Was it a whole unit? She let Joelle go and whispered, "Not another sound. They're Yankees—no telling what they'd do to us."

Joelle nodded.

The front door opened, then the voices and noise of boots faded into the house. Apparently they'd left the door open. Selah and Joelle sat there for a long time, cramped, sweating, shuddering, listening to the sound of glass breaking and furniture being dragged around in the parlor. If they found Papa's liquor cabinet—

Where was Mama? *Oh, God, let her be safe.*

The men were laughing now, the voices growing louder and the jokes more off-color. Selah didn't understand half of what they said and prayed Joelle didn't either. "Jesus, have mercy," she whispered into the top of her sister's head. Maybe they'd get so drunk they'd pass out. Then maybe she could sneak out and get Papa's hunting rifle from the office—

She jumped when a woman's shriek ripped from inside the house. Seconds later, a gunshot cracked, and Selah pressed Joelle's head into her shoulder to stifle her scream. What had just happened? That might have been her mother screaming, but it was hard to tell in the chaos of scuffling, furniture hitting walls, another gunshot.

"No, stop! Oh please, you cannot—" The frantic voice choked on muffled squeals.

The men burst into raucous laughter and cheers, while bumps and thumps shook the floor.

The noise went on and on, until Selah thought she might suffocate from rage and terror. Papa had taught her to shoot, and if she'd had a weapon she could have gone to her mother's defense. But she didn't, and anyway, she couldn't leave Joelle alone. They had to stay here, listening to the horror above their heads. The tiny space seemed to shrink around them.

Eyes squeezed shut, breath caught high in her throat, Selah prayed for it to end, prayed for rescue.

God, where are you? Strike them dead. I know you have the power.

He did, didn't he? Wasn't God able to annihilate entire armies? Maybe she wasn't praying in the right way. But Mama—or whoever that was, even one of the slaves—didn't deserve this. It was horrid. It was demonic. And if Selah ever got out from under this porch, the first Yankee she saw, she'd shoot him dead without a thought.

"Selah," Joelle whispered, "I hear someone else coming. You hear it?"

Selah listened. Horses galloping closer? "Maybe." It was hard to tell with the racket going on in the house. The woman had gone quiet, but the men were still laughing and crashing around. She'd heard boots going up the stairs to the second floor too. "Yes, you're right. Hush, honey, we've got to be quiet, so whoever that is won't find us."

In moments, the horses thundered to a stop, and the first

rider jumped to the ground, followed by the rest. Selah saw the leader's boots as he hurried past their hiding place. Blue pants this time, big spurs, clanking sword. An officer?

He ran up the porch steps, shouting, "Ho, you men! Form company! On the quick!" The voice was young, firm, with an edge of anxiety. He stopped somewhere close to the doorway above Selah's head, apparently encountering the brawl inside the parlor. Disjointed orders joined the shouting of the men, and even when the door slammed, Selah could still hear the young officer roaring above them. "I said halt! Stop that, you—" A gun fired.

Selah and Joelle both jumped, but the melee suddenly ceased. Eerie, uneasy silence fell.

The girls waited, clinging to each other, shivering. Selah knew that at any moment the officer or the rest of his unit could search the house, find them under the porch, and do anything they wished to her and Joelle. But at least he had stopped the horror that had been going on.

She heard the officer issue a series of curt orders, sending one of his men to bring a surgeon, their muffled and indistinguishable replies. The woman's groans faded, and Selah thought they must have moved her to another room. Maybe she had been injured by one of those gunshots. Selah couldn't stand not knowing if it was her mother or one of the slaves. All she could do was hold Joelle and pray.

At last they were gone, all of them. Darkness was falling, and the Yankees weren't likely to come back. But what if they did? What if this was a trick to coax survivors out of hiding?

Selah had sat under the porch with Joelle for another hour

or more before the doctor arrived. During the long wait, someone began to play the piano—someone very talented. The bizarre concert somehow exacerbated her anxiety, but it mercifully broke off with the arrival of the surgeon. Selah had no idea how much time passed before the young officer and his men got the looters bound and mounted and took them back to camp, but it seemed like forever.

"Selah," Joelle whispered. "Can't we come out now? I've got to . . . you know."

Selah herself was beyond uncomfortable. In fact, her muscles were so cramped she wasn't sure she'd be able to move at all. But they had to. She and Joelle couldn't stay here under the porch indefinitely.

She shoved away her terror, drawing on some reserve that hadn't been there before this morning. "Yes. Let's go."

Selah pushed at the latticework with her foot, put her hands on the ground, and crawled toward the opening, fighting skirts and short breath. She cautiously stuck her head out.

She didn't hear or see anything to indicate soldiers lingering on the property. No noise from the house or grounds. All was dead, ghostly silence, as if the Judgment had come and left her and Joelle behind. She wrestled her skirts out behind her and stood up on shaky legs, then bent to help Joelle.

They ran to the outhouse, took care of that business. Hand in hand, they climbed the back porch steps and stood looking at the door.

"Mama didn't come for us," Joelle said finally.

"I know." Selah swallowed. She knew what it meant, and her heart failed.

"Where do you think the men went?" Joelle whispered.

"I don't know." Selah shrugged. "Back to camp, maybe."

BETH WHITE

"Did you hear that man play the piano? Wasn't that strange?"

"Yes, very strange." Reluctantly she added, "But he was also good. Better even than Mama."

"Certainly better than me." Joelle gave a nervous giggle. "I don't practice enough."

"I'm afraid that piece would be over your head, darling." Selah sucked in a breath. "We've got to go in and see what the damage is. Clean it up before Mama—" She swallowed. "We need to look for Mama."

She reached for the doorknob.

Meekly, Joelle followed Selah into the house. "Oh, Selah." Joelle's voice broke.

The girls stood gawking at the mess in the breakfast room. There was just enough daylight left to see the broken table, chairs upended, smashed mirror over the sideboard, curtains yanked half off the rods. The two house servants must have run out the back to the slave quarters.

Selah pulled herself together. "We'll clean it up later. Let's look for Mama."

Together they walked through the breezeway into the rotunda. Joelle kept uttering little whimpering sounds as they encountered damaged furniture and floors and walls, but Selah tugged her grimly toward the stairs.

"Mama?" she called as they reached the second floor where the bedrooms were. "Mama, where are you?"

There was no answer.

At the top of the stairs, Selah stopped Joelle. "Stay here while I look around."

"Why? I want to come with you."

"Just mind me, Jo." Selah dreaded what she might find upstairs. She gave Joelle her fiercest glare.

15

"All right." Joelle sighed. "But hurry."

Selah headed straight for her parents' bedroom. The door was shut, and everything was utterly still. The fact that Mama hadn't come to get her and Joelle when the soldiers left could only mean that she had been taken by the soldiers or she was injured too badly to walk. Stomach roiling, Selah jerked the door open.

With the curtains pulled, the room was nearly pitch-dark, and Selah didn't have a candle or lamp. She closed her eyes for a moment to let her vision adjust to the darkness, then opened them. There was a dark form on the bed. "Mama?" She sounded childish to her own ears. Clearing her throat, she repeated more firmly, "Mama, it's Selah. Are you all right?"

Still no answer.

Then she knew. Everything she'd dreaded was true. Her mother was dead. They had killed her—those rotten, heartless Yankees with their loud, drunken voices, their crude boots and swords. They had taken and broken Selah and Joelle's one remaining anchor in life, their precious, beautiful, gentle mother.

The world upended, and she fainted.

One

February 25, 1870
Near Oxford, Mississippi

The train's rolling rhythm had nearly put Selah to sleep when the coach suddenly slung her against the window and a jarring bounce shook her head off the seatback. She blinked and sat up straighter. Wriggling to adjust the corset bone digging into her rib cage, she bumped elbows with the stout lady beside her.

"It's all right, dearie." The woman patted Selah's arm. "I can't get comfortable either, but we're about to cross Buckner's Ravine. We'll be in Oxford before you know it."

"I hope so, ma'am." Embarrassed to be caught squirming like a five-year-old, Selah glanced out the window at the woods rushing past. The trip to Memphis yesterday had been long and miserable, and the return home had so far been no better. If only she could go to sleep and block out her grandmother's ultimatum. *Stop trying to hang on to*

*that albatross of a plantation. Let the railroad have it. Move
here, where you and Joelle and Aurora can live like ladies.*

She supposed she was still a lady in some sense of the
word. Definitely female, as evidenced by the corset. And
limited in options because of that happenstance of sex. But
this was 1870, a new decade. With the war over, laws and
social structures continued to shift with the wind. Surely
there was some other way out of her dilemma.

You're the practical one, Selah. She'd heard it all her life,
had spent the past ten years shouldering one responsibility
after another, until sometimes she thought she must collapse
under the weight.

But giving up, to live in semi-wealthy gentility and sub-
jugation to her grandparents, leaving her father to wander
about, drinking and starving himself to death—

No, that was not a choice she could make. Not until after
her meeting with the banker in Oxford, at least.

Putting a hand against the knot in her stomach, she turned
from the window, her gaze colliding with that of the young
man seated across from her. He nodded, then returned to
scribbling notes in the small leather-bound book he'd pulled
from his coat pocket after getting on in Memphis. She'd been
sneaking glances at him, wishing he'd look up and speak
to her. He had the cheekbones of a Viking prince and an
appealing upward curl to the corners of his mouth, but his
expression was guarded. Though the war had ended almost
five years ago, that hard look was all too common in men
who'd fought on either side.

Selah couldn't help wondering what he was doing with
that notebook. Maybe he was a reporter. Or maybe he was
writing a letter to his sweetheart. A man with a face like

that had to have a beautiful woman somewhere waiting for him. What would it be like, to receive a written expression of fondness and devotion, composed for no one but her?

Just imagining that possibility brought her courage, like the appearance of a bright red cardinal on a rainy gray morning. She took a long breath, oddly settled. She *was* the practical one, and God would give her wisdom when the time came.

Staring at strangers, however, was ill-bred. She turned back to her seatmate and found the woman watching her with a small, knowing smile. Blushing, Selah asked, "Will you be getting off in Oxford or going on to New Orleans, ma'am?"

"Going on. My son is getting married there." The woman made a face. "I'm sorry, my dear—I didn't introduce myself. I'm Mrs. Norton."

"I'm Selah Daughtry." Selah tipped her head. "Are you not happy about the marriage?"

Mrs. Norton heaved a sigh that all but pushed Selah off the seat. "I confess I'd hoped my son would find a Memphis girl and settle down closer to home. But that's what happens when you bear nothing but boys. They leave home and never come back." She chuckled. "My husband tells me I'm entirely too sensitive. I should be glad that now I'll have the perfect excuse to travel down to New Orleans and go shopping."

Selah laughed. "One can never enjoy too much shopping."

"True." Mrs. Norton addressed the man opposite them with mock severity. "Young man, I hope you will accept my advice and consider your poor mama's feelings when you choose a mate—if it's not already too late, that is." She shot an inquisitive glance at his naked ring finger.

To Selah's surprise, he closed the notebook and grinned, creating a shallow crease along one cheek that in a softer face might have been called a dimple. He was younger than she'd first thought.

"My mother would be thrilled if I married anybody at all," he said, tucking the notebook into his breast pocket. "She has all but given up on my settling down."

"Bless her heart." Mrs. Norton tsked. "Where are you from, sir? You don't sound Southern at all."

"I grew up in Illinois. I'm Levi Riggins." He touched the brim of his hat with a polite nod. Nice manners, for a Yankee.

Selah studied him, taking in the plain but neat clothing, the well-made suit tailored to fit his tall, muscular—well, she had no business thinking about his physical form. "So what are you doing all the way down here in Mississippi, Mr. Riggins?"

He pushed back his shallow-crowned hat and regarded Selah cautiously. "Was that a 'Yankee go home' kind of question?"

She bit her lip. "I didn't mean—"

The train gave another hard jerk, and the car rocked sideways, slamming Selah's shoulder against the window. Grinding metallic noises, screaming and shouting exploded all around her as the front of the car pitched downward. Selah's stomach lurched. She fell into Levi Riggins's arms as passengers came hurtling over the seat from behind, and Mrs. Norton flumped onto Selah's back. Riggins held on to her as the cars crashed together.

Struggling to breathe, Selah lay with her face smashed against Riggins's coat. His arms crushed her, but she couldn't move, not with Mrs. Norton screaming and flailing about.

"Ma'am, you've got to be still." Riggins's deep voice was strained but calm. "We don't know how we're situated, and if the car rocks and upsets the balance—I said *stop* it!"

To Selah's relief, the weight on her back settled, quivering. Riggins released a breath against her ear. "Are you all right, Miss Daughtry?"

"I think so. Yes." The top of her head throbbed where it had hit the slatted seat, but she was alive.

"Good. I'm going to see what I can do to get us out of here." Riggins raised his voice again. "Mrs. Norton, can you roll to your left?"

The weight on Selah's back shifted, relieving some of the pressure on her rib cage and lungs. She gasped a quick, grateful breath.

"There's a man lying in the aisle," Mrs. Norton said, "but I think I can step over him. Oh, mercy, he's bleeding—"

"I'll see to him," Riggins said. "Just move slowly so we don't jostle the car."

"All right." Mrs. Norton moved again, awkwardly.

Suddenly Selah could breathe freely. She turned her head and found herself staring directly into Levi Riggins's hazel eyes. They were narrowed with concern. Or perhaps pain. Involuntarily she looked at his mouth and found his white teeth gritted. She must be crushing him.

She started to push away, but he clasped her tighter. "No, wait," he said, "you have to move slowly too. I'm all right, just a little . . . winded." He winked, then spoke to Mrs. Norton. "Stay right there, ma'am. Miss Daughtry and I are going to try to stand up."

Selah took in their predicament. The three of them, seated toward the back, had escaped the worst of the damage, but the passengers at the front of the car were beginning to stir and call out for help.

"What do you want me to do?" she asked Riggins.

His eyes warmed with approval. "Push yourself up so I can slide out from under you. Then sit down again until I can figure out what to do."

"All right. Here we go." Struggling against gravity, tight corset, and voluminous skirts, she managed to get herself upright—though in rather humiliating intimacy with this complete stranger.

Don't think about it.

Riggins slid out from under her, her skirt going with him, though she supposed a flash of petticoat was the least of her worries. He bent over the man on the floor, then stood, mouth grim. "Stay here and try to keep everyone calm," he told Selah. "I'm going to climb out and see about getting help."

"I'll come with you."

"These people need you here. I promise I'll be right back."

Somehow she believed him, trusted him. She swallowed her fear. "All right. But hurry."

The tail of Levi's greatcoat billowed in the wind as he balanced on the window ledge, looking down. Climbing out the window proved to be the easiest part of escaping that death trap. If he fell now, he'd either break his neck or impale himself on the scrubby pines and bare-limbed yellow oaks poking up along the slope like the teeth of a broken comb. Swallowing, he reminded himself that Mrs. Norton and Miss Daughtry depended on him to bring help.

Miss Daughtry, with the brown-cinnamon eyes and a voice that reminded him of a Liszt nocturne, must not die.

Well, neither must Mrs. Norton.

With a deep breath he swung onto the top of the railcar,

righted himself, and crouched, panting in the freezing air. He took in the devastating totality of the train wreck. The engine had crossed the bridge, but the car behind it had come uncoupled and gone over, yanking the rest along with it. Three cars lay crushed and scattered at the bottom of the ravine like toys hurled by a spoiled child. The next two hung angled off the bridge, shattered but supporting the one out of which he'd just climbed. Only the caboose remained fully on the tracks.

It hit him that he should have been in the shattered car in the ravine, along with the man he'd been following. If he hadn't seen Miss Daughtry through the window at the station and impulsively exchanged his ticket with a gentleman who wished to ride in the executive car, he would likely be dead instead of contemplating this suicidal climb up to the top of the bridge.

Since he'd been providentially preserved for this event, he'd best get on with it.

He began the climb on hands and knees along the roof until he reached the back end of the car, which rested on the bridge. Jumping down, he staggered and righted himself to straddle the rail ties, legs shaking. He'd made it, but there was no way those two women—or anybody else still trapped in the car below, for that matter—would make that climb.

Picking through what he'd learned from civil engineering studies at West Point and from his wartime experience, he realized he needed a rope-and-pulley system. And some help. And he'd better tackle it now, before the train's balance shifted and the whole thing tumbled into the ravine. He leaned out to peer down the side of the caboose. Precious little room remained between it and the edge of the bridge.

Except for the trusses crushed by the wrecked cars, the bridge looked stable, but the cause of the accident could be out of sight on the other side of the bridge.

Cautiously he got to his feet, aware of the panicked noises of passengers below as he edged around the car.

Vaulting onto the platform of the caboose, he called, "Hello? Anybody in charge here? We need to start getting people out."

A uniformed porter, harried of face, appeared in the caboose's doorway. He blinked in obvious astonishment. "Where did you come from?"

"Down there." Levi gestured toward the coach he'd just climbed out of.

The porter's eyes widened. "You climbed all the way up here on your own?"

"Yes. There are people still alive in that car, and we have to organize a rescue before the train dislodges."

"We've sent to Oxford for help, but it'll be a while before the equipment arrives."

"Equipment? All we need is some rope and a couple of strong backs." Riggins was used to being obeyed, and this man's reluctance was maddening. He'd just have to find somebody else with a little gumption. He wheeled.

"Wait!"

Levi spared a look over his shoulder. "Yes?"

"I'm coming. Let me get us some gloves, and I've got rope in the storage bins."

"Good. Who else can help?"

"A porter named Lunsford. I'm Kerr, by the way."

"Levi Riggins. Lead the way, I'll follow you."

Within a short while, Levi and the two porters, equipped

with a heavy tool box and three stout coils of rope, edged along the bridge toward the derailed cars. By now people were leaning out the windows, crying out for help.

"Hang on, folks," he called. "We're going to find a way to get you out." He stopped to estimate the distance to the bottom, then turned to his companions. "It will be easier to get them to the bottom than to bring them up to the top. We'll make a harness and slide them down one by one."

Kerr scratched his head. "But there's probably water down there—cold water. The women aren't going to like that."

"They'd like falling forty feet even less," Levi said with a grimace.

The porter named Lunsford peered over the edge. "He's right. Even if we managed to bring them up to the bridge, there's a long stretch of track between here and solid ground."

"It's going to take some time to get the line secured," Kerr objected. "What if the car falls before we can get the passengers out?"

"That might happen anyway," Levi said. "Listen, there's no perfect way to do this. Either we stand here arguing until we lose daylight, or we give this our best shot." He explained what he wanted, praying that Kerr and Lunsford would come to the sticking point without getting anybody killed.

He knotted the end of the rope securely about the rail, backed over the edge, and lowered himself. Arms straining to control his descent, he felt with his feet for the trestles, occasionally looking down at the spikes of trees at the bottom of the ravine. The women were going to be terrified.

But the alternative didn't bear thinking about.

Bracing himself against a sharp, buffeting wind that made his coat flap about his legs, he kept going down, down, his reluctant gaze on the silent wrecked cars. He had come through the war with death-scars on his soul that he feared might never heal. But somehow this accident, so many innocent lives cut obscenely short, struck him as the ultimate tragedy.

At the bottom, he disconnected himself from the rope and moved to investigate the first passenger car. No survivors, including Priester, whose body he found in a heap of splintered wood and bent metal. That part of his investigation had come to a screeching halt.

Sickened, he assessed the scrubby underbrush, briars, and vines, and rotten dead wood clogging the space between the ragged trees. It was going to take some doing to hack out a navigable path for the surviving passengers to get on the road for Oxford. He hoped they wouldn't run into a flooded stream or other roadblock on the way.

Muttering a prayer for wisdom and favor, he climbed over scattered luggage and broken pieces of the train to the second passenger car. He was about to abandon the search for survivors as a lost cause when he thought he heard a scrabbling sound from the center of the car.

"Is someone there?" Galvanized, he hauled aside shattered train walls and seats, shoved away a couple of dead bodies. A voice, a young one, rose from somewhere below the pile of rubble, but the words were undecipherable. "Where are you?" Levi shouted.

"Hurry, mister, I can hardly breathe," the young voice gasped.

Levi kept working. "Hang on, I'm coming." Finally he flipped over a seat back to reveal a pile of bodies, beneath which a hand moved weakly.

"I'm here . . ." The voice was adolescent male. The grubby

hand, attached to a skinny arm in a threadbare coat, lifted again. As Levi pulled aside the bodies, the boy sat up with a gasp. "Oh, thank God!" He knuckled streaming eyes, clearly choking back sobs.

Levi squatted and took the boy by the shoulders. "Are you hurt? What about your legs? Can you stand?"

"I think so. My ribs hurt."

Levi helped the boy to his feet, keeping a critical eye on the long, coltish legs. A bit wobbly, freckles standing out on the pale face, but apparently in one piece. "I'm Riggins. Don't know how you survived that, son, but you're a lucky man."

The boy sniffed hard, lifted his chin. "My name's Wyatt. Thank you for coming for me. My—my father's dead, isn't he?"

Levi cast a reluctant glance about the scene of destruction. "So is everybody in those first two cars but you, I'm afraid. Wyatt, if you're sure you're all right, I'm going to leave you and climb back up to start bringing the other survivors down to safety."

"Yes, sir. I'll do whatever I can to help."

"Good man. Rest for a few minutes, then you can start clearing a path out to the nearest road. We'll have to get wagons in here for the women and children eventually."

"Yes, sir." The boy promptly folded to the ground, leaned over and emptied the contents of his stomach.

Shaking his head in sympathy, Levi left him. He walked over to the bridge, grabbed the rope, and began to pull himself upward hand over hand. By the time he got to the top, Lunsford and Kerr had completed a sturdy cradle harness. Levi and Lunsford strapped the pint-sized Kerr into it and lowered him to an open window about a third of the way from the back of the car. Levi could hear the voices of the passengers inside rising in excitement.

"Hey, folks, stay calm," Kerr said, grabbing the edge of the window to lean in. "I'm one of the porters, and we're working to get you out of here. One of you gentlemen climb up here to talk to me, will you?"

As Kerr conferred with a large bewhiskered gentleman, Levi tended the rope to make sure it held, all the while wondering how Miss Daughtry fared. He imagined her soothing those around her with that calm, magnolia-soaked voice. He'd been calling her "*Miss* Daughtry" in his mind, but she'd introduced herself as Selah without an honorific. Perhaps she was married.

Selah surely was a pretty name, for a very pretty woman. He hoped she wasn't married. Not that he'd ever see her again after today. He had a job to do, and she was going to . . .

Where *was* she going? She'd already been on the train when he boarded, so she'd come at least as far as Memphis. She was dressed like a lady, the suit modest in cut and design. He didn't know enough about fashion to determine if she was stylish or not, but her clothes had that ragged-edged look of hard times so prevalent here in the South. Still, there was something intriguing about her, besides the interesting shape of her face and figure (which had been so delightfully pressed against him in the aftermath of the wreck). There was intelligence and determination in her eyes. Something *awake* and lively that made him want to know her better. Perhaps he could gain her direction and look her up when his business was completed.

Assuming, of course, that she wasn't married.

"Hey, you two!"

Kerr's shout jerked Levi's mind from Selah Daughtry to the business at hand—that of rescuing a train full of frightened and injured passengers.

Kerr was peering up at them, looking irritated at the delay. "Let me down," he said. "Colonel Brice here will follow and help me with the clearing of the path."

And with that, the rescue operation commenced. By the time a few men had been lowered with the harness and had begun to assist in rescuing the women and children, several citizens from Oxford arrived in their buggies with mattresses in the back to help remove the injured. An hour or so later, a special train, notified of the disaster and sent on with rescue and medical equipment, chugged to a stop behind the wreck.

Levi found himself in the position of organizing the effort, coordinating railroad personnel, civilians, and doctors—including several former soldiers like himself. Perhaps that was because he had initiated things. Perhaps because, as his little sister had once told him, "Levi Riggins, you are the bossiest human I ever met."

Whatever the reason, he accepted the responsibility and stood atop the bridge marshaling his troops—until he saw a young woman, wearing a familiar sensible hat, leaning out the window of the wrecked car.

"Miss Daughtry!" he shouted. "Are you all right?"

She looked up, squinting into the weak sun. "I'm fine. Just waiting my turn."

And she was the last one left in the car, God bless her.

"Stay right there—I'm coming." Hastily giving instructions to an engineer who had come to him with a question, he abandoned his command post and swung down the rope to the cradle dangling just outside the window where Miss Daughtry waited, brown eyes anxious.

"No place else to go, Mr. Riggins." Her smile was tight and her hands shook, but at least she wasn't a screamer.

"True." He grabbed the window ledge. "All right, here's what we're going to do. You remember how we worked together to get ourselves out from under Mrs. Norton?"

She laughed, and some of the fear leaked from her expression. "I hope she's safely on the ground now."

He grinned. "She is. Busy telling the men exactly how to proceed. So now you and I are going on another adventure. Take my hand and climb into the harness while I stabilize it." When she flinched, he leaned toward her. "Look at my eyes, Selah. I promise I won't let you fall."

SPYGLASS PRESSED TO HIS GOOD EYE, Daughtry crouched behind a tree at the edge of the creek running through Buckner's Ravine. Some forty yards away, the first passenger car lay smashed into shards and chunks of metal and wood, crushed by the two cars behind and on top of it. The intrepid young man in Union blue who had climbed out of the last passenger car and then rappelled down from the bridge had poked about among the crushed cars. Apparently the only survivor he'd found was a gangly boy in his early teens.

The mission was complete. Daughtry watched as the Yankee hero rescued a young woman hanging from one of the precariously leaning upper cars. *A woman?*

What was a woman doing on a Union train—

He squeezed his eyes shut, trying to focus. The mission. Orders. Blow up the bridge, keep the Yanks from crossing. They mustn't cross into Mississippi. Tennessee was close to utter surrender, Memphis had already gone Federal, Grant wanted Vicksburg.

Explosives men like Daughtry had become vital assets to

the Confederate cause. His training at West Point, though he hadn't known it at the time, had prepared him to understand the engineering of bridge trestles, terrain, and above all, the composition of explosives—a feat of marvelous efficiency and spectacular beauty, as much art as science.

Indeed the boxcars and passenger cars draped down from the bridge reminded him of other defining events in his lifetime. The night he'd asked Penelope to marry him. The birth of his first child. The purchase of his first brace of slaves. The day his family moved out of the cottage into the big house.

Now he was part of the holy crusade to preserve that exquisite autonomy of the individual. The enemy must be sent running in respectful terror back to the kennel. Only then could Daughtry and his brothers-in-arms return to their children, mourn their losses, and reclaim their rightful places as masters of the homes they had built.

But it was so hard. The jagged agony in his head never left, and Penny wasn't going to like moving to Mexico. The girls would be fine. They had learned Spanish at that liberal school and he'd gotten them out just in time.

He collapsed the spyglass, slid to the ground at the back side of the tree, and lay down with the leaden sky rotating above him.

Something about the whole scene wasn't making sense.

The world exploded in a blast of purple and orange as he grabbed his head, succumbing once again to the pain.

Three

SELAH LOOKED UP and met Levi Riggins's intent hazel eyes. His tall, lean body coiled around the rope, reminding her of a troupe of riverboat circus acrobats who had visited the plantation before the war. Though her entire body shuddered, his confidence and humor settled her.

But she wasn't going to look down. She kept her gaze on Riggins's face. "What do you want me to do next?"

"Sit on the edge of the window with your back to me. Then swing over one leg at a time as you turn around. I'll keep the harness close to the side of the car so you can slide down into it. Don't worry, it'll hold."

She had to glance at the harness to see what he was talking about, and the dizzying plunge into the ravine below sucked the breath out of her lungs.

He leaned in close again. "Selah, trust me. I've got you."

Her heart galloped, but she could hardly stay on the train, waiting for it to go crashing into the ravine.

"All right," she said, releasing a long breath. "Here we go."

She turned her back and bunched her skirt up to her knees

as she sat on the window ledge. Trying to ignore her hot face and trembling limbs, she soon found herself awkwardly enveloped in the harness, dangling forty feet in midair with Levi Riggins's arms around her. Feeling as if she might be sick or faint, or both, she flung both arms about her rescuer's waist and hid her face against his chest.

"Hey, hey, you did just fine," he said in her ear. "Now all we have to do is let them lower us to the ground."

"Is that all?" she said with a weak laugh. "I can't look."

"You don't have to. I'll let you know when we're about to reach the ground."

"All right—" The word ended on a squeak as the harness jolted and began to swing with the rope's descent. "Oh, my goodness, we're going fast!"

"You're one of the bravest women I've ever met. Doing what you have to do when you're afraid—that's what courage is."

Riggins seemed like someone who would understand that in a most personal way. Curiosity about him overcame some of her fear. But before she could think of a suitable response, the harness jerked once more as their descent slowed. Daring to open her eyes, she saw that they were within a few feet of the ground, and that a circle of men waited to assist her. A long line of buggies and wagons snaked out of the clearing as far as the eye could see.

Riggins had already jumped to the ground and stood waiting to assist her out of the harness. Selah was soon on her feet, trying to control her buckling knees. When Riggins slipped a strong arm about her waist with no fuss or comment, she looked up at him with a grateful smile. "Thank you."

"I was a little weak in the pins after my first trip down

too." He winked and all but carried her toward a wagon waiting nearby.

"Really, I'm fine," she said breathlessly. His touch was far from intimate, but still . . . "There must be others who need you right now."

"All the survivors are out now. I'll stay and help with the removal of the poor souls who didn't make it out alive. The railroad will take over everything else." His arm about her tightened a bit, as if he wanted to comfort her. "I wish I could come with you, to make sure you arrive safely."

He'd had an extraordinarily stressful afternoon, and he must be exhausted, hungry, and frustrated at the delay. Yet he had gone out of his way to be kind to her. "Mr. Riggins, I can hardly tell you how deeply I appreciate—"

"I've only done what any man with an ounce of sense would have done, Miss Daughtry." He hesitated, then added, "Though I don't know if you're *Miss* Daughtry after all. Perhaps you have a husband who is worried sick about your failure to arrive—"

"No. I'm not married." Overcome with the awkwardness of the situation, Selah looked away and encountered the wide-eyed stare of a tall, skinny young teen standing beside a large wagon with "J. A. Spencer, Fine Musical Instruments And Piano Tuning" lettered along its side.

Riggins followed her gaze. "Miss Daughtry, this is Wyatt. He is one of a handful of survivors from the cars ahead of us. You and he will be traveling with—ah, here he is."

A bespectacled man with a graying beard rose from behind the horses and approached, smiling, as Riggins made the introductions.

"Mr. Spencer, meet Miss Selah Daughtry. Miss Daughtry,

Mr. Spencer is one of the fine Oxford citizens who has come to lend his aid in the emergency."

As Selah curtsied, Spencer touched his bowler hat. "Happy to be of service," he said warmly. "I'm very glad you were not injured. My wife and I would be honored if you'd stay the night with our family. No doubt the hotels are all full by now."

"Thank you for your generosity." Selah glanced at Riggins. "I don't want to inconvenience you—"

"Put it right out of your mind." Spencer waved a hand. "My wife takes the Good Book seriously and would banish me to the barn if I failed to extend hospitality to strangers in need."

Selah smiled. "Well, I wouldn't want to be the cause of marital discord. In that case, perhaps Mr. Riggins would give me a hand up. You must be anxious to get home."

Riggins gave her arm an appreciative squeeze, then held her elbow as she climbed onto the seat. Meanwhile, the boy named Wyatt scrambled into the back of the wagon.

Once she was settled, Selah looked down at him, suddenly bereft at the thought of parting so soon. "Thank you again for all you've done today."

Backlit by the sun going down behind the bridge, his face was shadowed. He touched the brim of his hat in a courtly gesture, then addressed Spencer, who had clambered onto the driver's seat and taken up the reins. "I'm certain your Good Samaritan deeds won't go unrewarded, but I'd be happy to reimburse you for any expenses you incur on behalf of Miss Daughtry and the boy."

Spencer waved away the offer. "Not necessary, I assure you."

Riggins glanced at young Wyatt, slumped in the back of the wagon. "Even so, I'd like to come by in the morning to see what else I may do for them."

Spencer stroked his beard thoughtfully. "As justice of the peace, I'll be responsible for contacting the boy's relatives. I'd appreciate any help in locating them. Maybe I can convince Miss Daughtry to linger until you come by. What do you think, Miss Daughtry?"

"I should be glad to see you again, Mr. Riggins," she said with what dignity she could muster.

Spencer nodded. "Then, it's settled. Breakfast with the Spencer clan at eight." Waving at Riggins, he gave the horses leave to start.

Selah resisted the urge to look over her shoulder at her rescuer. Maybe something nice would come of this awful day after all.

Oxford, Mississippi

By the time they arrived in Oxford, Selah and the loquacious Mr. J. A. Spencer had become fast friends. She discovered him to be, besides the purveyor of an up-and-coming music business and justice of the peace, married to his childhood sweetheart and father to a quiverful of boys and girls aged fourteen down to an infant still on the breast. As they entered his tidy home near the business district, his bustling, energetic wife welcomed the two unexpected guests with open arms. After providing them with nightwear and a comforting mug of hot milk each, she settled Selah in for the night with her two eldest daughters and Wyatt with the little boys.

As she listened to the girls whisper in the dark about the accident until they fell asleep, Selah lay praying for Wyatt. The boy had endured the ride to Oxford in stoic quiet, his arms propped on bony knees and chin on his chest. He struck Selah as a little too sober and mature for his age, like a college professor in a fourteen-year-old body. Though he hadn't shed a tear, she couldn't believe he was not traumatized by the loss of his father.

Finally she slipped out of bed, pulling on the wrapper Mrs. Spencer had loaned her, and tiptoed to the living room. Maybe she could find a book and read by the fire until she got sleepy.

At the doorway, she stopped short. Wyatt sat on the hearth, wrapped in a blanket.

"Hullo, Miss Selah," he said softly. "You not sleeping either?"

She approached and knelt on the rug at the boy's feet. "I keep thinking about . . . today."

"I know." He shrugged.

They sat in companionable silence for a time, then she gently touched his bare foot. "Wyatt, honey, are you hungry? I could probably find us something to eat."

"No, ma'am. But if you are, go right ahead. Also you don't have to stay awake with me. I know you must be tired."

The oddly correct speech pattern, not to mention unusual concern for an adult's well-being, went to her heart. "I'm tired, but I don't think I can sleep yet. Why don't you tell me a little about your family. Sometimes talking about it will ease the pain. Mr. Riggins told me you lost your father today."

"Yes." He sighed. "You're going to think I'm hard-hearted, but I didn't know him very well. It's just that I'll need to work somewhere, and I'm worried that nobody is going to hire a fourteen-year-old kid—"

"Wait. Start over. Where's your mother?"

"She's dead. Died of scarlet fever just before Christmas."

"But you didn't know your father . . . ?"

"It's a bit complicated. My mother and I lived up in the Tennessee hills with her folks. Pa was a railroad man and gone a lot. He was a Union sympathizer too." Wyatt swallowed, glancing at Selah as if not sure how much to reveal to a Southern gentlewoman.

Selah nodded. "What happened?"

"Well, when I was about seven or so, some Rebel soldiers came through, looking for what they called traitors. Somebody turned Pa in, and the Rebs came after him. I was watching from the hayloft when they marched him away. I thought we'd never see him again, but he returned one night about a week later to say goodbye. He said he'd escaped and had to leave until after the war, when it would be safe to come back for us."

Fighting tears, Selah stared at the boy. She and her sisters had experienced a good deal of hardship, but at least they'd been old enough to understand what was going on, and they'd had Uncle Frederick as a buffer through the worst of it. She couldn't imagine what this child had been through, living in war-torn Tennessee. "When was the next time you saw him?"

"After the war, he went to work for the railroad in New Orleans. He sent money every now and again, but never came back to Tennessee. After my mother died, I wrote to Pa to let him know. He came for me a couple of weeks ago."

"I'm surprised he didn't come back for you sooner."

"Of course I asked him why he didn't, but he wouldn't give me a straight answer." Wyatt's mouth tightened. "He seemed to be afraid people were still looking for him." The boy looked away. "Frankly, I think he was a little crazy."

Selah thought so too. "But now . . . Perhaps you'd better go back to your relatives—"

"I'm not going back to Tennessee." Wyatt's voice cracked on a stubborn note. "I want to go to school and learn to be a doctor. Do you know how I could do that?"

Selah blinked. "Well . . . I could perhaps find out. I have a good friend at home in Tupelo who is a physician. I imagine he could steer you in the right direction."

Wyatt's body straightened with excitement. "That would be—oh, ma'am, I'll do whatever you need me to do, to earn my way!"

Selah restrained her impulse to exclaim that Wyatt had misunderstood her—that she hadn't meant she'd take him home with her. How on earth would she pay an extra fare when she could barely afford her own? And where would he stay? Unable to keep up the big house, she and Joelle and their second cousin ThomasAnne had been living in cramped quarters in the tiny agent's house, subsisting on next to nothing—to the point that it looked like they would be forced to comply with their grandparents' demands that they come to Memphis.

Words boiled on her tongue, ready to spill out and dash the flare of hope in the boy's tired, sad eyes.

"I'm not sure how we'll do it," she heard herself say, "but we'll manage something."

She said good night to Wyatt, went back to bed, and lay there for a long time. Despite her concerted effort to "let today's worries be sufficient unto themselves," an ocean of worries flooded in, through, and over her. Her father, crippled mentally and physically by his losses, living like a vagrant in the woods. The strong possibility—in fact, the near inevitability—of being forced from her home. Her worry over Aurora's flibbertigibbet ways.

She struggled with hopelessness, an enemy who roared against her on a nightly basis. Almost unable to breathe, she grasped for verses she'd learned as a child. "The LORD is my Shepherd. I shall not want. He maketh me . . ."

At last she fell asleep.

Levi sat by the fire in the constable's home, chewing on the tip of his pen, notebook open on his lap. He couldn't stop thinking about the broken bodies. He'd spent a grim, grueling couple of hours helping to recover the last of the train wreck victims and send them off in the mortuary wagon. By the time they'd finished, darkness blanketed the ravine, so he'd gladly accepted the constable's offer of a ride into town and a roof over his head.

Now every bone ached with weariness, and his injured shoulder was on fire. He rubbed it, remembering days during the war when he'd been encamped in much less hospitable circumstances. Nothing to look forward to on the morrow but another breakfast of hardtack, fatback, and boiled beans—and the privilege of being shot at by a fierce, cunning enemy motivated to protect home and property at all costs.

By God's grace, he'd survived. Following Lee's surrender at Appomattox, he'd resigned his commission and gone home to Illinois. At first he'd been all right, working for his father, recovering his humanity under the gentle, prayerful hands of his mother and sisters. But Lincoln's assassination had come as a bitter blow, setting him adrift in grief that even his music couldn't reach. Finally his father saw an advertisement in the local paper for Pinkerton agents and in desperation sent him off to Chicago.

"Keep your mind busy as well as your hands, boy," Pa had said. "You'd be good at this." When Levi protested that he was needed in the store, Pa brushed him off. "You're scaring off all my customers with that sour face."

Levi laughed for the first time in months and agreed to go.

As usual, his father turned out to be right. Allan Pinkerton expressed himself glad to have a man with such high recommendation from the esteemed Brigadier General Grierson, and from that point on, Levi was too busy to think about the losses in his life—or the shifting winds of the national landscape, for that matter.

Until today. Watching a beautiful woman sitting across from him in a train car, he'd suddenly become aware of how lonely he was. Tonight he would sleep knowing that, if he chose, he could see Selah Daughtry again in the morning. He could discover where her home was and maybe—

Maybe what? He dipped the pen in his inkwell with angry force. How delusional had he become, thinking of seeking out and courting a woman he'd known for less than a day? The men of his unit would roast him until he was fork-tender.

Breakfast. It was only breakfast. There wouldn't be time to woo her and win her, even if she'd consider taking up with a broken-up ex-soldier like him. A Yankee soldier at that.

He'd served with Union soldiers who hated everyone with a Southern accent, assuming they were all slaveholders and hypocrites. Levi wouldn't have gone that far, preferring to reserve judgment and treat individuals as he found them. Still, he found his rather dim view of Southern gentlewomen—a class to whom Selah indubitably belonged—belied by her self-deprecating humor and demonstrable courage.

He couldn't help comparing her to the woman he'd rescued seven years ago. Looking down at her lying on the canopy bed, aware of his dirty boots leaving marks on the rug, he'd tried not to look at the blood on her skirt. She was still breathing, though the bruises on her thin, aristocratic face stood out on the ashen skin.

He'd wanted to hang his head out the window and empty his stomach, but duty demanded that he stand there and face what his unwanted men had done. There was no excuse for abusing a female, even if she was a slave-holding rebel who probably thought she was better than all of them and undoubtedly hated his very soul. It was there in her tear- and pain-drenched blue eyes regarding him from beneath the gaunt arm she'd flung across her brow. And her recoil when he'd picked her up to carry her up the stairs. He'd wanted to assure her that the renegades would be tried and disciplined, sentenced to ten years or more for what they had done to her and the two Negro girls in the kitchen.

But that didn't seem enough.

"Ma'am," he said instead, "I'll send our surgeon back to look after you, if you want."

She closed her eyes and turned her head.

"All right then," he said. "But you should know that those men were Union soldiers who'd been recruited by the Confederate Army out of Andersonville prison. They were caught deserting back to our lines after the Battle of Franklin and allowed to rejoin—against my better judgment, I must add. We're all exhausted and short of rations, but this sort of raiding is—well, ma'am, as I said, there is no excuse for breaking the code of human decency."

Again the woman remained silent. Perhaps she'd fainted. He leaned down to lay two fingers against her neck, felt a pulse. Relieved, he stepped back, bent to swipe his hand at the dirt on the rug—a pointless exercise—then left the room, closing the door behind him.

He'd sent for the surgeon, waited more than two hours for him to come and see to the injured lady and her two slaves— time he couldn't really afford, with other orders to execute. He'd sent for the surgeon, waited more than two hours for him to come and see to the lady and her two slaves—time he couldn't really afford, with other orders to execute. During that miserable interval, he'd found himself irresistibly drawn to the piano in the parlor and allowed himself to sit down and play a sort of elegy to his own idealism.

He didn't know if the woman survived, but he hoped so. So many things he would do differently if he had the chance—starting with not trusting those men, savages that they were, on their own. Then maybe his conscience wouldn't have commenced eating his soul by slow degrees.

Returning to Mississippi, thinking about that woman, made all those memories come roaring back. Maybe he should return to that plantation and find out what had happened to the family. He didn't even know who they were or if they were still in the area. Many planters, having lost their homes, simply moved away to live with relatives elsewhere.

Well, anyway, Selah Daughtry had nothing to do with his assignment. He had a gang of train robbers to track

down. The firelight flickered across the report he'd begun—
Pinkerton expected daily briefings—and wasn't this a frustrating development? His only lead dead, and now days lost
in finding another. But there had been one odd thing he'd
noticed while climbing up and down the bridge trestles, clearing out the rubble of the train wreck as the sun went down.

He'd picked through the remains of what looked like explosive materials near the shattered central truss. His search
was conducted in near darkness, and he couldn't tell how
old the materials were. Besides, accidents weren't unheard
of, especially in this part of Mississippi where Union troops
had perpetrated heavy damage to rail lines. Levi himself had
early on learned to tie a "Sherman's Necktie" with speed and
cunning, heating rails and bending them around trees and any
other available stable object. Impossible to tell whether the
truss had collapsed due to a gradual weakening or sabotage.

But he made a note anyway. Pinkerton's training insisted
upon careful attention to details, which often broke open
a case when pieces came together after long investigations.
Of course, rabbit trails also cost time and money, and the
previous robberies hadn't involved explosives. As far as he
knew, nothing of value had been taken in this wreck.

Still, he'd best put Selah Daughtry out of his mind and con-
centrate on what he'd come to Mississippi to do. He finished
his report, sealed it in an envelope to be mailed to Pinkerton
at the first opportunity, and put the travel desk away.

Rolling out his pallet of blankets, he lay down, firmly
closed his eyes, and fell asleep.

And dreamed of brown eyes.

Four

THE NEXT MORNING, Levi knocked at the Spencers' front door, then stood shifting his weight. The dream from last night lingered in the back of his mind, adding to his discomfort. He had work to do, no time for socializing. So what was he doing here?

He'd turned to leave when Spencer himself opened the door. "There you are! We were just talking about you! Come in, my boy, come in! I hope you've brought an appetite, since Mrs. Spencer has fried enough bacon and eggs to feed Lee's army!"

Which left Levi with nothing to do but take off his hat and follow his host to the kitchen. There he found Selah rocking an infant in a chair by the fire, Wyatt amongst the older Spencer children gathered around a large farm table. Their noisy conversation and giggles stood out in stark contrast to Wyatt's subdued sadness.

Mrs. Spencer, a comfortable housewife in a ruffled calico apron, turned from the stove to greet Levi with a smile. "And here's the young man who rescued all those people—my, aren't you handsome! And look at Miss Selah blush! Marcus, stop drumming on the table before I send Allie out to the muscadine vine to fetch me a switch—I just *wish* I could have been there to see the heroics!"

Finding nothing suitably self-deprecating to say, Levi simply nodded.

Selah rescued him. "Mr. Riggins was certainly heroic, but so was your husband—driving all the way out to the scene of the accident and back, then offering to let us stay here with you all. Wyatt and I are fortunate to have survived, when so many didn't."

Mrs. Spencer's face softened as she went back to poking at the bacon. "Indeed you are."

"Have a seat, Riggins." Spencer pulled out an empty chair, then plunked himself down at the head of the table. "Miss Selah tells us she has an appointment at the bank at ten. Perhaps after breakfast you might escort her there?"

Selah looked at Levi in alarm. "Oh, I wouldn't want to—I'm sure you must have other obligations—"

"Nothing that won't keep for an hour or so," he said, quashing a surge of pleasure at the prospect of a little more time spent in her company.

"See?" Spencer chortled. "Fate seems determined to throw the two of you together."

"Fate? James, you might *try* to make your matchmaking efforts just a tad less obvious." Eyes twinkling, Mrs. Spencer turned to Selah. "The baby seems to be asleep, my dear. Why don't you put him in his cradle and come to the table? I believe we're ready to eat."

In the hubbub of children giggling and scraping chairs, dishes rattling, and food going round the table, Levi covertly watched Selah lay the baby down and pat his bottom until he stopped squirming. She seemed comfortable in this domestic situation, not at all rattled by their host's teasing. But when she caught Levi staring at her, she averted her gaze. Apparently, Spencer had observed the exchange as well but contained himself to a smug smile at his wife, who merely rolled her eyes and passed him another biscuit.

When the gargantuan breakfast had been consumed, Spencer brushed crumbs from his vest and wiped his beard with his napkin. "Allie! Caroline! Come here and give Papa a Yankee dime before you go out and feed the chickens." He laughed as his two youngest daughters each gave him a smacking kiss on the cheek.

"Really, James," his wife said with a good-natured frown, "stop tickling the girls, or you'll wake the baby. Eugenia, you may check the fireplaces, and Marcus, we need more wood chopped. Perhaps Wyatt wouldn't mind helping you with that."

As the uproar subsided, the children dispersing to morning chores, Spencer cleared his throat. "As reluctant as I am to break up this gathering, I'd better go down to the telegraph office to make some more inquiries regarding Wyatt's relatives before I open the store."

Selah, who had gotten up to help with straightening the kitchen, hung her dish towel on a hook and slid into a chair across from Levi. "I think I should tell you what I discovered from talking to Wyatt last night and this morning."

All her movements, Levi had noticed, were precise and economical. He wondered if she ever got flapped—but considering her behavior yesterday during the crash, he didn't think that likely. If that didn't do it, nothing would. He couldn't help smiling.

She wrinkled her nose. "What? Do I have something on my face?"

"Just a pretty smile." Levi ignored Spencer's snort and Mrs. Spencer's giggle. "So what did Wyatt tell you?"

Selah held his gaze, though her cheeks were pink. "Apparently Wyatt's father was a ranking official with the Mississippi Central, out of New Orleans. A Mr. Priester."

Levi put down his coffee abruptly. "Wait—Priester—from Tennessee? He was *that* Priester?" Connections began to fire. Two of the robberies he'd been investigating had resulted in the deaths of rail executives. Perhaps the gang's motive had been more than simple theft. And perhaps this accident was no accident.

Selah nodded. "Wyatt's mother died a few months ago, and he seems to think there is no one back in Tennessee who would take him. Now with his father dead, he has no place to go."

"Poor darling." Mrs. Spencer gasped. "Oh, James, do you think—"

"No, I do not!" Grimacing, Spencer moderated his tone. "My love, we cannot take in another child, not now, when we've just expanded the store. We'll do all we can to find him a place to go, but—" He shook his head firmly. "We cannot keep him."

In the ensuing silence, Levi steepled his fingers under his chin and watched the wordless tug-of-war between the married couple. They clearly enjoyed a marriage based upon mutual respect and admiration.

Mrs. Spencer huffed. "I suppose you're right. But what is the poor child going to do?"

"I'm going to take him with me."

Levi and both Spencers looked at Selah.

Levi laughed. "What did you say?"

Selah sat bolt upright, flushed and defiant. "You heard me. I promised Wyatt I'd take him home with me."

Apparently she could get flapped under the right circumstances.

Levi held up a hand. "Nobody's disagreeing with you. But what is your family going to say to you bringing home an orphan?"

"I'll cross that bridge when I come to it."

Spencer slapped a hand on the table. "I think that's a fine idea, Miss Selah. Since I have the authority to make the decision, you have my blessing. The boy already seems attached to you. Of course, if his relatives are found, we can rethink the situation, but for now . . ." He smiled at Selah. "I believe we can even find funds to purchase his fare."

Selah looked relieved. "I didn't know how I was going to—but Providence seems to have ordained this situation, so I shouldn't be surprised." She rose, shaking her skirts into orderly folds. "Well, I really must leave for my appointment. Mrs. Spencer, I'll come back here to collect Wyatt in time for us to meet the afternoon train."

"All right, my dear." The matron rose as well. "I'll make sure he knows you'll be coming back for him."

Spencer pushed away from the table. "I'll fetch our coats. Riggins can escort you to the bank while I head to the station."

A short time later, Levi and Selah parted ways with Spencer at the town square and turned onto a narrow alley just past the livery stable. Now was his chance to ask about her business with the banker, find out where her home was. He was acutely aware of her gloved hand lightly tucked into the bend of his elbow, the way she kept glancing up at him as if expecting him to speak.

A professional in the art of interviewing ought to have more address than this.

He cleared his throat. "I trust you slept well last night. I mean, of course we already talked about that at the table, but—" He took a deep breath. "Forgive me, but I'm trying to figure out how to discover your home direction and make sure this isn't the last time I see you."

She laughed and squeezed his arm. "And here I'd been biting my tongue to keep from offering it unbidden. I'm afraid I'm a bit too forthright as a rule. My family accuses me of a lack of ladylike sensibilities."

He halted abruptly. "Then I hope you'll forget their strictures, so that we may be honest in the little time we have remaining. Where *do* you call home, Miss Daughtry? And would you indeed have any objection to my calling upon you in the near future?"

Her laughter faded and he felt, crazily, as if his life balanced on a pin and could go bouncing off into ecstasy or misery. *Only a chance acquaintance, Riggins. Don't be dramatic.*

She nodded slowly. "I'd have no objection. But you should know that my sister, my cousin, and I might be forced to leave our home in the near future. My father was a high-ranking Confederate officer, and to make a long story short, our property—which is quite considerable—has been subject to confiscation under reparations laws." She met his eyes again, injured pride in every angle of her body. "We spent our last penny fighting it, and I'm hoping the bank will advance us enough to pull us out of debt. If they don't . . ." She shrugged. "I'm not sure where we'll end up."

He impulsively took her hands. "Selah—Miss Daughtry, I appreciate your honesty. After that accursed war, most folks find themselves at sixes and sevens. Thank God it's over, and we can begin to rebuild relationships and livelihoods."

Her eyes glossed with tears. "That has been my prayer for some time. It's just that at the very moment we seem to be breaking out of this—this hole, something else happens to knock the pins out from under us. And now there's Wyatt—"

"We'll think of something."

She sighed. "You just can't help rescuing, can you?"

"One might say the same of you, Selah Daughtry."

"It's a curse of being the eldest." She gave him a rueful smile. "My sister Joelle calls it interfering."

"Tell your sister the world needs more of that kind of interference."

"Joelle does, certainly. She's the kind of person who walks into walls with her nose in a book, while the rest of us endeavor to keep food on the table." Selah pulled her hands free and took his arm again. "Which is why I must hold on to our plantation."

"But . . . surely you have extended family. Someone to take you in if you lose the property?" He hoped that didn't sound too inquisitive.

She sighed again as they walked on. "My grandmother wants us to come to her—my youngest sister has been there for some years now. That's what I was doing in Memphis—something of a command performance."

"Ah. The Southern grand dame. I've met a few of those."

Selah laughed. "Indeed. Everyone is quite terrified of Grandmama. Capitulating to her would mean not only leaving the only home I've ever known, but giving up the independence I've gotten used to." She wrinkled her nose. "To be blunt, Mr. Riggins, I'm twenty-six years old. I can't imagine putting myself back under my grandparents' thumb, my every move scrutinized and questioned, forced to sip tea and embroider samplers—while our home is parceled out to strangers."

"Hmm. I wouldn't have guessed you to be such a relic of antiquity." He glanced down at her face, cheeks flushed by the chill air, eyes bright with indignation. Despite the maturity of her words and expression, she could have passed for sixteen. "Do you mind my asking why you haven't married? Or perhaps you have, and lost someone in the war . . ."

"To answer that question, you'd have to meet my sister Joelle." Her lips pursed with humor. "Any female in the same room with her simply pales to insignificance."

"Until I'm introduced to this paragon, I'll have to take you at your word." They stopped in front of the bank. "But perhaps you could give me the direction of your home, so that I might call upon you? I assume your destination is somewhere between here and New Orleans?"

"No, my home is just outside of Tupelo, about fifty miles east of here."

"T-Tupelo?" The stammer that still occasionally plagued him chose that moment to surface. "What is your family's plantation called?"

"Ithaca. Have you heard of it?"

Numb, Riggins stared at her. "I've—yes, I have," he finally said. "I was engaged in action nearby during the war." He proffered a stiff bow, bringing her gloved hand briefly to his lips. "I imagine I'll be able to find it after I've concluded my business here. Until then, goodbye, Miss Daughtry. May fortune smile upon your efforts to keep your property."

He dropped her hand and walked away, forcing himself to neither run nor look back.

Sometimes it was best if one's questions went unanswered.

Selah watched Riggins walk away with the athletic gait of a horseman, his broad back ramrod straight. What on earth had she said to offend him? Usually it was her sister's beautiful face that caused men to suddenly drop her hand and drift away. This time . . . this time he'd asked Selah all manner of personal questions, so that in less than twenty-four hours he knew almost all there was to know about her—then walked away before she could discover so much as his reason for traveling on that train.

Now that she thought about it, yesterday before the wreck he'd sidestepped that very question. He, on the other hand, demonstrated a knack for eliciting information from everyone around him. The thought left her both uncomfortable and puzzled to the core.

Well, there was nothing she could do about it. Either he would follow through and come to find her later . . . or he would not. Mentally dusting her hands, she opened the door to the bank and went inside.

He hadn't lied to her.

But as he entered the telegraph office, Levi admitted to himself with a certain amount of self-disgust that he'd led Selah to believe he'd seen action near her home without actually setting foot onto her family's property. And oh, how he wished that were true.

One thing he knew: she hadn't been there on that day long ago. Selah would have been in her late teens or early twenties back then, and he had not seen any young white women. He'd seen only one white lady, the one in the upstairs bedroom. The one his men had—

No, *not* "his men." They were deserters he'd been sent to apprehend.

And he hadn't gotten there in time to prevent the atrocities they'd committed. No matter how many times he tried to force the memory of that day back to its proper blurry state, nearly every moment was crystal clear. The woman had been middle-aged, forty at least, with deep blue eyes nothing like Selah's. Her hair might have been the same color, though, a deep mahogany brown with lustrous red undertones. And the bruises and swelling of her face would have concealed its shape and bone structure.

Could that woman have been Selah's mother? He didn't really want to know.

Where would Selah and her sisters have been when the attack came? They might not have even been on the plantation— perhaps they'd been with the grandmother in Memphis she'd mentioned. But what if they'd been watching from some hiding place, had seen the deserters coming? Then they must have also seen Levi arrive, too late to stop it. But if that was true, wouldn't she have recognized him?

Generally he got looks of suspicion when Southerners heard his natural pattern of speech. That was why he either stayed quiet or, when conducting an interview, adopted a fairly spot-on drawl. But yesterday on the train, and this morning, for that matter, Selah had not batted a single one of her long eyelashes at his Northern accent. She had treated him like an interesting stranger, not at all like an enemy.

She didn't know who he was.

The questions went round and round. What was he going to do about her? Pursue her, using the excuse of helping Wyatt? Pretend they'd never met and go on with his life?

He'd never struggled with physical cowardice, but the thought of provoking the scorn and disgust of one lovely Southern belle filled him with terror.

Action. The requirements of his job had saved his soul in the past, and now . . . It was all he knew to do.

He focused on his surroundings. Oxford's telegraph office should be a source of speculation and rumor—both of which often led to real information—if one persisted in asking the right questions.

The rectangular office—twice as wide as it was deep, with a long counter at the back—was decorated along bare-bones lines, with a row of sturdy chairs along one wall and a desk with writing supplies and telegram forms stationed against the other. It appeared he had arrived at a fortuitous time. Behind the counter a clerk in a dark suit stood taking down the message of a man accompanied by his wife and two small children—the only customers in sight.

Levi waited until the family had completed their business and left the office, then approached the clerk. "Good afternoon, sir." He leaned over the counter confidentially. "I'm surprised to find Oxford so quiet on the day after such a tragic event as the wreck at Buckner's."

"Yes, sir. Our folk are used to the disruptions of the rail industry—though not typically of such a dramatic turn of events, I'll grant you." The clerk did not quite meet his eyes, a fact which struck Levi as odd and somewhat evasive.

Levi decided to dig a little deeper. "Having met several of the Mississippi Central employees and other Oxford citizens, I've established quite a positive impression of your 'folk.' You are acquainted with Mr. Spencer, Justice of the Peace, I'm sure."

"Indeed I am! In fact, he owes his election in large part to my handling of his campaign. Good fellow, Spencer. In what regard are you acquainted, sir?" The clerk's bushy eyebrows rose above his spectacles.

"I met Mr. Spencer while assisting in the removal of passengers from the scene of the accident. In fact, I just came from his home, where his excellent wife served a most filling pot of grits."

"Belinda Spencer is one of the finest cooks in five counties. She and my wife are thick as thieves." The clerk grinned and put out a hand for Levi to shake. "Ford Scully at your service," he declared. "Was there something I could do for you?"

"I do want to send a telegram to my boss shortly, but first I'm hoping you won't mind answering a few questions. There's a man who died on that wrecked train, name of Priester. I'd like to locate any relatives who may be asking for him."

Levi watched Scully carefully for signs of surprise or recognition. But the clerk shook his head, expression only mildly curious. "I'm afraid not. But if someone else does come looking for him, who shall I tell them to apply to?"

"Here's my card." Levi reached into his pocket and laid the card on the counter. It simply read "L. E. Vine, Esq.,

Attorney at Law. Chicago, Memphis, New Orleans." The address was a Chicago post office box. "Please tell any interested parties to leave their name and direction with you. I'll try to check back sometime in the next few days, or you could always write to the address on the card."

Scully, interest clearly piqued, nodded. "Yes, sir, Mr. Vine. So you're a Chicago man. I thought that accent sounded a bit, shall we say, north of the Mason-Dixon line."

Levi chuckled. "I'm glad you are not one of these Southerners prejudiced against everyone without a drawl."

"Oh, there are plenty of those about!" Scully snorted. "You Illinois crackers rather ran rough-shod over us, after all. But a body with common sense won't cut off his nose to spite his face. Yankee money spends just fine."

"And there might just be some of that to go around, if Priester's connections can be located."

Scully shrugged. "Like I said, I don't know anything about that. But anybody will tell you there's a Mississippi Central executive from the New Orleans office by that name."

"That's what I hear," Levi said. "This wreck is going to put a bad taste in the mouths of potential customers, if even their own officials aren't safe on the rails. In fact, I'm changing my own travel plans, heading over to Tupelo to buy a ticket on the M&O."

"I hope you won't do that, Mr. Vine! The Mississippi Central will make right any inconveniences caused by this accident and do their utmost to discover its cause and rectify the situation. In fact—" Scully scowled. "I wouldn't be surprised if the Mobile and Ohio is discovered to be at fault somehow. They've been trying to buy us out since Christmas, and their board is ruthless."

Levi noted Scully's shaking hands, fumbling to set straight the spectacles that had gone askew. *Pay dirt.* He shrugged, as if unconvinced. "Perhaps."

"I'll tell you what—" Scully leaned closer—"that young Beaumont whelp has been in town for the last two days, up to no good, I'm sure. When he was a student here, everyone knew what a wild rapscallion he was."

Levi quirked his eyebrows. "Beaumont?"

"The younger of the two Beaumont brothers—Schuyler, I mean. Their pa has been on the board of the M&O since before the war. Schuyler always was a troublemaker, trying to outdo his big brother, but he generally only succeeded in costing his pa a bushel of money."

"Hmm." Levi had no idea which part of the man's blather could be trusted, if any, but at least he had some new leads to investigate. Conflicting testimony could always be compared, timelines developed to establish facts and root out the lies. He withdrew his notebook and pencil to record the names. "Any idea where I might find Beaumont? Have you seen him today?"

"I saw him driving around the square earlier today, no idea where he was going. But when he's here, he generally puts up with friends from university days, since the Oxford Inn—along with half the town—burned during the war." Scully sniffed. "The new Thompson House just opened, though, and I read in the *Falcon* that they're hosting a hop for the young people tonight. That would be just the sort of entertainment Schuyler Beaumont would patronize."

"Thank you, sir. Should you hear anything else, I'd appreciate it if you'd send me word." Levi tapped a finger on his card on the counter. "Now I've a wire of my own to compose, if you'll excuse me." With a smile, he turned and headed for the desk across the room. Pinkerton, who generally gave his agents great latitude in following trails of information, would likely carp at such a frivolous expense, but Levi counted on the value of this new lead outweighing the price of a ticket to a dance.

Tupelo, Mississippi

Getting herself and Wyatt home to Tupelo involved riding a spur line from Oxford to Holly Springs, then taking the connector home. They arrived that evening at the Tupelo station, tired, sore, and not a little anxious about the future. Grateful to find her feet firmly on the wooden platform and her shoulders no longer jarred by the rumbling of wheels on rail, Selah disembarked with Wyatt close on her heels. As she thought of her last sight of Mr. Spencer waving her off from the Oxford station, his stocky figure receding through the smeared train window, she fought an absurd mixture of nostalgia and regret. How could she have grown so fond of people she'd encountered for the first time only yesterday?

Now, with Wyatt hovering close to her elbow, she scanned the noisy, milling crowd for her sister. If Joelle hadn't managed to find transportation, they were going to have a difficult time getting home. "Wyatt, let me know if you see an empty livery wagon—"

Suddenly, above the heads of all the other women and some of the men, she caught sight of bright strawberry-blonde curls blowing in the frigid breeze from beneath a shapeless felt hat.

"Joelle!" Selah dropped her valise and waved her hand. "Over here!"

Joelle waved, and the ugly brown hat began to make its way through passengers and train personnel.

A few moments later, Joelle burst into sight, blue eyes shining like sapphires, a welcoming smile banishing her habitually preoccupied expression. "Selah! We were worried to death when we heard about the wreck!" Joelle snatched her close.

Selah gave her sister's shoulders an affectionate squeeze before pulling away. "You should know a little thing like a train wreck wouldn't keep me from coming home. How did you get here?"

"Gil's waiting with the wagon." Joelle gestured vaguely.

Selah stood on tiptoe but didn't see the tall, gangly preacher anywhere. Generally he followed Joelle around like a lost puppy. "Where?"

"I don't know." Joelle looked guilty. "I was thinking of something else . . ."

Joelle's brain functioned on a different level from anyone else she knew. One minute she'd be talking about milking the cow, the next she'd be off on some philosophical tangent espoused by Aristotle or Socrates or some other long-dead Greek fellow, and who knew when or where she'd come out.

Selah snorted. "Of course you were. One day Gil is going to talk you into getting married when you're not paying attention."

"I'm not *that* absent-minded! But he did mention it again on the way over here. Honestly, Selah, he's the funniest thing.

But can you see me as a pastor's wife? I can't cook, I don't like social things, and I'd say something outrageous without thinking and he'd get fired!"

"We certainly wouldn't want that," Selah said dryly. She looked around for Wyatt and found him listening to their conversation with a wrinkled brow, as if trying to interpret some foreign tongue. "Jo, I want you to meet Wyatt. He's going to be staying with us for a while." She pulled the boy closer.

Joelle blinked and looked down at the boy with little more than a quirk between her beautiful red brows. "Is he indeed?"

On the train, Selah had been working out how she would present this situation to her sister and ThomasAnne. Even the oblivious Joelle knew how stretched their household funds had become of late.

"Yes," Selah said firmly. "He was involved in the accident with his father, who didn't survive. So I've brought him here until his guardianship can be sorted out."

Joelle's blue eyes filled as she put her hand on Wyatt's shoulder. "Well then, I'm glad to meet you. My name is Joelle."

Wyatt stared, slack-jawed and wordless, at Joelle.

Joelle smiled. "You look like a college man. Are you on holiday?"

Wyatt's chest puffed. "I'm only fourteen. But I plan to go to medical college as soon as I can get my prerequisites in." He swallowed. "Are you really not married?"

"Well," Joelle said with laudable gravity, "I've yet to meet a man more interesting than Alexandre Dumas. Have you read *The Count of Monte Cristo*?"

Wyatt brightened. "Yes, did you know Dumas is one-quarter Negro?"

"How do you know that?"

"I dunno. Picked it up somewhere, just thought it was interesting." Wyatt shrugged. "Anyway, I like science better than literature."

Of course Joelle wasn't going to take that lying down. Ignoring the ensuing debate, Selah scoured the crowd in search of Gil. At last she found him—a tall drink of water with an oversized nose and lugubrious expression—holding the horses in a long line of wagons hitched in the shade of the station. She lifted her hand to wave to him, then turned to Joelle. "All right, you two, continue this later. Wyatt, can you get our bags?"

"'Course I can." The boy slung his smaller case over his shoulder and reached down to pick up Selah's.

Joelle took Selah's arm and led the way toward the wagon. "So how did the battle with Grandmama go?"

Selah let out an inelegant whistle. "She was loaded for bear."

"I'm surprised she didn't lock you in the attic and forbid you to return home."

"If I hadn't left you and ThomasAnne here, she would have."

Joelle looked at her sideways. "I don't know who's more stubborn—you or Grandmama."

"That's easy. I am." Selah frowned. "I'd rather eat pig shucks for the rest of my life than find myself a prisoner in that place!"

"Now, Sissy, it's not as bad as all that."

"Yes it is! Don't you remember the last time we visited, when Grandmama made us all dress alike and sip that nasty concoction of lemon juice and cider vinegar because she said it would improve our complexions? And we had to go to those crushing parties and dance with pimply boys who'd never ridden anything more spirited than a mule in their lives!"

Joelle laughed. "She's desperate for us all to marry, isn't she?"

"Yes, and she doesn't care to who, as long as he has the right pedigree—as if we were brood mares!"

"Selah, don't be vulgar. Don't you want to get married one day?"

"Not unless I can find a man I can't boss around."

"You don't ask for much, do you?"

"Actually, yes. I do. I want it all, Jo, and I'm not settling for second best." Selah gave an explosive sigh. "Which means I'll probably never marry at all. I'll be crazy Aunt Sissy, sitting on the porch, spitting snuff into a coffee can."

"That is a horrid idea, and you mustn't even think it. Besides, *I'm* the one who's not going to marry." Joelle's lips tightened as her gaze flicked to Gil Reese. "No matter how many times he asks."

Selah patted her sister's wrist. "It's your choice."

"Indeed it is," Joelle said tartly. "How is Aurora? She never writes."

"I think Grandmama won't let her. She gave me an earful of complaining about restriction and boredom. She doesn't seem to understand how much better off she is in Memphis than here with us. Don't get me wrong—I miss her. But we've got to get the creditors off our backs before she can come home."

"What did Grandpapa say about interceding for us with the bank?"

"He claims it would be a waste of time and energy."

"Did he know you were going to Oxford to apply for a loan?"

"I certainly hope not. As far as he knows, I came straight home to Tupelo through Holly Springs. He won't even know I was on the train that went off the bridge, so don't you dare write and mention that!"

"How can I possibly keep something like that from them? What if your name lands in the paper?"

"We'll just pray that it won't."

Joelle's brow clouded as if she wanted to argue, but they'd come within earshot of Gil. Selah smiled at him, and the business of greetings and introductions began all over again.

Gil's gentle gray eyes clouded with dismay as he stared down at Wyatt. "I applaud your humanitarian impulse, Selah," he said, "but where are you going to put another body in that little house?"

Selah had been wondering that very thing herself, but resented Gil questioning her judgment. "There's a sofa in the office that will suffice until we can make better arrangements."

"That's all very well," Gil said, "but how are you going to feed a growing boy?" He winked at Wyatt. "We eat rather a lot, don't we, son?"

Wyatt grinned. "Yes, sir, but I come from Tennessee. If there's a rifle and a fishing pole handy, I'm pretty good at feeding myself."

Gil slapped him on the shoulder with a laugh and, to Selah's relief, dropped the argument. Gil was a good man, and Joelle could do worse. But Lord knew, Selah herself wouldn't have wanted to marry into the glass house that was the lot of a minister's wife.

Settled in the back of the wagon with Wyatt and the luggage, Selah watched Gil at the reins and Joelle jouncing along as close to the outside of the seat as she dared. Just over a year ago, Gil had been sent over from the seminary in Jackson to shepherd the new Methodist church in Tupelo. It had taken him exactly one Sunday to fall head-over-heels in love with Joelle. Selah was amused, but Joelle found the situation maddening. Not being one of those girls who enjoyed manipulating men, Joelle resisted having to ask him for help. For his part, Gil took in stride his status as rejected lover, remaining as close as he was allowed and accepting every crumb of his beloved's attention with humble gratitude.

Selah shook her head. The human heart was a strange and fickle thing. If only Joelle had another potential beau, Gil might give up and move on. But Joelle had already rejected (for a wide variety of reasons) the attentions of every eligible single man in the vicinity, and unless some cataclysmic event occurred to change the situation, Selah was afraid the two of them were destined to become the crazy old maids they had laughed about.

As they drove through town, she watched Wyatt taking in the routine of a Saturday evening small town as it shut down in preparation for the Sabbath. Through his eyes she saw Whitmore Emporium—grandiose of signage, boasting a couple of rockers and a table for checkers on the front porch. The post office with its American flag flapping in the stiff breeze, the barber shop (she made a mental note to take Wyatt there at the first opportunity, as his eyes were barely visible under the mop of curly brown hair), the saloon across from the emporium—also owned by Oliver Whitmore—and finally the Gum Pond Hotel, so named for the tupelo swamp at the edge of town.

She had lived here for her entire life—mostly on the plantation, of course, though the people and places of Tupelo had helped shape her intellect, her morals, her values. The older she got, the more clearly she saw the flawed nature of that influence. Perhaps it was time she took on the job of influencing those around her and those who would come after her. Her gaze swung back to Wyatt. Taking one adolescent boy into her family would be a start. It was a responsibility she did not want to tackle on her own. She would need Joelle and ThomasAnne and, yes, even Gil.

A wistful image of a strong, handsome face with broad shoulders and a pair of intense hazel eyes marched through her mind and refused to go away, even when she shut her eyes. *God, where is Levi Riggins? Why did we cross paths if that was all there was to be? Would you bless him and give him favor in whatever brings him to Mississippi?*

The brief prayer comforted her. She opened her eyes and smiled at Wyatt. They were almost home. The danger of losing Ithaca was real, but God had a plan for them all, and anxiety was a sin. She would just have to trust that she'd know what to do when decisions had to be made.

The alternative was too frightening.

Levi dismounted outside the livery stable behind the Thompson House. His stomach told him suppertime had come and gone. It had been a long day of interviews all over town and waiting to hear back from Pinkerton, who had just now confirmed Levi's decision to follow Schuyler Beaumont. Continuing to catalog what he knew, discarding what he could only suppose, he tossed a coin to a stable boy as he handed over the reins and walked around to the hotel's broad front porch.

He had much to think about, most of it in a frustrating, dissatisfactory vein—the disparate pieces of a puzzle, none of which fit the other or made any sense when laid side by side. Inevitably he came back to his promise to help Selah take care of Wyatt Priester—the surviving son of a rail executive who happened to have been his main suspect in the express robberies. The wreck *could* have been the result of sabotage, though there was no definite proof that it was related to the robberies.

As he entered the bustling lobby, he couldn't help thinking Wyatt must know something. He just had to ask the right questions.

"Good evening, sir. You've come just in time. I've but one room left for tonight, if you'd like to sign the register?"

Levi blinked and focused on the well-dressed clerk who stood behind the heavy mahogany hotel desk. He was suddenly aware of resplendent decor, a massive bronze chandelier overhead, marble floors, the smell of new paint. "Yes, of course." He scribbled his name on the register, then handed over the pen. "I'll only be staying tonight, and I'll want dinner. I assume there's a restaurant?"

The clerk beamed. "Indeed there is. We employ one of the finest chefs in the state. And in honor of our grand opening, there's quite a to-do in the ballroom upstairs. Lots of the local ladies invited as well. If you hurry, you'll have time to eat dinner and change."

Levi ruefully looked down at his dusty clothes and boots. "I don't normally dine in all my dirt, but I confess I'm a bit peckish at the moment."

"Nothing to worry about, sir," the clerk reassured him. "Just tell the maître d'—"

"Thank you, but maybe you could help me with some information first. You seem to be a man who keeps his finger on the social pulse of the town, if you know what I mean." Levi slid a dollar across the counter.

Looking gratified, the clerk palmed the coin. "Of course, sir. We at the Thompson House are always ready to serve."

"Excellent." Levi leaned in and lowered his voice. "I wonder if you're acquainted with a man by the name of Schuyler Beaumont. Student here at one time, I believe?"

The clerk's face broke into a genuine smile. "Schuyler is a great favorite with everyone—particularly the ladies. *That's* no secret!"

"I understand he's in town. Do you know where I might find him?"

"Why, he's coming down the stairs right behind you."

At the clerk's gesture, Levi turned to find a tall, lanky young man descending the curving staircase. Perhaps in his early twenties, he was dressed in the height of fashion, an expensive-looking beaver top hat tipped at a rakish angle over thick, wheat-colored curls. Exactly what Levi would have expected.

But Levi had been an investigator long enough to know that people seldom presented their real motives on the surface.

"Mr. Beaumont!" the clerk called. "Over here, if you please—I've a visitor who would like to meet you."

Beaumont's brilliant blue gaze took a moment to find the voice, then a charming smile spread across the handsome face. "Mr. Dean, my good fellow! I missed you when I checked in this morning." He crossed the lobby in three long strides and reached to shake hands with the clerk. "Happy to see you've found employment here." Beaumont turned, curiosity evident in his open, genial expression. Removing the hat and performing an elegant bow, he offered a hand to Levi. "Schuyler Beaumont, at your service!"

"Levi Riggins." Levi shook hands, noting the garnet signet ring on Beaumont's index finger and the gold chain of a watch fob hanging from his vest pocket. Wealth here, but not the ostentatious sort.

"You're not from around here, are you?"

Levi sighed. "Illinois."

"Don't worry, half my family was Union." Beaumont made a wry face. "We've learned to get along."

"After five years, I should hope so."

Beaumont laughed. "Southerners are good at holding a grudge."

"True." Levi tipped his head in the direction of the dining room's open doorway. "You've been recommended to me as a man who might answer some questions I have regarding yesterday's rail accident. Would you care to be my guest for dinner?"

Beaumont looked puzzled. "I've been in Oxford for several days. Wasn't involved in that wreck at all."

"I'll explain that if you'll hear me out."

Beaumont shrugged, eyes twinkling. "A free meal is always welcome."

"Indeed," Levi said dryly. "Thank you, Mr. Dean," he said to the clerk. "If you'll have someone take my bag to my room and order that bath for me, I'll be up in an hour or so." He slid another coin across the desk.

"Yes, sir!"

Levi and Beaumont headed for the dining room, where a maître d' greeted them. Momentarily they were seated at a window table, scanning elegantly printed menus.

After they'd ordered, Beaumont propped his elbows on the table. "So you want to know about the wreck. It's big news hereabouts. Heard there was some army major rescuing people, scaling the tops of the cars and performing a circus act up and down the bridge trestles. Did you see?"

Levi scratched his jaw. "Not exactly."

Beaumont stared for an awkward moment. "That was *you?*"

"It wasn't as dramatic as you make it sound."

"Of course not." With a short laugh, Beaumont shook his head. "But I wish I'd been there!"

"No you don't," Levi said flatly. "It was a gruesome scene."

Beaumont quirked one eyebrow. "I thought that's what you wanted to discuss."

"I'm more interested in the background of the railroad. I'm told your father is an executive with the M&O, correct?"

"Since early days. He's finally given me leave to branch out on my own, see what I can do before he brings me into the company."

"The M&O is headquartered in Mobile, yes?"

"That's right. I'd been to visit my older sister and her family in New Orleans." Beaumont winked. "Pa doesn't know I'm here looking up investors for a new branch line between Oxford and Tupelo. Student travel should be quite lucrative—" Abruptly he broke off. "Pa says I talk too much. Are you with the Mississippi Central?"

Levi smiled. "Don't worry, I'm not the competition. I want

to know about the rail lines competing for federal contracts. And how they decide where to build."

Beaumont's stare was suspicious. "Not the competition? Then what *is* your business?"

"I'm an attorney specializing in hotel management." Levi could not have explained how or why those words popped into his brain and out of his mouth. But when his instincts took over during an interview, he'd learned not to fight them.

Beaumont's clever young face cleared. "That's a wondrous coincidence! One of the properties I'm interested in purchasing is a derelict plantation on the direct route of our proposed new line from here to Tupelo. The house would make a perfect luxury hotel."

Levi saw the hesitation. "But . . . ?"

"But the property is entangled in legalities. The family who owned it—own it, I should say—has so far refused our every offer. Can't afford to keep it up, but they don't want to let it go. The feds tried to oust them under war crime confiscation laws but ran into a judge with Confederate sympathies—"

"Wait." Levi held up a hand. "Are you perchance talking about a plantation known as Ithaca?"

"Well, yes, as a matter of fact. You're familiar with it then?"

"I've heard of it." Levi didn't much believe in coincidences. And Pinkerton had taught him that the motivation for most crimes could be traced to money or power—or both. But probing for information was a delicate affair. He simply waited, as if casually curious.

The young rail baron gave Levi a searching look, then lifted a shoulder. "I'm not surprised. The place is pretty famous in this area. The old man—Colonel Daughtry, I mean—was quite a cog in the Southern machine in his day, and probably destined for state office if the war hadn't quashed everything. He and my father were acquainted, as my old man wanted the railroad to go by Ithaca. But the Colonel dug in, wouldn't sell, and we spent a small fortune rerouting."

Friendly enemies, then. The entanglements grew by the minute. "What happened to Daughtry?"

"Quite a story." Beaumont settled in his chair, adjusting the fold of his tie. "Commanded a Mississippi regiment deployed to Tennessee early in the war. Chickamauga campaign, I believe. From what I understand, he and his men went chasing down a posse of Union sympathizers who had raided a Confederate general's farm. Managed to catch them, but the thing went sideways when the Colonel got impatient. Shot the prisoners without a trial and left 'em in a ditch."

Levi couldn't help wondering what the Colonel would have done had he found the men who pillaged his own plantation. "That's cold, even for a Johnny Reb."

"The Union outriders who caught him shortly after that thought so too. Daughtry was arrested, tried, and sent to Camp Douglas. He was there at least until the end of the war, then he escaped in the confusion, and the family stopped hearing from him. At least they say they did. Nobody knows if he died or left the country, but he never came home again."

Levi whistled. Poor Selah. A convicted war criminal for a father surely added to the complications surrounding her claim on the property. No wonder she'd been reluctant to trust a stranger with her family's difficulties.

He studied Beaumont's face. There was ambition in the blue eyes, a hint of arrogance about the fine mouth, but no real malice or bitterness. Still, like Selah, Levi knew better than to trust a stranger's good intentions. "I take it the property was left to Mrs. Daughtry?"

"She's dead too, and the entire estate went to the three sisters. I've been dealing with the eldest, Selah." Beaumont blew out a disgusted breath. "She's returned my correspondence unopened and marked 'trash'—in bold red letters."

"I happened to share a seat with Miss Daughtry on the train. She's quite a formidable young woman."

"She's a money-grubbing little harridan."

Levi raised his brows at the man's vehemence. "I found her to be quite charming. She isn't likely to give away her family home just because you ask for it."

"I made a perfectly fair offer." Beaumont folded his arms. "Enough to get her and her sisters out from under the debt and taxes attached to that great pile of brick and marble. I understand they have grandparents willing to take them in and provide for them. I just don't understand why she's—they are being so stubborn."

Levi restrained the urge to punch the man in his aristocratic nose. "No understanding a woman's motives."

"Isn't that the truth? My own sister eloped with a Union scout."

"But you've learned to get along," Levi reminded him with a small grin.

To his credit, Beaumont laughed. "Which is why I was just in New Orleans. Thanks to my turncoat sister and her Yankee husband, I have a brand-new niece, and I went to inspect her."

"Er. Congratulations?"

"Yes, of course, although she is a squirrely little mite, I must say. And they saddled her with the name Delythia, after my grandmother. The poor child will probably grow up with an uncontrollable urge to run the world, just like the old lady."

"In my experience, it's just what grandmothers do. Perhaps you can understand why Miss Selah and her sisters don't wish to subject themselves to the permanent management of their own grandmama."

"Good Lord, I do believe you have a point." Beaumont surveyed Levi with respect. "Since you seem to have developed something of a rapport with the elder Miss Daughtry, I wonder if we might strike a mutually beneficial arrangement. I'd be willing to pay your expenses—plus a tidy commission—if you'd travel to Tupelo, meet with the sisters, and convince them to sell their mausoleum to my company. Then, if you're interested, I'll entertain the notion of retaining your services for the purpose of developing the property and getting the hotel ready to open for business."

Six

Oxford, Mississippi

With his ruined features concealed by the starless night, Daughtry slouched past the burned-out shell of the Oxford courthouse—target of a series of Yankee bombs during the Late Unpleasantness. He'd heard rumors the building was going to be rebuilt and its clock tower replaced, now that the state had received federal reconstruction funds.

Life moved on, enemies expected to kiss and make up.

He bared his teeth. But not him, and not Scully. Long ago, when Daughtry was sent to Camp Douglas for nothing more than executing wartime justice, Scully had promised that when the war was over and things settled down in Mississippi, he would do anything he could to help his commander. Daughtry had already taken care of the two murdering rapists who had escaped in Tennessee. Now he was on to the ones who had ruined his own plantation. A man could spend half his life building an empire from nothing, and the minute he turned his back, a collection of lazy, jealous villains did their best to rip it to shreds. Intolerable.

But he was going to put it back together. Even if he couldn't run it himself—somehow, some way—his daughters would stand on his property, rebuild his kingdom. He'd lasso the wind and ride it to hell and back if he had to.

He ducked down the first alley he came to. Scully had better not argue with him. They might no longer be military, but Daughtry still pulled rank. As the commanding officer of their decimated little unit, Daughtry had been the one to order the firing squad, and he would do it again—let the Federal governor be cursed. He'd taken full responsibility for the incident, making sure his men went free. That was the price of responsibility. Scully, God bless him, had kept up a sporadic correspondence, letting him know his girls were safe with their maternal grandparents in Memphis. And after Daughtry escaped in the transfer to Fort Macon and made it to Mexico, Scully wrote to advise him of the general amnesty of Christmas 1868.

There was some question as to whether or not the amnesty would apply to war criminals, but he'd decided to risk coming back. He touched the patch over his empty eye socket. Even with his appearance significantly altered, it had seemed advisable to change his name. There were people in Tennessee, the families of the men he'd executed, who wanted him dead.

The light was on in the last little row house on the street. Daughtry had no idea if Scully lived alone, or whether his parents still lived. It never entered his head that the man might be married until he knocked, and the door was answered by a little dumpling of a woman wearing a fussy gray dress.

She clutched the broom in her hand across her body in an absurd gesture of protection. "Can I help you?"

"I'm sorry to bother you so late, ma'am." Daughtry removed his hat. "I'm looking for Ford Scully. I was told he still lives here."

"Mr. Scully!" the woman called over her shoulder. "Come here, if you please. We've a visitor."

"I'd be obliged if you'd let me in, ma'am. It's a mite brisk out here." Daughtry took a step toward her, but before she could respond, Scully himself appeared, folding a newspaper.

"Who is it?" Scully moved his wife aside and peered at Daughtry. His mouth tightened. "What are you doing here?"

"Now, Scully, I thought you'd be happy to see me."

Looking anything but happy, Scully stepped outside and shut the door in his wife's face. "What do you want? You were going to stay in Tennessee."

"You said you'd help me get settled if I came back." Daughtry paused, tugging on his damaged ear. "Carson and Priester are both dead, but I want the Yanks who raided my plantation and murdered my wife."

Scully glanced back at the closed door of his house. "Colonel, I got a family of my own now. Things are different."

Daughtry smoothed his beard, not quite as full or neatly trimmed as it had once been. "Does the little lady know what-all you were involved in during the war?"

"Are you threatening me?"

"I'm reminding you what I did for you, you ungrateful son of a gun. I have to set things right, and I need your help."

Scully looked down. "I know what you did, and I know what I did. It was justified, and I'd do it again. But this has to end somewhere."

"It will end when my plantation is mine again." Daughtry clenched his fists. "And when I kill that two-faced crew and their boy commander."

"How do you know who they are and how to find them?"

"There are records. People in the area know who was stationed there in the battles."

"Colonel, the raid on your plantation didn't happen during a battle. It was just a bunch of looters attached to Grierson's band of thugs."

"That's where you come in. I'm going to hide out in the woods on my property. I'll give you two weeks to make inquiries. When I come back, I'll expect an answer."

Scully stood there batting the rolled-up newspaper against his palm for a long moment. "I'll try. Did you know your daughter Selah was on that train?"

"She was not! She's safe at Ithaca."

"I saw her myself. Wouldn't have recognized her, but she sent a wire to her sister to let her know she was safe and sound. She'd been to Memphis and then came down to meet with a banker—" Scully swallowed hard. "Colonel, I would never have given you that information—you know this has gone too far, when our own families—"

"Enough!" Daughtry struggled through a red haze of horror. His memory, the headaches, right and wrong colliding like storm clouds. Events *had* gone too far—too far to go back. Breathing hard, he replaced his hat, then stepped off the porch and backed into the dark. "Every mission comes with a certain amount of risk. Just stay on the job and keep me informed. What else have you come across?"

Scully's jaw shifted as if he might refuse to answer. Finally he said sullenly, "There was a man came through the office this morning. Asking questions about Priester, wanted to talk about the accident—*said* he was a lawyer. But he sent a wire to Chicago. I'm pretty sure it was coded, I've seen that kind of thing before."

"What kind of code?"

"Words substituted, I'm almost certain. Now tell me, why would you go to the expense of sending a wire about continuing a search for a lost dog, unless it stood for something else?"

That had the ring of truth. "You think he's a crook or a law man? What did this man look like?"

Scully reached into his pocket and withdrew a business card, which he handed over to Daughtry. "Like I said, he claimed to be a lawyer, but he didn't have the slick look you'd expect. Dressed well, but nondescript—dark blue wool coat, military-style hat, plain boots but good leather."

Daughtry gave an impatient slice of his hand. "A man can change his dress. What about the face and build? Young? Old? Any scars? How tall?"

Scully closed his eyes, as if reviewing a mental picture. "A little over six foot, built like a fireman. Young with old eyes, so my guess is war vet. Admitted he was from Illinois, so undoubtedly a Yank. I didn't see any scars, but he favored his left upper arm. Slight stammer when he spoke."

Daughtry looked down at the card, though the night was too dark to distinguish its lettering. Didn't really matter what it said, anyway, since it would unquestionably be an alias. "I want the exact wording of the message he sent."

"You know I'm sworn not to reveal message information. I've already told you more than I should."

"That's right. If I whisper a word of this conversation, you lose your job." Daughtry let that sit in the frozen air.

"'Lost dog in Tupelo. Following female.'"

"You think he was following my daughter?" Daughtry had a sudden mental image of the hero from the train, rescuing a beautiful young woman. She would have been about Selah's age. He wanted to choke Scully, to somehow erase the information that now infused his brain.

"I don't know, Colonel." Scully's voice was weary. "Like I told you, he asked after Priester's kin, and we talked about the Beaumont whelp. He never mentioned a girl."

"Beaumont? Which Beaumont?" The Beaumont clan was known to be seeded with traitors and spies. Daughtry's rather simple plan now seemed to have as many tentacles as an octopus. He was going to have a hard time bringing it to a close.

"The youngest one, Schuyler. Don't ask me what one has to do with the other, because I couldn't tell you. I'm just the messenger."

"Maybe he's the dog our agent is following to Tupelo."

"Maybe. I've told you everything I know. I'll send word when I get the names you asked for. If I get them." Scully opened the door behind him with a jerk. "Don't ever come back to my house," he said and disappeared.

Cogitating on everything he'd just heard, Daughtry strolled across the yard and headed for the square. That could have gone much worse. Scully was so easily intimidated.

It was clear that this old wandering dog must follow the lion to Tupelo and find out why his rebellious eldest daughter had gone to visit an Oxford banker. Past time to go home. Like the Good Book said, a living dog was better than a dead lion.

Seven

Ithaca Plantation

"I suppose he could prove to be useful after all." Thomas-Anne stood at the kitchen window, watching Wyatt skin a rabbit he'd trapped the previous night.

Selah, in front of the mirror tying the ribbons of her hat under her chin, paused to exchange amused glances with Joelle, who was at the stove. "Of course he will. You'll be amazed how smart he is."

"But he's such a—such a—*boy*!" Letting the curtain fall, ThomasAnne flung her hands wide.

Joelle dumped onions and turnips into a bubbling broth on the stove. "Next you'll tell us he likes to belch and go fishing. Of course he's a boy! And it won't hurt to have someone around who doesn't mind chopping wood and mucking out the mule's stall."

"That's true." Selah wasn't surprised that Joelle and brainy Wyatt had hit it off in short order. ThomasAnne had proven to be the more difficult party to convince. She frowned at her sister's back. "You shouldn't have started that. You'll have to turn it off while we go to church, or you'll burn the house down."

"I thought I'd stay home with Wyatt today." Joelle's voice was suspiciously perky, and she didn't turn to look at Selah. "We can get lunch ready for everyone. I'll even make cornbread as a treat."

"Joelle! That's two Sundays in a row you'll have missed services. What's the matter with you?"

Joelle shot a guilty glance over her shoulder. "I just . . . don't feel quite up to the mark this morning."

ThomasAnne put her hands on her hips. "Joelle Alexandra Daughtry. Are you avoiding the Lord? Or are you avoiding the preacher?"

"Neither." But the side of Joelle's cheek that Selah could see was a violent shade of pink. "It's true that I sometimes feel Gil is preaching right at me, but I would never—I'm not a child, ThomasAnne. If I don't want to go to church today, you can't make me!"

Joelle was clearly avoiding Gil's romantic overtures, but Selah knew her sister well enough to know that she wouldn't admit it to their older cousin. She'd never had reason to doubt Joelle's spiritual depth, but she didn't want to argue in front of ThomasAnne. She shot ThomasAnne a cautioning look. "You're right, Jo. You're an adult. Perhaps you can get out your Bible and read to Wyatt, after the stew gets to simmering."

"That's a good idea." ThomasAnne, perennial avoider of arguments, reached for her own hat and cape. "And with that broken-down axle on the wagon, if we're going to get to church on time, Selah, we'd better start walking."

The weather was cold but clear this morning, and Selah

enjoyed the exercise. Letting ThomasAnne carry on a mono-logue involving speculation as to Joelle's sudden heathenish reluctance to attend services, Selah walked along nodding and "hmming" at appropriate pauses, while keeping an eye out for ruts in the road and hoping someone would come along and offer them a ride. There was rarely any traffic on the plantation road, but a couple of farmers still leased acreage from the Daughtrys, and the neighboring McCanless family were also members of the Methodist church—had in fact hosted the fledgling congregation in their home for the first year of its existence. Perhaps they would happen by.

They were still a mile from the wooden church build-ing, and she'd developed a painful blister on her instep, when the sound of approaching wagon wheels made her turn eagerly.

She waved. "Horatia! Mose!" The former slaves were dressed in shabby but fastidiously clean and neat Sunday best. "We're so very glad to see you!"

Horatia Lawrence's dark face broke into a broad smile as she waved a gloved hand. "Miss Selah! It's been quite a time since we laid eyes on you ladies."

Mose slowed his mule, pulling the wagon to a halt beside Selah and ThomasAnne. He touched his hat in a courtly gesture, eyes twinkling. "Guess as a general rule we don't head to church at the same time. I told Horatia we was gon' be late this morning if she didn't hurry up and make a de-cision on which hat ribbon to wear. They need me to lead the singing. And the later we start, the longer old Reverend Boykin gon' carry on into dinnertime."

Selah laughed. "And here we are, making you even later!

I don't suppose you'd drop us off at our church on the way to yours?"

"Why certainly we will!" Horatia started to climb down. "Miss ThomasAnne, you come sit up here with—"

"Mercy, no!" ThomasAnne gave Selah a horrified look. "We wouldn't dream of putting you and Mose out."

Selah ignored her cousin's frantic hand-fluttering. "Of course we wouldn't. ThomasAnne and I will sit in back. Horatia, you stay right where you are."

"Well, if you're sure." Horatia sat back down and elbowed her husband. "Mose, give me the reins and go help the ladies into the wagon."

In short order they were jouncing along the rutted road behind a mule with a gait like a square whiskey keg. Maintaining conversation would have been difficult under the best of circumstances, but ThomasAnne seemed frozen by mortification. Selah knew why, of course. It just wasn't done, associating with one's former slaves, particularly in the back of their wagon.

But she didn't care. Her feet hurt, and besides, Mose and Horatia were the two kindest people she'd known in her entire life and she *missed* them. Horatia had been her mammy during her childhood, a source of comfort and wisdom and instruction. And after Mama died, the Lawrences hadn't run away like most of the field slaves. They'd chosen to stay and make sure the Daughtry girls didn't starve. Even when they were freed at the end of the war, they'd taken Selah's offer of a little house of their own, about a mile from the big house. It wasn't the same as having them right at hand, but knowing they were close by provided a reassurance that Selah barely understood.

She stared at the back of Horatia's straw hat covering the neatly braided hair. The former slave sat ramrod straight, thin shoulders braced against the motion of the wagon. Did she and Mose have enough to eat? He was a knowledgeable farmer with a wealth of stored wisdom, Horatia a capable home manager. But if Selah and Joelle and ThomasAnne were struggling to make ends meet, how much harder must it be for the Lawrences?

"Horatia," she said suddenly, "would you and Mose like to join us for our meal after church?" She ignored Thomas-Anne's squeak of dismay.

Horatia glanced over her shoulder at ThomasAnne, then frowned at Selah. "That's very kind of you, Miss Selah, but we're having potluck at the church."

"Oh." Selah swallowed, feeling oddly relieved and disappointed all at once—and consequently disgusted with herself. "Well, then we'll do it another time. Maybe one evening later in the week. And Charmion and Nathan can come too." In for a penny, in for a pound. The Lawrences' daughter had been a playmate for the Daughtry girls until Charmion got old enough to serve as a maid and seamstress. Selah hadn't had a conversation with her since Charmion and Nathan married about a year ago.

Horatia didn't answer, perhaps aware that ThomasAnne would intervene to make sure no such thing happened. And that thought cemented Selah's determination to make sure it did—because Miss Mercy Lindquist of the Holly Springs Female Institute had done her work well.

"So you can see why I'm eager to make sure Ole Miss students have adequate transportation to all parts of the state." With a cheerful whistle, Schuyler Beaumont checked the horses, sending the hired carriage tooling around the corner of a graceful Greek Revival–style building. "And if someone's going to turn a profit on their accommodations at either end of the line, it might as well be me."

Levi's opinion of Beaumont had undergone several adjustments as Sunday morning progressed. Eager to pursue the conversation begun at last night's dinner and continued during the hotel's entertainment, he'd accepted the young entrepreneur's invitation to attend services at the Old Chapel on campus. Certainly he'd begun the day in a state of deep suspicion as to both the young man's motivations and his ability to bring his plans to fruition. But Beaumont's hearty joining of the hymn singing and sincere reverence during communion hinted at greater depth of character than Levi had first surmised. And it was not likely that degrees in mathematics and engineering from this highly regarded university would have been bestowed upon an intellectual lightweight. Beaumont was fluent in both Latin and Greek, and had held up his end of a discussion of the structural implications of Friday's catastrophic accident with ease.

In short, the more he thought about it, the stronger grew Levi's conviction that Schuyler Beaumont might hold an important key to solving his case. He just had to figure out the right questions to ask. "Well," he said, "there are profits, and then there are legal profits."

Beaumont laughed. "There's nothing illegal about buying a tumble-down pigsty and turning it into a thing of beauty that might make us all a fortune."

"Who, exactly, is 'us all'?"

"My father and m'brother and me, to begin with. And you, if you join us in the venture."

"I'm considering it." Levi paused to admire a three-story domed building which proclaimed itself, in large gold lettering, the Barnard Observatory. "But I'd want to inspect the property before committing myself."

"Naturally. But you'll have to operate around the Daughtry sisters. They've virtually—ahem—banned me from the property."

"What are you going to do if I decline the offer?"

"Something always works out," Beaumont said with an insouciant grin. "Government loans are at the ready, especially for development of the rail system. And managers—" he snapped his fingers—"a penny a dozen!"

"Is that so?" Levi felt a hundred years older than this man-child, who was probably only a few years his junior. "I can't help wondering why the Mississippi Central hasn't availed itself of those loans you mention. I walked nearly twenty miles of track with the constable yesterday morning, and their ties and rails—not to mention the bridge trusses—are in deplorable shape."

Beaumont sobered. "You're right. And that will be the first thing we address when we take over."

"When you—" Levi stared at him as though he'd never heard of this apparent bombshell. "What do you mean? Is there a merger in the works?"

"Nothing official, of course." Beaumont glanced over his shoulder, though they were bowling along at a rapid clip, and the streets of Oxford were all but bare on this quiet Sunday morning. Still, he lowered his voice. "But the Central is struggling to stay afloat, and merging the two lines would be to our advantage, if you know what I mean."

Levi knew exactly what Beaumont meant. In fact, he'd

just confirmed the telegraph operator's hints yesterday. The M&O Railroad was highly motivated to make sure the Mississippi Central was forced out of business. His low-key investigation of a $60,000 series of robberies had taken a sudden swerve toward corporate sabotage of mind-boggling proportions.

"You can depend on my discretion, Beaumont, and you've certainly got my interest piqued. I'll take the next train up to Holly Springs and then down to Tupelo for a visit with the Daughtry ladies. Perhaps after I've greased the wheels, so to speak, you might be invited to join me there."

Beaumont laughed in delight. "Now that's what I had in mind! I knew you were a right fellow the minute I laid eyes on you at the hotel. We'll deal together splendidly. Let us stop and give this nag a rest so I can show you around the physics department. There's a professor who's got quite an interesting take on locomotive design, and I want to show him some drawings I've been cooking up."

Levi agreed to this plan, mentally making a note to follow up on the Beaumont family's interest in the booming transportation industry. He had no doubt that Pinkerton would find the interconnections amongst the Priester family, Selah Daughtry, and Schuyler Beaumont of deep interest.

Tupelo

"I'm thinking this is a rash decision, my dear." ThomasAnne hovered like a lemon-colored butterfly at the foot of the church's front steps.

"Don't be ridiculous." Selah took her cousin by the arm

to keep her from fluttering off. "The Baptist church is only a block away, and Dr. Kidd will have to walk past us to get home. It's a simple request. If he says no, we won't have lost anything, but if he says yes, then my promise to Wyatt is fulfilled."

"Simple!" ThomasAnne's soprano squeaked up an octave. "Your grandmother would be scandalized! To ask a man—a bachelor man—to take in a strange fourteen-year-old boy is—is—it's the height of presumption!"

Selah stared at ThomasAnne. During the time she and Joelle had lived with their grandparents after their mother's death, she'd grown close to her mother's much younger first cousin, who was also taking refuge in Memphis. Because ThomasAnne was a model of respectability at the mature age of thirty-three, her chaperonage was the only reason the Daughtry girls had been allowed to return to Ithaca. Selah couldn't imagine what could have prompted such extravagant protest. "ThomasAnne, has Dr. Kidd said or done something to hurt your feelings?"

"No!" ThomasAnne looked as if she might dissolve into tears. "No, in fact, I hardly know the man—" Suddenly she went from brick red to white. "Oh, mercy. There he is—"

"ThomasAnne! Don't you dare faint!" Selah lunged to grip her cousin's wrist.

But Dr. Kidd reached ThomasAnne first. Dropping his medical bag, he caught her in long, sinewy arms just as she crumpled, eyes rolling backward. He stood there clutching her awkwardly, looking at Selah with his eyes wide behind their spectacles.

"Oh, dear," Selah said. "It's—it's a good thing you are here."

"Indeed it is," the physician grunted. He turned and negotiated the church steps with his ungainly burden. Tall and large of bone, ThomasAnne was not a mere slip of a woman. "Follow me, and we'll see if we can revive her," he ordered Selah over his shoulder.

Selah gathered herself and hurried after him.

Dr. Kidd laid her cousin down on a pew. "I need my smelling salts. Fetch my medical bag from the sidewalk."

Selah ran to obey. After handing over the doctor's bag, she hovered close, tenderly smoothing ThomasAnne's thick reddish-brown hair. Her cousin's forehead, she noted, was so pale that the freckles stood out in bright orange spots.

When ThomasAnne failed to revive with the application of the salts bottle, Dr. Kidd frowned at Selah. "Has she been fainting regularly of late?"

Selah shook her head. "I don't know what's wrong with her. But I'm so glad you were right there! She could have hurt herself badly—"

"She certainly could have. I haven't noticed Miss McGowan being of a particularly fragile temperament. Are you sure she hasn't been ill?" The doctor hooked his stethoscope in his ears and placed its bell against the pristine bodice of ThomasAnne's blouse.

"Not that I know of." But then again, Selah had been gone for those few days, and she'd been distracted by worry for quite some time. Quiet ThomasAnne had been very much at the periphery of her attention.

Dr. Kidd removed the earpieces of the scope. "Her heart is beating regularly, and there isn't any noticeable hitch in her breathing." He picked up the smelling salts vial and plied it again.

To Selah's relief, ThomasAnne suddenly sucked in a huge gasp, then coughed. She stared up into Dr. Kidd's clever face for a moment in utter horror, then slammed her eyes shut again. "Oh, dear, I'd hoped I was having a nightmare."

Laughter transformed Kidd's acerbic expression into something resembling boyish charm. "I'm sorry the sight of my face distresses you, Miss McGowan, but relieved that you've returned to consciousness. No, don't sit up just yet." He took ThomasAnne's hand and patted it with unexpected gentleness. "No more fainting spells for now."

ThomasAnne moaned. "I'm so embarrassed."

Selah met the doctor's twinkling eyes. "Don't be silly, it's not your fault," she said bracingly. "Your color's coming back. Are you feeling better?"

"Of course! I don't know what came over—but perhaps we should go home after all. Immediately." ThomasAnne sat up, swaying. "Oh, mercy!" When the doctor reached for her arm to keep her upright, she snatched it away and seemed about to leap off the pew. "Oh, mercy, mercy!"

Selah put her arm around her cousin. "Don't get up just yet. Sit quietly and rest for a moment while I talk to the doctor." With a jerk of her head, she motioned him aside and walked with him toward the church entryway. She lowered her voice. "Dr. Kidd, I'm sorry for interrupting your afternoon. But we were waiting for you because I needed to talk to you about something important." Selah and her sisters had known the doctor all their lives. But as he was at least ten years her senior and a bachelor, the relationship remained on a professional, neighborly level. And that made the request she was about to make of him, no matter what she had told ThomasAnne, presumptuous.

Kidd glanced back at ThomasAnne. "Are you and Miss McGowan in some difficulty—something that perhaps brought on her attack of nerves?"

"I confess, I'm mystified as to what precipitated my cousin's sudden anxiety, though it did come on just after I mentioned speaking to you. ThomasAnne is a dear woman, but normally very private as to her emotions." She shook her head. "At any rate, I hope you won't mind my getting straight to the point so that we can get home for lunch."

The doctor raised thick eyebrows. "Of course."

"Well then. It's this. Perhaps you are aware that our family *has* been in rather dire straits of late." When he nodded, compassion clear in his eyes, she sighed, picking at the threadbare cuff of her sleeve. "I was afraid of that. But you might not know that we have also taken in a young boy, an orphan who was involved in the train wreck over in Oxford last week. As much as I would like to continue fostering him, it's becoming increasingly clear that we cannot afford to do so for much longer. So I wondered if you'd ever thought of taking in an apprentice." She looked up at him.

His eyes, blue and guileless, widened. "The idea has never entered my mind."

"Well, you should consider it. He could run errands, keep your firewood chopped, fetch water . . ." Enthusiasm—she refused to call it desperation—strengthened Selah's voice. "He even knows how to hunt for game, though, to be perfectly honest, he's not as good a shot as—"

"Does this paragon have a name, Miss Daughtry?" the doctor asked with a trace of laughter in his voice.

"Wyatt Priester. He's fourteen, smart as a whip, and determined to become a doctor. I can't think of a better way for him to—"

"Miss Daughtry. Selah. Please, slow down a moment." Kidd held up a hand.

She peered at him. He still looked amused, but at least he hadn't walked away in disgust. "I'm not being rash and impulsive. I've thought about this a lot."

"I can see that. And I'm not entirely opposed to the idea, but surely you realize I couldn't make such a decision here on the spot, without even meeting the boy."

She felt her face break into a smile of joyful disbelief. "Then you will think about it?"

He nodded. "But your cousin's health is the most critical issue right now. Perhaps we should return to her before her head turns right around backward with anxiety."

"Of course." Selah glanced over at ThomasAnne guiltily. "But would you mind reassuring her that you aren't offended at my boldness? I'm afraid she thinks I've lost all sense of breeding."

The doctor laughed. "On the contrary, I admire your charity. Do you ladies have conveyance back to the plantation?" He glanced over at ThomasAnne, who had lain down on the pew again with an arm across her face. "Your cousin won't be up to a long walk today."

"I'm afraid you're right." Selah bit her lip. "I suppose we'll just have to wait here until she regains her strength."

"But she needs food and something to drink. In fact, I'm wondering if hunger and dehydration caused her lightheadedness. I'll go for my horse and buggy, and take you home."

"But that's too much—"

"I insist. Make sure she doesn't move until I return." Kidd wheeled and disappeared through the open church door.

Selah stared after him, feeling a surge of gratitude and something like hope. If her own life and that of her sisters seemed to be spiraling out of her control, at least compassionate gentlemen like Dr. Kidd and Mr. J. A. Spencer and Major Riggins existed in the world.

Eight

March 1, 1870
Ithaca Plantation

Levi tied his hired mount to an iron hitching post cast in the shape of a horse's head and stood looking up at Ithaca, Selah's home. He tried to see it through her eyes—not just a once-grand Greek Revival–style mansion gone to seed, and not the place of his own shame and undoing, but a beloved place of growing up.

The giant live oaks and spreading magnolia were as beautiful as he remembered, of course, but the weedy flower beds had been overrun by free-ranging chickens that had also pecked holes in the boxwoods and other shrubs. The porch floor had collapsed behind the marble steps, and drooping, scabby shutters framed faded curtains that hung behind broken windows.

Lord, the paint it would take to cover the square footage of that house. Ladders, tools, carpenters, and a blacksmith.

The project would be both expensive and time-consuming,

and it was a good thing Beaumont would be funding it. Pinkerton agents often disguised their identities and immersed themselves in communities for long periods of time in order to extract information from citizens who wouldn't divulge anything to strangers. Still, there was no guarantee his boss would approve this rather off-the-beaten-path plan.

Shaking his head, he walked up the pathway toward the sagging front porch. That would be the first thing he'd take care of, to make sure nobody fell through upon entering the house. Stepping carefully to avoid rotten planks, he lifted and dropped the front door knocker with a bang.

Nothing happened.

He stood there listening to the horse behind him chomp on weedy grass, the occasional bird whistle, the rustle of wind in the trees. There was not a sound from inside the house. In fact, he could not imagine three women living in this mausoleum alone.

Frowning, he made his way back to the yard. "Hello? Anyone here?"

Utter silence greeted him.

Of course they might be away. There had been no way to discover whether the ladies of Ithaca would be at home before he came. Well. At least he could walk around the outside of the house, make notes of structural damage that would need to be repaired—assuming, of course, that his plan came to fruition.

He turned and walked back toward the porch, this time with the eyes of an engineer. He'd been at West Point for nearly two years when the war began, and he'd not finished his course of study. But service in the army had given him invaluable experience, and he knew enough to see the cunning construction of the house's undergirdings, the quality of the basic structure and materials. It might have fallen upon hard times—like its owners—but Ithaca had a solid foundation.

Noticing a cleverly camouflaged door in the latticework under the porch, he walked to the right of the marble steps and tried the latch. When it opened easily under his hand, he squatted to peer in. Besides the expected cobwebs and residual dirt, he found a brick floor and the wooden walls of a small storage space. It was empty, except for—

A handkerchief? He reached for it and spread the delicate square of fabric over his hand. Though yellowed and smudged with dirt, it had been hemmed with tiny, fine stitches, a pink rose in the shape of a script *S* intricately embroidered in one corner. How on earth would such a beautiful item have found its way under the porch?

Frowning, he rose, absently tucking the handkerchief into his coat pocket, and closed the door to the cubbyhole. If he hadn't been looking directly at it, he might not have ever seen the door. It would make a perfect hiding place for children.

He continued his inspection around the east side of the house and came to a small brick one-story building situated some twenty yards from the main house. Approaching an uncurtained window, he peered in and saw that it was a kitchen, from all appearances long abandoned. With a shrug he walked on and soon reached the back of the house, where another broad porch looked out on a deep swale of lawn. A large, shabby pagoda stood some twenty yards directly ahead. He didn't remember having seen it when he was here before—but then again, he'd been occupied with events inside the house.

He stopped to look around, listening to the birdsong coming from the woods in the distance, imagining the family living here before the war, the women sipping iced tea on the porch swing. Or menfolk cleaning guns before a hunt, while children played in the dirt below the steps as servants came and went from the kitchen behind him. It must have been a genteel, placid kind of life—at least for the white folks. As always, the thought of the Negroes' bondage rankled. He could not conceive how Christian people could justify such cruelty—or, at the very least, indifference.

But war.

It had come, it had destroyed, burning down the rotten Southern plantation economic system. Now something new and better and stronger could rise from the ashes.

He walked down the gravel path toward the pagoda. Weeds sprang in ragged insolence from every crevice, choking the old flower beds that lined the path. The women who lived here clearly spent little time maintaining the landscape. He could see how it would take a dedicated gardener and a small army of servants to keep up with it all.

He was halfway down the path when a noise made him wheel and crouch, looking for the source. It sounded human, like someone calling out in desperate need, and reminded him of the train wreck. Had he come upon an attack of some kind?

Then he saw a peacock come strutting around the corner of the house, tail feathers fanned and head tucked in hauteur.

Levi relaxed and chuckled. "Greetings, your majesty! My sincere apologies if I disturbed your morning constitutional."

The bird screamed and preened, magnificent opalescent colors glinting like jewels in the sun.

Shaking his head, Levi turned and walked up the pagoda steps. These people had had more money than sense, spending it on beautiful but useless yard birds. Give him a good old-fashioned chicken or turkey any day.

The raised platform of the pagoda provided a view of the lawn sweeping down toward a burbling creek to the east and woods to the west. Fallow cotton fields lay beyond, with the old slave quarters and work buildings nearby. Levi had spent most of Sunday afternoon with Schuyler Beaumont, poring over maps of the plantation. Everything looked exactly as he'd pictured it, except more starkly abandoned.

He shivered as a bone-chilling breeze blew off the river and cut straight through his wool coat. Even so, he was glad he didn't yet have to go inside the house, face the scars of that calamitous day spent here during the war. He dreaded it, but Pinkerton had hired him for his Welsh hardheadedness and refusal to back down from a challenge. Since he couldn't change the past, the only option was to march forward, putting right what he could.

At a sudden movement in his peripheral vision, he turned and saw a second freestanding building on the west side of the big house, this one boasting a tiny railed porch fronted by four white columns. A slender female figure stepped off the porch and hurried toward him, the ends of her shawl fluttering behind her.

Levi straightened. He'd settled that he wouldn't see Selah today.

As she got closer, her gait slowed as if she were apprehensive of some confrontation. Then she stopped altogether, clutching her shawl close. "Mr. Riggins?" She sounded incredulous.

"Selah! Miss Daughtry!" He bounded down the steps. "I knocked on the front door but decided you weren't home—"

"Everyone local knows we moved into the plantation office." She stopped short, watching him approach. "I didn't think you would come."

"I wasn't sure I would." He stopped as well, studying her guarded expression.

Her head was uncovered, the mahogany-colored hair mostly confined in a knot at the back of her head, long tendrils escaping to blow about her face. Dressed in a simple dark blue skirt with the paisley shawl drawn over a white collared blouse, she shivered in the cold. "Why did you?"

He might have been offended by the blunt question, but he saw that she was genuinely curious. *I wanted to see you again. I needed to exorcise my demons. I'm afraid you're involved in a scheme against the M&O Railroad.* None of those things could he say aloud. "I wondered whether you and Wyatt arrived safely. And then I ran into a good excuse to find out."

Her fine eyebrows rose. "Then perhaps you'd better come inside and tell me about it." She turned and led the way back to the office. On the porch, she waited, looking back over her shoulder, a hand on the doorknob. "Wyatt will be glad to see you."

Are you not? he wanted to ask.

But Selah had already opened the door and stepped inside, so he followed and found himself in a large, cozy office with a fire burning merrily in a corner grate. Selah cast her shawl across the back of a chair near a large oak desk, then faced him, hands clasped at her waist. She was not as calm as she would like to appear. "Would you like tea?" she asked. "Or coffee? I'm afraid we don't have liquor in the house—"

"Nothing, thank you. I don't wish to inconvenience you in the least."

"It would not be—that is, please, sit down, Mr. Riggins, and tell me why you're here."

So they were back to "Mr. Riggins."

He sighed and chose a wingback chair beside a table piled with books. The office was, in fact, floor-to-ceiling books, on every wall except the fireplace and where the desk sat under a series of cubbies stuffed with papers. If Selah had read even a tenth of these, it explained the extraordinary depth of her intellect.

She turned the desk chair around and sat on it, folding her hands neatly in her lap. Her expression remained polite and inquiring, if not exactly warm. Perhaps her grandmother had taught her the trick of making adversaries squirm. The thought made him smile.

"Do you find my impecunious circumstances funny, Mr. Riggins?"

He sobered. "Of course I don't—Selah, don't put me off this way!" he blurted. "You know I wouldn't—"

"I don't know anything about you, short of what you told me," she said coolly, "and even that is subject to verification."

She had a point. He wouldn't want one of his sisters to take any man's blandishments at face value. Controlling his emotions, he spoke reasonably. "You are of course correct, but I bring you a letter from someone who is, I believe, well known to you. Someone with whom we share a mutual interest."

"Indeed?" Her tone was suspicious. "And who would that be?"

He withdrew Beaumont's letter from his coat pocket. "Here. See for yourself." He handed the letter to her.

Selah desperately tried to control the shaking of the folded and sealed paper in her hand. When Wyatt had come skidding into the office on a gush of cold air, she'd opened her mouth to reprimand him, then remembered Wyatt rarely got excited about anything.

"Miss Selah!" he'd panted, bent over with hands on knees in the attempt to catch his breath. "I ran all the way from the big house because there's a strange horse tied in front. I didn't see anybody, but I thought you'd want to know you got company. Want me to get the rifle and come with you?"

She laughed, told him it was probably a neighbor, and put on her shawl to see who'd come calling.

And found Levi Riggins standing under the pagoda.

Now he was here in her office, her home. Big, powerful shoulders and long legs taking up space the way her father used to do, smelling of cold air and horses, his hazel eyes intent on her face. He sat relaxed, the hat he'd removed resting on one knee, free hand tapping a tattoo on the arm of the chair.

She tried to focus on the letter, written in a masculine scrawl and signed at the bottom.

She looked up at Levi. "Schuyler Beaumont? You brought me correspondence from that—that vulture?"

He laughed, that engaging dimple flashing. "Now, Selah. Even you would have to admit that Beaumont is quite the golden-haired dandy, with no resemblance to black birds."

She crumpled the paper without reading it and tossed it into the fire. "You know what I mean," she said through her teeth. "He is no friend of mine. I told you how he expected me to hand over my property at the price of one-third its value."

"Well, of course he would *try* that—that's what smart businessmen do—but it doesn't mean you can't come back with a reasonable counteroffer. In fact, I'm here as a sort of intermediary. I told you I would try to find a way to assist you out of your difficulty."

"How did you meet Mr. Beaumont? I don't recall telling you his name."

"We happened to share a meal at the hotel Saturday evening. When Beaumont described his business plans, I saw the opportunity to act as agent for you in what could be a profitable venture for everyone concerned." Levi held up a hand, forestalling the protest burning on her lips. "No, listen. I've thought this through, and I think you'll like my idea—if you'll let me explain."

She sat back, frowning. "All right. Go ahead." She was inclined to throw Levi Riggins out on his presumptuous ear. But since she owed him her life, perhaps she could at least give him five more minutes.

"I knew you were an intelligent woman as well as a brave and generous one. What one has to do is think long term about real goals, avoiding the pitfalls of pride and immediate satisfaction."

"I'm not—" She stopped herself. If she were honest, pride had been a motivating factor in resisting her grandparents' offers of assistance and giving up the plantation. A niggling conscience had brought the issue to her prayer life often of late.

Levi seemed to understand her dilemma. "Selah, what is it you want out of life? Do you really want to live it out in this little cottage next door to your home, while it gradually disintegrates to rubble right before your eyes?"

"There is no shame in living in a small cottage," she said, chin up.

"True. But you haven't answered my question. What is driving your refusal to sell?"

"As you've never been inside the big house, you wouldn't understand." For some reason, he flinched, but she ground on. "You don't know how hard my parents worked, designing and building and furnishing every square inch of the place. Yes, it's excruciating to watch it decline, but that has been going on for nearly ten years, from the day we were invaded by Federal soldiers. You won't find many of us left here who don't acknowledge that the institution of slavery had to go. It was a horrible blight on our state and our nation. But now that it is gone and we've paid the price, there is nothing to be gained by throwing away every bit of beauty and heritage remaining."

"I'm not suggesting—"

"Aren't you?" Blinking away useless tears, she faced him, back straight and fists clenched in her lap. "You asked me what I want, so I'll tell you. I want to bring my home back to its glorious ability to feed and clothe an entire community. I would love to employ the people who were my father's slaves, giving them decent wages for honest work. I want to help Joelle in her passion to educate them so that they can start their own businesses and farms. I want to bring my little sister Aurora home, so that she can learn to become a woman of intellect and usefulness, rather than the china doll my grandmother would make of her."

"Selah—"

"I'm not done!" Hardly recognizing her own passion, but unable to contain it any longer, she jumped to her feet and glared at her visitor, who stared up at her with the beginnings of a grin curling his mouth. "What do I want, Levi Riggins? I want to be fearless! I want to climb out of train wrecks and take in orphans and use my head for more than a hat rack!"

Sitting down again with a plop, she pulled her handkerchief from her skirt pocket and dabbed at her suddenly hot face.

Levi leaned toward her, elbows on his knees. "In that case," he said quietly, "let us discuss what was in that letter you just burnt."

Because she had used all the words that had been churning about in her mind and heart for quite some time, she simply nodded.

"From what I understand," Levi said, "Beaumont doesn't want to tear down the house. On the contrary, like you, he wants to return it to its former glory—and he has the cash and credit to make that happen. What he didn't grasp, at least until I pointed it out, was that no one knows the ins and outs of running such a large place like one who has grown up here and learned the minutia of its daily operation, literally from the ground up."

Selah straightened. "Exactly—"

"Which is why I proposed a long-term lease, rather than a buy-out."

She stared at him. "What on earth are you talking about? I'm not going to lease my home to a railroad executive's wastrel son."

"Well, here's where things get a little outside what you have probably envisioned." Levi's tone had taken on a somewhat oily persuasiveness that Selah instinctively mistrusted. She felt like a cat with its fur rubbed the wrong way. But before she could object, he continued. "Beaumont has what you need—money. You have what he needs—a good head for business and a working knowledge of the facility and its neighborhood, not to mention solid relationships with potential employees and suppliers."

"*Facility?* What kind of facility?"

"The hotel, of course. You knew that's what he wanted the property for. But I've convinced him that unless you and your sisters are allowed to remain on site in a managerial role, he has little chance of avoiding the complications of litigation."

Selah's hackles definitely rose. "Managerial role? I'm to stay and help turn my home into a wayside inn?"

"Not just any wayside inn. Beaumont has in mind an exclusive resort hotel for only the wealthiest of clientele. And if you negotiate the contract wisely—which I'm here to help you do—you will find yourself in absolute control of most elements of the daily operation of the business. It seems to me you'd have the best of both worlds—the satisfaction of bringing Ithaca back to its original beauty without having to pay for it. On top of that, you'd actually get paid to live here, drawing a salary as manager. Listen to me, Selah," he said more gently. "I don't expect you to jump on this right now. In fact, I'd be disappointed in you if you didn't take several days to think about it before you make a decision. But I hope you'll see that the advantages of the arrangement far outweigh the negatives." Levi pulled a second folded paper from his pocket and laid it on the desk. Then he stood, replacing his hat upon his head. "This is a copy of Beaumont's letter. And now if you'll excuse me, I'll take my leave. I believe I've given you enough to ponder for the moment." He gave her a short bow and stepped toward the door, where he stopped and smiled over his shoulder. "I'll come back in a few days for your answer. Perhaps then you'll agree to show me through the house so I can see this legendary place for myself."

He was gone, leaving a blast of cold air in his wake.

Selah stared at the door. What in the world had just happened?

Tupelo

Levi pocketed Pinkerton's response to his explanation of
the current status of the investigation, peripherally aware
of the telegraph operator going back to his mail-sorting
duties. Besides the code of ethics that prohibited revealing
information contained in any telegraphed message—be it
ever so incriminating—operators in small Southern towns
like Tupelo were routinely required to perform a multitude
of tasks for long hours, and this fellow appeared too busy
and preoccupied to have time for memorizing his customers'
transmissions.

Convinced that the clerk had no interest in the personal
business of a Yankee businessman, Levi stepped out onto
the porch to read his telegram.

UPDATE RECD STOP PROCEED STOP WILL WIRE
FUNDS STOP ORIG ASGMT TO HODGES STOP KEEP
INFORMED STOP

Gratifying to have Pinkerton concur with his plan of action. He wondered what the famous detective—a brilliant judge of character—would have thought of Selah Daughtry. Levi wanted to trust her, but frankly feared his own attraction. Beautiful women had been used from the dawn of time to cozen susceptible males. Even their own agency employed women trained for that very purpose. And he'd known female spies on both sides of the late conflict between North and South who had used their charm to trade in information.

For a moment he stood pondering all the shades of Selah Daughtry he'd witnessed yesterday afternoon, beginning with her flustered embarrassment when she brought him into the cottage—not exactly a warm welcome, but rather a stunned surprise that he'd kept his promise to visit. It made him wonder what sort of men she had been accustomed to in the past.

Then there was her obvious suspicion and ire when he brought up Beaumont's offer of partnership. There was bad blood there. Beaumont had warned him, and he hadn't taken it seriously.

But he'd never forget the final breaking of the dam of her reserve. Something in that impassioned declaration of yearning—the desire to reach out beyond the restrictive scope of expectations for an impoverished gentlewoman—caught his admiration and made him want to help her. He knew it wasn't just talk, because he'd had to force it from her.

He didn't know many men with dreams that big.

With a frustrated shift of his shoulders, he stuffed the telegram back into his pocket and headed for the mercantile across the street. After leaving Selah and Ithaca, he'd returned to town and settled into the Gum Pond Hotel, located on

Main Street just a block away from the train station. It was a decent establishment for a town this size, but there were a few personal items he'd need to purchase if he was going to be here any length of time.

And it looked like he would be.

Whitmore Mercantile proclaimed itself (according to the sign on the door) the purveyor of every description of new and desirable items, including white goods, hosiery, notions, and a long list of other merchandise Levi hadn't time or interest in reading. Hurriedly gathering some personal grooming supplies, two pairs of socks, and a batch of writing paper, he headed to the counter to settle up.

He was met by a short, pudgy man of middle years, wearing wire-rimmed spectacles. A bad toupee, matching neither the ring of hair at the base of his head nor his extravagant mustache, tipped rather crazily to one side of his bald pate. "We were just about to close," this gentleman said, as if he'd conferred a great favor upon Levi, merely to address him instead of booting him out on his ear. "You must be new in town."

"I am," Levi said mildly. "Thank you for taking my money."

The merchant stopped in the act of figuring prices. "And from northern climes, if I recognize that accent. Michigan? Iowa?"

"Illinois. How much do I owe you?"

"A dollar forty-nine. But don't imagine I hold a grudge against you Yanks. Let bygones be bygones, I always say— and money is green on both sides of the Mason-Dixon! Haha!"

Levi grinned and relaxed. "It is indeed. I won't keep you, Mr. . . . . Whitmore, is it?"

"I'll admit this is my own establishment—and trust me when I say that I keep a weather eye on every detail for my own self, for no hired man guards the sheep like the shepherd, am I right, Mr.—and what am I to call you, young man? For I hope you'll give me your return business while you're in our fair city!"

"I'm sure I will. The name is Riggins, sir. I'm putting up at the Gum Pond, which is, if you ask me, a rather unfortunate name for a hotel."

Whitmore chuckled. "Some fool wanted to name the community after the tupelo gum trees in the swamp that was drained to make way for the first saloon. But when we came to incorporate last month, someone else"—he puffed out his chest—"had the better notion of using the more felicitous first part of the appellation."

"I salute whoever that was," Levi said dryly.

"Yes, but the name of the hotel unfortunately stuck. Haha! *Stuck*—get it?"

Levi laughed, handing over six two-bit pieces. "Mr. Whitmore, you've been very kind to put off your dinner while waiting on me, but perhaps you could answer one more question. I'd like to know where I might secure workers for a large construction project."

"I'm afraid the news isn't encouraging." Whitmore shook his head. "Most of the men who returned home after the war are maimed and sick, and the healthy ones are busy rebuilding what property they have left. The ones who never went— well, let's just say they wouldn't be real reliable workers." He paused. "I don't reckon you want colored men working on your project. Do you?"

There was judgment in the question. Levi had spent four

long years in hell for the right to answer truthfully. "I wouldn't mind it, if they're willing to work hard."

"At least they'd work cheap." Whitmore shrugged. "If you want to go that route, the best blacksmith in town is Nathan Vincent. He was a slave at Ithaca Plantation, but now he's got his own shop over on the colored side of town near the ponds. He'd probably put you in touch with others who need work."

Levi nodded. "I've heard of Ithaca. Run-down place near the river?"

"Yes. Sure ain't what it was before the war."

"I hear there's talk of a new rail spur going in from here to Oxford. You know anything about that?"

Whitmore straightened. "I thought that was just an unfounded rumor. Wouldn't that be a boon for business? Speaking of . . . what line of work did you say you're in? You're not actually working for the railroad, are you?"

Levi laughed. "Can't put anything past you, Mr. Whitmore. Just between us, the M&O sent me in to smooth the way—which is why I'm particularly interested in Ithaca."

"Ha. Well, you'd better come up with another route. The old Colonel never would sell to the railroad when the M&O first came through here, and I can't imagine Miss Selah going against her father's wishes—be she ever so deep in debt. That bunch would rather starve than give up one inch of soil from that plantation."

Ithaca

Selah went looking for Joelle and found her in her favorite spot, curled up in her mother's rocker by the kitchen fire.

Red-blonde hair falling in disheveled glory from a waterspout atop her head, a smear of ink running the length of her elegant nose, she sat scribbling in a leather-bound journal left over from their days at the Holly Springs Female Institute.

Rattling the paper in her hand, Selah cleared her throat.

Joelle looked up, blinking. "Oh, hello, Sissy, I didn't hear you come in. Did you say something?"

"No, because I knew it would be pointless until I had your full attention. I hope I'm not interrupting some world-changing composition."

"I daresay not, though one can always hope." Joelle shut her journal and put her feet on the floor. "What did you want?"

"I should tell you to go and wash the ink off your nose, but that too would be pointless, as it would reappear in less than five minutes." Smiling as her sister absently rubbed her nose, creating an even wider purple swath, Selah pulled a chair out from the table and sat down. "Where are Thomas-Anne and Wyatt?"

Joelle waved a hand in the vague direction of the kitchen yard. "I think they went to the barn to see the new goat twins. Or feed the peacocks. Or something—"

"Never mind. I wanted to talk to you alone anyway. We just had a visitor."

"Really? Who?" Joelle yawned. She clearly couldn't have cared less if the First Lady had come to call.

"Remember the man who saved my life in the train wreck?"

"I don't believe you mentioned him."

"Maybe I didn't." Selah frowned, trying to think back through what she'd told Joelle in the aftermath of her trip to Memphis. "Anyway, there was a man who helped me escape from the car before it fell into the ravine."

"He just came here? And you didn't introduce me to him?"

That sounded terrible. But she'd just been so taken off guard by Levi's sudden appearance. "Says the queen of the absent mind. His name is Levi Riggins, and he's a Yankee carpetbagger of sorts."

"Is he now?" Sitting up, Joelle tucked her notebook behind her back. "What was he doing here?"

"Well, while we were in Oxford, I revealed to Mr. Riggins some of our difficulties—with Grandmama and our creditors, you know—and he offered to help. I didn't take him seriously, of course, but apparently he meant it, because he came to present a rather harebrained idea for recovering our fortunes."

Joelle possessed quite a good mind for absorbing and synthesizing information when she chose to focus it. Her expression went from surprise to curiosity to amused incredulity over the space of a moment. "Selah Daughtry, you have, against all odds, acquired a beau."

"I have not!"

"How old is this Mr. Riggins?"

"I've no idea." Selah pictured the hard, clear hazel eyes, the creased cheek, the military horseman's carriage. "Perhaps thirty."

Joelle rolled her eyes. "And what was his 'harebrained idea'?"

"It seems he had somehow become acquainted with Schuyler Beaumont."

"Somehow? What does that mean?"

Selah had not considered the implications of that chance meeting. Now that she thought about it, perhaps it was not so coincidental after all. "I had told Mr. Riggins that we stood to lose our property to creditors and that I planned to meet with a banker in hopes of securing a loan. I also informed him that the railroad wanted to buy us out at an unrealistic price—though I did not mention Schuyler by name."

"Selah! It's not like you to divulge such personal details to a stranger."

Selah sheepishly put a hand to her forehead. "I think I must have been more shaken by the accident than I wanted to admit. Anyway, Mr. Riggins says he and Schuyler happened to be staying at the same hotel in Oxford and were paired for dinner. My name came up in the conversation, Riggins put two and two together, and he seems to have talked Schuyler around to offering a sort of partnership, rather than an outright buyout—"

"Wait. What was Schuyler doing in Oxford, anyway?"

"I don't know." Selah shrugged. There seemed to be an embarrassing lot she had taken for granted.

"And Riggins has convinced you this partnership is a good idea? I don't like it." Joelle's gaze was razor sharp now. "What if Schuyler was there to visit the bank ahead of you—to make sure you didn't get that loan, so that you'd be forced into accepting his offer?"

Selah gasped. "He wouldn't dare!"

"He absolutely would, that despicable rake! Remember the bath house incident?"

Selah studied her sister's tight expression. She had a reason to distrust Schuyler, but childhood pranks didn't necessarily lead to adult villainy. "Jo, don't let's reject it out of hand. We need to think this through. Mr. Riggins had some good points in favor of the arrangement." She proffered the paper Levi had left on the desk. "We would lease the big house and its surrounding hundred acres to Beaumont Enterprises for ten years, on a renewable basis. We could stay in our home—in fact, eventually move back into our old rooms in the big house—and wouldn't it be good to see Ithaca come back into its own? We would have gainful employment, me as manager, ThomasAnne in charge of the kitchen, and you with—with, well, whatever you wish."

"Correspondence," Joelle said promptly, scanning the paper in her hand. "That's what I'm good at."

"Exactly!" Selah grinned at her sister. "Anything word-related would be your responsibility."

"And we could bring Aurora home?"

"We could . . ." Selah wasn't so sure of the wisdom of that move. Aurora had become a bit of an unknown quantity since taking up residence with their grandmother all those years ago.

"Are you going to tell ThomasAnne?"

"Not right away. I don't want to deceive her, but neither do I wish to unnecessarily worry her. You know how she frets over change."

Joelle nodded. "Then we pray about it, just the two of us, until we're sure. I'm still not convinced we can trust Schuyler at his word, not to mention Mr. Riggins, a man we don't know at all. How long do we have before we'd need to give an answer?"

"Mr. Riggins mentioned a few days." Selah strode to the window, twitched the curtain aside, and pressed her nose close to the glass to stare at the big house. "I wonder what Papa would make of it."

"He wouldn't like it. But he's gone, Selah. We have to do what's best for us." Despite her dreamy nature, Joelle had a practical streak that seemed to surface when Selah most needed it.

Selah turned. "Do you remember how it came about that we went to boarding school in Holly Springs?"

Joelle shook her head. "I just know how much I missed Mama, how homesick I was."

Selah remembered her sister slipping into bed with her at night, crying in her arms, for weeks. "It's my fault we went."

"What do you mean?"

"I wasn't a boy."

Joelle laughed. "That's the kind of thing that isn't exactly under one's control."

It wasn't funny. "True. But Papa wanted—*needed*—a son. I knew it in my bones. I followed him around the plantation, watching everything he did, wishing I could . . ." She caught Joelle's gaze. "One day—I suppose I was nine or so—I snuck into the office and opened the account book he'd left on the desk. To my surprise, it made sense to me. But I found a mistake, where he'd transposed a figure. I found a piece of paper and copied everything, making the correction."

Joelle's eyes were wide. "What happened when he found it?"

"Well, at first he went roaring around, wanting to know who'd been trespassing in his office." That had been a terrifying sight, but when no one confessed and Papa had offered to punish one of the slaves, Selah had taken her courage in both hands and admitted she'd written the correction. "When he realized I'd fixed his error, he laughed. And said I was better than a boatload of knuckle-headed boys." Papa's bear hug that day was one of her warmest memories.

"What did that have to do with us going to boarding school?"

Selah sighed. "Papa insisted that he wasn't going to let such a fine mind go to waste, and he started looking for the best girls' school in the South. He wanted to send us to Mobile, but Mama pitched a fit, so he settled for Holly Springs."

Joelle's expression was unreadable. "I was barely seven when we left home."

Selah stared at her sister for a moment, then burst out, "But think how our lives would have been shaped so differently if we'd grown up here, sequestered in the big house, waited on by slaves like princesses in a castle. Yes, I got the maths and sciences I craved at school, but, Jo—we were allowed to read! We were taught to write, to think, to develop arguments." Her favorite teacher, Miss Lindquist, had settled for nothing less than Selah's best.

Joelle nodded slowly, gaze inward. "And the music."

"Yes! Papa would never have bought that piano if you hadn't learned to play in Holly Springs. He was so proud of you."

"He was proud of you too."

"Until I got us expelled and Miss Lindquist terminated."

Joelle uttered a short bark of laughter. "Even then, Papa was secretly pleased that you wouldn't back down."

"Mama was mortified. An abolitionist in the family."

"Two of us," Joelle said quietly. "I just wasn't as articulate as you."

A pensive silence ensued. Selah broke it with another sigh. "It was a good thing for us to go away, but nearly impossible to fit in here with eyes open and mouth shut. And not be able to do anything about it."

"I loved Mama and Papa so much. How could they have been so wrong?"

Selah shook her head. "Everyone around propped them up in their beliefs. When everyone *knows* something is true, you don't question it. 'Everyone knows Negroes don't have feelings like we do. Everyone knows Negroes are happier here than in Africa.' Which doesn't make any sense. If they don't have feelings, how can they be happier?" She flung her hands wide. "Like you said, what's done is done, we can't change the past. And the fact is, it's going to take a lot of money and elbow grease to repair the damage Uncle Frederick did when Papa left for Tennessee."

When Selah returned from school, Papa had begun teaching her how to log crops, sales, and purchases, and she could have run the plantation in her sleep. But Uncle Frederick could not be convinced that a young woman—be she ever so possessed of a scandalous amount of expensive education—should be allowed any responsibility for such a massive holding as Ithaca.

Selah had been forced to watch in growing frustration as profits dribbled away under her uncle's stewardship—slaves sold, valuable breeding livestock dying of disease or butchered for food. Vegetable gardens and cotton fields growing up in weeds that fed the local wildlife but did little for the struggling family. Two years into the war, Uncle Frederick himself had wasted away to a bitter shell of a man, then finally succumbed to scarlet fever.

The assault on the big house by those Union renegades, followed by Mama's subsequent death, had left the girls with little prospect of attracting suitors who might have rescued them from their dismal circumstances. Selah and Joelle had moved to Memphis for the duration of the war. Compounding their misery, at the end of the war federal agents had threatened to confiscate the property under reconstruction laws, and the legal battle had ensued.

"You're right. Like I said, we'd best make a covenant to pray." Joelle crossed one hand over the other. "Clear eyes, pure hearts."

Selah matched the gesture and laced her fingers with her sister's. Their family watchword had brought them all through more than one crisis. But it was based on prayer and faith in the One whose holiness provided that purity of heart.

She bowed her head. "Dear Father, Joelle and I need you right now . . ."

Ten

March 2, 1870
Ithaca Plantation

As dusk fell, the light of an oil lantern bobbed in the woods about half a mile east of the Tupelo train depot. The terrain seemed not to bother the man carrying the lantern; he trudged along, quite familiar with the area.

Truth be told, Daughtry knew this land as well as he'd known his prison cell at Camp Douglas. His limping pace was sober, contemplative. During the day, he'd hidden out in a rotten shelter left by Union soldiers after the Battles of Tupelo and Old Town Creek. He'd even found an old rifle, not too rusty, and some ammunition that might prove useful—both practically and as a reminder of the seriousness of his purpose.

He'd been hunting this land since he was a young man, two years married and a new father, determined to make his mark on the world. And he had done that. He had taken his father's gift and turned it into a property of mythic proportions, with that house the glowing central jewel in the crown.

The idea that the railroad—the Beaumonts—could come in and take it away rubbed him raw, much like the bone spur that distorted his gait. Fresh pain was useful, anyone could tell you that. A man must *feel* in order to be alive. Rage had kept him alive in prison, had facilitated his escape, had brought him back from exile. Now it would enable him to destroy the destroyers on his land.

He'd batted the railroad away once, a long time ago. It appeared he'd have to do it again.

Scully had served his main purpose of obtaining information. Armed with knowledge of exactly where the new rail line would be going through, the fact that his girls were eager to keep their inheritance, Daughtry could accomplish the second prong of his mission. Maybe he couldn't come out in the open, but he could make sure Ithaca never slipped into enemy hands. No one but the legitimate owner would protect this land. His father had entrusted him with it.

It was his inheritance. His legacy.

Eleven

March 4, 1870
Tupelo

Rubbing his aching upper arm, Levi paused outside the hotel—which turned out to be much less comfortable than the Thompson House in Oxford. He'd shared a room with a drunken salesman who'd snored half the night and sold shoes in his sleep the other half. Clearly there was a need for upscale lodging in the area.

The sky was overcast, heavy with the portent of something cold and wet—echoing yesterday's dismal failure to uncover further information regarding Ithaca and the Daughtry family or the Beaumonts' push to increase their influence in the rail industry. He'd spent two days hanging about at the three saloons in town, pretending to drink with inebriated and loose-tongued patrons, to no avail. Southerners, even under the influence of alcohol, tended to protect their own. The "Daughtry girls," as they were known hereabouts, and their father "the Colonel" were virtually untouchable.

His gaze fell on the sign beside the front door of an establishment across the street: DR. BENJAMIN KIDD, MD. It was one of only a handful of businesses he hadn't approached.

Why not talk to the doctor? He had nothing to lose except time.

The man who answered his knock looked like none of the stodgy physicians of Levi's previous acquaintance. Perhaps in his late thirties, Kidd exuded extreme eccentricity, pale blue eyes blinking in childlike innocence behind rimless spectacles, wheat-colored hair rumpled. His clothing seemed to have been randomly chosen in the dark.

The doctor looked irritated. "Yes? Can I help you?"

"Dr. Kidd?" Levi extended a hand. "My name is Riggins, and I'd like you to take a look at my arm, if you have time."

Kidd looked over his shoulder with a grimace, then slowly shook hands. "I suppose I can give you a few minutes. Come on in." He walked over to close an interior door, then gestured for Levi to sit upon an examining table on one side of the room. "What's the trouble?" he asked, his focus suddenly, sharply on Levi's face.

Ah. Now *here* was the scientist Levi had been looking for, the carnival-barker's attire notwithstanding.

Levi sat on the table, removing his heavy outer coat. The room was warm from the heat of a small potbelly stove squatting in the far corner of the room. "I've a piece of a bullet in my upper arm."

"Let me see." As Levi took off his dress coat, the doctor added, "How long has it been there?"

Levi unbuttoned his waistcoat. "Nearly six years. Since Brice's Crossroads."

Kidd gave him a sardonic look. "Union, aren't you? You've got nerve coming back here."

"The war's over. You going to refuse to treat me?" Levi stripped off his shirt.

"I advise you not to make assumptions." The doctor took hold of Levi's arm. "Does it hurt now?"

"Some." The injury only hurt on cold, raw days like today, and he'd come to accept the pain as part of life. He endured Kidd's examination of the ruined, scarred flesh of his shoulder without flinching.

"This was infected," the doctor muttered, pressing his thumb against the center of the scar.

Levi nearly came off the table as pain seared him unawares. "Yes," he managed. "I wouldn't let them amputate."

Kidd suddenly grinned and released him. "I don't blame you. Blasted army sawbones. I suppose they gave up looking for the bullet."

Levi nodded. "Said I was losing too much blood, they needed to sew me up or amputate. I said sew away, then left the hospital and reported back for duty before they could change their minds."

"If it hasn't killed you by now, it won't. I advise leaving it in."

"But it hurts like the devil on cold days."

Kidd thrust his hands into the pockets of his trousers and tipped his head. "If I go digging around in your arm, you'll hurt a lot more and likely die sooner."

Levi considered him for a moment, then looked around the room. Books towered in piles on every available surface, including the armchair in front of the stove, and papers littered the small table by the window. However, all was free of dust and dirt. Rigid rows of medical implements, lined up on a wheeled cart near the examining table, gleamed with metallic purity. A diploma on the wall behind Levi's head, from the Medical College of the University of Louisiana, proclaimed that Kidd was a distinguished fellow of surgery and pharmacology.

"I graduated first in my class," Kidd said in answer to Levi's apprehensive gaze. "I know what I'm talking about, ask anybody in town."

"That will be difficult, since nobody else in town will talk to me." Levi reached for his shirt and pulled it on over his head. "In light of that, perhaps you wouldn't mind me asking you a few questions on a different subject."

The doctor gave him a shrewd look. "I imagine you're having a bit of difficulty blending in."

"A bit." Levi smiled as he continued to dress. "But you seem to be a man of letters as well as common sense. And the fact that you haven't yet thrown me out tells me a lot about your sense of justice and compassion."

"People don't like me because I tell the truth."

"You have no idea how comforting I find that."

Kidd laughed and pulled a ladderback chair away from the kitchen table. He straddled it, facing Levi. "So what do you want to know?"

"How long have you lived here?"

"All my life, except for the five years I spent in medical college."

Levi nodded. "Then you're familiar with the Daughtry family?"

The doctor's eyebrows went up. "Yes, Selah is the eldest sister, and the best brain of the lot. When her father left for the war, she and her mother ran their plantation until debt brought it falling down around their ears."

"Ithaca."

"So you've heard of it?"

"I hear there's potential for a partnership between the Daughtrys and the Mobile and Ohio Railroad."

Kidd gave him a sour smile. "When hell freezes over."

"Most of the town would appear to agree with that assessment."

"We're rather proud of our landed royalty around here. Ithaca is a landmark of somewhat mythical status, if you'll pardon the pun."

"Would the citizens of Tupelo prefer their mythical landmark to crumble into ruins? To give her credit, Miss Daughtry has agreed to at least think about it."

The doctor went still. "Has she? I take it you are involved in the negotiations."

"I am. Doctor, please divorce your emotions from the issue. Renovating Ithaca would provide work—steady, *paying* work—for a crew of at least fifteen men. Plus, if Selah agrees to the terms and stays to manage the hotel, it would provide an income for the foreseeable future for her, her sisters, and her cousin—not to mention whatever house- and groundskeeping employees they hire."

"And you want these ladies to work—for wages—at the home from which they were evicted? So that strangers can come and sleep in their former bedrooms and eat at their dining table? That seems outré, even coming from a Yank."

Levi partially agreed. But he also had an investigation to pursue. "The ladies are on the point of eviction by their creditors. Which scenario would be worse?"

"What is your interest in these negotiations, Riggins?"

"As a friend to Selah—she entrusted me with her difficulty, and I offered to find a solution. When I found out about the Beaumonts' interest in the property, I saw the opportunity to bring them together for mutual benefit."

"Do you *know* the Beaumonts?" Kidd's expression was skeptical.

"I've had several conversations with young Schuyler. In spite of appearances, he seems a shrewd businessman."

"As is his father. His brother was one of the most skillful sea captains in the Confederate navy. But I wouldn't say that any of them are particularly committed to ethics when it comes to gaining an edge on an opponent."

"I don't disagree." Levi shrugged. "Which is why I sought your input before I use undue influence with Selah in such a partnership. She wants to stay at Ithaca, Beaumont is offering an infusion of cash to bring the property back to capacity. As long as all parties are satisfied, I don't see it as a bad deal."

"I repeat—what do you stand to gain? I won't let the Daughtry ladies be taken advantage of."

Levi considered his words. "I met Selah quite by chance during the accident outside Oxford last week. I was impressed by her courage, determination, and intellect in spite of her clear vulnerability to difficult circumstances. Since I find myself with business ties to the community for the next several months, I have taken it upon myself to ensure that she is properly settled. Beyond that, Dr. Kidd, I'm afraid I cannot say more until we are better acquainted."

The doctor's expression remained acerbic. "Well then, we agree to watch one another on behalf of the Daughtry ladies. I hope you'll understand if I take the side of caution in whatever advice they ask of me."

"Certainly. As I said, Selah has agreed to think about it." Levi slid off the table. "If you're not going to rid me of my bullet, Dr. Kidd, I believe I'll see if I can find someplace that serves a decent meal." He shook the doctor's hand. "I bid you good day."

The Gum Pond Hotel had been from its founding before the war quite a bustling establishment that, during the day, catered to customers breaking their rail journeys for lunch or libations. It also provided a livery stable for local transportation and, in the late evenings, card games in back-room gambling parlors for the more unsavory element. Though she had only been inside it a handful of times, Selah observed dinnertime at the Gum Pond to be a time of transition, with businessmen entertaining customers, families sharing a meal before retiring to their rooms, and here and there a single gentleman wining and dining a lady.

Since she and Joelle happened to be none of those, the two of them hovered awkwardly at the front desk, waiting for the clerk to finish with another customer. ThomasAnne, violently opposed to their errand but unable to dissuade Selah from her intent, had accompanied Wyatt to the Emporium, where he planned to sell a couple of pelts he'd trapped and cured, in an effort to contribute to his bed and board with the Daughtrys.

Joelle was the one who had precipitated this expedition. For two days Selah had put it off, stewing in the throes of indecision, until Joelle, exasperated, took matters into her own hands. She apprised ThomasAnne, who promptly threw a hissy fit, catapulting Selah off the fence, so to speak.

And here they were.

"There he is." Joelle gabbed Selah by the arm.

Selah followed her sister's gaze into the dining room. There she found Levi Riggins occupying a corner table, writing in the same journal he'd had on the train, while consuming a solitary meal.

"It is," Selah whispered. "But how did you know that?"

"He looks exactly the sort of man who would cause my eminently practical older sister to lose her mind."

"What does that mean?"

Joelle laughed and hauled Selah toward Riggins's table. As they approached, he looked up, did a double-take, and lurched to his feet. "Selah! Miss Daughtry! Wh-what are you d-doing here?"

Somehow, that slight stammer gave Selah courage. "I came to give you an answer to your proposal."

"Did you?" His gaze flickered to Joelle without undue interest, then returned to Selah. "Did you send me a message? I didn't receive one."

"I did not, because I expected you to contact me first."

"Did you?" he repeated, clearly off-balance. "I'm sorry— that is, would you ladies join me?" He looked wildly around for a waiter. In the process of settling chairs and seating Selah and Joelle, he regained his composure and smiled at Joelle. "You are the second Miss Daughtry, I presume. I'm Levi Riggins."

Joelle gave him an uncharacteristically incisive look. "So I see."

Levi seemed not to know what to make of that cryptic response. He looked at Selah. "Please, let me buy you dinner."

"No, thank you, we are only here to talk." When Joelle huffed and elbowed her, Selah relented. "Well, perhaps a cup of coffee."

The waiter returned with refreshments—to which Levi had added a plate of sugar cookies—and once more departed.

"Now, Mr. Riggins," Joelle said, sitting back with her coffee cup cradled in her palms, "I wish you to convince my sister of the wisdom of partnering our home and our family with the business interests of a young man who has, to this point in time, demonstrated not one scintilla of success in managing either hotels or railroads, other than his position as the scion of a man who has gained a monopoly in a rapacious industry designed to force out every private home in its path." She flirted her extravagant eyelashes in wholly unconscious appeal.

At least Selah was fairly sure it was unconscious.

But Riggins frowned. "If you're hoping to throw me off with that mouthful of jawbreakers, Miss Daughtry, you're fair and far off. And it is not my place to advise you or your sister in any business venture. I credit the both of you with enough sense to know when you're given a fair offer. Did you even look at the details of the contract I gave your sister?"

"I did, and if it involved anyone other than Schuyler Beaumont, I'd be inclined to jump on it."

"Any business venture involves some level of risk," Levi said levelly. "But to reassure you, the bank in Oxford—which Miss Selah had already approached on her own behalf—will be your main creditor, not Beaumont. His family's interests are merely securing the loan. Furthermore, I will personally remain on site to keep an eye on developments for some time."

"Forgive me, Mr. Riggins," Joelle said, "if I remind you that I don't know you *at all*."

"And you should know that there is at least one man capable of appreciating a razor-edged brain behind a beautiful face." Humor and challenge glinted in his hazel eyes. "Though I suspect Schuyler Beaumont may find himself set back on his heels before he knows what hit him."

He was, Selah thought, entirely too charming for his own good. And for hers as well, apparently. "Spring is upon us," she said, entering the conversation at last. "If we're going to have a garden, we'd best be planting soon. And we'll need cows and pigs too, if we're going to feed ourselves and a crew of workers. The only livestock on the property are a mule, a handful of chickens, and a muster of utterly useless peacocks!"

She found the full effect of that crooked smile turned on her. "Muster?" he said. "That's an army term with which I'm quite familiar, and 'useless peacocks' would describe a large number of officers to whom I've had the misfortune to report." He sobered, though his eyes still twinkled. "Does this mean you're ready to sign the contract?"

"Not so fast! The dairy and garden are only the beginning of our needs." She reached into her reticule and withdrew both the list he'd left her and a second one she'd been working on with Joelle. "Running a plantation—even in the guise of a public house—is a deal more complicated and costly than Mr. Beaumont seems to understand."

To her surprise, he glanced over the list and nodded in approval. "Which is exactly why we need your expertise. The investors are willing to put in the funds necessary to bring the plantation back into production. Industry begets revenue, which in turn promotes reinvestment. If we are patient and diligent, everyone involved will benefit." He leaned toward her. "Miss Selah, you strike me as an eminently patient and diligent young woman, if a bit on the overcautious side. I think we shall deal together quite well."

She couldn't decide if she should be flattered or insulted. "How you can possibly call me overcautious, when I allowed you to drop me out of a train window forty feet from the ground on a rope harness—"

"Selah!" Joelle gasped. "You didn't tell me the danger was that great!"

Selah jerked her gaze from Levi's mischievous grin and shot her sister a guilty look. "It must have slipped my mind." She stared at Levi again. "I would like it in writing that my sisters and I, along with my cousin and servants, will receive room and board for the next six months, plus fifty dollars a week to be deposited to our account at the bank. The railroad and the bank—or Beaumont, if he is truly funding this mad venture—will agree to absorb all expenses related to the renovation and upkeep of the house and the property, the accounts of which I will maintain under your weekly audit. As manager, I will consult with you, but I reserve the right to have final say in all decisions regarding the staffing and daily running of the house."

"Hotel."

She flattened her lips. He was going to make her say it. "Hotel."

"Done." He extended his hand.

She stared at it. It was well-shaped, an artist's hand, the nails neatly trimmed, with a fine carnelian agate ring on the smallest finger. But that same finger was bent midway at an odd angle, and myriad scars marred the back of his hand. What a contradiction this man seemed to be. Heroic saving angel, hard-nosed businessman, charming flirt. What was she to make of him? And what sort of noose would she be entering into, along with everyone under her wing?

On the other hand, what if God had sent Levi Riggins in the nick of time, to keep her from splintering her family—just as he'd been put there to fetch her out of that train wreck?

Taking his hand, she closed her eyes and prayed. *God, please don't let me regret this.*

His fingers—warm, firm and callused—closed around hers. For the first time in quite a long time, she felt utterly safe. And wildly abandoned, exactly as she had while swinging in his arms over Buckner's Ravine. She made herself open her eyes and look into his. "I'll expect you at Ithaca first thing in the morning for an initial inspection."

He gave her a sympathetic smile. "I promise you won't regret it."

Twelve

As Levi entered the rotunda with Selah, every detail of April 20, 1863, flayed his brain—the rush of fury as he shouted for the men to come to order, the pop-shatter of breaking glass, the crunch of broken furniture, his pulse pounding in his ears as thuds and muffled shrieks came from a back bedroom. During the ride over this morning, he'd tried to prepare himself, rehearsing the fact that he'd stopped it and made what reparations he could. But the iron-red stain of shame marred not just his career and reputation as an officer but his spirit—a shadow that maybe God could forgive, but he himself could not.

He blinked. What was wrong with him that he would voluntarily summon this nightmare? Thank God Selah could not see into his mind.

Pushing away the memory, he reached out to trace the gold lyre melted into one of the red stained-glass windows set on either side of the door. Dust motes swirled about him in the light pouring from the windows of the domed cupola three stories overhead. He turned, head tipped back for that breathtaking view of stairs spiraling upward, tier after tier. A few splintered spindles would have to be replaced, but the crystal prisms of the chandelier, dangling all the way down to the bottom of the second floor, seemed to be miraculously intact.

"Are those gas fixtures?" He pointed to the ornate brass candle brackets on the walls of the staircase.

"Yes." Selah followed his gaze, her tone stoic. "It was a rare extravagance in those days, but my father was so proud of this place and insisted on only the best materials. The ornamentations on the stairs are hand-carved, and the furniture is almost all imported."

He thought of his own simple, working-class upbringing, but couldn't bring himself to be critical in the face of her grief. "How long has it been since you moved out of the house?"

"Several years now." She hesitated. "Right after my mother died, in fact. We went to live with our grandmother in Memphis until the war ended. We couldn't have stayed here anyway. There were broken windows, a leaky roof, and other things Jo and I just couldn't afford to fix."

"What happened to create such damage?" He braced himself.

She looked at him as if weighing whether he merited the trust of an honest answer. "Union soldiers were here three different times during the war."

She didn't ask whether he'd been with them, and he didn't volunteer. The question hung between them.

"Other homes in our area were burnt to the ground, but ours was left," she finally said, as if absolving him somehow. "I still don't know why, but I'm grateful."

He could have told her why. "A lot of things didn't make sense to me either. I'm glad the outcome was that we are both still Americans. We have a chance to rebuild."

Slowly she nodded. "I suppose so. I want to show you the dining room. It was my mother's favorite place—she loved to entertain." Selah led him through a doorway to the left.

He stopped and stared at the portrait hanging on the wall facing him—not one of the ubiquitous paintings where the artist had simply painted heads onto pre-formed bodies, but a quality oil painting full of light and clear color, the brushstrokes delicate yet somehow assured. Whoever the artist was, he had captured three beautiful little girls, all in white dresses, clustered about a lovely red-haired woman in a yellow dress. The broken woman he'd moved upstairs all those years ago. The sight of her, young and beautiful in her prime, made his throat close.

The girls all possessed varying shades of their mother's red hair—one dark mahogany, one copper-brown, and one glittery red-gold like the last streak of sunset. He recognized Selah right off—the dark one seated just a little apart from the others, as if determined to support her own posture, self-sufficient to the core. Perhaps eleven years old, intelligence and humor in the eyes and mouth, eyebrows straight and cleanly marked, the hair pulled into a fierce chignon much too mature for the thin, preadolescent body.

The golden girl in the middle, next to her mother, was obviously Joelle.

"Tell me about your sister Aurora. You said she's been with your grandmother?"

She smiled, and he wondered if his reaction to the picture was that obvious. "Yes, in Memphis. She's been there since shortly after my father left for the war—she was only ten, and Grandmama insisted it was too dangerous here for a child." A pensive look crossed her face for a moment and then she sighed. "More than eight years ago. How can that much time have passed? She's a young lady now."

"One would think, after all this time, she'd be reluctant to leave the familiarity of her friends and home."

Selah's chin went up. "*This* is her home. Perhaps you don't have siblings and wouldn't understand the closeness of sisters. Pete—my papa's nickname for her—was like a baby doll for Jo and me. She followed us everywhere, copied everything we did. We were heartbroken when my mother gave in to Grandmama."

"My brigade was quartered in Memphis for a while. I might have met your grandparents at some point—though the citizens of the city weren't overly warm toward us Yanks." He remembered being spat upon during a return to quarters along the streets of Memphis in the wake of Sturgis's disastrous retreat.

"Grandmama wouldn't have been warm, that's for certain. She still loathes anyone who wore a blue uniform."

"Perhaps I'll meet her one day and change her mind." When Selah shook her head, he smiled. "Your mother was a beautiful woman. I can see why she attracted company."

"We used to have the most wonderful parties. Mama and Papa would send us girls to bed early, but we'd sit at the top of the stairs and listen to the music and laughter." She caught his arm and tugged him toward a second doorway into the front parlor. "You have to see the piano. One of the first things I want to do is get it tuned so Joelle can play again."

He'd been dreading this. There it was, a hand-carved rosewood Steinway grand, dusty like everything else, waiting to be cleaned and put back to use. Without even touching it, he could hear its rich tones in his head. In fact he'd dreamed about it for the last few nights, woken up with music filling his ears.

General Grierson—his teacher, mentor, and commander—would have loved that piano, would have insisted that Levi sit down and play a sonata or at least a Bach invention. But long years had passed since he felt like a musician, so long that he was afraid to try, lest he spoil the work.

He who was afraid of nothing.

"It's a beautiful instrument," he said more stiffly than he meant to. "I shall look forward to hearing Miss Joelle play." He sucked in a deep breath and offered her his arm. "But we have a rather large project to finish inspecting. Should we move on to the second floor? Of course the roof and windows must be repaired right away, but I want you to show me which rooms to set aside for you and your family. We'll need to refurbish those first."

She slipped her fingers into the crook of his arm. "Joelle and I can share a room, but we'll need a second one for ThomasAnne and Aurora." They reached the landing of the stairs, where Selah shook the bottom of her skirt, sending dust flying. "Ooh, things have gotten out of hand here. There used to be a broom in a closet off Mama and Papa's room. I'll get it and sweep on our way back down."

"Don't worry, I'll send someone to start the basic cleaning this afternoon." He coughed as they went on up to the second floor. "You'll have more important things to do. Show me the master bedroom first, please." He wanted to get it over with.

"What we called the 'master' is the guest room downstairs.

My parents' room is this way." She led him around the mez-zanine to a room at the eastern front corner of the house. She halted just inside, blinking as though seeing ghosts. "Mama and Papa slept here until he left for the war. My mother died here."

Selah couldn't have said why she'd volunteered that in-formation to Levi, except that he was looking around with an odd expression on his face—as if he were seeing ghosts too. Or maybe he was simply horrified at the decay she'd allowed to develop in her home, without the least attempt to stem or correct it.

One corner of the bedstead sagged on a broken leg. The wing chair's upholstery had been eaten by mice, and the in-laid mahogany armoire was smothered under a thick coat of dust. Selah didn't remember there being this much damage, but it had been a very long time since she'd been in this room.

Levi cleared his throat. "Perhaps after it's cleaned and re-furbished, this could be your room. As manager, you should have a comfortable place to retreat to at the end of the day. We'll put Joelle and your cousin elsewhere."

She managed not to shudder. "We'll . . . discuss it, Mr. Riggins. Thank you for your kindness."

"Couldn't you call me Levi?" he asked. "Or even Riggs, as my friends do? We'll be spending quite a bit of time together in the next few weeks, and 'Mr. Riggins' sounds too much like my father."

"I could use a friend." She sighed, looked away. Once she left school, friends outside of her family had been a rare commodity. Before the silence got too awkward, she met his eyes and smiled. "I'm trying to think what my mother would have me say."

His gaze held hers, defenseless and open. "I hope she would agree that in order to have a friend, one must *be* a friend. I promise I will never deliberately hurt you. And I will do my best to protect your reputation and that of your sisters. Please, Selah, let us begin to trust one another in this small way—at least when we are alone."

She swallowed a lump in her throat. "I believe my mother would like you, Levi Riggins," she said raggedly. "I'm sorry to be so weepy. I didn't expect to be undone by standing in my parents' room." Swiping at her eyes, she turned her back to him.

"I take it that's a yes," he said in a lighter tone. "Selah, Selah, Selah," he sang. "I have a friend named Selah."

Selah recognized the tune of "Holy, Holy, Holy," a new hymn she and Joelle had learned right before the war started. Levi's irreverent substitution of the words made laughter bubble over her emotion. "Yes, but we have a lot of ground to cover before the sun goes down." She beckoned him toward the mezzanine. "I haven't been up to the cupola in years. You have to see the lookout. The panorama is amazing."

She led the way up another set of narrow stairs to the attic, then on up to the very top of the house. Out of breath and laughing, they climbed out of the stairwell.

And stopped, ears assaulted by the roaring buzz of bees swarming about a gigantic beehive wedged behind the railing on the opposite side of the cupola. The hive, dripping golden honey onto the floor, stretched at least four feet from top to bottom, and was nearly that wide. Selah didn't even try to estimate the number of bees.

She felt a scream rise, but Levi took her by the shoulders. "Shush," he whispered urgently. "We don't want to startle them. Back up slowly, and we'll go downstairs."

The hum faded as they went down, and to Selah's relief the bees did not follow. When they reached the rotunda, she craned her neck to stare up at the dome. The beehive wasn't visible from here, and the hum of the bees didn't reach the ground.

"Well," she said. "I wasn't expecting that. Bats. Mice maybe. But bees? What are we going to do?"

"I'll have to pay someone to kill them," he said, shaking his head. "They'll be a danger to the workers and everyone who lives here."

"Wait." Selah put a hand on his arm. "I think they can be moved. The honey is valuable, and Papa always said crops grow better where there are bees."

"I don't suppose you know how to do that? Move them, I mean?"

"No, but Joelle probably does, or she could find something in Papa's library. She reads about all kinds of odd subjects."

Levi laughed. "All right, then. I've other business to attend to this afternoon, but tomorrow we'll have a conference and see what we can come up with. The Daughtry sisters to the rescue!"

Thirteen

WHITE-HOT RAGE blinded Daughtry, crouching inside a copse of overgrown trees and brush. Selah's letter was true. The Yanks had been inside his house. He'd seen it with his own eyes, when Penelope came to the door of the cottage, greeted the tall, broad-shouldered man—the one Scully had described, blue coat and all—and walked with him into the big house. They'd been inside for nearly an hour before emerging to stand on the porch. Penny stood waving her hands in uncharacteristic agitation, and the man responded by laying a presumptuous hand on her shoulder.

With shaking hands, he put the spyglass back to his eye, saw that a proper distance had come between the two as the Yank walked her around toward the cottage.

Where were his daughters? Were they safe? Something wasn't right. He shook his head hard, staggered into the woods, deeper and deeper like an animal seeking its lair. He remembered. Selah said her mother had died.

That couldn't be true, he'd just seen her.

He began to run, not *away* of course. Always toward the battlefield. Ever vigilant to protect what was his.

He tripped, landing hard on his knees, and fell face forward onto the ground.

Sometime later he awoke in the darkness and found himself at the edge of the small burial ground he'd created many years ago to inter his first and only son. All was quiet, leaving only the night sounds of animals in the woods, the occasional hoot of an owl or crack of dead limbs under foraging deer. A sliver of moonlight pierced the tops of the trees that ringed the little glade, illuminating the tiny headstone. He squatted and traced the letters as he'd done many times before.

Jonathan George Washington Daughtry III

Penelope had insisted on naming the infant, though he hadn't even lived three days, and they'd known from the outset that he was flawed. Daughtry had tried to talk her out of it, because what if they had another son and the name was already gone? It had seemed to him a prediction, almost a curse. No more sons.

Sometimes he suspected that the privations of prison, days on end in the mines, had bent his mind after all. But he could see that it was the world that had got twisted, when a father could not even protect his own daughters. He'd not been here to protect his wife.

It was not his fault. He'd been serving his homeland, the great state of Mississippi, where a man was free according to the Constitution to order his own business. He and other patriots had been working to drive out usurpers who would take away that freedom. Then the enemy had taken over his own plantation, violating his beautiful Penelope, so he'd punished Union-sympathizing rapists and pillagers in Tennessee.

Now they were back to do the same to his daughter.

But not while he had breath in his body.

He half rose, moved to squat in front of the bigger headstone just a few feet away. Sweet Penny. Red-haired, fiery, filling him with pride of possession, though it was she who owned Jonathan Daughtry's marrow and blood from the minute he saw her standing at the top of her father's stairs, glowing like the sun at noon.

He'd built Ithaca as his act of silent worship, bought the piano because she missed her music, imported a desk from Italy because she needed a place to write her invitations, paid for endless dinners and dances that he despised because she adored making others happy. He'd tolerated the girls' fripperies because they each, in myriad ways, reminded him of her.

He laid his hand on the frosted ground at the base of the headstone, sorrow reaching the bottom of his soul and wringing it dry. How was it possible to miss someone so much after so long a time? Where was God, that he could turn a blind eye to one who represented everything good and pure in the world, condoning this blasphemy?

He fell to his knees and sobbed.

Fourteen

"WE NEED THEIR HELP." Selah shot a defiant look at Thomas-Anne, who stood next to her on Mose and Horatia's front stoop, a jar of fig preserves tucked into a basket over her arm.

ThomasAnne pinched her lips together. She had insisted on accompanying Selah to visit the Lawrences and even agreed that the figs were a neighborly touch. Her disapproval at the purpose of the errand, however, was abundantly clear.

Well, she was just going to have to get over her delicate sensibilities. Selah knocked on the door, loudly.

"Why would they want to help us?" ThomasAnne hissed.

"I don't know that they will. But we'll never know if we don't ask. Joelle agrees the bees should be moved, not killed, and if anyone knows how to do that, it will be Mose."

She didn't tell her cousin about the main reason she wanted to talk to the Lawrences. The idea had come to her last night while she lay tossing and turning beside Joelle. She couldn't sleep for that insistent grain of excitement at the thought of making something new and wonderful out of the sadness that was Ithaca.

Of course her wakefulness had nothing to do with the somewhat conspiratorial nature of her dealings with Levi Riggins. In her head, she experimented with the idea of calling him by his given name, as he'd asked her to do. Levi. It fit him—sturdy, dependable, and biblical, but somehow slightly exotic. She had to keep reminding herself that he would be here long enough to launch the hotel, and then he would move on to his next project. She'd best not get too comfortable with their friendship. Besides, she'd never had a man for a friend. The notion seemed somewhat scandalous.

Before ThomasAnne could express her next objection, Mose Lawrence opened the door. He removed the corncob pipe from between his teeth to smile at Selah. "Miss Selah! And Miss ThomasAnne! What a nice surprise!" As he absorbed the obvious tension between Selah and her cousin, his smile faded. "Is something wrong down to the big house? You need a ride to the doctor?"

"Oh, mercy, no, I'm perfectly fine now," ThomasAnne said, overriding Selah. "Although how you knew about that—well, in any case, no one is ill, and we don't need a ride. Here, we brought you and Horatia some preserves." She thrust the basket at Mose.

He took it with a wink at Selah. "Thank you kindly, Miss ThomasAnne. Horatia will be pleased. She's in here working on a quilt . . ." He looked over his shoulder, as though considering the next proper social move. White ladies did not enter Negro cabins unless it was for some charitable purpose.

Selah took the bull by the proverbial horns. "I'd love to see what Horatia is working on, Mose, but you're actually the one I wanted to speak to. Do you suppose we could come in for a minute?"

He blinked but moved back politely. "Of course. Horatia! We got company!"

Selah and ThomasAnne stepped past Mose into a small sitting room with a quilt frame taking up most of the space in its center. Horatia jumped up from one of the four ladderback chairs set around the quilt. She was dressed in a simple brown cotton dress with a red knitted shawl pinned about her shoulders, her hair covered by a brown calico scarf. "Hello, Miss Selah, Miss ThomasAnne. How—how nice of you to come by." Horatia looked, Selah thought, more horrified than delighted, but recovered quickly. "Mose, go get two good cups out the kitchen, if you please, and refill the kettle so we can make more tea. Ladies, would you like to sit down?"

The room was toasty warm from the heat of the fireplace, so Selah unbuttoned her cloak and slipped it off. "I wanted to see the quilt. I still have the one you made for my doll when I was a little girl." Hanging her cloak over the back of one of the chairs, she leaned over to examine the intricate stitches of the quilt's wedding ring pattern. She didn't recognize any of the fabrics and wondered where they'd come from. "Is this Charmion's wedding gift?"

Horatia glanced at ThomasAnne, who had pulled one of the chairs away from the quilt and primly seated herself. ThomasAnne shrugged, as if to say, *Don't look at me, I can't do anything with her.*

Horatia shook her head. "It belongs to a friend at church. She got real sick, and I told her I'd finish it up for her daughter."

"Oh." Selah watched Horatia bustle about with the kettle and cups when Mose came back from the kitchen. She wished she could ease the former slave's discomfort. Perhaps she shouldn't have come after all. But that was so silly. Horatia used to boss her around, and kiss her cuts and bruises, and give her a ferocious frown when she disobeyed. Why on earth should things turn so awkward, now that Horatia was a free woman? "How is Charmion? I miss her."

"She fine, I reckon." Horatia didn't turn around.

"What do you mean, 'you reckon'? Where did she go? Has she left the state?"

"Selah, don't be nosy," ThomasAnne said.

"But—"

"Charmion married that boy against our wishes," Mose interrupted, "and we ain't seen her since, except maybe passing on the road."

"What?" Selah felt as if she'd been slapped. "But—why? She's your daughter!"

There was a brief silence. A log fell in the fire. Sparks flew up the chimney.

Mose exchanged glances with Horatia, then sighed. "I believe you came to see me about something, Miss Selah. What is it I can help you with?"

Selah felt shaky, as if something important had shifted in the world around her. She sat down in an empty chair. "Bees. We have bees in the cupola."

"The cupola?" Horatia handed Selah a cup of herb tea. "What you doing up there?"

"We were doing an inspection of sorts—a hotel agent named Mr. Riggins and myself. I'm thinking of—that is, we're definitely going to go into a partnership with—with a mutual acquaintance, to make the house livable again and convert it into a hotel suitable for rail customers who need to stay overnight in a more gracious and upscale environment than they can get at the Gum Pond Hotel." She had practiced that line all the way home from church this morning, thinking it would make a grand advertisement slogan.

Horatia turned wide eyes on ThomasAnne. "Miss Thomas-Anne, did you approve this chicken chase?"

ThomasAnne snorted. "I most certainly did not. But it is not my house, and I no longer have the place of authority over the young misses that I once had."

"And I call that a blessed shame." Horatia glared at Selah. "And you've let bees set up a hive in the cupola too?"

"I didn't *let* them!" Selah said. "Mose, there's honey dripping everywhere, and we've got to get rid of them, or no one will be safe walking through the house. I told Mr. Riggins you'd know how to do it."

Horatia rolled her eyes. "Mose got all kinds of useless knowledge in that bean head of his. But a hotel! What you gon' do with the rest of the property? There's eight thousand acres!"

"Well, now, that could all be put to good use." Mose, who had been quietly puffing on his pipe by the fire, leaned forward. "What does your Mr. Riggins say about it?"

Selah squirmed at the term "your Mr. Riggins" but let it go. "He suggested leasing it out to farmers who will provide the hotel with meat and vegetables and other foodstuffs and supplies. The tannery, sawmill, molasses mill, brick mill, and the gristmill will all be revived. We can draw people who want to fox hunt and bird hunt, and—" She stopped, suddenly aware that everyone else in the room stared at her as if she'd grown two heads. "What?"

"Selah, you're talking about our—your *home*," Thomas-Anne said. "Turning it into a public establishment."

Selah grabbed the quilt frame, jolting it. "Listen to me. Somebody around here has to think in practical terms. We cannot afford to be sentimental. Mr. Riggins, with the backing of the railroad, is going to turn Ithaca into a hotel, no matter what we do—because if I don't take this deal, we're going to lose the property. I went all the way to Oxford to get a loan, but the bank turned me down. We can sit here and be all prissy and aristocratic, but that would not change a thing." She drew herself straighter. "Also, ThomasAnne, Grandpapa is aware of our circumstances and prepared to come for us at any moment—unless we give him a good reason not to. Do you really want to go back there?"

"But Selah," ThomasAnne said faintly, "all that aside, ladies simply do not go into business. What gentlemen will want to marry three young women who have so lowered themselves—"

"ThomasAnne! Look at us! I am twenty-six years old, an old maid. In five years' time, has anyone offered marriage to any of us?" When ThomasAnne's blue eyes teared up, Selah gripped her hand. "Please, I wouldn't hurt you for anything, but facts are facts. We are already beyond the pale. Taking on legitimate employment can hardly make a difference in our prospects, and it might even help Joelle and Aurora in the long run. A little money makes any young woman more attractive."

While ThomasAnne sniffled in distress, Horatia stared at Selah for a long moment. "You ain't the same soft little girl you was when we left at the end of the war." It was not a question.

Selah felt flayed naked but somehow relieved that all pretenses were down. "No, I am not. I can never go back, and

I wouldn't if I could. I want to learn what you have to teach me, Horatia—and you too, Mose. Having to scrabble for every meal, to repatch patched clothes, has made me see things I wouldn't have seen any other way. I didn't come just about the bees. This opportunity has landed in our lap, and I wanted to invite you to take it in with us."

"What you mean?" Horatia's expression remained cool.

Selah folded her hands, calm now. "I've thought about this a good deal. Three women cannot do this by ourselves, and I don't know anyone more qualified to oversee the daily operation of a hotel than two people who did it for nearly thirty years." She hesitated, then blurted, "Would you and Mose consider coming to work with us at Ithaca? We'll need a cook and someone to manage the grounds. Of course you have every reason to turn us down, but I'd make sure you're well paid for your work. Would you absolutely hate going back there?"

Mose sat back, pulling on the pipe. "I don't mind at least talking about it. Ray, how 'bout you?"

"We have our own home, Mose. I won't give it up."

"No one says we got to." Mose glanced at Selah. "Do they, Miss Selah?"

She straightened. "Of course not! You'll have regular days off to spend however you wish, in addition to Sundays. In fact, it's fine if you want to continue to live here and travel back and forth to Ithaca. My plan is to find a few other young men and women you can train, so that the staff can rotate. I'm not going to pretend we won't all have to work very hard for quite a while to make the venture succeed. But I'm not afraid of hard work. It's better than the alternative."

Eyes downcast, Horatia picked up her needle and plunged

it into the quilt. A long moment went by as the former slave continued to sew without a word.

Selah's shoulders sagged under the realization that she had lost this battle of wills. She'd known forgiveness couldn't be forced, and she was going to have to live with the consequences of what her father had done. Little though she'd personally had to do with his sins, it had taken her too long to make the effort to rectify them.

She was about to stand to go, when Horatia looked up. "I'm not afraid of work neither, Miss Selah. I'm afraid of slipping back into the habit of obedience without thought. Mose and me, we're just getting over the resentment you mentioned, and being close to you all stirs it up again. That's a hard thing to shed. You see?"

"Yes, I see." Selah spoke through a tight throat. "Maybe it will help you to know that Joelle and Aurora and I need you. We need you so much. The older I get, the more I see your influence on me, the ways you shaped my heart and my spirit. I know you don't owe us anything. But I want to continue to be your student in any way you can allow."

"I just don't know that I got anything to give right now, honey—"

"You a good woman, Miss Selah." Mose went to stand behind Horatia, putting his hand on her bent shoulder. "And so are you, Ray. It be good for us to wrestle with bitterness. Throw it off to the pit of hell, where it belong."

Horatia looked up at her husband. "'Be not entangled again with the yoke of bondage.'"

It was a Scripture Selah had heard all her life. Now fresh meaning dawned on her. She'd never been bound by physical shackles, but guilt and anxiety had been dragging her down for quite some time. "Perhaps if we all pray for one another, those yokes will come off to stay."

"There you go." Mose sat down and took up his pipe.

"That's all well and good," ThomasAnne said, looking a bit lost, "but none of this is going to happen unless we deal with those bees. Will you help?"

Mose nodded. "Smoke," he said around the stem of his pipe.

"We know you're smoking." Horatia rolled her eyes. "In fact, you're stinkin' up this quilt, and I wish you'd go outside."

Mose removed the pipe long enough to point it at Selah. "Not me, the bees. Smoke makes 'em drunk and too lazy to sting." He aimed a twinkling glance at his wife. "Too bad it don't work on women."

"Oh, you," Horatia said mildly.

Selah smiled. "That sounds like a good idea, Mose, but how will you get smoke up in the cupola without setting the house on fire?"

Mose drew on the pipe and let out a long puff. "Now that's a good question. Might have to think on that a spell."

"Please do," Selah said. "And in the meantime, I'll get Joelle to continue her research. The sooner we get those bees moved, the sooner we can fix the roof."

And the sooner they could move out of that tiny cottage back into their home. She couldn't have said why that thought didn't bring a thrill of joy.

"I'm not asking you to leave your shop permanently." Levi unbuttoned his greatcoat and considered removing it. The blacksmith shop doors stood wide open, inviting in the chilly gusts of early March, but the forge beat them right back out again with a blast of heat so powerful that Nathan Vincent's brawny black shoulders and bare chest glistened with sweat.

Slamming his hammer down on a wagon wheel rim with a crashing clang, the tall young blacksmith seared Levi with a sardonic glare. "Ain't you?" Vincent tossed the giant hammer onto a nearby table as if it were a child's toy. "Then what exactly do you want?"

Levi looked around the shop, noting the tools hung along one wall at precise angles, graduating by size and function. Scrap iron lay stacked in a corner, and implements in all stages of repair lay waiting on shelves on the walls. The forge and its chimney, plus the anvil and worktable, took up the entire center of the room. The shop had clearly been designed by someone who had been well trained and continued to take a great deal of pride in his work.

The hotel would need a man with this level of skill and work ethic in order to succeed.

Levi picked his words carefully. "I want a smith who knows tools and understands how to use them. I want someone familiar with the property, enough to bring it back to smooth operation. I'd like to hire you through opening week at least. If you decide you don't want to stay after that, at least I'd have time to look about for someone to replace you."

"Can't nobody replace me," Vincent growled. "I'm the best in ten counties."

Levi laughed. "I believe it. Whitmore at the emporium told me so, and Miss Selah frankly won't have anyone else—"

"Miss Selah?" Vincent looked arrested. "What's she got to do with this?"

Levi now saw what he should have led with. "She's going to be the manager."

"What about her sisters and Miss ThomasAnne?"

No telling where these questions came from or led to, but Levi saw no reason to lie. "You know Selah wouldn't leave them behind."

"No, she wouldn't." Vincent's expression became, if possible, even more opaque. "Is she gon' hire the Lawrences too?"

"Who're they?"

"Mose was the groundskeeper, and Horatia was the family cook—slaves like me, but they was near about family to the girls. They didn't run far when they was set free, built a little house a mile down the road from the big house." Vincent pulled a rag out of his back pocket and began to wipe his hands. "Their daughter Charmion is my wife."

Levi whistled. "Well, I don't know who Miss Daughtry had in mind to bring in as staff, but I would think she'll be glad if you agree to come back to work at Ithaca. What about Charmion? Would she like a job too?"

"I bet she would. She and Miss Selah was good friends until—well, until the older girls went off to boarding school. Things changed then."

Levi scratched his chin, thinking. "Well, we'll need a cook, a groundsman, and several maids. There will be a livery and gardens to tend, as well as livestock to care for. In fact—" Levi paused, assessing the guarded interest on the blacksmith's dark face. "I suspect you could help me fill most of those positions within your acquaintance. I'd appreciate your sending good candidates my way."

Vincent slowly drew the sooty rag through his hands. "All

right. I'll come, on two conditions. First, I want my own house."

Levi squinted at him. "Where do you live now?"

"I rent a cabin here in Gum Pond. But I want a piece of land with a title free and clear. I don't mind building my house."

Levi thought about it for a moment. "I imagine we can arrange that. What else?"

"Don't tell Mose and Horatia you talked to me until after they agree to come."

"What? Why?"

"Just don't, not if you want us both." With an unexpected grin, Vincent reached for the hammer once more. "Let me know what they say. I'll have a lot of work to do if I'm gon' move my shop."

"That's true." There was something odd going on between Vincent and the Lawrences, but he needed a blacksmith. "I'll send someone to help you cart everything over to the plantation when you're ready. But before I go, do you happen to have any experience with honeybees?"

Fifteen

EARLY THURSDAY MORNING, nearly a week after she had agreed to turn Ithaca into a hotel, Selah sat at her father's desk, her thoughts seesawing between the bees in the cupola and the accounts she'd been trying to balance. Workers would arrive any day now to start reshingling the roofs of the three main buildings. They would have to be paid. She hoped the Lawrences would agree to be the hotel's cook and groundskeeper. They must be paid as well.

Shivering in the chilly office—she'd sent Wyatt to cut more wood, but he hadn't come back yet—she stared at the list of linens and cleaning supplies that must be purchased before the hotel could take in guests. Absently she reached for her shawl, which had fallen onto the threadbare, faded carpet, and sighed. Replacing the carpet was low on the list of priorities—the roof would have to come first. She couldn't help wondering if an infusion of Beaumont cash would pull them out of this dismal hole. Levi had made it sound as if she would have unlimited funds at her disposal. It would be nice to talk to him, but he hadn't been back since they'd found the bees. It almost seemed he'd been avoiding her.

With a huff she pushed away from the desk and rose. Perhaps she could cure her restlessness by walking over to the old freestanding kitchen to start some cleaning.

Putting on a hat and pulling the shawl close, she called out her intentions to Joelle and went out the front door. She hesitated on the porch, struck by the sun glaring off peeling white paint on the back porch columns of the big house. She vividly remembered the day the family had moved out of the cottage. Aurora was barely two at the time of the move, but at eight and six respectively, Selah and Joelle were old enough to be both attached to their old home and deliriously excited to have their own rooms in the new one. It had been like moving into a palace, and Joelle had insisted on being called Rapunzel as she glided up the gleaming curved staircase with a blanket about her head and trailing behind her for "hair."

Smiling at the memory, Selah felt something of the same ambivalence now, emotions bouncing from elation to melancholy and everything in between, depending on whether she was feeling nostalgic for her childhood or apprehensive about her future—or simply determined to overcome the challenge of the day.

She hadn't heard from Horatia and Mose since Sunday—another unbalanced equation to worry about. If they decided not to accept her job offer, she would have to rethink much of her renovation strategy. Many of her plans depended on their experienced assistance.

Well, Papa had always called her hardheaded, and not for nothing. All she could do was forge ahead, one foot at a time, taking control of what she could, letting go of what she couldn't.

She'd stepped off the porch and started across the backyard when the rattle of a wagon coming from the other side of the big house stopped her. She lifted her hand to shade her eyes. When the horse and wagon got close enough, she made out two tall male figures, one in a flat-crowned military hat and long dark coat, the driver more eclectically dressed in top hat and shooting jacket with plaid breeches and tall boots. Levi Riggins had apparently made time to visit at last, but what was he doing with—

"Dr. Kidd!" She took off across the yard, waving to attract the doctor's attention and shooing an indignant peacock out of the way as she went. "Over here!"

The doctor pulled up on the reins, his lean face creasing in his rare smile. "I was in the neighborhood delivering a baby and thought I'd stop by to check on Miss McGowan. Passed Riggins on the road and took him up with me."

Selah noted the horse tied behind the wagon, as well as Levi's relieved expression and the haste with which he vacated his seat. She suppressed a smile. The good doctor was famous for his somewhat erratic driving skills. "ThomasAnne seems to have recovered quite nicely, thank you," she said. "I believe that episode on Sunday was as much an upset of the nerves as anything." Clutching her shawl together, she nodded to Levi. "I had been wondering if you'd decided to abandon us to the bees."

Levi glanced up at the cupola. "They're still there?"

"Mose Lawrence said he could move them, but I haven't seen him since Sunday."

The doctor began to unhitch the wagon. "Riggins says you

ladies and the Beaumonts have worked out a business plan for bringing Ithaca back. It sounds like things are well in train." He looked over his shoulder as he turned the horse loose to graze. "I've been thinking about your request for taking on your science-y boy. Presumably you've got the means to house him here and don't need me any longer, but I wanted to at least meet him. Maybe he'd enjoy meeting with me a couple times a week for a discussion of whatever interests him."

"Oh, how kind of you!" Selah put up a hand to hold on to her hat, which had nearly been ripped from her head by a sudden gust of wind. "Why don't you both come over to the kitchen, where I was headed, and I'll introduce you. Wyatt will be so excited."

As Selah and the two men crunched across the frozen grass, chatting about the doctor's newest patient, she could hear the regular *chunk chunk* of Wyatt's ax from the back of the little building that had served as the plantation kitchen since before the mansion's construction. Four thick columns supported its broad, deep front porch and steep gabled roof. The kitchen had always been one of Selah's favorite places as a child, warm with tempting aromas, the occasional sugared treat, and Horatia's rather acerbic love.

She noted the sad state of the kitchen garden. Horatia would want to dig up the weedy plot and plant some herbs and a few vegetables. They would have to go into town soon to buy seed, then put Wyatt to work with a hoe. He would more than earn his keep with such simple chores.

Rounding the back corner of the kitchen, the three of them encountered Wyatt working on a pile of wood. No one could call him a lazy youngster.

In the act of tossing a stick onto the little wheelbarrow

kept for that purpose, Wyatt looked around and grinned. "Hello, Miss Selah. Mr. Riggins, it's good to see you again." He sent a curious glance at the doctor.

"Why don't you call it a day, Wyatt?" Selah said. "I brought a friend to meet you. This is Dr. Kidd, our local physician."

Wyatt's brown eyes lit. "A real doctor! How d'you do, sir! Honored to make your acquaintance." He swung the ax down into a chunk of wood, then brushed off his gloved hands and offered one to Kidd.

Kidd returned the greeting, then glanced at the pile of wood. "I like to see a man who's not afraid of hard work. Miss Daughtry says you aspire to the medical profession."

"Yes, sir! Miss Selah told me you might be willing to help me study for college entrance exams." Wyatt looked down, suddenly bashful. "I expect I'm a little behind, but I've tried to keep up as well as I can on my own."

"We'll discuss the matter," Kidd said easily. "Before I commit myself, I'll want to give you a basic test of grammar, mathematics, history, and the like. I imagine Selah and Joelle can help with that."

"Of course." Selah hugged Wyatt's bony shoulders. "But why don't we go inside for refreshments? Then you two can get to know one another better while Mr. Riggins and I confer about the hotel." She glanced at Levi, chin up.

With no noticeable chagrin, he nodded and fell into step with Selah as she led the way back to the office, Dr. Kidd and Wyatt following at their own pace. Wyatt's lively questions, the doctor's deep, quiet voice in answer, helped soothe some of Selah's unsettled emotions.

"You're angry with me," Levi said.

She looked up at him. "What makes you say that?"

"You're very quiet." He smiled when she bristled. "I know it's been a few days since I was last here. I've been making arrangements with the bank, wiring back and forth with Beaumont, and trying to locate workers and supplies for the repair phase. I thought you'd want some of that settled as quickly as possible."

"I did. I do." She bit her lip. "I wasn't angry, just a little anxious. I was hoping Horatia and Mose would have said yes or no by now. I can't make many decisions until they do."

"I met their son-in-law."

"Nathan? You did? He's such a kind man, and I don't understand why—" She didn't know how to describe Horatia's inexplicable antipathy toward her daughter's husband.

"Why what?"

"Did Nathan tell you Charmion's parents haven't spoken to her since she got married?"

Levi whistled. "I wondered why he asked me not to tell them I'd hired him as our blacksmith."

"That's a—I mean, I'm glad you did. I told you I like him. But you should consult me on such major decisions, Mr. Riggins."

"He was recommended as the best in town." He sounded perturbed.

"He is. But still—"

"All right, duly noted." He heaved a sigh. "Forgive me, *Miss Daughtry*."

They walked on, stiff and silent until they reached the office cottage. He reached to open the door for her, gave her an ironic bow, and stepped back to let her pass. Inwardly stewing, she gathered ThomasAnne, Joelle—who had to be dragged away from writing some piece of correspondence—Wyatt, and the two men around the kitchen table, providing coffee for the adults and a tall glass of milk for the boy.

ThomasAnne served a plate of tea cakes she'd just pulled from the oven, then sat down across from the doctor, who engaged her in conversation and even had her laughing at a description of the new baby's pointed head.

Marveling at her cousin's heightened complexion, Selah found her gaze colliding with Levi's. The amusement in his eyes faded.

He looked away. "I really should have waited—"

"No. You were right to go ahead and engage Nathan. You know more about the construction part of this project than I do." She hid her face behind her coffee cup. "I'm used to making the final decision on everything around here, and it's very strange to have help."

"I imagine so." His voice was gentle. "It's fine to lean, just once in a while."

Unable to answer for a moment, she cleared her throat. "We've got to get rid of those bees."

"Nathan says he knows how."

"Really?" Her eyes flashed to his. He looked just a bit smug, and she laughed.

"He'll be here tomorrow to take care of them." Leaving her vacillating between chagrin and relief, he turned to Wyatt. "It looks like you're settling in quite well here, young man. But one of the errands keeping me away all week has been following up on inquiries about your family."

Wyatt looked alarmed. "I told Miss Selah I don't want to go back to Tennessee!"

"As it turns out, that's a good thing," Levi said dryly. "I'm not saying nobody wants you, but I've been encouraged to leave you where you are for the present."

Wyatt swiped at the milk on his upper lip. "That's no surprise. My aunt and uncle only took me because they felt sorry for me, and they really don't need any more mouths to feed." He looked guiltily at Selah. "Not that you do, either—"

She put a hand on his arm. "Wyatt, we've been over this. You're more than welcome to stay here. We've got plenty for you to do, helping out, and now that Dr. Kidd has—" She glanced at the doctor. "That is, you *are* going to tutor him, aren't you?"

Dr. Kidd laughed. "I'll be glad to offer whatever assistance I can. It will be interesting to have another scientific brain with whom to confer on occasion."

Wyatt's chest puffed noticeably, and Selah silently blessed the doctor for his kindness.

"In fact," Kidd added, "why don't you come to me tomorrow morning—early, if you please, before I begin my rounds—and I'll get you started on algebraic equations and Latin. We might look into theories of electromagnetism that I've been reading about as well."

"Yes, sir!" Wyatt's eyes glowed. "I'll get up with the chickens and get my chores done first, though, Miss Selah."

She resisted the urge to assure him that chores weren't necessary. Boys thrived on responsibility. "That will be just fine," she said.

Levi gave her an approving look, then leaned back in his chair. "Wyatt, before we leave the subject, I wondered what else you can tell me about your father. Perhaps he left you provided for—"

"I don't want anything of his." Wyatt's freckled face had suddenly gone hard. "He left me and my ma alone for years without a word. I don't think he'd've come for me at all if she hadn't passed. And—except for landing with you folks—I'd have been better off without him."

"That may be true," Levi said matter-of-factly, "but you've nothing to lose in tracking your heritage. And you don't want to turn down anything that might help these ladies here, now do you?"

Wyatt looked down. "No, sir, I reckon not."

"Do you have any idea where in New Orleans your pa might have been taking you?"

"He wrote down the address and stuck it in my bag, but that got busted up and scattered in the wreck. I'm sorry, I didn't memorize it." Wyatt paused, thinking. "Maybe in the Garden District somewhere?"

Levi nodded. "I'll send someone to make inquiries there. And you say he met you in Humboldt? How long had he been there before you got on the train for New Orleans?"

Wyatt scrunched his face. "About two weeks, I guess. I know it was the middle of February, and we'd just had a big ice storm that tore up a bunch of trees and bridges."

"Huh." Levi looked interested. "That's about when a train robbery in the area that I heard about happened. Your pa involved in that?"

Wyatt shrugged. "If he was, he didn't say anything about it. Like I told Miss Selah, my pa was always sure somebody was out to get him."

Levi glanced at Selah, eyebrows up. She couldn't remember if she'd mentioned that to him when they first discussed Wyatt's situation at the Spencers' home. And she didn't know why he would care. There was something oddly pointed about Levi's questions.

Maybe he realized that, for he chuckled, relaxing farther in his chair. "Oh well," he said, "all kinds of intense emotions left over from the war. I admit to looking over my shoulder now and again myself."

Selah had been watching Wyatt closely, alarmed at the shadows deepening in his eyes. She was about to intervene when she felt Levi's hand close over her wrist. Her gaze flashed to his, and he shook his head.

Indignantly she pulled free.

But Wyatt had already leaned forward. "Pa made me watch out for this one particular man," he told Levi, his voice thready. "A big man with a scar through one eye. He said this man could hide anywhere, and if I saw him I was to run for the closest law officer."

"Did you see him on the train?" Levi asked quietly. Not careless, but matter-of-fact. "Or since then?"

"No, sir." Wyatt swallowed. "But I dream about him. Because I think I saw him once before, a long time ago during the war."

Levi's father had always told him that when you want to help people, you tell them the truth. When you want to help yourself, you tell them what they want to hear. He repeated that to himself several times as he rode alongside Nathan Vincent's blacksmith wagon toward Ithaca.

The problem was, he could not tell the complete truth to anyone connected to this case. The whole investigation had turned into a Gordian snarl of complications from which he saw no way of extricating himself anytime soon. Objectively, a run-down Mississippi plantation seemed the least likely of connections to a string of train robberies in middle Tennessee. But the more he pulled at the strands of the knot, the more clearly he saw a path leading to Ithaca as the center of the maze.

As much as he wanted to take Selah into his confidence—maybe even ask her to further question Wyatt Priester—there was something that she wasn't telling him. Her reaction to Wyatt's description of the man his father had told him to watch out for—eerily similar to that of the leader of the train robbery gang—had been no more than a widening of the eyes followed by a quick glance out the kitchen window.

If Levi had been looking away, he would have missed it. In fact, he could be mistaking a simple response to a noise outside for what resembled guilt. But he'd had enough experience interviewing guilty people that the inevitable conclusion was that he'd best continue to hold his cards close to the vest.

"Hey, boss." Nathan was pulling the wagon to a stop on the lane just inside the plantation's broad front gate. "Something going on up there."

Levi reined in, following the blacksmith's gaze to the front of the mansion. Yesterday, as he and the doctor made their adieus, he'd told Selah he wanted to bring Nathan back with him in the morning. The plan was to move the blacksmith's tools and equipment into the old shop, which, once restored, would be vital to the rest of the renovation process. She hadn't said anything about other work being done today.

He squinted, unable to distinguish the identities of the two white women, plus a colored man and woman who stood gesticulating at the foot of the porch. "Well, let's go see."

He nudged the horse's ribs, while Nathan started the wagon. As he got closer, he identified Selah and Joelle, who held an open book in her hand, but the Negroes were strangers to him. But judging by Nathan's gradual slowing of the wagon behind him, they had to be Mose and Horatia Lawrence.

Well, this should be interesting.

As he dismounted and hitched the horse, Selah rushed toward him.

"Levi! You're just in time." Her hair, he noticed, was bound in its usual neat, practical coronet of braids. She wore a different dress than she'd had on yesterday, covered by the soft gray knit shawl she favored. Her cheeks were flushed, and she looked very glad to see him.

"Am I?" He looked over his shoulder to find a very reluctant young blacksmith drawing the wagon to a halt. "You remember Nathan Vincent, don't you?"

"Yes, of course." Selah collected herself and smiled at Nathan. "I'm so glad you could come. Maybe you'll be able to—" She broke off, clearly uneasy. "I wish I'd known—but it's too late now. They're here, and—" She gulped. "Nathan, Charmion's parents have agreed to come to work here too."

Nathan returned her smile. "That's good." The two words were slow, deep, measured. Levi got the feeling he'd been anticipating this meeting for quite some time. Nathan stepped around Selah and approached his father-in-law. "Mose. It's time you quit lettin' your wife wear the pants. I know good and well I'm too black and ugly for your daughter, but she took me on anyway. Ain't you ready to bury the hatchet?"

Horatia stomped toward him, fists clenched. "Who do you think you—"

But Mose stilled her with an upraised hand. "Where is

she?" His voice was calm, but his stance, half turned toward his wife, revealed his tension.

"At home. She'll be moving here with me, soon's we can build us a little house." Nathan paused, looked hard at Horatia. "She gonna have your grandbaby."

Horatia sucked in a breath. "When?"

"This summer. She gettin' big already."

"Oh, my." Horatia's hands went to her mouth. Her eyes went from the top of the tall young man's raggedly cropped head, over the brawny shoulders under a homespun brown shirt, down to his big feet clad in cracked leather boots.

Levi wondered if she also noted the pride in his posture, the injury and hope mingled in his dark eyes.

Horatia wheeled without a word and marched around the side of the house.

Mose watched her go, a slight smile playing about his lips. "That woman's neck so stiff she might as well got a broom handle down her back." He turned to Nathan. "She'll get over it when the baby get here. You been taking care of my little girl?"

"Yes, sir. You know I do." Nathan turned his huge, callused hands palm up. "Long's I got these two hands and my anvil, we gon' eat just fine."

"Well, it's what's between the ears that be the important thing," Mose said dryly.

"I got plenty of know-how, even if I ain't learned to read and write yet, if that's what you mean," Nathan said. "But I was thinking, Miss Selah, we might make something of a trade—for a while at least. Y'all teach me and Charmion our letters, and we'll work for just food and supplies."

If Levi could have been granted three wishes, the first

would have been for the ability to sketch Selah's face in that moment and have it to look at for the rest of his life. She blinked rapidly, cleared her throat, and said threadily, "Nathan, that's very generous, but I don't know how I'll have time—"

"I'll do it." Joelle stepped forward in her languid way, and Levi saw she held a thick book under one arm, with a finger stuck between the pages to hold a spot. "Of course I'll teach you both. We'll work for an hour in the kitchen, midday, when we stop for lunch." She fixed Selah with a look from beneath raised eyebrows. "That will be all right, won't it?"

"Certainly. That's a wonderful idea." Selah gave her sister a nod of approval. "But we've got to move those bees out of the cupola before we can do anything else. Why don't you show Nathan the picture of the smoker you found in the Quimby book. Maybe he could design one for us."

Looking intrigued, Nathan stepped closer, and he and Joelle sat down side by side on the steps to pore over the book's diagrams, with Joelle reading the description aloud to him.

Levi, Selah, and Mose stood for a pensive moment, staring at the red-gold head leaning near the rough black one. Levi had no idea what to make of it, other than satisfaction that a small hurdle in the process of reconciliation seemed to have been overcome.

Mose finally sighed, removed his pipe from his coat pocket, and began to pack the bowl with tobacco. "I was gonna suggest smoking the bees with this, but seems the old ways ain't good enough no more. Let me go see about the old lady, or I may have to sleep in the barn tonight." Winking at Selah, he turned to trace Horatia's steps.

Selah smiled, glanced up at Levi. "Thank you for bringing Nathan on."

"You're not angry with me anymore?"

"I was never angry . . . Well, not about that anyway." Now she grinned, giving Levi a glimpse of the mischief inside this beautiful, hardheaded rebel.

He laughed. "What were you angry about?"

"The fear that you'd launched me and my family into this monstrous, expensive, time-consuming project and then left me to deal with it alone." She sighed. "I have trouble trusting people."

He managed to hold her gaze somehow. "I know. I'll do my best not to let you down."

The almost certain failure of that promise filled him with despair.

Sixteen

"THAT'S IT?" Selah bent to examine the contraption Nathan, Mose, and Joelle had been working on all weekend. It sat on the dining room table, magnificent in its homeliness—a series of square frames that would slide in and out of grooves notched into the sides of a wooden box.

"Doesn't look like much, does it?" Joelle smiled at Nathan. "But it looks exactly like the diagram, and the measurements are perfect. Nathan even hinged the lid so we can open and close it when we're moving the bees out to the woods. And look." She picked up a flat, scythe-like implement lying next to the box. "This will cut the comb into slices so they can be inserted into the frames. We can move the whole hive without it falling apart."

Selah shuddered and backed up a step, though there wasn't a bee in sight. "I can't imagine a swarm of bees letting you cut their hive apart."

Mose, who had been silently watching the inspection, drew on his pipe, then lowered it with a puff. "That's where the smoke come in. Keeps the bees quiet. And—" he jabbed the air with the pipe stem—"that's why it matter who take on this operation. The minute you gets nervous or loud, bees goin' on the attack."

Levi broke the silence ensuing from that ominous prediction. "Then who's going to tackle it? I confess, I've had little experience with bees."

Everyone in the room looked at Mose.

He scowled. "This old hide pretty tough, but I ain't hankerin' to be a pin cushion for no gang of insects. Besides, my hands ain't as steady as they used to be."

"I don't blame you," Selah said with a laugh. "But I agree that it needs to be someone with a steady hand, a relaxed demeanor, someone who can work quickly—"

"It was my idea," Joelle said resolutely. "I've been studying the process. If Mose will come up with me and operate the smoker, I think we can manage it."

"Now, Miss Joelle, I don't like that idea at all." Nathan looked horrified.

Selah's skin crawled too. She looked at Levi for corroboration.

After a pause, he said reluctantly, "I'm sorry, Selah, but I think that may be our best option. I don't mind coming up too, to help in case of emergency. What's needed here, though, isn't strength, but dexterity and common sense."

Until today, Selah wouldn't have accredited her sister with either of those qualities, but she supposed she had little choice in the matter. She met Joelle's gaze, all but willing her sister to change her mind. "Maybe we should just kill them all," she blurted.

Joelle laughed. "You know we can't do that. I've got a couple of veils at the cottage. I'll go get them for Mose and me. We'll cover up in several layers of clothes and gloves, and hope for the best."

Finding herself outvoted on the subject, Selah backed off. She paced the dining room, studied the brushstrokes of the portrait of herself and her sisters with their mother, sat down, and jumped to her feet to begin prowling again. Levi had wandered into the parlor, and she could hear him plunking random notes on the piano.

Just when Selah thought her nerves could no longer stand the wait, Joelle returned, wearing an outlandish collection of clothing that included her own blouse, an old gardening jacket and boots, along with a pair of Wyatt's breeches. Under her arm was a straw hat with her funeral veil dragging the ground.

ThomasAnne turned from the window and gasped. "Joelle! Remove those—those—men's nether garments immediately!"

Joelle glanced at Selah. "I could, but I doubt you'd like that any better." She reached for the button at her waist.

Predictably, ThomasAnne let out a scandalized shriek. Joelle grinned.

Levi's head appeared around the doorway. "Is everyone all right in here? Ah. Very practical costume, Joelle. And here's our other apian knight, set to vanquish the buzzing hordes."

Mose walked in, squinting dubiously at the veil draped over his own hat. "I think I may jus' take my chances with my bare face, if it's all the same to you, Miss Jo."

Joelle shrugged. "It's your face." She took a deep breath. "If you're ready, let's go and get this over with."

Everyone trooped into the foyer, where Nathan waited with the big frame box and smoker. Selah had examined the cool-air smoker and found it to be a fairly simple contraption made out of a tin red pepper can, a smaller tobacco can, some copper piping, and a small leather bellows. Joelle was to handle the bees and slice the comb, while Mose dealt with the smoker. Levi and Nathan would accompany them as far as the top of the stairs and handle any unplanned emergencies.

Selah could only pray there would be no such emergencies. She could only pray, period. She didn't know what else to do.

Moving a large hive of bees down three flights of stairs turned out to be about as easy as Levi had expected it to be. Not impossible. But pretty close to it.

What he hadn't expected was the atmosphere of unity and cooperation he found in working alongside a bookish Southern belle and two former slaves with as much reason to like each other as a fox and a bobcat tied by the tails inside a burlap sack.

Whatever his reservations, Levi found himself inching farther into the cupola so that he could get a better view of the proceedings. The bees, due perhaps to the intermittent puffs of smoke, perhaps to the quiet conversation between Joelle and Mose, remained calm and stayed close to the hive. By the time Joelle had cut most of the comb one slice at a time, transferring it to the frames—which Nathan attached and then slid into the box's grooves—Levi was near enough to appreciate Joelle's excitement when she captured the queen.

"Isn't she beautiful?" Joelle murmured, staring at the insect tumbling in the little net bag she'd created for the purpose.

"If you say so." Resisting a strong urge to scratch, Levi

backed up a step. He sure hoped her majesty didn't get loose before she and her vassals relocated to the woods.

Within another few minutes—Levi supposed the whole process had taken less than half an hour—the last of the comb had been detached from the ceiling and rounded wall. Nathan gently closed the lid of the box, trapping the bees inside. The four of them looked at each other.

And then the window behind Levi shattered. A loud buzz whizzed past his head, accompanied by a sting at the top of his ear. Instinctively he ducked, clapped his hand to his head. He stared at his bloody hand. That was no bee—it was a bullet.

He'd been shot.

Another loud pop exploded from outside, and a second bullet smashed the glass on the opposite side of the cupola.

"Get down!" He yanked Joelle to the floor and crouched over her.

The other two men were already crawling for the stairs.

"Come on, let's get out of here." All but shoving Joelle toward the stairs, he followed, blood dripping from his ear.

Then he realized there were smeared puddles of blood ahead of him. One of the others had been hit too. He kept going, hearing more gunfire behind and above him, windows shattering.

He was armed with a pistol, but that would do no good against an assailant at a distance with a rifle. If the shooter had a Spencer repeating rifle—assuming there was only one— he had used five rounds, with two to go before he would have to stop and reload. Levi might have time to secure his own carbine from his horse and get the women to a safer location before any renewed attack.

Sure enough, the firing stopped, but Levi was beginning to feel lightheaded. He paused, panting. "Mose—Nathan, which one of you is hit?"

"It's Mose," Nathan replied from the floor of the attic. "He fainted. Looks like he was clipped in the head. Whoever that was, he a good shot."

"We're lucky he missed you and Joelle. Jo, you all right?"

"Yes." Her breathing was ragged, but she sat up and removed the hat and veil. She surveyed Levi, her blue eyes dark with worry but not panic. These Daughtry women were made of stern stuff. "You're bleeding." She reached for him.

"It's just a nick." Levi slid past her and reached Mose, whose head wound bled freely but seemed to be only surface. Laying two fingers on the pulse point beneath the Negro's ear, he found a strong heartbeat. *Thank God.* "You two see what you can do for Mose while I go down for my rifle."

"Who *was* that?" Joelle demanded. "Nobody goes hunting in the middle of the day this close to someone's house."

Leaving her fuming, Levi hurried down the stairs. His heart pounded, anxiety and unanswered questions drumming through his head. He'd heard the women screaming from the ground floor and prayed they were safe. That was no hunter outside, but a sniper with a lethal aim. If that first bullet had hit him an inch or two to the left, he would be dead.

Unfortunately, he hadn't anticipated the gory sight he must have presented with blood dripping from his ear onto his shirt and Mose's blood all over the knees of his pants. Eyes wide with horror, Selah stood in the foyer clutching a sobbing ThomasAnne. Horatia, standing in the breezeway, emitted a strangled shriek as Levi got to the bottom of the stairs.

"Where's Wyatt?" he asked Selah.

"He took the shotgun and went out the back door. Is Joelle all right?"

"She's fine. Mose was hit. You ladies get under the stairs. I'm going for my rifle."

"But you're—"

"It's nothing. Do what I said—get away from the windows!" As they moved to obey, Levi flattened himself against the doorframe and reached to turn the doorknob. When no further shots rang out, he picked up a bowl on a side table, opened the door, and tossed the bowl out. Nothing happened. Leaning into the doorway, he took a quick look across the collapsed porch. His horse stood quietly grazing, as if the volley of gunfire had never happened.

For several minutes Levi stood baffled, trying to ignore the pain in his ear, as he worked through what had just happened. Apparently the assailant had run out of ammunition or given up. Why? What had he hoped to accomplish? Had someone involved in the robberies discovered his identity and decided to eliminate him? That seemed unlikely, though not out of the question.

He stepped over the rotten boards in the porch and made his way to the horse. "You need some water, old fellow," he said, running a hand down the horse's withers and legs, double-checking for injury. He seemed perfectly fine. "I'll send Wyatt back for you in a minute." With a last pat on the horse's neck, he unsheathed the rifle from its scabbard and took it with him back to the house. No sense taking any more chances.

He had to find Wyatt before the kid stumbled on the assailant's lair without any backup.

The minute Levi turned his back, Selah deposited her weeping cousin under the stairs. "ThomasAnne, you're going to be fine. The shots have stopped. But Mose is hurt, and I have to go check on him and Joelle." She shook the unresponsive ThomasAnne. "Do you hear me?"

ThomasAnne wiped her streaming eyes. "You need to stay here until Mr. Riggins gets back. What if—Selah!"

But Selah had already bolted around the newel post to run up the stairs. At the sound of footsteps behind her, she turned her head to find Horatia in her wake.

"He my man," Horatia said defiantly.

Selah nodded. As they reached the second floor, she followed the sound of a deep moan, overlaid by Joelle's lighter voice, into the east bedroom.

There was blood everywhere, smeared across the floor all the way to the bed, where Mose lay gasping in pain. Joelle bent over him, pressing a cloth to his head, while Nathan stood watching with his back to the window, fists clenched in impotent frustration.

"Mose!" Horatia's cry was guttural. She ran to her husband, firmly moving Joelle out of the way.

"I didn't know what to do." Joelle lifted a hand to push her hair out of her face, rendering her appearance, if possible, even more frightening. "He's bleeding so much—"

"Head wounds does that." Horatia lifted the cloth away to quickly examine the gash in Mose's head. "You've stopped the bleeding. He'll be fine, once we wash and treat it with herbs." She glanced over her shoulder, smiling at Joelle's uncomprehending disbelief. "Really, Miss Joelle, you saved his life."

"We need clean water, don't we?" asked Selah.

"Yes, but you can't go to the well—"

"I'll go." Nathan was already out the door.

Selah knelt beside Horatia, who continued to stroke her husband's ashy face. He had fainted from the pain and lay quietly, an occasional twitch drawing his body tight. "We'll call the doctor in," Selah said, laying a hand on Horatia's.

"Thank you." Horatia's voice was tight.

"It's the least we can do. This wouldn't have happened if y'all hadn't come to help."

"It's not that." Horatia turned her hand to grasp Selah's. "I'm glad we came. Mose and me, we talked about what you said, and you right. We neighbors. Jesus said a neighbor be anybody needs help. I'm just wondering why it's easier to forgive and help you and your family than my own daughter."

Bereft of words, Selah squeezed the coffee-colored hand in hers.

"It hurts to be rejected in favor of someone else. Especially by your family." Joelle's quiet words sank hard into Selah's chest.

Sitting back on her heels, Selah stared at her sister. What on earth did she mean?

Apparently Horatia misunderstood. Something like despair suffused her face. "I ain't reject Charmion. I's just trying to help her. I know she love that boy. I even know he a good provider," she added grudgingly. "But he also as black as a moonless night. Nathan Vincent was born on a boat from Africa, you can hear it in his accent. Now before you go arguing with me about what difference that make, now that we're free, let me tell you something. When I was a girl, even as a slave I choose my man real careful—and your mama, she love me, so she protect me and help me."

"She . . . helped you?" asked Selah. "Helped you do what?"

"She know the darker a Negro's skin, the harder his life gon' be. It's just the way of the world. I wanted light-skinned babies 'cause I want them to have every advantage I didn't have."

Selah looked from Horatia to Mose, bewildered. "But you love Mose! Are you saying you married him because his skin was paler than yours?"

"Of course I love Mose. But they was others I could've had. Your mama arranged for him to be close to me, so I could fluff my feathers in a timely manner. Men—they take the bait so easy." Horatia rolled her eyes.

"But, Horatia, Charmion chose Nathan and they're married! They're already expecting a baby—"

"I know that!" Horatia's eyes glistened with something that in a lesser woman might have been tears. "And that makes me—" She threw an arm across her bosom in a wholly uncharacteristic defensive posture. "Ah, it makes me ill and full of joy at the same time, so's I don't know myself no more."

Dense silence overtook the cold, once-grand room that Selah had slept in hundreds of nights, sometimes to dream of handsome suitors, sometimes in later years to sorrow over losses—but always with a prayer for God's protection and guidance. She couldn't fathom his purposes in today's circumstances. She felt neither safe nor wise.

Joelle suddenly let out a harsh sigh. "I'm going to the linen closet to look for some clean bandages. I'll be right back."

Selah watched her go. "Horatia, I think none of us really know for sure how to navigate this life, especially me. But I do know one thing. We've got to stick together, and we've got to trust God's Word to be true, or we're all going under."

Horatia took Selah's hand to her lips and kissed it. "You so much like your mama sometimes, it takes my breath."

"What? No, I—"

"Yes. You are." Horatia smiled and let her go with a brusque wave of the hand. "Now go out to the herb garden and bring me some yarrow. We gonna get this man back on his feet, chokin' us all with that dad-blame pipe."

Seventeen

LEVI CAME UPON WYATT, shotgun propped against his thigh, squatting at the base of a big oak tree situated some three hundred yards from the east side of the main house and angled to the right of the old kitchen. The boy was staring at something in his palm.

"Wyatt!" Levi called as he approached. "What have you got there?"

Wyatt stood up, showing Levi the spent shell casing in his hand.

Levi examined it. It was from a .56-56 bullet, ammunition for a Spencer rifle—one of the standard weapons issued to Union troops. One thing he knew for sure—it had been recently fired. He'd expected to spend hours looking for detritus from the shooter's weapon. "How did you find this?"

Wyatt pointed up at the cupola's smashed windows. "Traced the trajectory the bullet would have had to follow."

"Good work, son." Levi shook Wyatt's shoulder with affectionate roughness.

Wyatt shrugged. "I always liked science and mathematics. Useful, you know?"

The boy would make a good detective, but Levi couldn't tell him so. "All right. Let's look around for anything else the shooter might have left behind."

For nearly an hour the two of them searched the area, looking for human disturbance—footprints, snagged clothing, anything that might have identified the assailant—without announcing their own presence. Finally Wyatt asked Levi if he didn't want to go in and get his "head doctored."

Realizing he'd been unconsciously touching the aching ear every time an incautious step jarred his balance, Levi sighed. "Guess we'd better. I'd hoped we'd find something else by now."

Frustrated, footsore, and thirsty, they emerged from the woods in front of the house just as a horse and wagon came bowling up the lane from the gate. Dr. Benjamin Kidd, dressed in a bright blue coat buttoned over a red paisley tie, pulled up on the reins, letting out a whistle at Levi's armed and no doubt gory appearance. "Nathan came to get me. He said there's been a bit of trouble." Kidd tied off the reins and sprang down from the wagon seat. "Shouldn't you be lying down?"

Levi's hand went to his ear. "I'm fine. This is just a scratch. Well, I was about to wash up and change clothes—I'm sure I look a mess. Mose Lawrence is in bad shape, though. We'd appreciate it if you'd come look at him."

"Of course. My bag is in the wagon."

"I'll get it." Wyatt eagerly sprang to help.

"Nathan said there was an attack," Kidd said as he accompanied Levi into the house. "Any idea who would do such a thing?"

"Not yet. Selah!" Looking around, Levi propped his gun by the door. "Where is everybody?"

Selah appeared, looking down over the second-floor railing. "Up here, with Mose. Hello, Doctor! I'm *so* glad you came!"

"Of course I came," Kidd said, running up the stairs. "Somebody fill me in on the details while I attend to the patient."

An hour or so later Levi sat in the desk chair in the library, letting Dr. Kidd work on his ear with something he called an "antiseptic"—which hurt like the devil but would, in the doctor's words, "keep your ear from falling off." He supposed he should be grateful for small mercies.

Kidd had checked Mose, approving Horatia's herbal dressing, then left him resting quietly in the upstairs bedroom with Horatia standing as nurse. Meanwhile, Levi had marshaled his troops, sending Joelle, Wyatt, and Nathan to complete the transferral of the bees out to the woods. After coaxing Miss ThomasAnne out from under the stairs with the promise that the danger was past and she could help by rounding up refreshments, he'd made the trek up to the cupola to inspect the damage. It was a mess for sure, with golden sticky, fragrant honey on the ceiling and walls, blood stains on the floor, and shattered glass and wood everywhere.

But that wasn't the most interesting thing he'd found there.

His gaze rested now on Selah, who stood beside the doctor with a bowl of hot water and a tray of bandages. He didn't know whether or not to tell her about the spyglass.

None of them had noticed it during the process of removing the bees.

He tried to interpret her expression. Fading anxiety, undoubtedly related more to the harrowing experience she had just come through than personal concern for him. She was chewing on her bottom lip, a tell which he'd noticed on a few other occasions. She wasn't a flutterer, nor did she babble incessantly like a lot of women. That was one of the things he liked most about her. But he didn't like worrying her at all.

Finally he'd had all he could take. "All right, Doc, that's enough. I've had worse injuries and survived."

"Be still, you ingrate," said the doctor. "I'm trying to sew your ear back together."

"Huh. Feels more like you're splitting it down the middle." Levi was relieved to see Selah smile. "Miss Daughtry is undoubtedly a better embroiderer than you."

"I don't know," she said, bending to inspect Levi's ear and giving him a tantalizing view of her smooth throat. "Doc's developed quite a neat stitch."

Kidd chuckled and nudged her out of the way. "Despite my best efforts, I'm afraid he'll be left with a bit of a scar."

"A scar is better than the alternative." Selah scowled at him. "An inch closer to your head and you'd be dead, Levi. Joelle said it was a poacher. What do you think?"

Levi hesitated. She wasn't going to accept some off-the-cuff nonsense for an answer. And he wanted to trust her—in fact, it had occurred to him that he might be endangering her and her whole family by keeping her in the dark. But Pinkerton had been adamant about the security of his mission.

"Not likely a poacher would be aiming that high, five shots in a row," he said with a shrug. "But I'll keep looking around and make inquiries in the neighborhood."

The doctor gave one final tug of the thread in Levi's ear and snipped it off. "If that wasn't an accident, somebody here has got a powerful enemy. The war's over, but emotions still get riled when Yankees come in trying to make a dollar off the backs of locals."

Selah set down the bowl sharply. "Doc, you honestly think someone was shooting at Levi? Who even knows he's here?"

With a crack of laughter, Kidd bent to wash his hands in the bowl of water. "Everyone in Tupelo knows he's here. The fool's been all over town trying to find people to work on his new hotel."

"Levi? Is that true?" Selah searched his face.

"Yes, but that doesn't necessarily correlate to attempted murder."

Kidd turned, drying his hands on the towel he pulled off his shoulder. "It doesn't necessarily *not* correlate either. I'd be watching my back if I were you."

"Is that a threat?" Levi stood, wincing when his ear throbbed.

"More or less." Kidd grinned. "Would you like me to give you something for the pain?"

Levi shook his head. "If people are coming after me for offering employment, I'll need all my wits about me."

Suddenly the door knocker sounded—loudly and repeatedly. Selah lifted her hands. "What now? We're not exactly ready for company." She hurried toward the rotunda.

Levi heard the door open, heard Selah's intake of breath. There was a long silence.

Finally, an elderly female voice with haughty overtones demanded, "Well, aren't you going to let us in?"

"Grandmama! Aurora!" Selah sounded stunned. "What are you doing here?"

"What do you think I'm doing here? I've come to sort out this disgraceful business venture in which you seem to have embroiled our family." Grandmama pushed past, narrowly missing Selah's toes with the end of her cane. Clearly her opinion of the word *business* equated to that of brothels and voodoo rituals. "Reminds me of that Edmondson girl, cavorting with opera singers during the war and actually carrying messages tied up in her petticoat across enemy lines."

Aurora gave Selah a big hug and pulled back, eyes twinkling. "But Grandmama, everyone says Belle Edmondson was a heroine—"

"I'm sure she was," Grandmama said with a sniff, "but that in no way mitigates the *déclassé* nature of her behavior." She paused in the center of the rotunda to look up and around. "Well. If this place hasn't turned into a fine pigsty."

Suppressing a shudder, Selah thought about Mose asleep upstairs in her old bedroom, Horatia keeping watch by his side, and the library turned into a surgery, not to mention the blood, mayhem, and honeycomb in the cupola. She took her grandmother firmly by the arm and steered her toward the parlor. "It sounds like you had a difficult journey. Come sit down and rest your feet. ThomasAnne will be back any moment now with refreshments."

"I *did* have a nasty, sooty journey on that cursed train.

But I've been sitting for half the day, so I prefer to stand for a while, although some Lapsang souchong would be lovely, along with a nice teacake, if you please." Grandmama paused in the parlor doorway, absently tapping her cane, apparently carried mainly for effect. Her silver hair was coiffed in a mass of puffs and braids, with two great black feathers waving from the top of the pile every time she moved. Her suit of bottle-green linsey-woolsey, tailored in the current bustle style, showed off her tall, still straight figure in a manner that Selah could only admire. "Well? Where is the pretty one—and my pathetic niece, ThomasAnne?"

"Aunt Winnie," came a quavering voice from the doorway behind Selah. "How nice to see you. What a surprise."

Grandmama turned sharply. "If that isn't like you, Thomas-Anne, creeping up on one in that mousy fashion. How a woman of your size contrives to be so invisible defies all laws of nature. Come put that tray down before you drop it."

As ThomasAnne bit her lip and moved to obey, Selah charged into the fray. "Grandmama, I wish you had let me know you planned to come. I'm afraid there is no place adequate—"

"I'm quite sure that's the case, considering the forethought typical of this branch of the family. The Daughtrys always were a flighty lot. How you propose to run a hotel with no experience—"

"Grandmama!" Selah raised a hand. "Stop. I beg you, just stop."

Grandmama's thin eyebrows rose in astonishment at this unprecedented rudeness, but at least the impending tirade seemed to have been arrested. Temporarily, anyway.

Selah looked at Aurora. "How did you know about the hotel? We only just decided to take it on after we got home."

As Aurora opened her mouth to answer, the door knocker sounded again.

Exasperated, Selah stomped to the door and yanked it open to find Schuyler Beaumont standing there with a broad grin on his handsome face. "I heard there was a party," he said.

Selah stepped back to let him in. "So that's how they got here."

"You needn't sound so bitter." Schuyler removed his hat and laid it on a table. "They were going to come anyway, so I offered transportation as the price of admission to the show. I left the carriage next to the wagon and the other horse. I assume there's no livery service as yet."

Selah couldn't decide whether to laugh or slap him. As a compromise, she rolled her eyes. "When Wyatt comes back, I'll have him tend to the horses."

"Perfect. Who's Wyatt?" Schuyler laughed at her expression. "Never mind. Where's your redoubtable grandmama?"

"Terrorizing my cousin in the parlor. You might as well join her, I suppose." She turned on her heel.

"You're going to be just like her one day, you know," Schuyler observed.

Refusing to dignify that sally with a response, she poked her head into the library on the way past. "Gentlemen, it seems we're having tea in the parlor."

"Sounds like quite the soirée," Doc said, grinning at Levi, who was already on his feet.

Selah sighed and marched into battle with the three men trailing after her.

In the parlor, Grandmama had finally deigned to sit on

the dusty settee—after protecting her skirt with her handkerchief. She lowered her tea cup and fastened a freezing blue gaze over Selah's shoulder. "You must be the Yankee."

"I am," Levi said gravely. He took Grandmama's hand and kissed it as elegantly as Sir Walter Raleigh making his obeisance to Queen Elizabeth. "Levi Riggins."

She sniffed, but allowed it. "Mr. Riggins." Her birdlike gaze took in Levi's trim waist and broad shoulders, then moved on to the doctor.

Kidd executed a simple bow. "Ma'am. I'm Dr. Kidd."

Resigned, Selah moved to the tea service laid out on a small gated table under the window. "Gentlemen, this is my grandmama, Mrs. McGowan. Beside her is my youngest sister, Aurora. And I believe both of you are acquainted with Mr. Beaumont."

Aurora preened under the three admiring male gazes fixed on her glowing countenance. She smoothed her striped wool traveling dress, the color of which echoed the dark-copper curls tamed in a loose chignon at the back of her head. "Isn't this a lovely party? I think we should host a ball this month and invite the whole neighborhood."

Selah found herself staring into Levi's eyes, which mirrored her own horror at this insane proposal. She was about to blurt out something suitably dampening when Levi winked at her and said mildly, "And we shall, once the renovations are complete."

"How long is that going to take?" Schuyler looked around with undisguised skepticism. "I was hoping we could open this summer."

"Well, there's the roof . . . ," Selah began.

Levi gave her a cautioning look. "And I'm afraid the kitchen is a bit of a shambles." He smiled at Aurora. "We want to put our best foot forward, so to speak, don't you think?"

"I suppose." Aurora looked disappointed. "This *summer*? Really?"

"Or possibly in the fall, when the weather is cooler," Selah said firmly.

Into the ensuing depressed silence, Dr. Kidd said, "Miss ThomasAnne, I've been meaning to ask how you're feeling. No more fainting spells, I trust?"

Every eye in the room focused on ThomasAnne, who turned a violent shade of pink and nearly lost her tea cup. "I didn't—I haven't—"

Grandmama frowned. "If that isn't like you, ThomasAnne, drawing attention to yourself with these nonsensical fits."

"I assure you," the doctor said, "losing consciousness is nothing one has any control over. She could have been badly hurt if I hadn't been there." He smiled at ThomasAnne.

"If you hadn't been *where*?" Grandmama demanded.

"It was really nothing to worry over," ThomasAnne said, hands fluttering. "I'm just fine now. Selah and I were—" She looked wildly at Selah for rescue.

"We were just coming out of church," Selah said. "Thomas-Anne wasn't feeling well, and Dr. Kidd happened by."

"Hmph." Grandmama looked unsatisfied, but she could hardly object to churchgoing.

Aurora laughed. "That sounds interesting, and I'm sure we'll hear more about it later, but Selah, where is Joelle? Is she hiding in a corner with some dusty old book?"

Selah had opened her mouth to answer when the back door slammed. The sound of boots approached down the breezeway into the rotunda, and Wyatt burst into the parlor.

"Where is every—oh!" Wyatt halted to survey the three strangers, then shouted over his shoulder, "Here they are, Miss Jo! Looks like there's some kind of party going on."

Selah sat frozen, her worst nightmare fully realized as Joelle and Nathan appeared in the doorway behind Wyatt. All three were covered in honey, beeswax, dead leaves, and dirt. If she hadn't known that was her sister, Joelle would not even have been recognizable as female.

Nathan recovered first. "Wyatt, we best get these muddy boots back outside. We can eat later. Come on." He grabbed Wyatt by the sleeve and hauled him back the way they'd come.

Joelle was left standing there alone in her dirty male attire. "Hello, Grandmama." Removing her hat to let her hair tumble about her shoulders, she scowled at Schuyler. "What are *you* doing here?"

"I might ask you the same question." Schuyler sat back, looking amused. "This is not your usual bluestocking entertainment."

"Nor is this your usual gin-soused choice of companion," Joelle said sweetly. "Were you bored, poor dear?"

Schuyler laughed aloud while Grandmama thumped the floor with her cane. "Young lady, what is the meaning of this outlandish attire, not to mention such blatant discourtesy to a guest?"

"Bees," Joelle said through her teeth.

Selah jumped to her feet. "What she means is, we have been studying the age-old art of beekeeping, and Joelle has perhaps entered a little too enthusiastically into the natural aspect of the enterprise. She will go to the cottage and change immediately, won't you, Jo?"

"I suppose I'd better." Brushing a hand down her filthy

pant leg, Joelle glowered at Schuyler. "We seem to have become infested with all sorts of vermin." She quit the room with her nose in the air.

Grandmama thumped again. "Who was that boy? And the Negro?"

"That was Wyatt. He has come to live with us after the—" Catching herself just short of blurting out the truth about the train wreck, Selah glanced at Doc. "He is an orphan who will be apprenticing with Dr. Kidd. And Nathan is our new blacksmith."

"What was *he* doing in the house?" Grandmama sounded more confused than scandalized. "Is he studying beekeeping too?"

"More or less." Selah gathered herself. She was the manager here. Sticky situations were bound to occur, and she might as well practice getting herself out of them. Tact. She must exercise tact. "Grandmama, you know we're all glad to see you, but as you can see, we are not ready to entertain guests just yet. Perhaps Dr. Kidd would take you and Aurora back to the hotel in town, since he is going that way."

"I was just about to leave," Doc said, setting down his coffee cup. "I'll go retrieve my hat and bag from the library. You ladies can meet me out front."

"But I wanted to stay here!" Aurora exclaimed. "This is my home too."

"Of course it is, Pete," Selah said gently. "But the rooms aren't ready here in the big house, and we don't have any more bed space in the cottage."

Aurora's lower lip might have protruded just a bit, but to Selah's surprise, she sighed and said, "All right. But I'm coming back tomorrow with a broom and mop in hand. I'm going to help in whatever way you need me to."

The baby was growing up. Selah nodded. "We'll loan you some clothes so you won't ruin yours."

"But not Joelle's."

Selah laughed. "No. At least not the breeches."

Eighteen

IN THE DARK, Daughtry jerked rusty nails out of the boards across the door of the old hunting shack, tossing them out into the woods. He'd built this little deer stand when the older two girls were small, a refuge from the carping of a miserable pregnant wife and unending responsibilities. In following years, a few days out of each month during the winter, he'd come here with his gun, get his head on straight, and kill everything in sight, whether it could be eaten or not. Then he'd go back home to drive the plantation and work on the mansion.

His and Penelope's dream home, Ithaca. Cotton palace.

He had not planned to shoot in broad daylight. It had been a stupid, foolhardy thing to do, and he would never have done it if he'd known Joelle was anywhere near the cupola. He couldn't imagine what she was doing dressed in the boy's clothes. And why had she been in such companionable conversation with that young Negro blacksmith? The thought of that black hand touching his beautiful, golden daughter made his blood boil.

The other question he couldn't satisfy was the identity of the white boy. He could almost swear he was the same boy the Yank had pulled from the wreckage of the train car at Buckner's Ravine. The car in which Priester had died. The thought buzzed in his head like one of those angry bees: What if that boy had been with Priester? What if Priester had said something to him, told him he was being hunted?

Wondering, debating with himself, he'd slipped along behind them in the woods. He'd listened to the three of them discuss the noisy box of bees the Negro carried, how they'd removed it from the cupola, and their reaction to the gunfire. It sounded like one of Daughtry's shots had hit Mose—apparently the old gardener was still employed here at Ithaca—and maybe someone called Levi Riggins. That must be the name of the Yankee spy. Clever. "L. E. Vine," the name on the "attorney's" card, had been derived from "Levi."

Scully said the Yank was looking for Priester's kin. Then the boy turned up with him in Tupelo.

Coincidence? Maybe. Wouldn't hurt to find some way to question the boy.

No devil's spawn of a Yankee was going to lay claim to his home, not while he lived and breathed. So he hadn't been able to resist taking a shot at him when he had the chance. He'd missed this time. Well, he'd be more patient, wait for a better opportunity.

Then he'd blow his arrogant head off.

Nineteen

DURING THE IMPROMPTU TEA PARTY, Levi had learned a lot about the Daughtrys and their extended family. Selah had exaggerated neither her grandmother's strong personality nor the level of tension created by their impecunious circumstances.

As he followed Selah and Schuyler up the stairs to assess the damage in the cupola, he mentally ran through what he knew so far. Most crimes could be traced to the acquisition of money and materials, everyone involved had a clear motive, and they all possessed the mental acuity for planning, executing, and covering up any level of complex plot.

At first glance, dreamy, bookish Joelle seemed an unlikely conspirator. But today she had demonstrated the ability to literally get her hands dirty. The arrival of little sister Aurora, previously an unknown and distant quantity, reminded him that family loyalty could play an important role in whether or not people took part in extra-legal activity.

Which brought him to Selah, head of the household by default. She loved her home and seemed to be willing to do anything to keep possession of it. She loved her sisters and would protect them at all costs—preferably keeping them with her, but willing to let them go for their own safety.

He watched the straight line of her back as she climbed the stairs ahead of him, eschewing Schuyler's arm to advance lightly on the balls of her feet, one hand on the rail, the other lifting her heavy skirt clear of the dusty treads. Self-reliant, economical of movement and thought, she expected perfection from herself, if not from everyone around her.

And yet . . . the cynical wartime side of Levi's brain warned him not to take the evidence he saw at face value. Selah and Joelle both had expressed a certain disdain for Schuyler Beaumont, but that did not mean they weren't using him for more than the immediate supply of funds for renovating the mansion and grounds or, alternatively, helping him in a deeper plot to ruin or buy out a competing rail line.

Beaumont himself was a slippery case. Overtly playful and vain, the young entrepreneur still somehow left Levi feeling mocked in return—which he both resented and found fascinating.

And then there was the identity and motive of the mysterious shooter from this morning. What connection could such an attack have with train robberies and rail sabotage? The target would have to have been visible through the window of the cupola—shadowy figures at best, even in broad daylight, taking into account the glare of the sun off the glass. But supposing the assailant knew who would be in the cupola, the target would have to be himself, Joelle, Mose, or Nathan. Joelle had been somewhat disguised in her men's attire and broad-brimmed hat and veil. But tall, muscular black-skinned Nathan and the smaller Mose would have been clearly identifiable.

It all came back to motive—and Levi concluded that he simply didn't know enough about the personalities involved.

Of the four visitors who had arrived shortly after the attack, he could almost certainly rule out Mrs. McGowan and Aurora as suspects. Neither seemed capable of shouldering a rifle, much less aiming and firing it at such a small, distant target.

Doc Kidd probably kept a weapon for self-defense in his wagon. He seemed to have no reason to harm anyone on the plantation, but again, Levi had yet to uncover many details about his past. He would have to rectify that omission soon.

Reaching the top of the stairs right behind Selah and Schuyler, he watched the two of them for reactions to the utter mess in the cupola.

Selah put her hands to her mouth and drew in a deep breath of dismay. "Oh my."

Chunks of the wall had been taken out by bullets, and the carved molding around the dome was damaged in several places. The dome itself and the chandelier plate in its center were, by some miracle, intact. The two broken windows, of course, would have to be replaced.

Selah turned to Levi, her eyes shiny with tears. "How did you all make it out of here alive?"

He wanted to put his arms around her as he had on the train, to reassure her that he would keep her safe—as if he had the means to actually do so. He looked away. "The Good Lord watches out for fools and little children, they say. Beaumont, can you think of anyone who knew about this project and might want to stop it?"

Schuyler, peering out one of the broken windows, looked over his shoulder. "I can think of several people who spout things in the paper every day about how the government shouldn't be subsidizing the rails or any other kind of progress. My family, especially my father's influence, has long been a target of envy in the public sector. Now that he's announced that he'll be running for the House of Representatives—"

"What?" Levi straightened. "You didn't tell me that!"

Schuyler shrugged. "Didn't seem relevant."

"What difference does that make?" Selah asked.

"It means there's a large target on the company's back," Levi said. "It also means you'll have to be very careful about appearances of corruption."

"Oh, I'm aware." Schuyler turned to lean against the windowsill. "And it's true that North Carolina rail companies have funneled money to legislators in return for millions in state money for tracks that won't ever be built. But my pa's an honest man. His goal is reducing the tax load on land owners. But if he goes to Washington, that's going to leave my brother and me with a boatload of extra work. I wish he'd stay in Mobile and leave the politics to Grant and his drinking cronies."

Levi privately thought Ulysses Grant might turn out to be a much stronger president than his predecessor, the squishy Andrew Johnson. But he needed Beaumont to keep talking, not get defensive in a pointless debate. "Political figures of all stripes get hotheaded these days, especially here in Mississippi. Do you suppose someone knew you were coming here?"

Schuyler looked amused. "I would think a Yank carpetbagger would be a more likely target than a man whose family has had the run of this place for nearly two decades. Who, furthermore, is doing his best to take it into the modern era without destroying it."

Now that was interesting. "I suppose that's all a matter of perspective." Levi looked at Selah, who had knelt to quietly begin picking up glass and putting it in a pile. "But it reminds me of something I've been meaning to mention to the two of you. I've been thinking about the name of this place, which has become synonymous in the community with the plantation lifestyle and culture."

"It's a good name," Selah said. "Ithaca made my father think of homecoming and victory."

"Your father is gone," Levi reminded her, "and for so many this has been a place of sadness and death. Victory *will* come, though, as you rebuild it with a new vision."

Selah's head remained lowered for a moment. A gust of wind came through the open window, moving the chandelier chain so that the crystal prisms below tinkled like wind chimes. Finally she rose, brushing her hands together, settling her skirt. "That is a good thought. I should like to call the place Daughtry House. Plain and simple."

Schuyler shook his head. "I don't think the reference to your father is a good idea."

"It's *my* name too," Selah said firmly. "However much money you pump in, it's *our* property—mine and Joelle's and Aurora's."

"You've indicated more than once that your families have had longstanding ties. Yet there still seems to be a certain . . . tension in the relationship—with Joelle in particular." Levi sighed. "You two are essentially equal partners in this venture. Do you mind helping me understand the source of the difficulty?"

"I don't think—"

"It was a long time ago, Selah," Schuyler said. "It was stupid and it doesn't matter anymore."

Then she looked up, brown eyes glittering. Levi couldn't tell if her anger was directed more at herself or Schuyler. "It *does* matter. History always matters, because it impacts the present and the future."

"Of all the Greek tragedies!" Schuyler clutched at his lapels, as if he'd rather have put his hands over her mouth. "All right. Fine. But I'm not going to stand here and defend myself against a girl who can't get over a practical joke." He pushed past Levi and clattered down the stairs.

Selah was acutely aware that she and Levi were left alone, isolated in the remotest part of the house. True, they had been here before, and besides, she was hardly a young debutante who must protect her reputation. In their three weeks' acquaintance, Levi had never once offered any sort of disrespect in word or deed. In fact, he was such a gentleman that she wondered if her person presented any temptation to indiscretion at all.

Which was a ludicrous thought after Schuyler's dramatic exit.

"Are you quite all right?" Levi gave her a searching look. "Beaumont is a young peacock, but I won't insist on your breaking a confidence."

She stared back at him. There was something mesmerizing in those hooded hazel eyes, though of course she couldn't say so. "You're really easy to talk to."

"Am I?" His lips curved. "I guess I've always been better at listening than talking."

"Then sit here on the stairs with me for a while, and I'll tell you the whole ridiculous story. You may be sorry you didn't run when you had the chance."

The stairway was so narrow that Selah's dress and petticoats billowed over Levi's legs and feet, and she could feel every muscle of his arm against hers. She couldn't help remembering the shocking intimacy of the train wreck when she had fallen into his arms.

"Are you cold?" he asked.

Goodness, had she actually shivered? How embarrassing. "No, of course—" Glancing up at him had been a mistake, for there was a look in his eyes, a baffling look, almost like . . .

She couldn't even complete the thought. He was looking at her lips.

"You do that a lot," he said.

"What?"

"Chew the inside of your lip. When you are taken off-guard."

"I do not!" She put her hand over her mouth.

He pulled it away and kept it. His hand was warm, engulfing hers. "Yes, you do, and it makes me . . ." He swallowed. "Never mind. Tell me your story."

She couldn't think what she'd been about to tell him. She tore her gaze away and looked at his fingers gently curling and uncurling hers. Concentrating, she pulled her thoughts together. "Oh, yes. Schuyler and Joelle. Well, every few years, the Beaumont family used to come up from Mobile, to visit us during the summer. Camilla and I were friends at school in Holly Springs, though she's about a year older than me. I think I told you our grandmothers are cousins."

"That's quite a long way to travel," Levi said.

"Yes, but they'd take the train and get here within a day. About ten years ago—the summer before the war—we had one of those visits. I was so happy to see Camilla, because I'd had to leave school without graduating—"

"Why?"

"That's another long story. I'll tell you some other time." She dared to glance up at him again, found his head bent to hers, eyes intent. She blurted, "If you really want to know, I'd taken on some radically liberal views from one of my teachers, a Miss Lindquist. Joelle, too."

"What kind of views?" He looked neither disgusted nor offended, merely interested.

"About educating Negroes. Their human rights. I was leaning toward abolitionism, when someone wrote to my papa, and he made us come home. Miss Lindquist was dismissed."

"Selah. That was very brave of you."

She shook her head hard, pulling her hand from his. "I was *not* brave. I came home and obeyed my parents and looked away when I passed the cotton fields. I let Charmion dress me and fix my hair and clean my room." She put her head down on her knees. "At least I was kind to her. I would never think of hitting her or speaking harshly. I gave her my old clothes and shoes, which she seemed to like."

She felt Levi's hand on her head, comforting. "You were, what? Fifteen years old? How were you going to rebel? You were pretty restricted yourself. Here, look at me." His hand slipped to her ear, moved to touch her chin, and she sat up, eyes closed, leaning into him. "I can tell you have grieved over that. And I know you well enough to know you must've asked for forgiveness."

"I did." Her throat ached with tears she'd held back for years. "I'm not sure it's been granted."

"That will come—but even if it doesn't, you make what reparations you can, and trust God to work in the other person's heart. As much as we'd like to, we can't control someone else's response."

He sounded as if he knew that from personal experience. She opened her eyes to stare into his. She'd never known a man with such contained masculinity, who talked like a preacher and used his power to protect what was his. His hand was strong enough to have snapped her neck, but he cupped her cheek as if holding a bird. She wanted to know what it would be like to kiss him, just once, but she wanted his respect too. A lady didn't offer herself. She was about to go over the edge of what was acceptable, even for a twenty-six-year-old spinster who had no reputation to lose.

When she withdrew, he let her go, gravely if reluctantly.

She knotted her fingers together in her lap. "Please forgive this maudlin self-loathing," she said, trying to smile. "It doesn't hit me very often, but it's been rather a stressful day."

"No apology necessary." His tone was careful. "You were telling me . . ."

"All right. I believe I left off with the summer of 1860. The Beaumonts came, in spite of heated national rhetoric and threats of violence in some parts of the state. We would ride and play with the dogs during the day, the men went fishing in the creek, and then we'd fry it up for supper, with hush puppies and fresh vegetables and ice cream for dessert. We used to have a lovely swimming pool across the road."

"A swimming hole? Like a creek?"

"No, a real indoor pool. Mama had grown up swimming in the creek back at her home in Georgia, and she missed the daily refreshing of a bath in clean water. So a year after we moved into the big house, Papa partially dammed up the spring over there, to make a fresh-water pond, and had it lined with Italian marble. Mama was thrilled, of course. As soon as Joelle and I got big enough, Mama taught us both to swim and had lovely little bathing costumes made up in Memphis and delivered to the plantation."

"Is the pool still there?"

Selah shrugged. "I haven't been over there in quite some time. It's probably a slimy mess by now."

"We'll take a look tomorrow. Never mind. Keep going."

She nodded. "The reason I mention the swimming pool is because it was the cause of the . . . kerfuffle, I guess you could call it."

"I like that word," he said with a smile.

"My mama used it a lot. So one day, all us girls—Jo, Pete, and I, plus Camilla—decided to go for a swim. We took our swim costumes with us and dressed in the bathhouse, where we left our street clothes."

"I'm surprised your father allowed that."

"It hadn't been a problem, since the company was generally female. The area would be off-limits to any male visitors who happened to be onsite, you know. But this particular day, Schuyler apparently got bored with sitting still on the creek bank with the men. He snuck into the bathhouse, took our dresses and shoes, and hid them. Then he thought it would be fun to toss frogs into the pool. Big, disgusting bullfrogs with long legs and bulbous eyes and the ability to leap over walls."

Levi's eyes had lit as he followed her tale, but he winced now. "That could not have ended well."

"It did not. Camilla took it in stride. Having two older brothers, she had endured worse. And Pete—Aurora, I mean—rather likes reptiles and amphibians for some reason. But Joelle had been sitting on the pool steps reading, and one of those poor creatures found himself roosting atop her bonnet. Jo screamed and sent the book, the bonnet, and the frog flying into the pool, then tore down the road at a flat-out run."

"What about you? You're not laughing."

"I knew how terrified Jo is of frogs. You have to understand what an imagination she has. When we were little girls and first read the Bible story of the plagues of Egypt, she had nightmares for months. And then there was the 'Diamonds and Toads' fairytale Mama used to tell us." Selah shuddered. "I think it was the surprise of it all, combined with being in the pool when it happened and Schuyler laughing like a hyena. He went chasing after her—and I will say, she's quite a runner, because it took him a while to catch her—and only the two of them know what happened when he did . . . Joelle refused to speak of it, though Sky later apologized and groveled." Selah shook her head. "I assume he has grown up to some degree."

Levi's lips quirked. "If I told you some of the addlepated stunts I pulled around the age of twelve or thirteen, you'd wonder how I survived to adulthood. I take credit for the fact that my sisters are made of very stern stuff."

"You have sisters?" She'd wondered about his family but resisted the forwardness of inquiring.

"Yes, two—both a good bit younger than me."

She turned her head to study him. Getting to know him was like enjoying the novelties of a foreign country. "Are they still in Illinois?"

He nodded. "Anwen and her husband live near my parents, and Ceri lives at home." He hesitated. "Ceri was born deaf, which is why my parents chose to settle in Jacksonville after we immigrated. They'd heard about the school for the deaf there."

"Ah. I suppose that was . . . I mean, I can't imagine going through life without hearing music or laughter or . . ." She couldn't finish the sentence for the expression on Levi's face, so tender, so sad, yet filled with indescribable love for those sisters. "How could you leave them? Clearly you're very close to your family."

He nodded, looking down at his hands. "I'm sure I'll go back home at some point. I do miss them, but they write to me regularly, particularly my mother. And Ceri—she's quite an entertaining writer."

"So is Joelle. When we were growing up, she wrote little plays for us to act out. She loved to make our papa laugh."

"Our family entertainment was music. Even Ceri plays drums." He smiled. "Father is a bugler, Mother plays the harp, and Anwen was quite good on the flute."

"And you—"

"I took piano lessons when I was younger."

"Then we *must* get the piano tuned! I know Joelle would enjoy playing again too. Maybe you could play duets—"

"I don't play anymore." The flatness of his tone hit her like a slap.

"But why?"

"I just—j-just don't." She hadn't heard him stammer in

quite a while, but before she could press him further, he stood, abruptly, and offered her a hand. "Come, we'd best get downstairs and rescue Beaumont before he further antagonizes your sister."

Letting him help her to her feet, she accompanied him down the stairs. Just when she'd thought their friendship might be deepening, she'd apparently said something to make him withdraw again. She couldn't help wondering what was so off-putting about playing the piano with her sister.

Twenty

March 16, 1870
Tupelo

Popping the daily newspaper against his leg, Levi walked along in the Negro residential area known as Shake Rag. Located near the gum ponds on the periphery of town, it was little more than a closely set succession of single-story shacks. Already the women of the neighborhood were out and about, singing as they washed laundry in tubs in the yards and pegged clothing on lines hung across the porches. Barefoot children dressed in ragged, drab-colored cotton played in the muddy road with whatever toys could be found in nature—sticks and acorns and pine knots—with the occasional knife for a game of mumblety-peg. Nathan had thought Levi would be more likely to secure the workers he needed if he conducted personal interviews at the forge. Negro distrust of white carpetbaggers was second only to that of their previous captors. Concurring that the strategy made sense, Levi had readily agreed.

He'd turned onto a dirt alleyway between two little cabins when he heard someone behind him whistling a tune he recognized. Looking over his shoulder with a smile, he saw a young colored boy of about ten following him, hands in pockets, ragged straw hat tilted at a jaunty angle.

"The Union forever! Hurrah, boys, hurrah!" Levi sang along. "Down with the traitor, up with the star; while we rally round the flag, boys, rally once again—shouting the battle cry of freedom!"

The boy laughed and caught up with Levi. "You know that song, sir?"

"You bet I do." Levi whistled another verse, harmonizing with the boy, who could hardly purse his lips for grinning.

They walked along companionably for a while, then the boy looked up shyly. "My name's Tee-Toc, sir. You mind me asking what you doing in this neighborhood?"

"Not at all. I'm Levi, and I've got business at the forge. Am I headed the right way?" He knew he was, but had learned the habit of asking casual questions to encourage conversation.

"Yes, sir! I'll take you my own self." Tee-Toc swaggered, adding ingenuously, "Mr. Nathan, he give me a penny when I bring him business."

"That's very enterprising of you," Levi said. "As a matter of fact, I'm here looking to hire fellows who don't mind a hard day's work."

"Oh, that would be me! I'm a lot stronger than I look." Tee-Toc flexed a skinny arm. "What kind of jobs you got? I can hoe weeds and chop wood and card cotton and shell butterbeans or just about anything that comes along." He looked over his shoulder. "I don't much care for wringing laundry, 'cause that's women's work."

"I have to agree with you, son." Levi winked. "You hang tight with me, and I'm sure we can find you a job that will require a little muscle and a good male brain."

Before long they reached the forge, and Tee-Toc ran ahead, shouting, "Mr. Nathan! Hey, Nathan! I brung you a customer. He's a Yankee, but he's real nice. And I don't even need a penny—lest you just want to give me one—'cause he's gon' give me a job."

"Alright, you hush that rattletrap," Nathan was saying to the boy in his measured way as Levi walked in. Laying his tongs aside to wipe his hands, he nodded at Levi, a twinkle in his eyes. "Morning, Mr. Riggins. I had this one last project to finish before I pack it all up and haul it over to the plantation forge."

"That's just fine," Levi said, walking over to examine the ax head Nathan had been working on. It was perfectly shaped and looked like it could sever anything from trees to hogs' heads in a stroke or two. "I'd buy this," he said, "if it's for sale."

"Already sold. Boy, don't you touch that," Nathan said sharply to Tee-Toc, who had inched a little too close to the fire.

"Yessir, I'm just looking." But Tee-Toc took a judicious step toward Levi.

"I put out the word all day yesterday that you was coming to talk to men who need work." Nathan walked over to the open door and peered out. "Here they come. Tee-Toc, go grab a few of them buckets and put 'em out, so folks can sit while we talk."

Levi nodded. "I'm depending on you to steer me to the ones who can be relied on to do good work."

Shortly Levi found himself in front of a group of mostly stone-faced Negro men, trying to explain why they should risk life and limb repairing the roof of the plantation home of a young white woman whose father had once called himself the owner of hundreds of their brethren. In fact, Levi was pretty sure many of these very men had worked the cotton fields at Ithaca.

He got halfway through his prepared speech, stopped, and lifted his hands. "Gentlemen, you all look hungry, and I've got several months' work for up to thirty at a time. I understand why you'd be reluctant to abandon your own crops to take on a short-term job, but think of it this way—you'll be paid well enough that you should be able to afford to buy a nice piece of land that you can do with as you wish. Or, after Ithaca's house and grounds are brought back to productivity, Mr. Beaumont tells me the railroad will have jobs available for those who don't want to farm.

"I can pay $1.50 a day, beginning at daylight and ending at dusk, three meals a day, plenty of water. You all may know Mose Lawrence, who will be the supervisor on-site. I'll be there off and on, overseeing the project, but you'll be largely independent, working on your reputation. If the roof goes well, there will be other jobs related to bringing the other buildings back to functionality. We'll work out a rotation of shifts so that everyone has a day off once a week, and there will be no work on Sunday." He paused, encouraged at the murmur of enthusiasm swelling amongst the group. He glanced at Nathan. "Nathan here has already hired on as our blacksmith, and we've had extensive discussions about how payday and benefits like education will work. He or I can answer your questions."

There was a long moment of stunned silence. "Wait just a minute, sir," said one man standing in the back. Tall and skinny, he stood head and shoulders above everyone else. "Did you just offer education?"

Levi nodded. "The middle Miss Daughtry, Miss Joelle, has offered to spend an hour every day, during the noon meal, working with those who want to learn to read and write."

The man let out a long whistle. "Shoot, I'd be willing to work dawn to dusk, just for that." He pushed his way to the front of the crowd. "I'm Shug Pogue. Where do I put my mark?"

Though he'd expected most of the men to be illiterate, Levi had prepared a labor contract with the details enumerated and plenty of room for signatures. Conscripting a barrel as a desk, he laid out the contract and handed his pen to Shug. The tall Negro drew an *X* at the bottom of the paper with elaborate flair, then passed it to a friend. By lunchtime, Levi had collected more than enough help for his construction crew, with several on a waiting list in case others dropped out. Nathan approved all the men as being trustworthy.

When everyone had gone home, leaving him and Nathan alone in the forge, Levi traced a finger over the last scrawled *X*. "I don't know how to thank you for this," he said, looking up at Nathan. "Selah will be so relieved that we can start in the morning."

Nathan nodded. "You a good man, Mr. Levi. Miss Selah's a good woman. These men need the work, and we're grateful you didn't overlook us. Since the war ended, we all been pretty anxious, thinking we might have to go north to the factories or out west to work on the new railroads to feed our families. Might have to eventually, but it's good to have a little more breathing time." He held his head up. "You treat us right, we'll work hard for you."

Levi extended a hand. "We will, and I'm confident we'll have that place sparkling like a new penny before summer." The two men shook. "Now let's start gathering up your tools and get you moved out to the . . . hotel."

He wasn't going to call it a plantation, ever again. It was time to move into the future. The future of Daughtry House.

Thursday, midmorning, Selah leaned over the piano, rubbing furniture oil into its rosewood top. She smiled as the memory of her mother and Joelle's duets played counterpoint to the chaotic rhythm of hammers banging on the roof. Levi had brought a large crew that morning to start the biggest project on their list. She was relieved to see him, of course—he hadn't been back since Monday, when he'd reacted in such a peculiar fashion to her suggestion that he play the instrument. His manner this morning had been perfectly normal, though he hadn't stayed to talk. Instead he'd pulled on a pair of gloves and climbed up on the roof to supervise the job.

Selah was pleased with the progress over the last two days. Aurora had arrived on Tuesday as promised, along with Schuyler and Grandmama, who had refused to be left behind. To Selah's astonishment, all three city-dwellers had been willing to tackle any assignment, no matter how grubby or menial. Schuyler, who proved to be handy with a hammer and saw, helped Mose replace the broken windows in the cupola and repair the walls, and Grandmama suggested scrubbing away the honeycomb residue with vinegar to eliminate the odor. Aurora, attired in one of Selah's old dresses, worked like a Spartan, joining the other women in taking the rugs and curtains outside to be beaten and aired, brushing upholstery, and sweeping and mopping the wood floors.

Schuyler, Aurora, and Grandmama had yet to arrive today, but Horatia and ThomasAnne had been in the kitchen all morning, making note of needed household supplies, while Joelle worked in the library. Selah still had a long list of projects to be completed—including furniture repair, replacing broken spindles in the staircase, and thorough dusting and polishing of lamps and light fixtures—but she was confident it could all be done well before the heat of summer arrived.

Hearing the rattle of wheels coming up the drive, she glanced at the grandfather clock ticking away in the corner of the parlor. It was nearly ten o'clock, when Doc Kidd had made a habit of coming by to collect Wyatt for a tutoring session. The boy had accompanied Mose and Nathan to the old forge to help clean, refurbish, and settle the blacksmith's equipment.

Putting the cloth and polish on the entryway table, she opened the front door and stood shading her eyes against the sunlight. That wasn't Doc's wagon and horses, but an unfamiliar pair of matched sorrels, pulling a beautiful spanking-new covered carriage. Schuyler held the reins, and Aurora, dressed to the nines, bounced on the red-velvet seat next to him. In the rear passenger seat, Grandmama clutched the side of the carriage as if in imminent danger of being thrown out.

Aurora clapped her hands with excitement as the carriage rolled to a stop. "Look what we bought, Sissy! Aren't they beautiful?"

Schuyler threw the reins to Mose, who had sauntered around from the back of the house. "Take the carriage to the barn and unhitch the horses, will you, Mose? Give them a drink and show Wyatt how to rub them down." He turned to help Grandmama down, then reached for Aurora. "Come on, Pete."

But Aurora gave his shoulder a playful shove. "No, I'll go with Mose and make sure the horses are settled."

As she and Mose took the carriage bowling around the side of the house, Grandmama shook off Selah's hand on her elbow with a sniff. "Do you see what I've had to put up with for the last eight years? I'm getting too old to have to restrain such unbridled energy, and your grandfather is no help at all. All the girl has to do is bat those long eyelashes and he gives her whatever she wants."

Selah smiled. "Grandmama, I tried to get you to let her come home with me three weeks ago, and you refused!"

"That's because I wanted you to stay, you goose! I should have known you'd call my bluff." She began to stump her way up the steps. "Just like your father, ornery as a mule!"

Selah sighed and turned to find Schuyler watching the show. He was fashionably dressed in a black coat over a red-and-black-striped vest, with white shirt, black trousers, and a neat string tie. Clearly he had not come to work today. "She's right, you know," he said with a broad grin.

Selah ignored the hit. "I had thought Aurora might have turned into a lady by now, but she seems to love animals as much as she ever did. When she was little, she used to follow Papa around everywhere on her pony. She's always been a better horsewoman than me or Joelle."

Schuyler chuckled. "There's no denying she knows her way

around horseflesh. She did most of the negotiating today and probably saved us a hundred dollars on that pair of sorrels."

"I'm glad she was helpful to you," Selah said, hands on her hips. "At least that's something."

"She's a bit of a flirt," Schuyler said with a shrug. "But I wouldn't take it too seriously. Where's Lady Bluestocking?"

"Joelle? In the library, where else? Schuyler, please don't pester her."

He grinned. "Someone's got to keep her stirred up so she doesn't atrophy like one of those petrified trees over near Jackson."

"I think you've mixed your metaphors—" But he'd already gone running up the steps, so she called after him, "Make sure Grandmama gets her tea, would you?"

Schuyler waved a hand and disappeared into the house.

"It must be a lot of work, keeping the world from crashing in on itself."

The voice came from overhead, and Selah looked up, squinting into the sun. Levi squatted on the edge of the second-story roof, forearms on his thighs, hands dangling between his knees. He looked perfectly comfortable, but her heart bounced at the thought of him falling and hitting the ground.

"If you need to talk to me, use the ladder and come down," she said, perhaps more sharply than she'd intended. "I'm getting a crick in my neck."

He laughed. "There's a wisteria vine right here. Don't move."

"Be careful!" she exclaimed, but he was already on his way down. She waited for him at the bottom of the vine, remembering the day she'd met him, the way he'd clambered up and down ropes and bridge trestles and balanced along rails like a trapeze artist. Heights didn't bother him, she knew that. Still . . . "I once got stuck in the middle of that vine, it started coming loose from the house, and—"

"So that's why you don't like heights." He swung to the ground, landing on the balls of his feet, knees bent, then stood there looking at her, a smile curving his lips. He'd dispensed with a coat, and the open neck of his shirt revealed his strong brown throat and collarbone. A long V of sweat darkened the front of the shirt. "Selah, don't wear yourself out trying to do everyone's job. You'll have to put up with some disasters, but people will sort themselves out and everything will eventually get done."

"I don't know how to slow down! Besides, it seems the more I have to do, the more I *can* do." She stopped, puzzled by the startled expression on his face. "What's wrong? What did I say?"

"It's just . . . my commander said something like that all the time." Levi ran his hand through his hair and let it fall even more rumpled than before.

Selah didn't know what to think. It was true that from the moment she opened her eyes every morning until she lay down on her cot in the office, she found herself at the center of a vortex of questions and decisions. As manager and recognized source of authority, she dished out encouragement, answers, and discipline with nearly equal frequency. The family and servants had taken to calling her "the general," with as much irritation as admiration and humor. She had laughed and answered to the sobriquet without objection.

But she reminded Levi of his *commander*? Was she that

masculine? That overbearing? It sounded like a serious character flaw.

Perhaps sensing her hackles going up, he winked. "Grierson was one of my favorite people. After all, somebody has to have a plan. Listen, Shug has got things going just fine on the roof. Since you're out here, why don't we look at a couple of places I haven't gotten to yet." When she hesitated, he quickly scanned her garb. "Unless you want to change into some other clothes first . . ."

"No, I'm ready for any amount of dirt, I'm afraid." She pulled her old shawl closer, suddenly shy under his regard. She'd taken more care with her hair today, dressing it in a coronet of braids, but there was nothing to be done about her depleted wardrobe. Everything she owned—except the travel dress she'd borrowed from Joelle for the trip to Memphis—had been turned, patched, and remade until she was hardly fit to appear in public. She wore her usual simple black skirt, faded to a murky blue, with a yellow print blouse whose only decoration was a double row of self ruffles around the neck. It was the last garment Charmion had made for her before the end of the war.

"You look beautiful," Levi said with apparent sincerity, for his cheeks turned ruddy, and he cleared his throat. "So I wanted to start with the ice house. If we're going to compete with hotels in town, we need amenities that will set us apart. That and the swimming pool—" He wheeled off in the direction of the side of the house, forcing Selah to skip to catch up. "How are things going inside the house?"

"Everything is as clean as I can get it, but I need to send ThomasAnne to town with the supply list she and Horatia have been working on. The kitchen will be our next project."

They rounded the back of the house. "I don't suppose you've run across a capable carpenter, have you? We need to repair the broken furniture in the master bedroom."

Levi's stride faltered for a split second. "Yes, there's a fellow Nathan recommended, who's up on the roof at the moment. When we all break for lunch, I'll send him in to talk to you."

"All right. Mr. Riggins—Levi, would you slow down? I'm all but running."

By now he was on the path to the pagoda, which stood on a natural rise, with the roof of the two-story ice house just behind it. Halting to let her catch up, he looked over his shoulder with an easy smile. "Sorry. My long legs." He extended his arm.

She took it out of habit, though she could have walked up the pagoda steps on her own. The two sides of her upbringing and education waged civil war inside her brain. Mama would have said, *Behave like a lady, and you'll be treated like a lady.* Miss Lindquist would have said, *Don't let others do for you what you can do for yourself.*

The curl in the pit of her stomach created by the feel of Levi's powerful forearm beneath her palm had nothing to do with manners or personal ability. It was, she was aware, simple attraction. Nothing else. Therefore she refused to entertain it.

She walked over to the wooden swing Papa had had built a couple of years before the onset of the war. After brushing it off with her hand, she sat down. The morning breeze was stiff enough that she was glad of her shawl, but she could close her eyes and remember a late spring when she'd sat here with a boy from the Hankins plantation, pretending to be grown enough to need a chaperone. He'd tried to hold her hand, but she'd given him a glass of lemonade instead, chilled with ice from the ice house. He'd promptly spilled it all over his trousers—

"What are you smiling about?" Levi asked.

Her eyes popped open, and she found him leaning against a peeling, splintered post, legs crossed at the ankles. He looked scruffy and masculine and interested in what she had to say. She lifted her shoulders. "Just a silly incident from a long time ago." She looked around. The two wrought-iron benches across the way, on either side of a small round iron table, were a bit rusty, but she supposed they could be painted. The wooden columns, floor, and railing would all need paint as well. "I haven't sat out here in a long time, but we used to have lovely garden parties in the summer when it was too hot to stay in the house. Mama always took such good care of her flowers." She glanced at the ice house looming over Levi's shoulder. "If you want to go in and look around, go ahead."

"Don't you want to come with me?"

She avoided his eyes. "It's just an ice house, no different than a hundred others in the South—except the bricks were made in our kiln right here on the property. I'll wait for you here. I'll trust your assessment." It had been years since she'd been down into the ice house. It had been the milieu of the servants, she and her sisters having been discouraged as children from risking injury on the narrow stairs, not to mention the danger of getting accidentally locked in. After Papa left, they hadn't been able to afford ice, even if it could have been smuggled down from the North on the black market. Now you couldn't pay her a hundred dollars to walk down those stairs.

There was a short silence. "You'd best tell me about it." Levi's voice was gentle.

"I can't."

"Selah, you can tell me anything."

"Not that. You're—Union, you wouldn't understand."

"I understand more than you think."

"I've learned to deal with it," she said between her teeth, "but I can't say it out loud. Pulling it up, talking about it, makes it real."

He moved, in one step reaching the swing. It jarred as he sat beside her, but he seemed to know better than to touch her. "Yes, it will make it real—not some monster that can stalk you in the night. Look at me." She did, reluctantly, and saw that his eyes blazed with pain. "Don't you think I saw and did things during that cursed war that still make me sick to my stomach? There was a pastor at home, in Illinois, who had been in my unit. We listened to each other. And it got easier to bear. Though sometimes I just—" He swept a hand over his face, looked away, then fixed his eyes on hers again. "I could tell you about it sometime. If you want."

She fought an insane urge to crawl up into his lap, to hold him and be held. "You're going to think me the veriest coward, but small, enclosed spaces . . ." She shuddered. "Worse than heights."

"Why? What happened?"

The words burst as if from a sprung dam. "It was April of 1863. Joelle and I were on the front porch—she was reading and I was sewing. Mama had been tending the flowers out by the gate. She came running up the front lane to the house, said horses were coming, a lot of them, men she didn't recognize, and we were to hide. Under the porch, there's a

. . . crawl space, covered with latticework. We used to hide there as children sometimes."

Levi's hand went to his chest as if he were looking for something in a pocket, then remembered he wasn't wearing a coat. It was an odd gesture, quickly covered when he clenched his hand and dropped it on his thigh. "Go on," he said. "I'm listening."

She swallowed. "We heard Mama run back in the house and shoo the servants out the back door. Then the horsemen, about five of them, dismounted right in front of us. We heard them clatter up the porch, saw their boots and breeches. They were in butternut, so I didn't know if they were Union or Confederate, but Mama made us promise to stay put until she came for us. We sat there listening to them tear the house apart, breaking windows, and we could hear Mama trying to reason with them at first, then she started to cry and then scream."

Selah doubled over, remembering, feeling the suffocating closeness of the hiding place, the fear that they would be found, the shame that she couldn't go to her mother's aid, the rage at her helplessness.

Levi shifted beside her, and she knew if he touched her, she would break into a million shards. He murmured something that sounded like "I'm so sorry." But he didn't touch her.

She sat up with a deep breath. "Someone came to stop them, apparently an officer—I knew he was Union because of the blue pants. There were a couple of gunshots, and we wondered who'd been hit."

"Probably just fired in the air to get everybody's attention."

Selah looked at Levi.

He shrugged. "That's what I would have done."

She nodded. "So we stayed where we were, a long, long time, until late in the afternoon when they all rode away.

Finally we decided it was safe to come out. The house was empty, so much damage . . . We went upstairs, calling for Mama. She didn't answer, but we found her lying on her bed, and it was—" She gulped. "It was too late."

"You and Joelle—you were both safe? No one molested you?" Tears stood in his eyes, and nothing had ever comforted her like his genuine concern.

"No, I told you, we were under the porch the whole time. Two girls who were in the house with Mama were raped but survived—" Selah's voice broke. "They told me later that the officer who came and stopped the ransacking—they said he sent for a Union surgeon and waited while he tended to everybody. That's why they were in the house so long. He was very kind, they said, and didn't want to leave Mama there alone, but she insisted."

"You never saw the faces of the men who were there?"

She shook her head. "All we saw were boots and spurs and pant legs and swords."

"I'm sure the looters were prosecuted."

"I doubt it." She heard the bitterness in her own voice. "Both Union and Confederate troops pillaged plantations until the end of the war, and it got steadily worse. Of course, Jo and I didn't have to worry about it, because Grandpapa came to get us as soon as he heard. And Grandmama never let us forget that we had a chance to come to Memphis when Aurora did, but Mama insisted on staying at Ithaca. But of course we wouldn't leave her alone here."

Now Levi took her hand. He threaded his fingers through hers, held it on his thigh, and looked her in the eye. "Selah, I promise you nothing like that is ever going to happen to you again."

Twenty-One

IT WAS AN EXTRAORDINARILY PERSONAL THING to say, Levi knew it, and he didn't care. She had just trusted him with the most private, heart-wrenching event of her life. She must know that he would guard it, guard her, until one of them died.

One thing that he could never tell her was that he had been partially to blame for that terrible scar on both their souls.

When she didn't answer, just squeezed his hand a little, he sighed and let her go. The place was crawling with people, and he wouldn't expose her to comment or ridicule.

"Well," he said, "I'll go take a quick look, just to satisfy my curiosity, maybe make a few notes—" He stopped in the act of reaching for the notebook in his pocket, reminded again that he'd left his coat on the back porch. "Mental notes," he amended. "I'll be right back."

The ice house was a tall, narrow but sturdy little two-story brick building. The warped, rotten wood of the outside door would have to be replaced but at least made it easy to get in. Leaving the door open, he stood there for a minute, letting his eyes adjust to the comparative dimness of the interior. Stairs ran along the wall to the upper story, presumably a storage loft. "Should have brought a lamp," he muttered, noting the empty hook by the door.

His gaze fell on a three-foot hinged square in the floor—access to the underground ice storage. Its rusty hasp having long since broken apart, Levi threw it aside and laid the door back on the floor. Peering into the opening, he found more narrow steps spiraling downward into the dank darkness. He'd have to come back with a light. Just as well, since Selah was waiting.

He started to rise, but a flicker of light from below stopped him. "Who's down there?"

The light doused. All right, a scavenger. Since the incident in the cupola, though he could hardly carry around a rifle, Levi had kept his old Army Colt revolver tucked into the back of his pants. He drew it and pulled back the hammer.

"I'm armed," he said quietly, "and I'm not going away. Come up with your hands in the air."

He heard a distinct gasp. Holding the gun steady, he waited. Slow footsteps ascended the stairs, getting louder until the top of a curly brown head appeared out of the darkness.

Levi slowly lowered the hammer. "Wyatt, what are you up to?" Putting the gun away, he reached down to haul a very chastened Wyatt Priester into the light of day.

"I'm sorry, Mr. Riggins," Wyatt said as soon as his feet hit the floorboards. "I wasn't bothering all that stuff, I promise."

"What stuff?"

The boy glanced down into the trap opening, then back at Levi, wide-eyed. "You didn't know it was there?"

"Clearly I didn't. What are you talking about?"

"Somebody's got an explosives lab down there."

Levi stared at Wyatt. "Give me that lamp." When Wyatt started to follow him, he snapped, "Stay here."

Five minutes later he came back chilled to the bone, though not from stored ice. In one hand he grasped the necks of three small canvas bags.

"Come with me." Levi stalked out of the ice house and up the steps of the pagoda, where he dropped the bags onto the iron table, then yanked Wyatt by the sleeve to stand before Selah. "Look who I found snooping around in your ice house."

Selah rose, all sorts of questions in her eyes. "Wyatt? You're supposed to be helping ThomasAnne clean the kitchen."

"She told me I was underfoot." He clamped his lips together.

Selah studied his face. "You've been down there before, haven't you?"

Wyatt hunched his shoulders. How had she known that? What an interrogator she would make.

She looked at Levi and sighed. "He could have gotten hurt, I suppose. But it's just an old empty ice house."

"Full of explosives."

"Full of *what?*"

Levi studied her. "You didn't know there's an explosives lab in your ice house?"

She gaped at him. "Of course not! Are you sure?"

"Some of the materials look similar to what our troops used to mine Confederate earthworks during the war." And identical to the shell pieces he'd found under the bridge outside Oxford.

Selah branded Wyatt with a piercing glare. "Wyatt, it's not

like you to go poking around where you haven't been given permission to go. What were you thinking?"

Looking down, lips pressed together, Wyatt shuffled his feet. "I don't know."

Selah looked at Levi. "When you say 'explosives lab,' what do you mean? How dangerous is it? Are the elements assembled into actual bombs? What exactly are we talking about?"

She knew enough to ask good questions—something for him to think about later. He wished he had his notebook.

"Unassembled." Levi gestured toward the bags on the table. "I brought some of what I found up here. But other things I'd never seen before in this context. Lime and other odd chemicals, for example, and wax." He was fairly confident the boy hadn't been buying and stockpiling explosive ordnance. Nor was he capable of manufacturing torpedo casings and fuses on his own. But that was not to say that the boy had no information about the real culprit.

Wyatt shivered in his thin jacket. A little physical misery would do him good, Levi thought.

Selah apparently agreed. She stood in front of Wyatt, hands fisted at her hips in remarkable resemblance to Horatia at her sternest. She glanced over her shoulder at the sample items from the ice house. "What do you know about those?"

"N-nothing!" Wyatt stammered. "I don't even know what that is!"

Levi took his flint from his pocket. "Then you won't mind if I strike a spark and test it out—"

"No!" Wyatt yelped. "You'll blow us all to—" Wildly he shook his head and swallowed. "I mean, I don't think that's a good idea if you don't know what it is."

"I know what it is, you young knucklehead. And so do you."

Wyatt folded his arms and slumped. "Yes, sir. It's everything you need to make a torpedo. Powder—saltpeter, charcoal, and sulfur—fuses, shell casings, safety caps. I've seen it done up in Tennessee when the Yankees came riding over our land. Neighbors used to plant them under the bridges, and us kids had to know how to recognize them."

Selah sucked in a breath, and Levi shot her a warning glance. *Let me handle this.*

She bit her lip, but lifted her chin. *Be careful with this child.*

He turned back to Wyatt. "All right, we're going to Selah's office, and you're going to explain to me how and when you first discovered this stuff, along with anything else you might have noticed or moved or removed while you were down there."

They marched Wyatt over to the office in the cottage, where Selah had left a fire burning low in the grate. No one thought of asking for refreshments. Wyatt hunched into himself, bony shoulders pulled up to his ears, freckled face pale and pinched. Selah sat ramrod straight on the edge of her chair, hands folded and expression sober. She watched Wyatt with maternal compassion in her brown eyes.

Levi sat with elbows on his knees and fingers steepled. At this point, he figured he'd get more out of the boy with a soft interrogation. There was something odd going on here. If Wyatt were innocent, there would be no need for this excessive reluctance.

"We're listening," Levi told him quietly. "No one's accusing you of anything. We just want to know how long that lab has been in the ice house."

Wyatt shrugged. "I don't know. The other day I came across that trap door. It had been broken into, so I took a light and poked around. Nothing in the upper level, but when I went on down into the second one . . . well, there it all was, just like you saw it. I swear, Mr. Levi, I didn't mess with it. Well, I picked up the charcoal and sniffed at the sulfur to make sure that's what it was. None of it's dangerous on its own, and I left the lantern on the nail by the doorway—I'm not stupid."

"Wyatt, nobody thinks you're stupid," Selah said with a note of humor in her voice.

Levi exchanged glances with Selah. Wyatt was indeed no one's fool. And Levi still couldn't think of any motivation the boy might have for making homemade torpedoes. "Very well," he said, frowning. "So who do you think left the materials there? No dust or mice droppings on them, so we know they haven't been there long."

Wyatt's gaze slid to the side, and Levi knew a whopper was about to emerge. "I have no idea, sir," Wyatt said. "I haven't seen anybody go in or out of that door, not even any of the Negroes. And I've been watching to make sure."

Negroes? Levi blinked. *Who said anything about Negroes?* "That's good that you were watching." He gave Wyatt an encouraging nod. "What day did you say you first found the ice house?"

"Saturday."

Today was Thursday, which left several days unaccounted for. "How do you know nobody went down there while you were at school or church?"

The boy squirmed. Perhaps he was too close to the fire, but Levi didn't think so. "Well, I guess I don't know for sure, but yesterday I walked over to the blacksmith shop and watched Nathan work for a while, and he showed me how to make a fox trap, so when Miss ThomasAnne ran me out of the kitchen I decided to take the trap out to the woods and try it. But then I remembered the ice house and thought I'd better make sure nobody had been in it since yesterday. That's when you found me down there." Wyatt paused in his ramble. "How did you know about it, sir?"

"You might just say I had a feeling. So Nathan has been in the forge all morning?"

"Yes, sir! He was really busy." Wyatt dramatically grabbed his stomach. "Miss Selah, I'm hungry. Do you think I could go to the kitchen and ask Horatia if she's got some cheese or a biscuit or something?"

Selah had been frowning as she listened to Levi question Wyatt. "That would be fine. Would you mind telling her we're about finished up here, and we'll all need lunch in about an hour?"

"Yes, ma'am!" Wyatt bolted from the room.

Levi and Selah looked at each other. "What do you think?" he asked. He knew what he thought.

"You should question Nathan."

He smiled at her. "Somebody taught you to spot a liar."

She nodded. "Wyatt's not a bad boy. He's covering for someone."

"I agree. May be Nathan, may not be. But explosive devices don't magically appear in underground ice houses that haven't been in use in a decade. Something funny's going on here."

"Levi, I've got a nasty feeling in the pit of my stomach. Combine this with the shots at you in the cupola, and we've got a dangerous situation here."

He nodded. "How well do you know the workers who are making the repairs?"

"Most of them came off our plantation, so I know them all at least by sight." She spread her hands. "It's possible someone could hold a grudge against us."

"Maybe." He pulled at his lower lip. "I'll go over to the forge and talk to Nathan. Meanwhile, you make sure Wyatt knows that ice house is off-limits." He winked at her. "One thing's for sure—your life hasn't been boring since you met me!"

March 21, 1870

Selah met Mose and Horatia in the front yard, rejoicing that the roof was done, the front porch repaired, and the marble steps put back in place. They were still going to need a coat of paint over the whole outside of the house, but at least the family could now come and go without risking life and limb.

She watched in concern as Mose climbed down from the wagon, a large bandage still covering his head wound.

"I don't know why she wouldn't let me drive," Mose complained, eyes twinkling at his wife.

"You can't hardly drive with two good eyes," Horatia said, tying the mule to the hitching post.

Selah laughed. "We're glad to have you back. Levi's gone to town, and he'll be sorry he missed you."

"I'll be around all day," Mose said, pulling on his pipe. "Ray says the big house is clean top to bottom, and she's been working on the kitchen. What we gon' do next?"

"We'll look at the list together and I'll let you help me

decide. But first, I have a surprise for you." Selah avoided Horatia's eyes. She had a feeling Mose was going to be a lot happier about this than his wife. But it was good. Surely this was a good thing. "Come on around to the kitchen."

The three of them made their way around the left side of the house, Mose moving a little slower than usual and Horatia watching him like a hawk for any dizziness. As far as Selah could tell, he'd suffered no debilitating or lasting harm from the attack. They had a lot to praise God for. Now she had to trust him with this little complication that had arrived today.

Like in most large plantations, Ithaca's kitchen was a freestanding brick building, constructed at a distance to reduce the possibility of fires spreading to the main house. Finished before work started on the big house, it was equipped with a large woodstove, an ample pantry, and plenty of cabinets. Most of the cookware, kitchen tools, and small appliances had been stolen by squatters and vandals while the Daughtry sisters were in exile in Memphis. But Levi would be bringing a shipment of replacements back from town later today.

Selah couldn't help a little jolt of excitement at the thought of her home once again running at full capability. This time, though, its staff would be working for honest wages. *Be careful*, she cautioned herself. *We're not there yet . . .*

As she walked across the kitchen yard with the Lawrences, Horatia clicked her tongue in disgust. "The herb garden needs tending, Mose. And the vegetables shoulda done been planted already."

"I know that, woman," Mose said. "A man only got so many hours in a day. Miss Selah, I'm thinking that boy Tee-Toc, always underfoot, he would make a fine assistant and get some of that done. What you think?"

"That's your province, Mose. You take on whoever you want and train him up." Selah took a deep breath and pushed open the front door. "Charmion? You still here? Look who I brought!" She stood aside to allow the Lawrences to enter behind her.

She'd expected Horatia's angry intake of breath, Mose's soft, joyful laughter. She hadn't expected to find the obviously pregnant Charmion to be standing on a chair hanging curtains.

Horatia rushed past Selah. "Girl-child, get yourself down off that chair before you hurt yourself and my grandbaby! Have you lost whatever little sense you was born with?" Horatia took her daughter's hands in support as she stepped down off the chair—and held them, face working. "Oh, little honey-pie. I'm so glad to see you!"

With a sob, Charmion flung herself at her mother. "Mama. Oh, Mama."

Selah backed out of the kitchen, dabbing her eyes with the hem of her apron. She had done the right thing, encouraging Nathan to bring Charmion on over, early this morning. He'd been working on their little cabin down the road, in the earliest hours before dawn and into the darkness of dusk, so that it was almost ready for its young mistress to turn it into a home. Charmion had walked all around it with her hands pressed to her cheeks. "Oh, Nathan! Is this really ours? I'll put the baby's cradle over here by our bed, and the stove can go there, and—" She'd started to cry. "It's so beautiful, and I want my mama to see it!"

"She will, darlin', she will." Nathan took her into his arms, looking over Charmion's head at Selah.

And so Selah had made that happen.

As she shut the kitchen door now, she watched Mose walk over to pat Horatia on the back.

Yes. It was good.

Levi had left the boardinghouse early that morning. His landlady had prepared her usual breakfast of cat-head biscuits and a slab of salted ham, along with a couple of eggs fried over easy. With his belly pleasantly full, he'd sat playing checkers with an old-timer on the front porch of the Mercantile, waiting on Whitmore to open up. No discussions of politics, just listening to an old man's stories of Indians, bears, hacking a home out of a wilderness, and watching the wonders of modern life roll in on train tracks.

Yawning, Whitmore arrived around eight, unlocked the door, and invited Levi to come in and browse while he got the coffeepot going.

Levi leaned on the counter and proffered a paper covered in Selah's neat script. "I would, but my boss said I was to purchase the items on this list, nothing more, nothing less."

Whitmore pulled his spectacles down to the end of his nose and peered. "We've got everything there, plus some special orders for Miss Daughtry that arrived on the Saturday afternoon train. If you'll wait, I'll be but a moment."

Levi nodded and watched Whitmore putter around, stoking the woodstove, pouring water, grinding and measuring coffee, and setting it to boil.

Whitmore looked over his shoulder. "You've stayed in Tupelo longer than I expected you to, Mr. Riggins—certainly longer than most Yanks do. You must be finding the company congenial out at Ithaca."

"I am, as a matter of fact." Levi nodded at the list on the counter. "Miss Selah is a careful, straightforward manager, for all her high standards. I like that in a woman."

"Selah's not everyone's cup of tea—my wife, for one—but she's easy to look at, and a man always knows where he stands with her." Whitmore's eyes twinkled. "Since she hasn't run you off, I presume your standing is on solid ground."

"We get along well together, and she is very pretty." For the sake of Selah's reputation, Levi forbore mentioning that he still found it a modern miracle that Selah Daughtry remained unwed. After a slight pause, he said, "Would you mind telling me what your wife finds objectionable in such a virtuous and godly young woman?"

"It's nothing that would bother you and me, Riggins. But that straightforward manner you mentioned can express itself in some . . . shall we say, tart pronouncements from time to time. Miss Selah does not suffer a fool, and she will not tolerate any sort of criticism of her sisters or of her cousin, Miss McGowan."

"Has your wife had reason to be critical of Selah's family?"

Whitmore sighed. "My wife does love gossip. But even though it's harmless, I never repeat such nonsense."

Whitmore clearly wished to share whatever it was he knew.

"Now, Mr. Whitmore, you know I won't believe anything salacious about the Daughtry ladies. You might as well tell me what you mean."

"It's nothing that everyone in town doesn't already know." Whitmore looked around and lowered his voice. "Did you know that Miss ThomasAnne came to live with the Daughtrys for a brief time while the two older girls were away at boarding school?"

"I don't know much about her at all," Levi admitted. "She's a bit like dust in the corner of a room, blown here and there by movement around her, but making little impression on her own."

Whitmore nodded. "And she's been a good companion for the Daughtry girls—highly respectable, impeccable manners, decorously dressed. But she originally came from Georgia, I believe. And that first stint at the Daughtrys' plantation was covered by a certain . . . cloud of scandal. She'd recently ended an engagement with a soldier, and they say Miss ThomasAnne came to Ithaca to recover from a broken heart."

"I see." Levi pulled at his lip. What a sad and frankly boring little story. Women broke engagements or got jilted every day.

"Well, you wanted to know what Mrs. Whitmore had to do with it. I'm afraid my wife made a rather unkind assessment as to the reason for Miss ThomasAnne's previous stay with her cousin, and happened to repeat it in Miss Selah's hearing one day at church. Selah lit into poor Mrs. Whitmore like a dog protecting a favorite bone, and—" Whitmore's eyes rolled behind his spectacles. "Neither one of them has ever gotten over it. Miss Selah seems to have rather a talent for holding a grudge."

Levi could well believe that might once have been true. But he'd seen the tender heart beneath her toughness, and he suspected that life had lately softened her rigidity a good deal.

"She is definitely protective and loyal," he said, "and with all due respect to your good wife, I find it difficult to believe any salacious talk about ThomasAnne. I am interested, however, in Selah's father. She seems to revere him, but there are no portraits of him anywhere in the house. What can you tell me about him?"

"Colonel Daughtry?" Whitmore let out a low whistle. "Now there was a man larger than life, wasn't afraid to take what he wanted and hang on. He loved his wife and those girls and the plantation, and literally died protecting them."

"He is dead, then? There seems to be some question."

Whitmore scratched his head, shifting the toupee. "Most people assume he is, because if he was alive, he'd be here trying to stop this merger between the M&O and the Mississippi Central. He did keep the M&O from coming across his land once, in the late '50s, which is why Gum Pond—Tupelo, that is—wound up here. Daughtry wasn't stupid, though. He managed to buy property across the street from the train depot and put up a saloon."

"Selah's father owned a saloon? What happened to it? Who gets the profit now?"

"Nobody knows. Not sure Selah even has any idea her pa owned it. All his business interests were run through a bank in Oxford. I imagine it was sold or mortgaged, though, to buy Confederate bonds, like most people of property did." Whitmore leaned over the counter, settling in to gossip. "Before the war, Ithaca was one of the most profitable plantations in the state. Had its own tannery and brick kiln and forge, Italian marble seats in the privies, the swimming pool, and ice house. The Colonel kept dogs and horses, and I was invited out there to hunt on occasion." Whitmore preened a bit at this evidence of his own social standing. "You should have seen it when it was all decked out for Christmas. All those fancy mirrors and tables and serving dishes must've cost twelve fortunes. And sending the girls to boarding school . . . My lands, that family had connections, and the man was a genius at making money."

Levi could well believe it, considering what it was costing to bring the place back. "But Daughtry left it all, to enlist in the Confederate army. A lot of planters paid to have others serve in their places."

"True. But the Colonel was a fighting man. Which is why what happened is not surprising, when you think about it. I know you've heard by now about the raid on the plantation—I think it was in the spring of '63—gang of galvanized Yanks took off and went on a spree foraging for food. They found Ithaca and tore the place up, violated poor Mrs. Daughtry, and she died that same day from shock and injury. Just miraculous they didn't find those beautiful girls. Story is, they were hiding under the porch the whole time."

Levi's hand went to his pocket. "Thank God," he said. But where was God for Selah's mother? Did God pick sides? Or did he simply take his hands off the reins and let people destroy themselves willy-nilly?

"Indeed. They wrote to their grandfather, he came to get them, and word was sent to the Colonel. That's when things got interesting. He was in Tennessee, commanding a Mississippi regiment during the Chickamauga campaign, so he couldn't just up and take leave to come home. But he did go a little crazy when he heard something similar happened at General Maney's plantation outside Chattanooga. Daughtry took his men riding out after the Union sympathizers that plundered Maney's place, rounded them up, and then went after their families, breaking fingers until the women gave up the locations of a bunch of other traitors. The Colonel—" Whitmore blew out a breath—"shoo, you didn't want to mess with him. The governor ordered him to bring the men in for trial, but Colonel Daughtry was beyond reason at this point. When some of them escaped, he just up and shot the rest and left 'em in a ditch."

Levi had heard some of that story from Schuyler Beaumont, but he wanted details and perspective that Whitmore might provide. "What happened then?"

"Who knows what would have happened if he'd simply surrendered? But by that time Union forces in the area heard about the massacre, tracked the Colonel down, and arrested him. After a proper trial, he was sentenced to life. Then another twist in the story!" Whitmore chortled. "The Colonel apparently escaped as the Federals closed down Camp Douglas after the war."

"You think he left the country?" Levi's gut was telling him that Selah's father had played some part in the sequence of events leading up to his own investigation. But big chunks of it made no sense. Especially if he was dead.

Whitmore laid a finger beside his nose. "I don't know. But I tell you one thing. Jonathan Daughtry wasn't a man to fade into obscurity. And if his daughter Selah has a long memory, her pa was one to never forget a slight. And you can take that to the bank."

DAUGHTRY SLIPPED THROUGH the woods behind the boy. He was done with shooting from a distance. He believed in the elegance of using the right tool for the right job. Blowing a bridge required explosives. To take out a nest of Yankee soldiers, you needed artillery. Eliminating a spy was a little more subtle.

The Yank was well trained. In daylight he managed to stay too close to one of the women, usually secreted in the house, and he would come and go under the cover of darkness. Getting rid of him meant Daughtry was going to have to get up close and use a knife—or some other clean, quiet method with his hands.

Right now it was the boy he was worried about. Like his pa, a traitor and Federalist sympathizer, no telling who he would turn on. He had found the explosives, the little sneak-thief.

In prison they'd talked about what they were going to do when they got out. Everybody knew of arms stashes—places where the Confederacy had managed to keep weapons out of Union hands. A barn here, an ice house there. So on his way to Mexico and back, he'd collected what he thought he would need, then made his way back home. He'd expected to have the place to himself, with the girls safe in Memphis, the slaves scattered.

He should have known Selah would come back. She was too much like him, a man's mind in that willowy female body, a calculating, straightforward temperament that would never allow anyone, even her domineering grandmother, to order her life. Now that she was here, Daughtry wanted to help her keep the place—but not on the dime of that scoundrel Beaumont. The Good Book spoke against families that would devise evil and work iniquity upon their beds. Those who would covet a field and oppress a man and his heritage. The Beaumonts were tainted with abolitionism; the youngest, Camilla, had nearly corrupted his own girls, though he'd removed them from danger just in time.

Hadn't he? Yes. His girls might be tenderhearted, but they weren't stupid, even Joelle, who forever had her head in a book.

The boy's footsteps slowed, and Daughtry kept pace. What was the kid up to? Generally he took off early in the morning for town, to spend the day with that milk-toast doctor, or he was out at the forge with Nathan. Daughtry hadn't forgotten his connection with the train accident and the Yank. Perhaps he should question the boy first. One could never have too much information.

Better yet, perhaps he could be turned into a spy. Threaten to harm one of his benefactors. Elegance. Yes.

Twenty-Three

"DID YOU SEE THE HEADLINE in this morning's paper?" Schuyler popped the newspaper open in Selah's face the moment she opened the door.

"I haven't read it yet, but please, do come in," she said to his back as he stomped past her into the rotunda.

"Well here!" He wheeled and tossed it at her. "Read it now!"

She straightened the pages, focused her gaze, and cleared her throat. "'A vessel has arrived at Mobile on Friday last with 3,500 bags of coffee consigned to a house in that city.'"

"Not that!" Schuyler snatched the paper and thumped a large headline midway down the front page. "This one. 'The Mobile and Ohio Railroad has once again overreached itself in taking subsidies from worthless government bonds issued to a gullible public—' Have you ever read such utter nonsense? And on and on it goes, with contrived allegations of funds misspent by board executives wining and dining themselves at taxpayer expense! Who writes this kind of thing?"

"I don't know," Selah said, trying to look over his shoulder. "Is there a byline?"

"Just 'A Concerned Citizen.' *Concerned*, my eye! One of those radical Republicans beyond doubt!"

"Why do you say that? Shouldn't we all be concerned about our taxes being fairly and wisely spent?"

"Well, of course we should, but is there any reason to target the M&O?"

Selah regarded him, suddenly uneasy. "Schuyler, is this true?"

"No!" he roared. "Do you see me wining and dining anybody? And even if I were, there are legitimate expenses attached to running a business."

"Is—are those bonds attached to Ithaca? Is that where the money is coming from?"

"No. I've saved my money, pinched pennies until they scream bloody murder. I've made a few investments. The money is mine, the bank credit is mine." Schuyler's face flamed with controlled rage. "But don't you see, if the railroad fails, Daughtry House will fail too! People read tripe like this in the paper, they believe it, and they vote. They write their congressmen and laws get changed. I've got to find out who wrote this and make them retract it."

"But Schuyler, it's just one article. Surely it can't have that much influence." She took the paper from him, found the editorial, and read it again more slowly. "Besides, it's very contained and reasonable, compared to some of the other—"

"Oh, never mind. I'll deal with it myself." He took the paper from her again and crammed it under his arm. "What I really came over to talk to you about is the house party."

"What house party?"

"The one we're going to host in two weeks, as a pre-opening introduction of Daughtry House to the public."

Selah reached up to place the back of her hand against his forehead. "It's funny, you don't seem to have a fever."

"What do you mean?"

"Well, clearly, you are raving with some sort of debilitating disease. We won't be ready to introduce Daughtry House to the public for at least another month."

Schuyler spread his arms wide, flourishing the paper. "It's going to have to be sooner than that. I want to start by drawing attention to you three beautiful sisters running the place—in fact, we're going to have your picture done, all dressed in ball gowns, to use for publicity. So start looking for a seamstress. Go shopping! Whatever it is you women do to get gussied up for a special occasion. Because that's what this will be—the most special occasion you've ever had in your lives."

"I don't object to seamstresses or shopping. But—Schuyler, two weeks? No." She laughed. "No!"

"I say yes."

Selah turned to find Aurora coming down the stairs. "What? I didn't even know you were here."

"I came in while you were out in the kitchen." Aurora reached the bottom step and paused dramatically, one hand on the newel. "I've been to take a look at the progress upstairs, and it's remarkable what we've accomplished just since Grandmama and I arrived. Oh, and Schuyler." She smiled at him. "He's right. We have to overcome the bad press someone has launched against us."

Selah shook her head. "But it never mentioned us by name—"

"It's there by inference. If I saw it, others will too." Aurora bestowed her dimpled smile on Selah. "Besides, a party is always a good idea, and the sooner the better."

Selah prided herself on never allowing anyone to talk her into something she hadn't thought through. "Schuyler, you made me the manager for a reason. I'm going to sit down and list all the pros and cons, see how the accounts add up. I'll talk to Levi and Horatia, see if they think the work on the ground floor and the yard can realistically be completed within two weeks. And someone has to think about feeding—How many people do you want to invite?" She was remembering the last Christmas party her parents hosted before the war. Her mother's feverish work to get everything ready. How many people that took.

Schuyler glanced at Aurora, his ally. "Eight or ten selected overnight guests. Fifty or so more for a ball—"

"Eighty," Aurora interrupted. "Or a hundred. We want the word to get out that Daughtry House will be the summertime destination of north Mississippi. We want to have to turn down reservations."

Schuyler beamed at her. "That's my girl! Sometimes you have to spend money to make money."

Selah pulled a notebook out of her apron pocket. "You people," she spluttered. "Oh you!"

Levi got back to Daughtry House around lunchtime, driving a wagon loaded down like a traveling peddler's caravan.

In his pocket was a telegram from Pinkerton that had thrown another twist in his investigation. Apparently an Oxford, Mississippi, telegraph operator named Scully had

written to the address on L. E. Vine's business card. Said he
might have information leading to the location of Archibald
Priester's kin, and would Mr. Vine please return to Oxford
as soon as possible to discuss the matter. Pinkerton wanted
Levi to make the trip to Oxford as soon as possible.

The timing couldn't have been worse. Now that Beaumont, his prime suspect, was here in Tupelo, and events
had heated up with the attack on the cupola and the discovery of those explosives in the ice house, he couldn't
help wondering what information the telegraph operator
could provide. Wyatt's involvement as Priester's son seemed
peripheral at best.

On the other hand, a wise investigator never ignored a
loose thread. He'd replied with his own message, updating
Pinkerton and asking how Agent Hodges was faring with
regard to the robbery aspect of the case. Weighing heavily on
his mind was the fear that he might be avoiding truth staring
him right in the face because of his growing attachment to
Selah Daughtry. There was tension between her and Schuyler Beaumont; Levi just couldn't tell if it stemmed from the
natural strain of partnership or from genuine antagonism
left over from that early clash between Schuyler and Joelle.
It was difficult to determine if he had one case with two
related angles—or two separate cases.

Teeth gritted in frustration, he drove down the rutted lane
from the main road to the house. Under normal circumstances, he would long since have begun to openly court Selah
Daughtry. But because he was operating under cover, as he
had during the war—ferreting out information for larger purposes than his own emotional well-being—he couldn't even
reveal to her his full identity. He was very glad he had used

his real name when he'd first met her. At least he wouldn't have to later undo an alias.

The case would eventually be solved, hopefully without her at its center, but the longer that took, the greater the risk of ruining their relationship with lies. How would she ever be able to trust his word, when he'd fooled her as to his very identity for months on end?

And if he broke every rule of common sense and revealed it to her now? She would still have good reason to think of him as a cheat, liar, and spy. Plus, if she was involved in the scheme to defraud the stockholders of the Mississippi Central Railroad, then he, Levi Matthew Riggins, would become known as the biggest dupe in the history of the Pinkerton Agency.

By the time he stopped the wagon in the kitchen yard, Horatia and her daughter, Charmion, waited to take charge of unloading. Horatia sent Mose to gather the men of the house to haul in the heaviest crates, and the lot of them emptied the wagon in short order.

Levi found Nathan's wife to be a lovely light-skinned girl, blooming with child, with a bright pair of dark eyes and a shy, pleasant manner. She deferred to her mother, but it was clear the sun rose and set for her in the tall young blacksmith. He could see how Charmion had been willing to forgo her parents' approval in favor of such a happy marriage.

When the last of the supplies had been disposed of, Levi called Nathan aside. "Have you got a few minutes to come look at something before you go back to the forge? I want to add a project to your waiting list."

"Yessir, of course." Nathan called to Charmion, "Don't you be lifting nothing heavy, girl. Your mama gon' tan your bottom, you try anything silly. Right, Miss Ray?" Winking at Horatia, who responded with her patented "Hmph," he followed Levi toward the pagoda.

"You familiar with the ice house?" Levi asked as he walked around the pagoda.

Nathan shrugged. "Back in the old days, I used to be the one have to haul blocks of ice from the river and stow it. You know, since I'm such a good-size boy. Been a long time since anybody been able to afford ice, though." He stopped in the path outside the ice house. "Why?"

"Selah and I inspected it the other day and found broken hinges in the trap door and other spots that need to be repaired before it can be used." Levi covertly studied Nathan's expression and the set of his posture. He seemed not to be uneasy, just curious as to Levi's purpose.

"Well, let me see what I can do." Without hesitation Nathan yanked open the outer door and poked his head in. "Pretty dark in here, since they's no windows. Got a lantern?"

"Hanging on a nail right there."

With the lantern lit, Levi showed Nathan the broken door and narrow, winding stairs.

Nathan hesitated on the top step. "You go down first, boss. I never did like this skinny staircase."

"I went down it the other day. The steps are intact."

"Still . . ." Nathan took a step back. "I'll fix anything you need me to. But I've growed a lot taller and broader than I was eight, ten years ago. Call me a chicken if you want to, but I ain't going down there."

Levi lifted the lantern to study Nathan's face. If the big blacksmith wasn't genuinely afraid of that dark two-level basement, he was a better actor than a lot of stage thespians.

Which meant he had not placed those explosives down there himself. Which meant Wyatt had been misleading Levi last week—or he had been referring to some other Negro. Mose, maybe? That was even more far-fetched an idea. Mose had been laid up in bed with a busted head.

"All right," he said. "So what can you tell me about a stash of explosives materials I found down there last Thursday?"

Nathan's mouth fell open. "A stash of what?"

"You heard me. I found Wyatt down there poking around with that stuff—chemicals, fuses, powder—and he very deliberately said you had been nowhere in the vicinity—when nobody had brought up any such thing. You know, a little too much protest? Which leads me to believe you might know something about it."

Stone-faced, Nathan returned Levi's stare. After a moment, his white smile broke. "I might at that. But it ain't what you think."

"Nathan, I frankly don't know what to think. I know you couldn't have been the one to take those shots up into the cupola. I know you've gone out of your way to help me and Selah get this operation up and running. So let's go sit on the steps, you tell me what you know about that stuff, and we'll see where we are."

Looking relieved that he wasn't going to be asked to descend into that dark hole after all, Nathan stepped outside and waited for Levi to follow. They perched on the pagoda steps, Nathan clearly uneasy and Levi working hard to figure out his strategy.

Before he could say anything, Nathan sighed. "First of all, Wyatt, he just a dumb kid. Doc shouldn't have let him see the project to begin with."

Levi blinked. So now suddenly Doc was involved in this mess? "Doc Kidd? Is that where Wyatt is right now? I thought they were studying for medical school. What kind of project?"

Nathan shook his head. "I don't know where Wyatt is right now. Doc's gone to Oxford to meet with Professor Quinlan, his partner in the electric magnet project. But please, boss, don't tell anybody else, or I could get in trouble."

Selah was fond of lists. In thinking about the wisdom of throwing a house party before said house was ready for public viewing, she had made several of them. One concerned everything to be gained from early publicity. Another took on all the possible disasters. A third enumerated the costs that a three-day house party and grand ball would entail.

In the end, she came to one of her mother's favorite Proverbs: "Without counsel purposes are disappointed, but in the multitude of counselors they are established." Tucking the lists in her apron pocket, she'd sought out Horatia and offered to help prepare supper for the family and work crew—to be served in the big house.

"Miss Selah, you do know when this place turns into a hotel, you folks not gonna eat in the dining room with the paying guests—don't you?" Horatia hoisted a tray laden with a big pot of chicken and dumplings and headed for the kitchen door.

As Horatia bumped the door open with her hip, Selah picked up the cornbread basket and butter. "Today we are all in need of a treat, if only something so small as a meal on a fine dining table, with real silver and china." She shot Horatia a straight look. "And the Lawrences will join us."

"Your grandmama would have a conniption. Besides—" Horatia sniffed—"the Lawrences don't need a fine table to enjoy a good pot of dumplings. The kitchen will do us right fine. That way Mose can smoke his pipe without me fussing about stinking up the linens."

Selah laughed and followed Horatia down the new covered walkway to the house. "I wouldn't want to spoil Mose's after-dinner pipe. But Horatia—" She hesitated. "I wanted to ask you about something."

"I knew they was something on your mind." Horatia stopped and wheeled so suddenly that Selah nearly plowed into her. "Last week or so, you been closeted with Mr. Riggins every time I turn around. Did he finally get up the nerve to court you like a girl ought to be courted?"

Why did everyone assume Levi must be the first and only thing on her mind these days? "Of course he hasn't—I mean, I have no idea what you mean!"

"Hmph. I ain't just fell off the turnip wagon. Everybody see the way that man look at you."

"What way is that?"

"Like he want Selah puddin' for dessert."

"That's just ridiculous."

"Yes, ma'am, it purely is. If I was a laughing woman, I'd be rolling on the ground with it."

Selah gathered herself and marched on into the house. "Mr. Riggins is very busy, he has said nothing untoward to me, has *done* nothing to make me think he regards me as anything other than an employee. Or at the very most, a good friend." Well, that was not precisely true. Did good friends hold hands? "Anyway, speaking of pudding, what I wanted to ask you about is the possibility of finding enough foodstuffs at this time of year to feed a party of ten—in addition to staff, I mean—for three days, and then refreshments for a large ball. Assume that cost is not a factor."

Horatia didn't answer for a moment, her broad, strong brow knit as she dealt with dumplings and cornbread on the serving counter. Finally she looked at Selah, expression bland. "You do know your pa kept five hundred turkeys on hand, plus the chickens and geese and ducks. We'd often butcher over four hundred hogs in a month. There was cows for meat and milk. And in the summer we'd harvest sixteen hundred bushels of peas in a day, then twelve hundred more two days later. And that don't take into account the fresh oysters that came up from the Gulf and other luxuries wealthy folks look for when they guests somewhere. I'm not sure where we're gonna get all that."

That was reality, Selah knew. Keeping her feet on the ground was the very reason she'd come to Horatia with her question. But on the other hand, she wanted to remain hopeful. It seemed to her, the more she thought about it, that the Christian life was all about hope. Maybe Horatia needed a little hope too.

"I'm not sure either," she said with a rueful shake of her head. "But I'm not sure we need to be that extravagant. Think about it. The reason we had to have all that food back then was to keep the . . . the slaves fed. When you own something, you're responsible for caring for it. I'm just going to say this, and you tell me what you think about it. Nobody owns you and Mose anymore, Horatia. You're responsible for sustaining yourselves. That's not to say I don't care what happens to you, and it's not to say that as your employer I don't have to pay you fairly for your work. But we can negotiate how much of your wages comes in the form of food and other nonmonetary goods. So what I'm thinking is, it should take a lot less food to run this non-slavery-based hotel than a cotton plantation. We're going to send most of our employees home at the end of each day and let them provide for their own bed and board."

A glimmer appeared in Horatia's dark eyes. "You want to know what I think about that? I can have chicken livers and onions for supper if I don't want dumplings. So I'm gonna find a way to help you make this house party happen if I have to send Mose all the way to Mobile for oysters!"

Twenty-Four

AFTER SUPPER, the entire company—tired from the long day and full of dumplings—adjourned to the back porch with tall glasses of Horatia's lemonade to watch the sun go down. The windows and doors of the house stood open to the evening breeze, and Levi imagined the music of Joelle's piano drifting down the breezeway from the parlor, as it must have all those years ago when the family gathered after similar congenial meals.

Tonight, elderly Mrs. McGowan occupied the most comfortable chair, a cane rocker whose cushions had already been remade by the nimble-fingered Charmion. Levi would normally have made his adieus and started for town, but he'd been thinking all day about the convoluted knot this investigation had become. It was time to get some answers. So he waited until most of the party had drifted to rockers, straight chairs, and the three-seat swing at one end of the porch, then chose the top step between Selah and Wyatt.

The boy had been very quiet since he'd returned from a hunting expedition with barely enough time to wash his hands before supper. During the meal, his gaze had stayed on his food, which he'd picked at with none of his usual healthy appetite.

Selah apparently noticed his abstraction too. "Wyatt, what's wrong with you? I know you missed your tutoring session today, but it's not like you to be so—so—" She waved a hand. "So unlike yourself."

Wyatt snickered. "If I'm not like me, then who do I remind you of? Oh, yeah, someone else."

She laughed. "That's more like it. Tease the people who don't have your giant vocabulary."

"Tell us a little more about what you and Doc are working on," Levi said. "I understand it has something to do with electromagnetism, I presume with medicinal applications?" He remembered the first time he'd visited Kidd at his office. The doctor's momentary irritation had undoubtedly been because of the interruption to some research or experiment.

Wyatt's face lit. "He told you about that? He's made me keep it quiet." He paused, but when Levi neither confirmed nor denied the source of his information—rather, simply made his interest apparent—continued eagerly, "Doc was initially interested in the uses of electricity and magnetics in the way that Aepinus worked with tourmaline in electro-therapeutics, which led to the discovery of the pyroelectric properties of sulphate of quinine and quartz. I immediately understood what he was getting at, so he let me read his books and papers on torsion balance found in Coulomb's law."

Levi saw Selah's glazed expression. "Coulomb's law," he said, "posits that the force between two small electrified bodies varies inversely as the square of the distance between them. I learned that at West Point."

Her lips quirked. "Of course you did."

"Exactly," Wyatt said. "So the next step was Volta's electric battery, Ampere's theory of electrodynamics, and then Ohm's law. Finally, we got to Faraday's experiments that developed electromotive force with electromagnetic induction. Doc is every bit as smart as any of those scientists, and what he's figured out is going to be enormously practical, but all that material costs a lot of money, which is why he had Nathan help us with the construction—" The spate of information came to an abrupt halt as Wyatt seemed to realize he was volunteering more than he ought.

"Wyatt," Selah said gently, "is that where that explosives material came from? Why would Doc store it in our ice house?"

"I don't know for sure that he did. All I've seen is his work at the lab in his office." Wyatt's brow wrinkled. "But I do know that Doc isn't cooking up bombs! How could you think that? He's trying to help people."

Levi nodded. "It's unfortunate how often scientific discoveries and inventions designed for progress can be used to destroy people and things as well. Who is Professor Quinlan?"

"He's some mechanics professor at Ole Miss that Mr. Schuyler told him about. He's gotten funding from . . . somewhere or other, for research related to moving objects with electricity."

Levi could guess where the "somewhere" might be, and that the research would benefit the transportation industry. He regretted that his questions had further distressed the boy. He gave Wyatt a little shove of the shoulder. "Don't worry, we'll get to the bottom of it. I'm sure there's a simple explanation."

"Yes, sir. Please don't tell Doc I spilled anything. He'd be very upset that I talked out of turn."

That was two warnings Levi had received in one day against angering the young doctor. Perhaps a trip to Oxford would be in order after all, not only to question telegraphmaster Scully but to look into Professor Quinlan's research. "Tell you what, son," he said, "if it's all right with Selah, I'll stay the night here and take you with me back to town in the morning. You can look in on the doc, while I take care of an errand or two I didn't get to while I was there this morning."

"Then you don't mind if I keep up my lessons?" Wyatt asked. "I'd be grateful, sir. Is that okay, Miss Selah?"

She met Levi's eyes, her expression puzzled. "I suppose so," she said to Wyatt. "Now you'd best get on to bed, since the sun's going down. You'll want to get up early to get your chores done before y'all leave in the morning."

The boy tore off toward the cottage without another word. Levi was about to slide along the step closer to her, but she glanced over her shoulder toward her grandmother's chair. Worrying about what someone else thought seemed a tad out of character for her.

Levi rose and bowed to the old lady. "Mrs. McGowan, your lemonade seems to be in need of replenishing. May I fetch you another glassful?"

She looked at him from under beetled brows. "Those are some mighty nice manners for a boy from north of the Mason-Dixon. What do you want?"

He laughed. "I want a few minutes' conversation alone with your granddaughter. I promise to stay in sight, right there in the pagoda."

"And don't you know it's getting dark enough I can barely

see past my own hand?" She kicked at the toe of his boot with her slipper. "Thank you, I've had all the lemonade I can hold for one night. But, yes, you can have your pick of granddaughters—though I guess I know which one you want!"

"I thank you kindly, ma'am." He winked and turned to find Selah on her feet.

"You've got a great deal of nerve, Mr. Riggins!"

"On the contrary, I find my nerves more faint than they ever were when I faced a whole regiment of Johnny Rebs."

There was a titter of laughter from the four women on the porch, and Schuyler bellowed, "Rally round the flag, boys!"

Selah gasped and ran for the pagoda.

"Wait, Selah, hold on!" Laughing, Levi caught up and took her hand to pull it through his elbow. "You'll fall in the dark on this bumpy path."

She tried to tug her hand away. "You didn't have to embarrass me! And I've walked this path hundreds of times, just fine, all by myself."

"Then *you* can keep *me* from tripping." He laced his fingers through hers and held on for dear life. "I'm sorry, I couldn't resist. Selah! Have mercy, slow down."

She did, reluctantly. When they reached the pagoda steps, she climbed two, bringing herself to his height. She stared at him and said quietly, "Is this a battle?"

"I hope not."

"What's in your pocket?"

"Wh-what?"

"You touch your coat pocket all the time. There's something in there that means something to you. If you want to get to know me, you have to tell me personal things about yourself."

264

"That sounds kind of backwards."

"I already told you more than you need to know. What's in your pocket?"

"I keep a journal." And she wasn't going to see it, because it had his case notes in it. Notes about Selah and her family. "But today I left it at my boardinghouse."

"That's a lie. Or a partial truth."

He was startled into laughter. "What makes you say that?"

"You looked away. Besides, I've seen you writing in that notebook. I watched you on the train before we met."

He whistled through his teeth. "You would make a very good lawyer. Or policeman."

"And you still haven't told me what else is in your pocket."

"How do you know there's something else?"

"I just know. A journal isn't a touchstone."

"That's a science word, Miss 'I don't have a giant vocabulary' Daughtry. You are a very hardheaded woman."

"Yes, I am. I've told you that, over and over. As I'm sure everyone else who knows me has as well. And you didn't answer me."

"Selah, I can't. Not now, anyway."

"But you brought me out here for some reason."

She was absolutely right. What had he thought was going to happen? "Do you want to sit in the swing? Or go around to the back steps?"

"It depends on how public you want this conversation to be. You promised my grandmother that we would stay in view."

"And she clearly gave me permission to take you wherever I wished."

"So what *do* you wish, Levi Riggins? Yankee-boy straight-arrow rescuer of damsels in distress, vanquisher of bees,

minstrel of hymns and battle songs? I already told you what
I want. Now it's *your* turn."

Levi was silent so long she thought he wasn't going to
answer. Finally he sighed, so close that his breath fanned
her cheek. "I want to kiss you."

She blinked, almost laughed. But he clearly wasn't joking. He was looking at her mouth as a starving man looks
at his first meal, his eyes narrowed and smoky with longing.
"Levi," she said in a cautioning tone.

"I know," he said, those eyes moving to hers, humor and
unaccustomed helplessness easing the tension in his expression. "We're standing where anyone could see. It's not the
place or the time, but the more I'm with you, the more I
think about it, and I feel as if—" He jiggled her hand a little.
"Have you ever wanted something so much you thought you
might actually implode?"

This time she did laugh. "Levi, really. All you had to do
was—"

"Ask? No, it doesn't work that way, at least not with me."
He put on a fairly polished British accent and leered at her
comically. "Pardon me, Miss Daughtry, would you mind puck-
ering up so that we can get this kissing thing out of the way?"

Laughter bubbled. "I see what you mean."

He looked at her, his face a study in frustration. "Here,
sit down. Right here on the step."

They sat looking up at the stars until everyone on the
porch had gone back into the house with the lantern, and
they were in the dark. Selah felt sleepy, tired from the long,
busy day, but oddly itchy and restless. She was aware of Levi's

muscular arm against hers, the sound of his breathing, the pleasant scent of his clothing.

"Are you still thinking about it?" she asked suddenly.

"About what?"

He knew what. He'd put the idea into her head and she wouldn't be able to sleep tonight if they didn't—

She jerked the thought to a halt. He was being a gentleman, and no lady brought up the subject of kissing a man who was not her husband, even if they'd been joking about it earlier. But it wasn't a joke, really. He clearly felt some sense of unworthiness, or he would have already acted upon his desire. He was such a good man, Yankee notwithstanding, and he did not deserve to feel unworthy. She must correct that misapprehension at once.

She reached up and cupped his face with her hand. "Come here." The scrape of late-in-the-day whiskers against her palm sent a rush of excitement through her belly. Her thumb brushed his mouth.

His lips parted. "What are you doing?"

"I said, come here." Sliding her hand to the back of his neck, she pulled his head down. She had no idea what she was doing, but instinct took over.

And then he took over. "Oh, Selah," he whispered against her lips and kissed her.

Finally she broke away to turn her face into his shoulder. One of his arms curled around her, his other hand in the hair tumbling down her back. "Is that the way it works?" she asked, shivering.

He chuckled huskily against her temple. "It'll do for a start."

"It's not enough, is it?"

He swallowed. "Selah, I want to ask you to marry me, but I cannot. Not when I'm—"

He was not free, maybe already betrothed to someone else. Or, worse, married, and she had thrown herself at him.

But before she could shove him away, he was kissing her again, breaking her resistance into waves of overpowering sweetness. Vaguely she wondered if this was a flaw in her character, a demon that had reared itself to effect her undoing. Or something that had only to do with this particular man, which, once he was gone, would retreat safely once more into slumber. *I don't care*, she thought.

But you must care. People count on you to protect them.

He must have felt her ambivalence, for he broke away from her lips and began to kiss her cheeks and eyelids softly. "I'm sorry," he whispered. "I knew better, but you're so beautiful, and I . . . I'm not at liberty to tell you why."

"Are you tied to someone else?" She braced for his answer.

"Yes, but not in the way you mean."

"That's no answer."

"I know." He let her go.

She sat, bereft and cold, arms wrapped about herself. "I'm such a fool."

"No you're not." Again, he held his peace, and she could feel unspoken emotion pulsing from him. She moved to rise, but he put his arm about her and held her still. "Wait. I'm going to show you what's in my pocket." He reached into the interior pocket under her shoulder and withdrew a square of fabric.

She took it, felt the fine lawn linen, ran her thumb over the nubbiness of stitching in one corner. "It's a handkerchief."

"Yes, do you recognize it?"

"Levi, it's dark, I can't see——"

"It's yours. At least I'm pretty sure it is. I found it in the crawl space under the porch, the first day I was here."

"Oh." She didn't know how to feel, so she shut off feeling for the moment. "Yes, I was working on it when . . . Why were you looking under the porch?"

"Just a routine inspection of a property I wanted to manage."

"And why did you keep this? Why didn't you give it to me right away?" Here was the central question. She knew it.

"Because . . ." His indrawn breath was ragged. "Because I knew it was something important. Because I suspected it was yours and meant something to you. Because already I was——" His hand tucked under her jaw and lifted her face. "I was already halfway in love with you."

"You couldn't have been. We barely knew each other."

"We still barely know each other. But listen to me, Selah. I'm doing everything in my power to straighten it all out, and if you'll just be patient, very soon I'll be able to explain and come to you as a man ought to. I'm asking you now to trust me, no matter what happens. Trust that I want the best for you and your family." He kissed her lips, gently, barely a brush, then pressed the handkerchief into her hand. "So keep this and remember what I just said. I'll ask for it back one day."

She stared up into the shadows of his face and said resentfully, "You didn't ask me if I——"

"I know you do." She heard the smile in his voice. "Call it Yankee brilliance."

Levi lay rolled up in a blanket on the back porch, using the rocker cushion for a pillow. It smelled like the old lady's lavender scent, and it made him think of his mother. Ma would love Selah. One day he would take Selah to Illinois to meet his whole family, but he would have to teach her sign language so she could communicate with Ceri. He closed his eyes and imagined an evening spent on a back porch of their own house—nothing as grand as Daughtry House, of course, but a modern cottage with indoor plumbing and gas lighting—showing her how to translate words into meaningful hand and arm movements, the facial expressions and body energy adding nuance and beauty. She was a quick study, and it wouldn't take her long to become proficient.

Oh, she was a quick study in lots of things. Kissing, for example. He turned over, pushing aside the natural direction of his thoughts. All of that in good time.

For now, he'd best focus on wrapping up this case.

So far, he had dribbles of information about several players in the drama. The starring characters seemed to be Schuyler Beaumont, Selah Daughtry, and Wyatt Priester—possibly in collusion—all of whom had been in Oxford at the time of the train wreck (though it seemed unlikely that either Wyatt or Selah would have willingly sabotaged the train on which they were passengers). All three had also been present on the day of the cupola shooting.

Wyatt had demonstrated skill with a gun, and Schuyler's arrival on the scene seemed suspiciously timed (though the presence of Aurora and her grandmother would take some explaining away). Another questionable arrival that morning had been Dr. Kidd. Levi wanted to like Kidd but had learned the hard way how deceptively charming the perpetrator of a crime could be.

Which brought him to the ice house explosives. There was a potential crime—or the possible source of the train wreck, since they matched the type of explosives found under the Buckner's Ravine bridge. Whoever had put them in the ice house had to know by now that they had been discovered. There was nothing Levi could do about that. But maybe he could lay some kind of trap by getting all of his suspects in the same room at the same time. This confounded house party Schuyler and Aurora seemed so determined to pull off might be the way to accomplish that.

He wanted to explore the link between the railroad—Beaumont in particular—and Kidd's experiments, which implicated this professor in Oxford. Levi knew he could make the trip to Oxford within the next day or two, in order to conduct a formal interview, but perhaps a better idea would be to allay suspicions by encouraging Schuyler to invite his mentor to the ball. That way, Levi could watch the interactions amongst the professor, the rail baron, and the local doctor. Of course Wyatt and Nathan would be present as well.

Levi flipped onto his back and put his hands behind his head. He liked it. And Pinkerton would approve of the efficiency of the plan.

With efficiency in mind, he hoped to receive a reply to the telegraph he'd sent yesterday to Mr. J. A. Spencer of Oxford. It was time to bring the curtain down.

Twenty-Five

March 22, 1870

Levi pulled the Daughtry House carriage into the business district hitch lot, settled the sorrels near a shady post, then hastened to hand down his two female passengers. "Watch your step there, Miss Joelle. Aurora." He glanced at Wyatt, who had already jumped to the ground. "I'm afraid you'll have to cut it a bit short today, son. I need to be back at the hotel by noon for an appointment with the tiler. But I want to talk to Doc, so I'll come get you around eleven."

"Yessir. I'll let him know." Wyatt scampered off down the street in the direction of the doctor's office.

The sisters already had their heads together, discussing their shopping strategy. That morning Levi had been somewhat taken aback to find the two younger Daughtry sisters waiting with Wyatt in the carriage house at the appointed departure time. Apparently Joelle—or more likely Aurora—deemed new dresses for the house party essential to its success. Levi had hoped to follow up on Wyatt's abstracted manner last night and discover details about his father's capture in Tennessee. Since he could hardly do that with an audience, he'd pretended to be glad of the charming company and handed the ladies up into the rear seat along with their reticules and the most recent issue of *Godey's Lady's Book*.

"Would you like me to escort you to the Mercantile first?" he asked now, quashing his impatience.

Aurora gave him her dimpled smile. "Oh, no, we can make our way just fine on our own. We plan to do lots of looking before we purchase, and nothing is more frustrating than hauling about a bored male while one discusses the advantages of braids over lace." She looked down at the watch pinned to her sash. "We'll meet you back here at . . . shall we say 11:30?"

He tipped his hat. "In that case, I shall wish you a successful shopping venture and take my leave."

He headed for the boardinghouse, where it took him less than half an hour to clear his room and settle the bill with his landlady. Since Schuyler, Aurora, and Mrs. McGowan had already relocated to Daughtry House, it seemed prudent that he should do the same. He wanted to keep a protective eye on the women; plus, if his plans came to fruition, his investigation was about to come to a boil there. Leaving his bag in the carriage boot, he tucked his journal into his coat pocket—highly conscious of the absence of Selah's handkerchief—and walked toward the telegraph and post office.

Encountering Selah this morning in the newly cleaned and refurbished breakfast room had proven to be a lesson in exquisite torture. Her appearance was neat and practical as always—the wavy dark hair contained in its usual severe coronet, a plaid fichu that matched her blue skirt pinned about her shoulders—but her brown eyes looked bruised, as though she hadn't slept well. When he questioned her, her response had been brief to the point of brusqueness.

He had wanted to draw her aside, to cajole her into talking, to make her laugh. He knew how to do that.

But for now he hadn't the right to take advantage of her obvious attraction to him. Not until his responsibilities with Pinkerton were laid to rest. So he'd settled for cutting a full-blown magnolia blossom from the tree in the front yard and dropping it into her lap before he walked out the door. Her gasp of pleasure had made him smile all the way to the carriage house.

For now his task was amassing every bit of information possible about the various suspects on his list. Inside the Tupelo telegraph office, Mr. Carpenter, the operator, greeted him as an old friend, informing him that a letter had come for him.

Levi took Pinkerton's neatly scribed envelope in hand and walked to the window to open it. The message comprised, as per Levi's request, a detailing of the Beaumont family's documented military background, filling in the gaps of what Levi had already ascertained from interviews with Schuyler and others acquainted with the family. Pinkerton's sources revealed that the Beaumonts had resided in Mobile since the early 1800s, building their fortune and reputation in the shipping industry. They had heavily invested in the M&O railroad but kept a hand in maritime trading. When the threat of war broke out, they had supported Southern interests by lending rail services to the movement of troops and using their ships as blockade runners—eldest son Jamie functioning as a quasi-pirate for five years—without sinking sums directly into Confederate coffers. Thus, when bonds went belly-up at the end of the war, the Beaumonts maintained real assets rather than the disastrous paper ones, and managed to rebuild their fortunes relatively painlessly.

All of that demonstrated a bold familial sense of adventure undergirded by cold, cunning self-preservation.

Or, depending on how one looked at it, a boatload of sheer good luck.

As for Schuyler's wartime service, there was little information. At the onset of the war, he had been too young for enlistment and, as North and South continued to thrash about in unresolved furor, had evidently never formally signed on. This led Levi to wonder if Schuyler's service might have been of a clandestine nature—for which side was anyone's guess. After all, his sister had fled the city as a known Union spy.

Levi mentally riffled through sources who might dig up further information for him. Time was of the essence. After a few minutes' thought, he sat down at the desk near the window and composed a coded telegram in answer to Pinkerton's letter. One name he'd unearthed himself, in that second conversation with Whitmore at the Mercantile, was Confederate General Maney—someone with wartime ties to Selah's father. Levi hadn't gotten around to researching further connections to postwar events in Tennessee or Mississippi. If Maney could be tied to railroad interests, then Levi might have something useful to work with. He added Maney's name to his request for information from his boss.

He addressed his next telegram to Mr. J. A. Spencer of Oxford. Halfway through a third, he snapped his fingers, wadded the form then and tossed it into the wastebasket under the desk. Whistling through his teeth, he approached the telegraph desk and handed over the two finished messages along with enough money to cover the requisite fees. "I'd be obliged if you'd send these to the persons addressed, Mr. Carpenter. I'll stop by on my way out of town to check for any replies."

Carpenter took the telegrams, studied them for a moment, then sat down at his key and began tapping.

Satisfied that he'd set several balls in motion, Levi sauntered out of the office. He glanced in the post office window as he passed. Carpenter had disappeared from behind the counter, but the back of his jacket was just visible, bent over the desk Levi had used to write his messages. Looked like he was fishing in the wastebasket.

Levi grinned.

I don't have time for this, Selah thought. She stared at the portrait in the dining room—her mother, herself, and her two little sisters—a frozen moment in times that were good.

Good for her, at least. It was a time when she'd been unaware of tension between her parents, unaware of the brewing storm of national debate. It had been painted during the summer right before she and Joelle left for boarding school.

Innocence.

She walked up to the painting, reached over the buffet to touch the canvas, followed the swirl of brushstrokes down her mother's favorite yellow gown. She could remember the sight of that gorgeous silk, the color of sunshine, draped across a boudoir chair the first time Mama put it on. Selah hadn't been able to resist picking it up to pinch it between her fingers while Horatia laced up Mama's corset so tight she could barely breathe. Even after three children, Papa could span Mama's waist with his two hands, fingers touching.

There was a fall of lace like lemon meringue along the low neckline, veiling the décolletage and drawing attention to the locket above it.

Suddenly Selah wondered what had happened to that locket. The time after Mama's passing had been a blur of grief and upset, packing bags and moving, leaving everything unessential behind. She hadn't thought to look for it upon her return after the war. Really, truly, she hadn't time to do so now, but a surge of nostalgia and curiosity drew her up the stairs to the attic. Passing through here with Levi, the day they'd found the bees, she'd been distracted by his presence, too much so to think about what was in the attic. And then so busy with the excitement of venturing into business.

Now it seemed crucial to find that locket.

Everything on the second floor was orderly, clean, awaiting new bed linens that had been ordered from Memphis. Peeking into each room, she walked around to the attic stairs, circling up from the second floor. The attic had been cleaned too—Horatia's work, no doubt. The floor was swept free of dust, just a few motes twirling in the light pouring down from the cupola above. Four sturdy cedar chests had been pushed under the eaves, leaving the central area open. A couple of rusty lanterns, a rocker with a horsehair seat, and two or three other pieces of discarded furniture took up the odd corner.

Where should she start? The two smaller chests against the back of the house proved to be unlocked when she tried the lids. Inside one she found baby clothes, diapers, tiny blankets, ruffled bonnets—free of moth holes, no doubt due to the strong cedar scent that wafted upward from the lid. All the things a young mother would treasure and save. Oh, Charmion would enjoy these so much, and Selah couldn't wait to give them to her. Smiling, she closed that trunk and opened the one next to it. No surprise, another stage of children's clothing, including small shoes and a few toys—a top, a corn husk dolly, and a set of jacks lay at the top.

Selah tucked the doll into her apron pocket and moved to the third trunk. It was locked, and she had no idea where the key might have gotten to, so she shrugged and pulled at the lid of the last one. It opened easily, and there lay the yellow dress, as if Mama had put it away only reluctantly. Once Papa left for the war, there had been no parties grand enough for such a garment. She laid her hand on it, felt the coolness of the silk, rubbed the fabric between her fingers as she had done as a child. It still had that lovely slip-slidey texture that made her want to brush it against her face or go waltzing—or both.

She stood up and shook the dress out—it had been rolled up with tissue paper inside it—then held it up to herself at the shoulders. Wrinkled a bit, of course, but it still fell in drapey folds around her feet. No mirror up here, but when she held the dress's waistline against her own, she thought it might fit with just a little adjustment. She was on the lanky side like Papa, unfortunately, without Mama's petite curves, but at least her waist was small.

Letting the dress shoosh to the floor, she dropped to her knees again to see what had been beneath it. Mama's rose-wood jewelry box lay under a pile of crinolines, a couple of nightgowns, and a gray woolen day dress. Holding her breath, she lifted out the box and thumbed open the latch.

There it was. The locket needed a good polish, but its gold

was lustrous in quality, the fragile chain piled in a careful coil. Setting the box aside, she picked up the locket and laid it cool in her palm. She closed her eyes, her mother's gentle presence palpable, not needing to open the locket to feel the sanctity of her parents' love.

Unbidden, she thought of the magnolia blossom that had dropped over her shoulder that morning. Temporary beauty indeed, but no less priceless.

Suddenly, she wanted Levi to see her in a beautiful gown, dressed to please him. She wanted to waltz in his arms, to feel his heart beating beneath her palm.

If Aurora insisted on having a ball, then Selah, as hostess, should have a nice dress.

Bundling the yellow gown over her arm, the locket still in her hand, she closed the trunk and headed back downstairs. "Charmion!" she called as she reached the ground floor. "Charmion, where are you? I want to show you something!"

Aurora had made it clear that Levi's presence was neither needed nor wanted while the women completed their shopping. But since he had a little time to spare before he needed to pick up Wyatt, some contrary imp pushed him to cross the street to the Mercantile anyway. Whitmore and his opinionated wife would make interesting additions to the upcoming Daughtry House festivities. He should definitely issue an invitation.

Inside the store, he located Aurora's feathered hat and coppery curls bobbing past a row of fabric bolts propped against the far wall. Waving at Mr. Whitmore, Levi headed that direction. "Aurora!"

She turned with a smile. "Levi! Are you done with your business? Would you like to come give me your opinion of this silk jacquard?"

"I can think of few things I know less about than patterns and weaves. I would think Joelle—" He looked around. "What have you done with your sister?"

"She said she had an errand to run while I narrowed down my choices. Come to think of it, she didn't say where she was going."

That was odd—and intriguing. "I'll see if I can locate her." Levi went back outside and looked up and down the street. Though perhaps not as analytical as Selah, Joelle was a reader, well-informed, and he'd had several conversations with her about politics and history and books they'd both read. Tupelo didn't have a library yet, but there was a bookstore next to the newspaper office. He headed that way.

He wasn't even aware that he had glanced in the newspaper office window until he'd stopped in his tracks and backed up. Joelle sat at the editor's desk, gloved hands clutching her reticule. She was talking a blue streak, her milk-and-roses complexion flushed. Finally she stopped her tirade and glared, bosom heaving, at the man across from her.

Jiminy. What in the world was going on?

The editor scowled, then reluctantly reached into a cubby behind him to withdraw a small cash till. He took out a bill—Levi couldn't decipher its denomination—and handed it to Joelle. She pinched her lips together, tucked the note into her bag, and rose. With a jerky nod, she turned and headed for the door.

Adjusting his position to make it look as if he'd just come out of the bookstore, Levi strolled back the way he'd come.

When Joelle all but plowed into him, he grabbed her arm to slow her down. "Joelle! What a surprise! Have you finished your shopping?"

Those electric blue eyes flashed to his face as she snatched her arm away. "I'm—I haven't—mercy, you startled me!" Wildly she looked over her shoulder. "I was just going to the bookstore. Aurora didn't want to come, so . . . here I am. For a little time *by myself*." Twisting the strap of her reticule, she edged toward the bookstore.

"You seem agitated," he said, moving to block her escape. "Has someone upset you?"

"Of course not. I'm perfectly fine. I just want a book. So if you'll excuse me . . ." She walked away.

He fell into step with her. Nothing like behaving like an obtuse male for a lark. "I wanted to buy something for Selah, but couldn't decide. Perhaps you could give me a suggestion." He moved to open the door of the bookstore for her.

She halted abruptly. "Mr. Riggins. Levi." Her gaze was level, defiant. "Nobody knows I come to town periodically to meet with the newspaper editor. I'd appreciate it if you didn't mention this to anyone. Especially Grandmama. Or Schuyler. Or anyone."

"Of course I wouldn't betray a confidence," he said, "not that there's anything particularly scandalous about buying a newspaper."

"I'm not buying newspapers."

"You're placing advertisements?" he said skeptically. "What for?"

"I'm not placing advertisements."

"Then what are you—oh." She was a writer. He should have seen it. "Does Selah know?"

"No."

"I don't think she'd disapprove."

"I can't take any chances. I need the money, and it's what I—it's just what I do. I can't help it."

She sounded as if she had just confessed to an opium addiction. He smiled. "What do you need money for? The hotel will be upside down for a year or two, most likely, but eventually you ladies should be set pretty well. And what about your grandmother—"

"Grandmama isn't as rich as she likes to pretend. Plus, she's cheap as stinking mackerel."

That caught him so off-guard that he laughed out loud. "What?"

"*Henry IV*," she sighed. "Why are Yankees so illiterate?"

"I'm not illiterate, and that is beyond obscure. Also, you didn't say what the money is for."

"This is a very public place for such a conversation."

"Would you be more comfortable jawing over a tankard of beer at the Rattlesnake?"

"I hate you, Levi Riggins."

He grinned at her. "One day when I'm your brother-in-law you'll appreciate me."

"I knew it! I knew she wasn't telling me something!"

He leaned in. "She doesn't exactly know it yet either. Come on, Joelle. Spill it."

"All right! Promise you won't—"

"Won't tell anybody," he finished with her. "I swear on my sainted granny, who is also cheap as stinking mackerel."

Joelle stared at him for a moment, then leaned back against the front of the bookstore, arms folded. "I want to buy books and materials for a real Negro school."

He let out a long whistle. "That's . . . quite an ambitious goal. But I don't see why you can't tell anybody."

"Because I'm a woman. The *Journal* makes me write anonymously."

"But women are published all the time."

"Not the sort of thing I write. Political commentary mostly." Joelle scowled at him. "So if you tell on me, I'll tell Selah you were a spy during the war."

Levi went cold. Did she know that for sure, or had she made a wild guess? He made himself laugh. "Don't worry, Joelle, you don't have to resort to making things up. Your secret is safe with me and my granny. Now you'd better get on back to Aurora before she suspects you've had a pint at the Rattlesnake after all. I'm going to get Wyatt, and we'll meet you ladies at the buggy in half an hour." He tipped his hat.

As Joelle sniffed and walked away with her elegant nose in the air, Levi shook his head and continued toward Doc Kidd's office. The things people did sometimes defied all logic.

So he should not have been surprised when Kidd yanked the door open before Levi even had a chance to knock. "I've been waiting on you, you slimy spy," the doctor said in a menacing tone.

Levi stood there with his knuckles in the air, considering the idea of plowing them into Doc's beaky nose. This made twice in a short while he'd been accused of spying. In the interest of deescalating tensions, however, he lowered his hand and raised his eyebrows. "I beg your pardon?"

"And well you should," Doc growled. "How dare you pump that kid, trying to worm my research out of him?"

Levi sighed. "He told you about our discussion, then."

"Yes, he told me you tricked him into confirming some

crazy suspicion of yours that I've been building *bombs* in my medical office? Have you lost your tiny Yankee mind?"

Levi was also getting tired of defending his education and intellectual capacity to these slow-talking Southerners. "Do you mind if we conduct this brawl indoors?"

Kidd blinked, nodded at a woman passing on the sidewalk, and stepped back into the office. "Come in," he said with obvious reluctance. "But I'm watching you."

Levi entered, noting Wyatt guarding the interior door—the one Doc had made sure to close when Levi visited the first time. "Wyatt," he said with a nod. "How did your lesson go today?"

Wyatt ducked his head. "Fine," he mumbled. "Dissected a fetal pig today."

"Charming," Levi said. "It seems somebody can't keep his mouth shut, and it wasn't me."

Wyatt addressed his shoes. "I felt bad—badly, that is— about giving away Doc's trade secret. I told him you misunderstood what it was all about, and those chemicals weren't—"

"Wyatt!" Doc said sharply. "Shut up."

"Oh. Yes, sir."

"Well, here's the thing, Kidd," Levi said. "You're the one who has misunderstood, apparently. I have no interest whatsoever in stealing your research."

Doc scowled. "Then what—"

"Come on, man, use your head. If *you* had come upon a cache of fuses and shells and chemicals and powder in a plantation ice house populated by a bunch of women, don't you think you'd be just a tad curious as to their origin?" Levi spread his hands. "Wyatt was there when I found them, but naturally denied any knowledge of how they got there. However, something he said made me question Nathan Vincent, who hinted that he was involved in a project having to do with electromagnetism. Which is a subject that I happen to be vaguely familiar with." He paused. "And you happen to be the only individual I've met in this godforsaken backwater town with the mental capacity to understand such a complex idea, let alone develop a practical use for it. It wasn't such a great leap."

One of Doc's eyebrows lifted. "Laying it on a bit thick, old son."

"I'm a hotel developer," Levi insisted. "What would I care about electrical wires and chemicals?"

"That's the question, isn't it? Why *were* you poking around in my business?"

Levi knew he'd better be careful with the rest of this conversation. "I'm always interested in making connections with innovators who are developing technical advances with applications for the service industries. Transportation, lodging, food, communication. From now on into the next century, people are going to be more mobile than ever. That type of development and research requires funding. Lots of it. And that's my specialty. Look how I connected Beaumont and the Daughtry ladies."

Doc stared at him, blue eyes piercing. Finally he released a disgusted breath. "I *hate* that part of the process. It does take money to purchase materials and equipment, and to feed myself while I'm testing and failing, analyzing and regrouping, and then testing again. But hobnobbing with people who understand nothing about my work, who just want to *use* it, is a waste of precious time. I'm not naive—I know that what I'm doing will make somebody wealthy. But I honestly couldn't care less if that somebody is me. I simply want to give people longer, more productive, less painful lives."

The longer Kidd's speech went on, the more convinced Levi became that he had not located his master criminal. But that did not mean Doc didn't have some information that might lead him to the right person—or group of people.

Levi held up a hand. "Wait. That's all fine. But it still doesn't explain those materials I found at Daughtry House. Most of it was Confederate issue, and I'm assuming you didn't sit out the war."

"Of course I didn't. I organized a battlefield hospital right here at the Gum Tree Hotel and treated whoever came my way—whatever the color of his uniform. But, Riggins, I'm a physician! What on earth would I do with ammunition shells?"

"Well, there's that," Levi admitted. "So let's assume you weren't storing materials at Ithaca. You did happen along there more than once—at suspicious times and with no plausible excuse."

Doc blew out a disgusted breath. "One needs an excuse for a social visit?"

"If one is an antisocial curmudgeon, one does."

"I'll have you know I get along quite well with my patients."

"That would be people who are too sick to argue."

They stared at one another. Finally Doc shrugged and looked at Wyatt. "Go sit on the porch for a few minutes, son."

"But Doc—"

"Obey me."

Wyatt left, slamming the front door.

Doc started to pace the room. "This goes no further, do you hear me?"

"Of course." Levi simply stood where he was. He would write down what he heard later.

"There's a lady I'm fond of who lives in the neighborhood."

"A what?" Ithaca wasn't exactly a neighborhood. It was several square miles of plantation inhabited by one white family. Of course it was possible that Kidd was involved in an interracial affair.

"You heard me." Doc's color rose. "She doesn't know I—that my feelings are engaged. That is why I insist that you respect my privacy."

Levi nodded.

"Swear it!"

"All right!" Levi raised his hands. "I swear not to tell a soul. But what's the problem? If you would simply tell her—"

"Riggins, you of all people should understand the complications of falling in love with a difficult woman."

"What do you mean?"

Doc paused in his perambulations, his expression sardonic. "Do you think no one knows you're head over heels for Selah Daughtry?"

Twenty-Six

DAUGHTRY PAUSED TO DUST OFF HIS JACKET and straighten his tie, then limped up the steps of the Tupelo post office. Off and on over the years, he'd wondered what postmaster Daniel Carpenter thought when a Wanted poster featuring a photograph of his old friend, one of Tupelo's most celebrated Confederate officers, landed on his desk. His appearance had changed enough in nine years that it shouldn't matter, but he was about to find out.

He knew his clothes were on the ragged side, and he needed a haircut and beard trim. He'd bathed in the creek this morning before daylight, though, so at least he shouldn't smell too bad.

Once he was inside, he stopped to look around. The telegraph apparatus was new, but the Wanted posters were still tacked on the wall above the writing desk. Thumbs tucked in his suspenders, he ambled over.

Reward: $1000 for the apprehension of Jonathan Daughtry, wanted for murder—escaped from Federal Prison October 1865.

No photograph of him in his uniform, just the bald, brutal words, as if he didn't even deserve the recognition of his likeness.

An angry buzz overtook his senses at the memory of that Yankee judge pronouncing sentence. Killing a pack of rabid dogs was not murder, and neither was ridding the world of a gang of raping thieves. The world had truly gone upside down.

In one swipe, he ripped the paper off the wall, crumpled it, and cast it into the waste bin beneath the desk. The red haze bled away as he stood there blinking at the blank space on the wall. At last he was calm enough to turn around and make his way to the counter.

Carpenter greeted him with a pleasant smile. "Good afternoon, sir. How can I help you?"

Good Lord, the man had grown old. *He doesn't know me.* Daughtry wasn't sure what to think of that. "I need to send a telegram," he said.

"All right. You're new in town, I see. Supplies are on the desk over—" The postmaster frowned at the wall with the missing poster, as if he knew something wasn't right, then glanced back at Daughtry. "—at that desk. Just fill out one of the forms with your message and bring it back to me." Before Daughtry could move, Carpenter squinted. "You seem familiar. Do I know you?"

"I'm just arriving," Daughtry said. "So maybe you could give me a little further information. I'm looking for a young Yankee officer who's been staying out at Ithaca."

"Oh, you must mean Riggins, though as far as I know he's not active duty anymore. Nice fellow. You just missed him. He was in here less than an hour ago."

"That right? Was he by himself?"

"He seemed to be."

He'd missed a perfect chance to get rid of him. "Any idea where he went from here?"

Carpenter scratched his head. "Do you mind telling me why you want to know? As a government employee, I have to be careful what information goes in and out of here."

Daughtry almost drew himself up to tell the fool who he was. Just in time, he caught himself. "As you can tell, I'm not swimming in the best of circumstances. I understand Riggins is a lawyer who specializes in helping war vets like me get on the right side of property rights."

"Oh, well, in that case, I saw him head across the street to the Mercantile. Of course I don't know if he would still—"

"Much obliged."

"What about the telegram?"

Daughtry was already at the door.

He entered the Mercantile, saw no one but loudmouth Oliver Whitmore behind the counter.

"Afternoon, sir!" Whitmore called out. "Let me know if you don't see what you need."

Fuming, Daughtry turned around and walked back out. Where had that blasted Yankee gone? L. E. Vine, aka Riggins, masquerading as a lawyer, but no telling what he was really up to.

"Who you looking for?" came a querulous voice just behind him.

Daughtry turned and found a wizened old man perched

in a rocking chair near a checkerboard on a barrel. He'd been in such a hurry, he hadn't even noticed the man on the way in. "Hello, Gramps! I thought I saw a man going in here a little while ago. I seem to have just missed him, though. Young fellow, name of Riggins. You seen him?"

"I beat him in checkers just yesterday. Don't 'pear to have time for games today. What's your business with him?"

People sure were suspicious today. Daughtry laughed. "Nothing serious. Little property dispute I want his help with."

"Smart young feller, Yankee and all, can't half understand him. I think I saw him over near the bookstore with that pretty Daughtry girl—the one got the preacher drooling like a young fool."

All his girls were pretty, but he didn't bother to pursue which one. "Thanks, old man," he said, taking the steps down, "I'll just—"

"Ain't there no more, though."

Daughtry stopped, frowned over his shoulder. "What?"

"They split up, she walked over here to the Mercantile, and he went on down the street." The old man waved a gnarled hand in a vague easterly direction.

Daughtry scowled at the oldster, who looked pleased at having frustrated Daughtry's search. "How long was the Daughtry girl in here?" That would give him an idea of how far away his quarry might have gotten by now.

Gramps settled back in the rocker and closed his eyes as if he'd gotten bored with the whole conversation. "Dunno. I fell asleep. You woke me up stomping past."

Daughtry grunted and continued on his original path. Looked like he'd have to resort to wandering around town like a lost soul.

Then an elderly cackle drifted from the porch behind him. "Glad to see the Yanks didn't manage to keep you down, Colonel."

Daughtry hunched his shoulders but didn't respond. At least somebody hadn't forgotten him.

Twenty-Seven

March 23, 1870

"I understand there is an instrument here that needs a tuning." The balding, bearded man standing at the front door, bowler hat in hand and baggage at his feet, grinned broadly.

Selah tried for a frantic moment to remember where she'd seen the man before. "Mr. Spencer!" She flung her arms around him, then quickly stepped back in embarrassment. "Forgive my enthusiasm. I'm just so surprised to see you— and glad, of course! Come in!"

Chuckling, Spencer laid his hat on a side table and grasped Selah's hands warmly. "The whole family send their regards, my dear. Apologies for dropping in without warning, but Riggins wanted it to be a surprise."

"Oh, it's wonderful!" She drew him into the parlor, calling for one of the new housemaids to bring coffee and petit fours. "Take Mr. Spencer's luggage into the master suite," she told the girl, then seated her guest in the most comfortable chair in the parlor. "So tell me, how is Mrs. Spencer? And the children?"

Spencer rolled his eyes. "All was well when I left. Though there was a slight to-do this morning when Caroline decided to start calling her rag doll Jezzy—short for Jezebel. What little girl names her dolly after the wickedest queen in the whole Bible?"

Selah laughed. "Caroline must be one of those creative types like Joelle. She once got her legs birched for yanking down the curtains in her room to make a wedding train."

"I'm looking forward to meeting your sister. Isn't she the pianist in the family?"

"Yes. Aurora, our youngest sister, is here now too—along with my grandmother and several other house guests. We've had quite the uproar since going into the hotel business."

"I'll enjoy hearing all about it. Riggins wrote to say that you were able to keep from forfeiting the property to the bank after all. I must say, the place is quite impressive, driving up from the gate."

"Thank you. We've been working hard to make repairs, and our gardener, Mose, is quite talented with the landscaping. He actually helped my mother lay in the plantings many years ago. Mr. Riggins has been . . ." She looked down. "We couldn't have done any of this without him. He helped us negotiate with an investor who was once a family friend."

There was a short pause while Spencer seemed to be waiting for her to elaborate. When she didn't, he asked, "Is Riggins hereabouts? I'd like to pay my respects before I get down to the business of tuning."

"I'm not sure where he is, frankly. I haven't seen much of him in the last couple of days. He's been working to clean out the overseer's old cabin, and I've been finalizing details for the party." She hadn't had much help from her sisters, who had come back from the shopping trip with armloads of dressmaking supplies and proceeded to commandeer Charmion. Selah sighed as she thought of the yellow ball dress languishing in the wardrobe in her room.

"I see," Spencer said with a puzzled look. "I was under the impression that the two of you . . . Well, my wife always accuses me of an overabundance of romanticism. I suppose I want everyone I meet to be as happy as we are!"

Remembering the abundantly romantic evening in the pagoda, locked in Levi's arms, Selah couldn't help wishing the same thing. She held her tongue, merely lifted her shoulders unhappily.

"In that case, perhaps you'll allow me to examine my patient?" Spencer glanced at the piano on the other side of the room near the window.

"Yes, of course." Selah jumped to her feet. "Gladys will be back with the coffee in just a moment, I'm sure."

Spencer rose as well. "No rush on that, my dear. My, my, what a beautiful instrument! That offset keyboard is rather a rarity."

"That's what I understand. Would you mind if I leave you to it? I've quite a few items to take care of this morning before lunch."

"Certainly, don't mind me. I'll just be plinking and plunking for a couple of hours."

"I'll find Wyatt and send him in. I know he'll be glad to see you again. And Joelle will want to meet you!"

"Excellent," Spencer said, lifting the lid of the piano. "I shall look forward to it."

Selah fled. The piano was the last thing on her mind.

Levi didn't know much about the previous tenant of the overseer's cabin, but it had turned into quite a nice little place, once he bleached the floors and built-in shelving, replaced the mattress, and made up the bed with clean linens. ThomasAnne turned out to be his ally in the task of locating furniture. In the attic she found him two oil lamps, a horsehair rocker with a side table, and a few kitchen items. He was also now the proud owner of a sturdy pine table and chairs made onsite in some distant past. There was even a picture of a dragon-slaying knight that some enterprising youngster had painted on a box lid. There was no signature, but he suspected Joelle might be the artist, judging by its lurid color palette and dramatic brushwork. He nailed it to the wall over his bed.

He was sitting in a straight chair tipped against the wall of his tiny front porch, enjoying the cool spring breeze sighing through the trees, when he spied Selah's distinctive swinging walk coming from the direction of the pagoda.

The chair hit the floor. She had been avoiding him as hard as she could for the last day or so, and he had just let her be. But if she needed him—

He hurried to meet her. "Selah! Is something wrong?"

She tilted her head. "No, of course not. Why would you think that?" But she was pleating the edge of her apron, and her gaze skated everywhere but his face. He wanted to kiss her.

Instead, he scowled. "No reason. I've got my place fit for habitation. And Nathan and Charmion's cabin is clean and set up too."

"I was looking for Wyatt. Mr. Spencer has arrived." She folded her arms. "Levi, I wish you'd warned me he would be coming. I look a perfect fright!"

He skimmed her tidy figure. She looked pretty much as she always did. "I'm sorry, I thought you would like—"

"Never mind. I'm glad to see him, and Joelle will be thrilled to have the piano tuned. It was very thoughtful of you. So where is Wyatt?"

"I assume he's with Doc. Would you like to see my place?"

"No! I mean—" She leaned past him to peer at the cabin. "It looks very nice."

"Selah, what is the matter with you today? Something is just . . . I don't know, off."

"I have no idea what you mean." She stepped around him, walked on to the cabin, and disappeared inside. By the time he'd reached the porch, she was back in the doorway with a funny look on her face. "Where did you get that picture?"

"ThomasAnne found it in the attic."

"It's mine."

"Joelle painted it for you? Do you want it back?"

"No, I painted it. Myself. Charmion and I were . . ." She put her hands over her face.

He reached her in one step and pulled her into his arms. "I'm sorry. I didn't know. I'll give it back—"

"Don't be silly," she choked out, clutching the front of his shirt. "It just caught me off guard. I remember the day I painted it. Papa had let me use his paints—a rare treat—so I took them out on the back porch. Charmion sat down with me, to watch. She's the real artist, so she was telling me which colors to pick and we were laughing, having so much fun." Her voice roughened, and she swallowed. "Then Papa came back from hunting with some other men, and he saw me sitting there with Charmion like two close friends do. He got so angry and sent her out to the kitchen, told her never to touch his paints, and he actually whipped me. I put the painting under my bed, didn't sign it, never wanted to see it again."

"How could he?"

"Oh, Levi, he was a good man. He just didn't see our slaves as people, and he didn't want me to be hurt. In his mind it was like, you teach your child that a beautiful snake can be poisonous, and you stay away." She sighed deeply, rubbing her cheek against his chest. "I knew it was wrong, but you don't question your father. At least, I didn't then."

He gave her a silent squeeze, letting her know he heard her, dreading the moment he'd have to let go. "Your father was an artist?"

"Yes, he painted the portrait in the dining room."

He was so stunned that he couldn't formulate words. "The—what? That exquisite—what?" He released Selah to stare at her.

"You see what I mean? How could someone with such an eye for truth be so blind? Later, when I came home from boarding school one Christmas, I tried to argue, using Scripture. He didn't want to see it and would counter with verses in Leviticus and Titus and Colossians about slaves respecting and submitting to their masters." Her lips twisted. "Pointless."

"Well," he said slowly, "it's a fact that changing the mind of someone who has believed a concept from youth is nearly impossible. Especially when the surrounding society supports that concept—or at least does nothing to change it. But I admire the fact that you personally haven't caved in to society's pressure to conform in that way. Do you have any idea how courageous it is, simply to hire your former slaves? To give them a chance to regain the human dignity guaranteed in the American Constitution? Certainly it took a long time for the nation to arrive at enough of a national consensus to spell it out in the 14th Amendment. And it took a bloody, hellacious war. But we did it."

"Yes, but my father and others like him—"

"He's dead, Selah. You can't change him."

"No. He's not. I've seen him."

He gripped her shoulders. "Selah, no. I realize you've been under a lot of pressure—mental, financial, all sorts of ways—and nightmares are normal. God knows I've had my share—"

"It wasn't a dream, and I didn't imagine it." She looked as if she might faint, though.

He put his arm around her again. "Here, sit down on the step with me. Tell me what you mean."

She sat down hard, as though her knees had buckled. Her eyes closed. "It started with Wyatt. The day you and I—the day we went to the pagoda. Remember?"

As if he'd ever forget that in a hundred years. He nodded.

"Remember how distracted Wyatt was that evening? And you got him to tell us about Doc's research. Somehow. I don't know how you do that, make people say things they know they ought not say." She looked up at him, her brown eyes naked in their pain. "But I knew there was something else, because I know fear when I see it. And Wyatt is *not* afraid of Doc. So yesterday while y'all were gone to town, I sent Mose out to the woods where he and Wyatt had been hunting before, and asked him to look around to see what might have scared Wyatt. A big bear, bobcat, anything unusual."

Levi nodded, a knot growing in the pit of his stomach.

"Well, Mose came back after a couple of hours. It had occurred to him to look in an old shooting house my father built years ago, deep in the woods. He said he knew my papa would go there sometimes to get out of the house, away from all the women." Selah gulped. "Mose said it was empty, but someone's been living there. It's not too far from a freshwater creek, there would be plenty of game. There was a blanket in the house, a recent campfire outside . . ." Her voice trailed off.

"That doesn't mean it was your father. Could have just been some vagrant—"

"No, *listen*. He'd come through here about a year ago, acting pretty crazy, so I gave him some food and made him leave. Because I was afraid—well, I knew the law was looking for him. So this time I knew he'd come back. I just knew. So I went myself last night—"

"Selah!"

"I took Mose with me. I'm not stupid. But I asked him to stand out of sight and watch, with a gun ready just in case. So I started calling Papa's name before I got too close, I didn't want to scare him. And he came out looking so . . . Oh, Levi, so old and broken—he's got a patch over one eye, and you can see the scar from his hairline to his chin. He called me Penny—that's my mama—but he must've thought I was a ghost, because he didn't try to touch me, just started to cry." Selah wiped her eyes, looked up at Levi, her lips trembling. "I don't know what to do. I know he's still a wanted criminal, but he surely wouldn't hurt anybody now. So I told him I loved him and I'd bring him some food and pray for him, and I just—just left."

Levi sat staring at her, stroking her arm in an attempt to comfort, while squaring everything he knew with what Selah just told him. Jonathan Daughtry was alive, living in the area as a ghostly vagrant. He had a patch over one scarred eye. Wyatt had seen him and was afraid of him, and had described a similar man involved in the Humboldt train robbery.

But why would Daughtry sabotage a train that carried his daughter as a passenger? Unless he didn't know she would be on it. And why would he take shots at the house where his daughters lived? So much of this still didn't make any sense.

Another question occurred to him. What if Selah truly had dreamed that whole event?

She must have seen his mental wheels turning. "Ask Mose. He'll tell you." Chin set, she returned his stare.

"And you think your father's presence might explain Wyatt's odd behavior? Why would you make that leap?"

"Because I asked Wyatt about it this morning, and he admitted he'd seen an old vagrant in the woods. I told him to be careful and let him go. Doc never came for him today. The more I thought about it, the more worried I got—"

Levi jerked to his feet. "I'll go look for him now." But that would leave Selah and the rest of the women in the house unprotected against an unseen, most likely insane antagonist. Then he remembered Spencer and Beaumont, Mose and Nathan. They would make a dependable little army of defenders. He looked down at Selah, sitting on the top step of his little porch, back straight as an arrow. There was the definition of grit, a woman who would track a known killer to his lair, in the dark, with only an elderly servant for protection. "Do you know how to use a gun?" he asked her.

"Yes."

"All right. Find one and make sure it's loaded. Tell Spencer and Beaumont that I've gone to look for Wyatt, and I want them to stay in the house, armed, until I get back. For that matter, keep *everyone* inside until further notice." He would post Mose and Nathan outside to stand guard. He pulled Selah to her feet and kissed her hard and quick. "Pray for me to be able to find Wyatt."

"I will." She turned and ran for the house.

He watched until she was safely inside, then retrieved his pistol and rifle from the cabin. He tucked the Colt into the back of his waistband and shouldered the rifle. It had been a long time since he'd taken on a manhunt. He just hoped he could bring Daughtry in alive. Killing Selah's father would not be a good way to start a marriage.

She must have been mad, thinking she could hide anything from Levi. He had an uncanny knack for reading people and, as she'd pointed out, bringing their secrets to light. Secrets she hadn't even wanted to think about. Now she had to not just think, but act.

Selah went straight to the parlor and found Mr. Spencer still bent over the open piano, from which a series of random tinny, harplike noises emanated. A cup still full of coffee languished, apparently untasted, on the table.

"Mr. Spencer."

He stood up, a hand at the small of his back, and smiled at her. "Please, Miss Selah, I think we've come to the point where you may address me as James. Did you find Wyatt?"

"No, I—something has come up, and I—but I did find Levi. He sends his regards." Mercy, that sounded limp. There was no way to start this conversation that wouldn't sound melodramatic. "Mr. Spencer—James, Wyatt is missing. Levi has gone to look for him."

"Missing?" Spencer laid down his tuning wrench and approached her in concern. "What has happened? Does it have to do with your father?"

She blinked. "As a matter of fact, yes. How did you know?"

"Riggins didn't tell you he'd asked me to find out what I could about your father's wartime activities?"

"No. Why wouldn't he just ask me? I could have told him—"

"My dear, I've uncovered things that I doubt you'd have any way of knowing. Details covered up by Confederate authorities who had good reason to hide them."

Selah felt for the closest chair and sank into it. "I know why he went to prison. And I know he escaped."

"Did you also know he went to Mexico with General Maney? And that since they came back to the United States, the two of them have been systematically hunting down the Union gangs who raped and pillaged their homes?"

Twenty-Eight

Levi crisscrossed the property, surrounding his mind with prayer, even as he combed through the possible actions of his quarry. There was no guarantee that Daughtry could be counted on to pursue any logical course of action. After all, according to his own band of accomplices, he had ordered the cold execution of several men without remorse. He wasn't likely to stand for the annoying interference of a fourteen-year-old boy.

Wyatt could be dead. If Daughtry's purpose was eliminating his perceived enemies, then the boy would be high on the list. His description of the train robber matched Selah's description of her father. Though Wyatt hadn't been an eyewitness to the robbery, there was no telling how Daughtry's twisted imagination might deal with the threat.

But a methodical search to eliminate the obvious was the place to start—then he could proceed on gut instinct.

He started at the blacksmith shop, where he found Nathan Vincent at the forge, pounding at an ax blade on the anvil.

Nathan looked up and smiled. "Afternoon, boss." Throwing aside his hammer, he used a pair of tongs to lower the blade into a bucket of water. "What brings you out here on this fine spring day?"

"Nothing good," Levi said. "Whatever weapon you've got to hand, take it and get over to the main house. I want you to post a circular guard around the house, don't let anyone come or go for any reason. We've got an intruder, could be dangerous."

"An intruder? Who you think it is?"

"I'm pretty sure it's Selah's father."

"The Colonel? Thought he was—"

"—dead? Yeah, we all did. But turns out he's been camping out in a shooting house in the woods." Levi paused, gave Nathan a straight look. "So you haven't seen any signs of him coming and going? Nothing out of place?"

Nathan scratched his sweaty chest. "Come to think of it, there's been some food gone missing here and there. I just thought it was varmints out of the woods. Could've been him, I guess." He began the process of putting out the fire. "You sure you don't want me to come with you?"

"I need someone to protect the women at the house."

"Yes, sir. I'll do that. Don't you worry."

"Good man. Where's Mose?"

"Said he was going to check on the horses."

Levi nodded and headed for the barn. "Mose!" he called. "You in there?"

Mose appeared, a pitchfork in hand. "Yessir. You need something?"

Levi stalked toward him. "How long have you known he was out there?"

"Sir?"

305

"You know what I mean. You took Selah out there in the dark to see her father, and you didn't come get me. Have you lost your mind?"

The old man wilted. "I seen him a time or two, creeping around with a rusty old shotgun. He's just pitiful, Mr. Levi, like a mangy old stray dog. Couldn't hurt nobody."

"He could, and it looks like he did. Wyatt's missing."

"Naw, sir!"

"Yes, so I want you to take me where you found him last night. He's likely gone by now, but I want to look around."

"Yessir, sure enough, but what about the ladies in the house? Horatia and Charmion be there too."

"I honestly don't think he'd try to storm the house, but Schuyler Beaumont and a justice of the peace from Oxford are inside, and I sent Nathan to watch from outside. So you're going to take me to his lair, then I want you to go stand guard with Nathan."

"I'm sorry I didn't tell you, boss. Miss Selah said for me not to." Trading the pitchfork for a rifle leaning in a corner, Mose followed Levi out of the barn.

"Selah wasn't thinking straight last night, but she understands the danger now." He stopped at the edge of the woods and gave Mose a level look. "Here's what I suspect about Colonel Daughtry. He's a convicted war criminal who believes the world owes him justice. I think he loves his daughters, but if they get in the way of whatever revenge he's got planned, they could be collateral damage. And I think he may just be crazy enough to not care."

"I dunno," Mose said slowly. "I saw him one night, laying across his boy's gravestone. Crying like a baby. That's when I started leaving him food."

"What boy? I thought there were just the three daughters."

"Infant son, born late to him and the mistress. Didn't live more than a few days."

Levi stared at Mose. "Where is the gravesite?"

Mose pointed east. "That way."

"All right. Take me to the hunting cabin first. Quiet now."

Nodding, Mose started off soft-footed.

Levi followed, listening with every step for another presence in the woods. Except for rustlings of birds and forest animals, all remained quiet. The sun filtered through the trees overhead, though soft clouds blocked some of the glare, and the crisp odor of new plant growth belied the serious nature of their mission. It was almost as if this search would have been more appropriately conducted in the dark or in a winter snow.

After a ten-minute walk, Mose halted behind a scrub oak outside a clearing, where a tiny rough cabin, little more than four walls with a door and three rectangular windows, squatted on three-foot pilings. Levi came abreast, controlling his breath, alert to every sound. Exactly as Selah had described it, the remains of an old campfire marred the ground off to one side. It seemed abandoned, but Levi raised his rifle and approached the cabin with extreme care.

"Colonel!" he called softly. "If you're in there, I just want to talk." He stopped. "Colonel!"

There was no answer, not a scratch of sound from the cabin.

Levi approached and climbed the short ladder propped against the doorway. The little house was empty, just some chicken bones left in a corner. He returned to Mose. "He's gone."

"I knowed he would be, boss."

Levi had halfway expected it too. What now? The ice house was a long shot, but maybe they should look just in case. Levi had replaced the broken lock with a new one Nathan had fashioned and left the explosives materials where he'd found them, thinking they could be moved when the ice for the party arrived from Nashville.

When they reached the ice house, Levi knelt and rattled the lock. Finding it tight, he almost got up to leave, but then noticed some odd scratches around the keyhole. A new lock shouldn't look like that.

"Mose, this lock has been jimmied. I'm going to get the key and check to see if the explosives are undisturbed. While I do that, I want you to go make sure Nathan hasn't had any trouble."

"Yessir." Mose took off at a remarkable clip for a man his age.

Levi ran for his cabin and grabbed the key off the hook. He had turned for the door when a flash of metal on the table beside his chair caught his eye. The spyglass he'd found in the cupola and slipped into his pocket the day they'd moved the bees and the shooter had attacked.

And Levi suddenly knew where Daughtry would have gone.

The gun stood in the corner where she'd left it, just at the edge of her peripheral vision.

She'd taken it out of the gun cabinet in the library, noting with relief that someone—probably Schuyler—had recently cleaned it. Now she sat quietly, aware of its cold strength, smiling at her sisters' flirtation with James Spencer. She would not tell them of the danger outside.

Perhaps Levi was worried for nothing. Maybe Wyatt had simply decided to walk to town and meet with Doc. Or maybe he had gone to check his traps. That wouldn't be good, though, for what if he encountered Papa in the woods? What if Papa were angry? If anybody understood his volatile temper, she did.

And then there was Levi himself in danger. Papa hated Yankees. And Levi was about as Yankee as they came. Papa would likely shoot him on sight.

How on earth was she going to sit here and smile, when any minute now—

"Selah, come and sing this with me." Joelle was beckoning, incandescent with joy at having her instrument restored to perfect pitch.

Selah shook her head. "No, I can't—"

"Yes, you can! You do the harmony so well, and Aurora says she doesn't know this one."

"Why, Miss Selah!" James turned to Selah, a finger wagging. "You neglected to mention that you are a musician as well."

"Truly I'm not," she said, wishing she could sink through the floor. "What song are you looking at?"

"'Aura Lee.'" Joelle's blue eyes pleaded. "Please, it used to be Mama's favorite."

If she continued to demur, someone was going to ask her why, and she might blurt out her worry. Wouldn't it be better to keep everyone distracted and entertained, right here in the parlor? Where was Schuyler? Shouldn't she tell him to be prepared to defend them all?

James was already giving her an odd look.

She shrugged and made her way to the piano. "All right. I suppose so."

Having won the point, Joelle smiled. "Thank you, Sissy. Here's where you come in. Remember?" She plunked out Selah's part at the chorus, smiling as Selah hummed along. "That's it. I knew you'd remember. Now let's try that together."

After a few minutes of starting and stopping, Selah and Joelle sang the song from start to finish, Joelle taking the first verse as a solo, Selah taking the second, and harmonizing on the chorus both times. At the end, their little audience clapped in enthusiastic approval.

Even Grandmama looked impressed. "Well done, girls. I can see that the music lessons at that liberal boarding school paid off to some degree."

"We should have a little concert at the party!" Aurora clapped her hands. "Mr. Spencer, perhaps you'll bring a band to play for the dancing too."

James looked pleased. "I'd be honored, presuming everyone is free that evening. We've been working all winter to prepare for the spring season, and this will be our first concert. What is the proposed date of the festivities?"

"April 2 has been discussed," Selah said. "I realize that is very short notice, but—"

"Miss Selah!"

Recognizing Horatia's distinctive voice, raised almost to a shout, Selah froze. The housekeeper would never interrupt unless an emergency had arisen. She rose, excusing herself, and hurried toward the foyer. "What is it, Horatia?"

She found Horatia all but blocking the entrance of a small,

wiry man with a pair of bushy eyebrows beetling over rimless spectacles. "This *gentleman* claims to be in search of a Mr. Vine, who I never heard one word of."

"Indeed?" Assuming a polite but regal air she'd observed in her mother many times, Selah touched Horatia's elbow, then took her place in the doorway. "Thank you, Horatia, you may go. I'm sorry to disappoint you, sir, but you seem to have arrived at the wrong address."

The man shook his head vehemently. "I'm *certain* I don't have the wrong address, though the name could be an alias. The man I'm looking for is an attorney—or claims to be such. He is a tall, strapping, youngish man, aged somewhere around thirty years, with dark hair. Claims to be from Illinois—though, again, accents can be assumed."

The description fit Levi. "I don't know anyone by that name," Selah said firmly. "Good day." She started to shut the door.

The man blocked the door with his shoulder. "I was sent here—directly here—by Mr. Carpenter at the Tupelo post office. My name is Scully. I knew your pa."

A frisson of fear walked up Selah's spine. The timing of this visit couldn't have been more eerie. A man who knew her father, who also seemed to be looking for Levi under an assumed name, showing up on the day after Papa came to light at Ithaca. She glanced over her shoulder. She wished she hadn't left the gun in the parlor.

"Miss Daughtry, I really think you should talk to me." Scully's voice was quieter, not so threatening. "I have some information that you will find of interest."

"All right, but not here. Let's go out on the porch. I don't want to disturb my family." She stepped outside, closing the door behind her. A bank of storm clouds had rolled in, casting a leaden pall over the early afternoon. A chilly gust whistled past the front of the house, and she shivered. How many more weird twists could this day possibly hold? She faced Scully, chin up. "Now what is the meaning of this intrusion?"

"Believe me, I didn't want to come. But I thought I'd better warn you that your father has returned from Mexico, and—and Miss Daughtry, I owe him a lot. He did some wrong things, for sure, but all that was, in my mind, justified by the cruel way the Yanks cut us down. He could've taken me and some others along with him to prison, but he wouldn't give us up, took the entire blame for ordering what we done. Anyway, he's not in his right mind, frankly never has been the same since your ma—since he found out what happened here in '63. You know?"

Selah took a step back. "You served under my father? So you participated in that massacre?"

"It wasn't like that!" Scully wiped his sleeve across his brow, sweating in spite of the chill. "It was justice. If you'd seen those women and children on General Maney's place—"

"They deserved a trial!" she cried. "Everyone deserves a trial."

"I won't stand here and argue with you—what's done is done." Scully's voice was strained. "And your pa paid for what we all did. I came because if you was my own daughter, I'd want you to know. That man, Vine, or whatever he calls himself, is one of the men that rode onto this plantation the day your ma died. And your pa is dead set on killing him."

312

Levi crouched at the bottom of the wisteria vine, now in full, glorious purple bloom.

With the spyglass in his pocket, the first thing he'd done was return to the ice house, light a lantern, and unlock the trap door. Leaving the rifle by the door, he'd crept down the stairs, the lantern in one hand and his pistol in the other. A quick inventory led to the disturbing but not surprising discovery that wires, powder, and shells had gone missing. Heart lurching, he'd vaulted back up the stairs, doused the lantern, and picked up the rifle.

Approaching the house from the rear, he'd found Nathan standing guard at the back porch steps. "Where's Mose? I sent him to back you up."

"Just went around to the office side. Boss, this place so spread out, I don't know how we can keep anybody from gettin' in, if they want to bad enough."

"I know. But it's worse than I thought. Daughtry's taken ammo from the ice house. You stay here while I make a perimeter check. When Mose gets back, tell him to wait so we can make a plan."

He'd gone around to the kitchen side of the house, where the wisteria climbed all the way to the roof. He remembered the day he'd clambered down from the roof to talk to Selah. The vine was old, gnarly, sturdy enough to support a climber, but now he couldn't tell for sure if the vine had recently been disturbed—there were no crushed blossoms, broken limbs, scrapes along the central bole.

He'd been so sure Daughtry was inside the house.

Then he heard Selah's voice, faint but clear, coming from the front porch. Outside? What was she doing—

He took off at a run. Clearing the corner of the house,

he saw her in deep conversation with a small, wiry man. As Levi got closer, their voices became more distinct until he clearly heard Selah say, "You are insane! He cannot have been. I would long since have known—"

"Miss Daughtry, I'm sorry, but it's the truth," the little man said. "I have no reason to lie."

"And neither have I any reason to believe you!" she replied, stamping her foot. "I insist that you leave my property this— Levi!" Her face cleared with relief as she saw him coming at a run. "What have you found? Is my father—" She broke off, glanced at her apparently unwanted visitor. "Where is he?"

"I don't know." Levi caught his breath. "I'm afraid he may have climbed the wisteria and gotten in through the cupola. Sir, Miss Daughtry has told you to leave, and—"

"So you don't remember me? I've told her who you are, you Yankee spawn of Satan! She doesn't believe me, but I'll prove it—"

Levi raised the rifle, aiming it at the man's chest. "Say another word, Scully, and I'll blow you back to Oxford."

Scully's mouth opened and closed.

"Now. You're going to sit right here and wait while I go in and deal with your old friend—" Levi jerked his head in the direction of a cane-bottom chair on the porch—"and if you're not here when I get back, I'll hunt you to the farthest ends of the earth. Do you understand me?"

Scully gulped and sat down.

Levi looked at Selah, sick with remorse. He should have told her the truth a long time ago. It was bound to come out, but he'd wanted it to be in his own time, the *right* time. Not like this.

"He's inside the house?" She looked incredulous.

"What? Oh—" He glanced up at the cupola. "Yes, I—I'm almost certain—" He got control of his voice. "It looks like he's planning to blow up the house."

"There's a room full of people in the parlor!"

"I know. I've got to get everybody out, quietly and fast. Go around back, where Mose and Nathan are waiting. I'll send the rest out to you. Don't explain too much, just say there's a situation we're trying to get control of, everybody needs to stay calm, and have them gather in the pagoda."

She picked up her skirts and ran.

There was no time to process what had just happened, no time to figure out what he was going to do about it. All he could do was shove his lacerated emotions into the corner reserved for battle operations. Most likely he was going to kill the father of the woman he loved, on top of feeling like he was responsible for her mother's death.

With a deep breath he entered the house.

Twenty-Nine

EMOTIONS TUMBLING, Selah reached the back of the house. She saw Mose and Nathan, both armed, waiting on the back porch.

"Miss Selah!" Mose met her halfway. "Where's Mr. Levi?"

"He's sending everyone out of the house, and we're to make them go out to the pagoda. I'm not sure—" She halted to catch her breath. She wasn't sure of anything. Was Levi her defender or her enemy? Had her father really put explosives in the house, threatening to demolish the very thing for which he had sacrificed his life and his freedom? Or was Levi manipulating everyone for his own purposes? Had that man Scully told her the truth? Why would she trust the word of someone she'd never set eyes on until today, above that of the man she loved, a man who had saved her life?

A flash of memory surfaced, of Levi holding her hand and telling her how brave she was. And of another time he'd reminded her that courage came with acting in spite of fear. But she also knew that, sometimes, one must hold fast through fear in order to protect someone else, as she had when waiting under the porch with Joelle. Living to fight another day.

The trouble was, none of them could fathom what stirred her father's troubled mind. Levi was acting according to what he knew. She had been avoiding what she intuitively understood. Both boxing at shadows.

What was true? God's Word was true. God, the author of life, source of love. God, who in Jesus had himself walked through every pain and difficulty she or Levi had ever experienced, and who had held her through her own losses.

And the blessings. She had so much to be thankful for. She would not give up fighting for her sisters, for her home, for this wide-open opportunity to help others.

"I'll be right back," she told Mose and deliberately walked up the porch steps, passing Nathan to open the back door.

The occupants of the house were coming through the breezeway as she entered. They talked in fearful whispers, Aurora supporting Grandmama, Joelle on James Spencer's arm. Gladys, Charmion, and Horatia followed.

"Miss Selah, where you going?" Horatia grabbed her arm. "Mr. Levi said—"

"I won't be long." Selah smiled as she gently pulled her arm away. "Keep everyone quiet."

The house was still now, eerily so. She walked under the stairs into the rotunda and looked up, turning a full circle to take in the now-sparkling chandelier, the polished staircase, the dome at the very top of the house. She didn't see Levi—he must have already gone up the stairs. Making a conscious decision to leave the gun where she'd left it in the parlor, she started to climb.

Afraid to call out, reluctant to disturb whatever evil held

her father in its grip, she took one step, then another, until she was at the second-floor landing. Quickly she scanned each empty room.

Well then. Keep going. In the attic, she paused, heartbeat thumping in her throat. Listened.

She thought she heard someone in the cupola above, the regular intake of breath after hard breath, but whether it was Levi or her father she didn't know. She took the last flight of stairs.

Emerging, she saw Levi crouched at the easternmost window, one hand on the low sill, the other holding a spyglass. His rifle was on the floor at his feet, a pistol stuck in the back waistband of his trousers. There was no one else in the room.

He turned to look at her, his expression puzzled. "I was sure he would come back here."

She walked over to stand beside him, looked over the roof of the kitchen to the edge of the woods. "Did you look in that shooting house?"

"Yes. Empty."

"The ice house?"

"He'd jimmied the lock and took some powder and wire and shells, then locked it back up." They were both silent, then Levi said, "I was going to look at your baby brother's grave, but I remembered I'd found this spyglass up here." He handed it to her.

Her throat closed. "You didn't tell me."

"No." He hesitated. "There are a lot of things I should have told you, but I couldn't because—" He rose to tower over her. "Well, it doesn't matter, except now it's more important you have the facts so you can help me figure this out."

"What facts? How did you know about my brother?"

"Mose told me. Selah, are you cold?"

His eyes were bleak with regret—for what?—and she was suddenly aware that she was indeed shivering, though the cupola was, if anything, stuffy.

"No. Explain what that man said." Wrapping her arms about herself, she looked up at him, braced for whatever he was about to say.

"All right." His voice was low, tense. "I was in Mississippi during the war. I rode with General Grierson as part of his raid through the center of the state down to Baton Rouge, and later served under Smith during the Tupelo and Meridian campaigns."

Of course she'd known he was Union, that he'd fought against her father, her uncles, her cousins from Memphis and from Georgia. She knew he'd been right here in Mississippi, and that Sherman had all but burned Meridian to the ground, practicing for Atlanta.

But Levi was *kind*, he was tender with children, and he was one of the few men with whom ThomasAnne was comfortable enough to carry on a coherent conversation. Aurora respected and obeyed him, Joelle had been heard to call him intelligent.

Selah liked him too. She more than liked him. She was falling in love with him.

She'd let him into her house, her mind and heart. She'd let him hold her and kiss her.

"I knew all that," she said, teeth chattering. "What else?"

He held the spyglass tight in both hands, twisting it round and round. "In the spring of '63, we caught a group of galvanized soldiers crossing over to Federal lines—they'd been Union prisoners of war, recruited out of Andersonville Prison into Confederate service, and they claimed they wanted to reenlist with us. Nobody really trusted them, and sure enough, one day five of them took off on a raid before daylight. My unit was sent to round them up."

"Those were the men that raped my mother and our slaves. They tore up Ithaca." Selah could barely breathe. "That's why they were in butternut."

"Yes. God help me, I got here too late." The grief in his eyes echoed her own.

"I can't—I can't—" She turned her back, unable to face him.

He took her by the shoulders, and she nearly jumped out of her skin. "Selah—"

"Don't touch me." She was shivering harder now, great wracking shudders.

"I'm so sorry, Selah." He suddenly wrapped his arms about her and pulled her back against his tall, warm body.

And to her unending shame, she let him. Hot tears rolled down her cheeks, and she bit her lips together to keep from sobbing aloud. This was how it felt to be comforted by someone strong. It would be too easy to get used to it. Her mother had depended utterly on her father's strength, had pined away without him.

Selah was not going to make that mistake.

She regained control, forced herself to relax, pulled in a raking breath. "It's all right," she said. "We survived, my sisters and I. We didn't have it as bad as most people, in fact. Now here we are, back home, with a way to make something good out of the rubble. I refuse to wallow in the past." She pushed against his arms.

"Wait, don't—" He let her go. "Selah, I know you believe in forgiveness."

Turning, she looked up at him without reply. In the silence

a guard slid between them. "We're not going to talk about the war ever again, do you understand me? It's too painful, and it stirs up things that ought not be stirred up."

His lips tightened, those fine beautiful lips that held his smile, before he shook his head and let her go. "All right. Have it your way. For now. We have to find—"

He fell as a gunshot blasted.

Fiery pain seared Levi's shoulder, and for a crazy moment he thought he was back at Brice's Crossroads. He blinked up at Selah. She wouldn't be here if—

He sat up, head swimming. "Where did that come from?" He'd been facing her, away from the eastern window. "Are you all right?" There was blood on her hands, her dress— "Get down!"

Instead she shoved him backward, leaned over him. Pressed down hard on his shoulder. He groaned with the pain.

"I'm fine," she said, teeth clenched. "It came from the kitchen roof straight across. No one there now, though."

"I'm going after him—"

"Here. Put your hand here." She moved his hand to stanch the wound. "I'm going to tie this up, then you'll stay on your back and keep pressure on while I go for Horatia." She used her teeth to rip off the bottom ruffle of her petticoat with an economy of motion he would have admired if he hadn't been struggling to remain conscious.

"Selah—"

"Shut *up*, you Yankee idiot! Save your breath."

He fainted.

Sometime later, he awoke with his shoulder still ablaze,

lying on his back on the floor, blinking up at the dome of the cupola. Something cold and hard pressed against his temple.

"I could've shot you like the dog you are, but I wanted to see your eyes when I send you to hell."

Levi couldn't place the gruff, Southern voice, though it sounded like any number of Confederates he'd faced in battle. He turned his head into the gun. He'd never seen the face before either, but he knew who it was. Long, greasy gray hair, unkempt beard, eye patch covering some disastrous mangling. The bone structure was aristocratic, the expression haughty. The good eye was a dark cinnamon brown, the pupil dilated as if he'd been a long time in a dark room.

Levi swallowed against a thick tongue. "Mr. Daughtry. I've been waiting a long time to meet you."

"And I you. The Yankee spy who's been chasing me all over Tennessee and Mississippi." The tone was taunting. "Congratulations, you were right after all. I was downstairs in the attic. You walked right past me." Daughtry pressed harder with the gun.

Levi struggled not to wince. "Then you didn't shoot me."

"Not this time. Must've been that bonehead Scully. Never could hit the broad side of a barn."

Levi studied the craggy, leonine face, looking for some shred of sanity. "I'm going to sit up," he said, "so we can discuss this like gentlemen."

"Go ahead. Looks like your shoulder is boogered up pretty good." Grinning at his own irony, Daughtry moved the gun but kept it aimed at Levi's head.

Levi sat up, sweating, agonizing jags of pain making his teeth rattle. He didn't know how long he had before Selah got back. All he had right now were his wits. And maybe the gun still stuck in the back of his pants. "You've been up here before, haven't you?" he asked.

"I wondered where I'd left my glass." Daughtry dangled the spyglass in his free hand. "General Forrest gave it to me early on in the war, as a special commendation."

"Your name is respected in these parts. Not many rich men gave up everything to join the cause."

"It's what my family does. I couldn't pay somebody else to serve in my place. My wife didn't understand, and the girls begged me not to go."

"Women aren't built for battle, that's true. But your daughter Selah—she's something else. I've never met a stronger woman. You raised her right."

"She's a pistol, sure enough. Could've married four or five times over, but she was hard to please. Not one boy smart enough or brash enough to bust down those walls of hers." Daughtry surveyed Levi, mouth grim. "I heard you making up to her one night, and if she hadn't been too close, kissing you like a whore, you'd be a dead man already. You must've been laughing to think you were right here in this house, just like before, eating our food and playing my piano while my wife lay dead upstairs, violated by your men."

"Daughtry, that's not what happened. You can read the official reports of the incident—"

"Incident!" Daughtry snarled. "My wife's murder was not an incident! And you think I'd trust the report of a Yankee officer with every reason to lie?"

Levi's reply was aborted by the sound of light footsteps running up the stairs.

He couldn't see Selah behind her father's crouching form, but he heard her gasp. "Papa!"

Daughtry jerked, the gun wavering as he turned his head. Levi grabbed for the gun but missed, and Daughtry quickly turned back, leveling the gun once more.

"Don't think I won't shoot you now that she's here," Daughtry said through his teeth. "She needs to see what a coward you are."

Selah was in the cupola, edging toward him with a bowl of water and some rags in her hands. Her face was pale, horror-stricken.

"Selah, stay back," Levi said.

She paid absolutely no attention to him, instead went around her father and knelt beside Levi. "You've broken this open again," she said. "I'm going to clean and redress it." She turned to look at Daughtry. "Papa, move. You're in the way."

To Levi's astonishment, Daughtry obeyed, letting Selah open Levi's shirt and begin to cleanse and rebandage the wound—a process which hurt like the devil.

Daughtry's eyes clouded, his expression confused. He seemed mesmerized by his daughter's capable, gentle hands, ministering to an enemy. "Penelope?"

Selah glanced at him, her smile gentle. "No, Papa, it's me."

"I know it's you," Daughtry said. "I saw you in the yellow dress. You wore it for me."

"I wore it for—" Selah met Levi's eyes, and he understood her plea for him to stay quiet. He saw her love. "I wore it for you," she said softly.

"I wanted the painting to be perfect," Daughtry said. "I wanted everyone to see how beautiful my girls were. All of them." He laughed softly. "All that red hair, all the shades of sunset."

"I know," Selah said. "I know you love us."

Daughtry blinked rapidly. "I do. Even when I'm roaring angry. I shouldn't have whipped Selah so hard, but she wouldn't say she was sorry, and you've got to quit letting the little darkies play in the house with the girls."

Selah's hand jerked. Levi caught it and carried it to his lips. He kept watching for Daughtry's attention to wander, another chance to grab the gun. Not yet.

"Charmion wasn't hurting anything, Jonathan," Selah said. "She just wanted to make something pretty."

"That's impossible," Daughtry said, frowning. "They don't—they can't—anyway, it wasn't right, she didn't have permission, and everybody was all upset over nothing."

Selah sighed as she began wrapping a long strip of bandage around and under Levi's armpit and shoulder. "Jonathan, I wish you'd put the gun down and get washed up for supper. We've got chicken and dumplings and butter beans, and coconut meringue pie for dessert."

Daughtry's eyes lit. "You know that's my favorite pie. You'll play 'Aura Lee' for me after supper, won't you?"

"I'll sing it for you now, if you'll put the gun down like I said." Selah sat back on her heels and began to sing, "As the blackbird in the spring, 'neath the willow tree, sat and piped I heard him sing, sing of—'"

"'Aura Lee,'" Daughtry finished with her. The gun dropped between his thighs, muzzle down. "'Aura Lee, Aura Lee, maid of golden hair . . .'"

Selah reached out to take her father's hand, slipping the gun away with the other. "'Sunshine comes along with thee . . .'" She handed the gun to Levi. "'And swallows in the air.'"

Daughtry was sobbing. Head down, as if he were weary to the bone.

Levi cast the gun out the window behind him. He looked over Daughtry's bent head and saw James Spencer standing at the top of the stairs, gawking at him.

"What in the name of all that's holy—" Spencer approached before Levi could react.

Selah leapt to her feet, a hand on her father's shoulder. "James, it's all right. Levi is—"

"He needs a doctor!" Spencer rushed forward.

Chaos broke loose. Daughtry felt the threat and lurched to his feet, Levi rolled to get out of the way, and Selah screamed.

The sudden movement wrenched Levi's shoulder, and his vision blurred with pain. Vaguely he was aware of Spencer wrangling with Daughtry right by the open window and Selah shouting, "Stop it! Papa, stop! Mr. Spencer is our friend!"

Gasping, Levi reached for his Colt, found it, squeezed his eyes shut in an effort to focus, then tried to follow the dancing motion of the two men. He couldn't shoot—what if Selah lunged into the line of fire? His aim was none too steady anyway.

At least Daughtry was no longer armed—but there was every possibility that, in his mania, he could shove Spencer through the window. Panting, Levi prayed for mercy, grace, miraculous intervention.

At last Daughtry gave one great shove, pushing Spencer away, toward the railing around the central opening of the cupola. In doing so, he lost his balance. He fell backward, tumbled out the window, and onto the steeply pitched roof on his back.

Levi had stood on that roof, knew how steep was the incline. The shingling was new and fresh, but Daughtry's footing was no match for gravity and physics. He went hurtling and disappeared from sight.

Selah's scream ripped into Levi, a sound he knew he would never forget if he lived to be a hundred. She rushed to the window, and he thought she might climb through. At the last second, some remnant of sanity made her instead fling herself across the windowsill, prostrate.

He crawled to her, wrapped his good arm around her waist, and pulled her back inside. Hauling her against himself, he held on while she beat at his face and chest, sobbing some incoherent, keening supplication. She gradually stilled, he kissed her hair again and again, and he realized her words had become a monotonous, raspy "no." Over and over and over. He let her cry until she was heaving in broken tearless gasps.

Levi looked over her head and saw James Spencer kneeling in prayer. He too was crying. Levi rubbed his own wet face against Selah's temple.

"It's over, sweetheart," he told her.

Thirty

IT WAS FAR FROM OVER. The men collected her father's broken body and laid him out in one of the upstairs bedrooms. James Spencer stood guard, his demeanor as solemn as if he were presiding over his courtroom in Oxford. They wouldn't let Selah in, so she huddled outside the door on a little ottoman from her parents' room, arms clasped about her middle, dry-eyed and aching with emptiness.

Scenes from her childhood rolled through her brain one after the other. Did his sins, his outright evil toward their slaves, rub off on her and her sisters? Could they ever do enough good to right the wrong? Now that he was dead, what would God have her do? What did he expect of her? The only answer she could come to was a verse that went something like, "He hath shown thee what is good; and what doth the Lord require of thee, but to do justly, and to love mercy, and to walk humbly with thy God."

A verse she would have wanted to live by in any case. And round she came back to the beginning again.

She'd been sitting there for some time and must have fallen

asleep with her head against the wall. She caught herself falling off the stool and found Charmion sitting cross-legged on the floor beside her, rounded belly cradled in her slender dark hands.

Selah straightened, rubbing her stiff neck. "How long have you been here?"

"A minute." Charmion's eyes were tender. "Mama thought you might need a little company."

Selah smiled her gratitude. "How is Levi?"

"That man don't never stop. There's something going on out at the bath house, but he said not to wake you."

"The—bath house?" She jumped to her feet. "What on earth?"

"I don't know." Charmion struggled to her feet as well. "Nathan didn't want me out there."

"That's wise, but—Stay here and keep watch for me, please, Char. I've got to go see—" She hurried out to the front porch and stood there, indecisive. The rain had started to come down in buckets, thunder booming like cannon fire, lightning bursting in jagged forks in the distance.

Too much unsettled. Scully, the man who had come here claiming to be her father's friend, had warned her that Papa was out to murder Levi. Then Papa said Scully was the one shooting from the kitchen roof. Of course the man was no longer in the chair where Levi had told him to stay. And as far as she knew, Wyatt hadn't been found. Maybe that was what was going on at the bath house.

Taking a deep breath, she walked out into the pouring rain. Within seconds she was soaked.

Selah supposed the pool and bath house were still in bad shape from the years of neglect, though Schuyler seemed determined to make it a featured amenity of the hotel. Uneasily aware of the dangers inherent in a pool and an electrical storm, she wiped her eyes as she reached the front gate. The minute thunder cracked, even if there was no rain, Papa used to make everybody get out of the water.

She was about to turn back for the house when, through the trees, she saw the new carriage and horses. Telling herself not to be afraid, she crossed the muddy road and found herself slip-sliding through weeds and underbrush. As she got closer, the sound of raised voices filtered to her. One was loud, angry, and very young—definitely Wyatt—and the other sounded like Levi. Heart hammering, she got in too big a hurry, slipped and fell. Not that it mattered. Her dress and petticoat were already ruined.

Scrambling to her feet, she stumbled on and made it to the carriage. To her surprise, Schuyler and Dr. Kidd stood beside it, maintaining an odd, anxious silence.

Doc turned with a cautioning finger to his lips.

As Selah quietly approached, Levi's calm, reasonable tone became clearer. "Wyatt, you've got to let us in to take him under arrest. The trap worked."

"Where are they?" Selah whispered to Doc.

"Wyatt's got that scoundrel Scully locked inside the bath house. He and Levi lured him in with rumors of stolen Confederate silver on that train that wrecked over at Oxford. But Wyatt apparently had a little more restitution for his father's death in mind."

"What do you mean?"

Doc grimaced. "When the boy realized your father and Scully had hunted down and murdered the men who escaped their firing squad at Chickamauga—that would be Wyatt's father and a man named Carson—he decided he was going to find a way to get even. So he cooperated with Levi's little hustle—"

"Hustle?"

"It was a set-up, Selah. Now, though, Wyatt's got his own little electrical trap set in there. All that water . . . if he pushes Scully into the pool, he's a dead man. We could break the door down, but the boy's a little out of his head, no telling what he'll do. He'd be tried for murder himself." Doc took a breath. "Levi's trying to talk him out of there."

Standing in the rain, wet to the skin, Selah felt like she'd been punched in the stomach all over again. "Levi's—*hustle*? What are you talking about?"

"Apparently our Yankee hotel agent is a Pinkerton detective who started out trying to root out a gang of train robbers and wound up mixed up in a series of murder investigations." Doc laughed softly. "I have to admit I was a bit taken aback when I realized *I* was on his list of suspects! And so were you, at least at the beginning. I presume you're cleared by now."

She should have seen it.

All those questions. His gift for eliciting information from anyone and everyone. The unexplained disappearances. The unfinished sentences, half explanations. A seemingly unending supply of funds for expenses incurred, without a real source of income. The notebook in which he kept detailed information on everyone he met. *Including me.*

Kissing her to get her to talk.

Scam.

She was a dupe, and on top of that, his part in her mother's death. That had been somewhat explained by the exigencies of war. He'd been under orders.

But this. This two-month-long lie.

L. E. Vine, or whatever he's calling himself.

He lied to me. Used me to find my father.

Reeling, she lifted her face to the rain, let it wash her in humiliation.

This whole thing was far from over.

Levi pressed his ear to the bath house door—praying for Wyatt, praying for himself, even praying for the man who'd less than an hour ago put a bullet in his shoulder. He wished he could ask Selah to pray too. She seemed to have the Lord's ear.

Wyatt had gone quiet. Levi could hear Scully's muffled curses and struggles against whatever bonds Wyatt had devised to keep him confined. The brain of a young genius housed in the body of a distraught teenage boy, bent on revenge—it was not a situation Levi had ever before encountered.

Levi realized his mistake had been in taking Wyatt's sanguine temperament at face value. The boy had seemed to be rolling with every punch thrown his way, jumping over hurdle after hurdle and landing on his feet. Perhaps there had been signs of this single-minded refusal to listen to reason. Levi Riggins, the great detective, successful solver of crime, capable of hoodwinking Southern rebels into believing he was one of them—

Double-crossed by a fourteen-year-old.

Without giving Wyatt too much information, Levi had asked if he wanted to help him in a little law enforcement sting. What teenage boy would refuse an offer like that? So

Levi, suspecting Carpenter's complicity in the ring, planted the fake telegram. Sure enough he took the bait and connected it to Scully on the other end. There was to be a casket of Confederate silver stored in the abandoned bath house at Ithaca.

But Levi had failed to anticipate Wyatt's plan superimposed on his own—setting up an electrical "experiment" designed to impress his mentors, Kidd and Beaumont, and their partner Quinlan at the university. Wyatt knew exactly what he was doing, setting up the trap that Scully sprang while Levi was occupied in the house. By the time Levi arrived on the scene, the door was locked and Wyatt was in charge.

And what was he going to do now? Talk his way out of this one? Pretend something else?

Truth. Maybe it was time for a little truth to illuminate the murky corners of this situation.

"Wyatt," Levi said quietly, "I'm going to tell you something I noticed about you, the first time I met you. You want to hear it?" He waited for a full thirty seconds, counting it down.

On beat thirty-two, Wyatt said, "Maybe. What is it?"

"I saw you had every reason to be scared and alone, but you made friends right off and took responsibility for yourself. I can't tell you how much I admire that."

"You're just trying to bluff me, Mr. Levi. It's raining and I'm tired, and I want to get this over with."

"Well, you could do that, but I hope you'll use that giant brain for some common sense for just a minute more. You and Doc, you're the kind of people who live to help others, and he says you're getting close to figuring out something really important. Are you sure you want to give that up?"

"What do you mean?"

"Well, if you, um, fry Mr. Scully in there, it's not going to go well for you. At the very least you'll be in prison the rest of your life, and all your experiments will be over. Doc will have to proceed without you."

"He deserves to fry."

"Aw now, Doc's pretty obnoxious but that's a little harsh."

Wyatt snorted. "Scully, not Doc."

"Maybe so, but that's for a jury of his peers to decide, not you. Kid, you're not God. I'm not God. None of us get to decide when or where someone else dies."

"You hypocrite, how many people did you kill in the war?"

Levi said as steadily as he could, "War is different. We were fighting for the rights of people who couldn't fight for themselves." He sucked in a breath. "And I'd do it again."

Wyatt was silent for so long Levi was afraid he was leaning into disaster. Finally, "This isn't war, is it?"

"Feels like it, I know, but it isn't. Let me take that sap-sucker in, and Mr. Spencer will see to it he gets tried for all his crimes."

Scully squealed like a pig.

"Oh, all right." Wyatt unlocked the door from the inside. His expression was vaguely supercilious. "Didn't you or Miss Selah have a key?"

"Right, I'm standing here arguing with you, key in hand."

"Oh. Yes, sir." Wyatt looked over his shoulder. "Well, come and get him. He's a little damp and scared, but none the worse for the wear."

Levi entered the bath house and found it, as Selah had predicted, a slimy mess, the marble pool black with age and mildew. Scully was tied to a chair, gagged with a bandanna, hands and feet bound with a strong, thin cord that Levi figured Wyatt had designed and constructed himself. The knots would have made a professional kidnapper proud. Levi cut the cords around the man's feet with his pocketknife but left his hands tied and the bandanna in place. He really didn't want to hear anything Scully had to say right now.

Marching him outside into the rain, Wyatt in the rear, Levi somehow felt less than victorious. Something still felt off, unfinished.

Kidd and Beaumont both looked relieved to see him but avoided his eyes as they helped haul Scully up into the carriage by the scruff of the neck and seat of the pants.

Prepared to walk back to the house with Wyatt, Levi held up the carriage with a hand on one of the sorrels' bridles. "What's wrong?"

The two men exchanged glances.

"You tell him," Beaumont said.

Doc shrugged. "Selah was here. I might or might not have told her you're a Pinkerton agent."

Levi winced. "Where did she go?"

"I don't know," Doc said, "but I'd give her a wide berth for a while."

The rain continued the rest of the afternoon, all night, and into the next morning. Selah woke in her little bed in the office cottage, feeling bruised all over.

Her father was to be buried today, between his beloved Penelope and their little son.

She dragged herself out of bed to wash her face and dress, then shortly after breakfast, the undertaker came from town. When the body was laid out in the parlor, Pastor Gil arrived

unannounced to sit with the three sisters as neighbors came by
to pay their respects and bring food. Selah found Gil's lanky
awkwardness oddly comforting, and even Joelle allowed him
to hold her hand as he prayed over them. Aurora started out
sitting a little aloof, as though not sure of her welcome, but
Selah beckoned her close, slipping an arm around her.

Aurora nestled into Selah's shoulder, whispering, "I missed
you both so much!"

"I know, darling," Selah said. "We need you too."

It was true. They all needed each other. At the gravesite
the three of them linked arms and watched as the casket was
lowered into the ground. Gil read a section of Scripture, then
prayed again, and several of the Daughtrys' former slaves—
now free employees of the hotel—shoveled dirt into the grave.
Something about that generous act of service soothed some
of Selah's misery, even as Charmion's company had helped
her the day before. When Joelle started singing "Nearer, My
God, to Thee," everyone joined in, concluding the simple
service, then adjourned to the house for a meal.

Selah had never felt less like eating in her life. She hardly
noticed when her sisters went ahead with ThomasAnne and
Grandmama, escorted by Schuyler, Gil, and Dr. Kidd. She
found herself thinking half-formed prayers that would skit-
ter off into memories bound up in recent events and slashed
by fears for the future. Whether she wanted to admit it or
not, the prospect of running this business without Levi was
overwhelming and frightening.

"Selah, I need to talk to you."

She jumped at the sound of Levi's voice—as if he could
read her thoughts—and found him right beside her, keeping
pace with her slow steps. "Levi, I don't feel much like—"

"I know you don't, but I'm leaving this afternoon." He took a breath, as though he wanted to add something else, then shook his head and looked at her.

She blinked. "Today?" On second thought, why would that be surprising? His case was solved.

"Yes. I'm going back to Chicago. Pinkerton has asked me to come back to debrief. But I couldn't leave without t-trying to—trying to—" He pinched his lips together, frustration evident in the hazel eyes. "I wanted to say I'm sorry."

"You're—sorry?" She laughed. "You found the criminals. We're all safe now. Everything could have been much worse. Thank you for that, by the way." She looked at his arm, bound up in a sling to keep the weight off his shoulder.

His lips parted as he stared at her for a moment. "You're not angry?"

She returned his gaze, searching for something, anything that would indicate his real feelings. If he had real feelings.

Meanwhile, she tried to figure out how she felt. "I'm not angry," she said truthfully. Angry didn't cover it. Hurt, burnt, *scalded* was more like it. "I wish you'd told me the truth from the beginning, but I suppose I understand why you didn't."

"I couldn't," he said, looking somewhat at a loss.

Good. He deserved to be as at sea as she was.

She turned and walked toward the house again.

"Wait! Selah!" He caught her in one step, took her arm, and turned her to face him.

She stepped back. *"What?"*

His hands clenched, those clever, artistic musician's hands that had cupped her face so tenderly. "Don't let us part this way. If I could undo all this I would, but—no, that's not what

I mean! I j-just wish I could m-make you trust me again, m-make you—"

"Well, that's the thing, Levi. No matter how good you are at manipulating people, you can't make people feel the way you want them to feel. Don't worry about me. I'm a big girl, way past the days of mooning over lost affections. I'll be really busy in the coming days, getting ready for Schuyler's ridiculous party. I'll write when I get a chance and let you know how things are going. I wouldn't have had the courage to go into the hotel deal without your intervention."

This time when she walked away, Levi let her go.

His palpable frustration provided a tiny bit of satisfaction. She hoped his regrets would keep him awake at night for quite some time to come. And if that was selfish, she'd ask for forgiveness at some later date.

Thirty-One

April 1, 1870

Levi sat in Pinkerton's anteroom, eyes closed, head back against the wall. After a sleepless two-day trip from Mississippi, his train had chugged into Chicago this morning, and he was looking forward to getting the debriefing behind him so that he could spend a few days at home in Jacksonville before his next assignment.

A man did not quit a job when it got hard or boring or frustrating. But leaving Selah Daughtry had broken Levi in a way that getting shot at, having to sleep atop a steamship's piano because of lack of space, and going hungry for days had never come close to.

He still couldn't get the image of her bruised expression out of his head. Of course she grieved her father's brutal death. But it was more than that. He, Levi Matthew Riggins, had torn a corner off her faith—surely he didn't have the power to destroy it completely—that only a miracle of God would rebuild.

She had changed him too. He'd never again hear a Southern accent without turning to see if it was someone he knew. He was through making judgments about people's intentions. And he constantly caught himself thinking, *I'm going to tell Selah that next time I see her*—and then remembering that there wouldn't be a next time. He had come as close to begging for forgiveness as a man ought to do, and she had slammed the door and nailed it shut. She'd told him he wasn't going to manipulate her feelings.

But as she'd pointed out, manipulation was part of his job. That wasn't going to change.

Pinkerton's office door jerked open, and the famous detective stuck his head out. "Riggins, come in! Sorry to make you wait."

Levi walked over to shake hands, then sat down in one of the extra chairs.

Pinkerton plopped down in his desk chair with his usual energy, folding his hands across his stomach. "Welcome back to civilization," he said with a grin. "Congratulations on your work on the Mississippi Central case. I like a man who can think on his feet, improvise when necessary."

"Thank you, sir."

"I don't hand out false commendations. You've earned a significant bonus with this one. Now give me your written report and let's go over it."

"Yes, sir." Levi handed over the document he'd written on the way home.

Pinkerton looked it over and asked for a few clarifications, then laid the report down and leaned forward, elbows on the desk. "All right, Riggins, that concludes your responsibilities with that case. As I said, I'm very impressed. In fact, your last couple of cases have been closed with remarkable efficiency. I'm ready to try you in a supervisory role—perhaps in our Southern division, since you got along so well there—if you're willing to consider moving."

Levi stared at Pinkerton blankly. "Supervisory? You mean sitting in an office? I don't know, sir—I like going undercover, mingling with people, interviewing, digging things up."

"Of course, and you're good at it. But I'd also like to see if you can use your head for planning and directing the top level of an investigation—sending agents out with leads, collecting and synthesizing information, keeping reports, and coordinating with this office in Chicago. I've been thinking for a while about opening up an office in New Orleans. You're young, but taking your wartime service with Grierson into account, you're also one of my most experienced agents."

Levi knew he should jump at this offer. It was a breathtaking opportunity, a chance to move up in a respected company, that undoubtedly would come with a significant pay raise—though salary hadn't been mentioned yet. Still, he hesitated.

"Could I think about it for a day or two, sir? I'd like to discuss the idea with my father."

Clearly not pleased, Pinkerton removed his spectacles and squinted at Levi. "I suppose so. But don't take too long. I want to get this settled by the end of this week, and if you turn it down, I'll need to interview other agents."

"Yes, sir. I'll telegraph within the next day or two." Levi rose, shook hands again, and left the office feeling like every kind of fool.

He'd planned to check into a hotel and get a good night's sleep before taking the next train down to Jacksonville. But blindsided by Pinkerton's offer, as tired as he was, he doubted he'd be able to rest. So instead he ate lunch at Henrici's, telegraphed his family that he'd be home tonight, and purchased a ticket to Jacksonville.

By suppertime, he was walking in his parents' door, being enveloped in warm and excited hugs, his injury exclaimed over, urged to sit down and rest. Later, with his belly full of Swiss steak with onion sauce, mashed potatoes, and green beans, along with his mother's rye rolls, Levi sat back and surveyed his family with sleepy satisfaction.

"You look like a drunken sultan about to roll off your palanquin," his sister Anwen said, translating her remark into sign language for Ceri. "You'd better go to bed and talk to us in the morning."

When everyone laughed, Levi said, "I will, but first I want to tell you all about an offer Pinkerton has made me, just today. He wants to promote me to field supervisor and send me to New Orleans."

His mother gaped. "You mean to live? Permanently?"

Levi nodded. "But I'm not sure I'm ready to leave Illinois." He looked around at them all—his father smoking a pipe, reminding him of Mose Lawrence; his mother, comfortably bouncing Anwen's eighteen-month-old Hugh on her lap, Ceri and Anwen giving one another anxious glances. How he'd missed them during the last two months. To consider parting again, especially with this new soreness in his spirit, seemed more than he could bear.

Ceri, always sensitive to his expressions, got up and put her arms around his shoulders from behind. She laid her cheek against his.

"Thank you, Ree," he said, comforted.

Ceri kissed his cheek and then calmly began to clear the plates.

But Anwen had never been one to let Levi go unchallenged. "What kind of crazy person considers turning down such a wonderful opportunity? Those Mississippi hillbillies have softened your brain!"

"Anwen!" admonished Mother.

"I've actually gotten pretty fond of those Mississippi folk." He glanced at his father. "Enough that I almost thought about not coming home at all."

Pa took the pipe out of his mouth. "You don't say."

Ceri set down the plates and clapped her hands. "Levi's got a girl," she signed.

He'd forgotten how good she was at lip-reading. "If I did," he said, "she would be with me. Unfortunately this girl won't have me."

"What's wrong with her?" Anwen said in high dudgeon. "Is she blind?"

"On the contrary, Selah is about as clear-eyed as they come. She has seen me in every possible negative light and is entirely justified in her skepticism." Delirious from lack of sleep, Levi blinked owlishly for a moment, then abruptly got to his feet. "I'm going to bed. I'll see you all in the morning."

He was asleep before his head hit the pillow.

The next morning, he woke to full sunshine glaring through his mother's filmy curtains that blew in the open window. Birds sang as if a new day were a glorious event to celebrate with the orchestra of nature—which in normal circumstances would be the case.

This day brought a heavy sense that he was headed straight into a dust storm, one that would blind and suffocate him, ultimately killing any vestige of joy. Dragging himself out of bed, he washed his face, shaved, and dressed for the day. After letting his mother fill him with pancakes and enough scrambled eggs and bacon to have fed his entire cavalry unit, he spent the morning taking care of a multitude of little projects she'd been putting off since the last time he was home.

Then he walked down to his father's store and helped stock the produce that a farm wagon had just delivered. Talking with his father and the clerks who had taken his place when Levi went off to West Point—the standing joke being that it had taken two men to replace him—he tried not to think about the decision he was supposed to be considering.

Then during his father's afternoon pipe and chess break, Pa mentioned it, sending the whole question crashing round his brain again.

Levi studied one of his knights, aware that he was about to lose this game to a master—and would have even if he hadn't had his "head full of rocks," as Pa liked to say. His father was good at patiently working the long game.

And Levi needed his wisdom right now. "Pa, I've fallen in love with Selah Daughtry. No, let me put that more truthfully. I might have fallen at first—thought she was beautiful and brave and bright and funny—just the first impression you get when you meet someone. Then I saw her fight through hard things, remain graceful and tender, admit her faults and ask forgiveness. I saw her love her family and outsiders in practical ways, stand her ground against a bully grandmother, do her best to redeem the unredeemable. Pa, she's not perfect, but I've *grown* to love her. I want to spend my life getting to know her, because I think she'll make me a better man."

Pa just looked at him. Then removed Levi's bishop. With

a little grin he said, "I would be all for that. Why don't you go and get her?"

"She sent me away! Besides, she would never leave Daughtry House—she has enormous responsibilities to a lot of people. I could never ask her to—"

"Son, when you saw your country falling apart around you, did you back off and let someone else deal with it? When Pinkerton gives you an assignment that seems more than you can handle, do you give up? Courage comes in a lot of different stripes, and being a man is fighting for what you want—whether that's in war or your livelihood or matters of the heart." Pa touched Levi's chest with the stem of his pipe. "Did you ever consider that your lady might be a little bit afraid of you too? Maybe she's wishing you would come back and knock down a few walls for her." Pa shrugged. "You won't know unless you try. Checkmate."

April 8, 1870
Daughtry House

At seven o'clock, an hour before guests were expected to arrive for the grand ball celebrating the opening of Daughtry House, Selah walked over from her bedroom in the manager's cottage. It was a fine, clear spring evening following a day spent flitting from room to room, checking and double-checking the placement of every item of furniture, every fall of drapery, the removal of the smallest speck of dust that might mar richly polished tables and gleaming fixtures and ornaments.

After serious thought, she had concluded that all family

and staff should live off-site, leaving the five bedrooms, dining room, parlor, and library in the main house available for paying guests. Joelle and ThomasAnne shared the second bedroom in Selah's cottage, while Wyatt took over the renovated overseer's cabin. For the time being, Grandmama and Aurora stayed in the main house. Selah assumed they would return to Memphis after the opening party; she'd avoided discussing the subject because she had neither the time nor energy to argue with her grandmother.

As she ascended the stairs to check the second-floor bedrooms one more time, she lifted the buttery yellow skirts of the dress that Charmion had surprised her with this morning. By some ingenious seamstress's trick, Charmion had removed the skirt of Mama's ball gown and put it back on, incorporating a tuck and bustle pattern from the current *Godey's*. The bodice's sleeves had been shortened to fluttery caps, the neckline dropping off her shoulders in a glamorous design that made Selah feel like a princess.

A working princess—which was, in her mind, an improvement on the ones who sat in a tower either asleep or braiding their hair in hopes that some useless, two-faced prince would come to the rescue.

Grinning to herself, she walked the circle around the mezzanine, peeking into each uniquely decorated bedroom. What a pleasure to finally see everything in place, ready for guests to relax and enjoy themselves. Over the course of the last week, as word had spread of the hotel's impending opening, she'd received visitors from newspapers all over the state of Mississippi, up into Tennessee, and over in Alabama. She'd given tours herself when she had time, but passed them on to Aurora when she didn't—and no surprise that her bubbly, gregarious baby sister turned out to have a strong talent for selling the amenities of a resort hotel in rural northeast Mississippi.

When she got back to the head of the stairs, she stood there for a moment, hands on the railing, looking down through the glittering prisms of the chandelier at the polished floor of the rotunda. She could hear the orchestra Mr. Spencer had brought from Oxford in the parlor. It had been a very long time since she'd danced a waltz, but maybe she hadn't forgotten how. She shoved away the thought that Levi Riggins would have been happy to remind her of the steps.

No useless regrets were going to spoil her enjoyment of this evening.

She sucked in a deep breath and was about to descend the stairs, when the random trills and scales of the orchestra stopped. After a brief pause, the piano began by itself, a haunting, leisurely solo stepping over a rippling triple-meter accompaniment. Selah stood transfixed. She'd heard that lonely melody before, but it wasn't something Joelle would have been able to perform with such tender artistry. Nor her mother. Where, where had she heard it?

Then she remembered. The day her mother died, during that terrible time she and Joelle sat beneath the porch, waiting for the soldiers in the house to leave. One of those unseen men had sat down at the piano to play part of that piece. At the time—actually until she'd discovered the delay was caused by the wait for the surgeon to come and tend to the injured women—she'd considered the impromptu concert to be horridly inappropriate.

Later, unable to get the melody out of her head, she'd discovered it to be Liszt's famous third nocturne. For a long time, the very idea of the song—based as it was on a German love poem roughly translated "Love as Long as You Can"—had scalded her heart every time she thought about her mother's sacrifice for her daughters. But over the years as the pain became acceptance, then finally healed, Selah began to look for ways to love the family she had left, with all the strength of her being, with every grace that God gave.

Now she collapsed on the top step, wrapped her arms around her knees, and listened, mesmerized. Grace. Mercy. Forgiveness. Wound from the beginning throughout Levi's counterpart to her family tragedy. When the final note resonated through the rotunda, she heaved a deep sigh and sat up. Something had come to an end.

But also . . . something new had begun. In spite of everything, she was glad she'd met Levi, glad for the things she'd learned from him, at peace with moving into whatever God had for her next.

She would begin by introducing herself to the pianist that James had brought to entertain her guests. Maybe she would find a new friend. She rose and went on down the stairs.

By the time she reached the parlor, the orchestra had disappeared, leaving just the pianist. He had torn into Mozart's Rondo alla Turca, and the first thing she noticed—because his back was to her—was the wide bulk of his shoulders, the straight line of the back, the flying fingers. Then he turned his head.

No. No no no no. But of course it was him, and why had he come back to burst through all the shattered windows that her heart had so carefully papered over?

She didn't know that she'd said his name aloud until he stopped with a discordant crash of the keys, standing so fast that he knocked the stool over backward. He turned with a jerk, and she saw that he wore a black evening dress coat and trousers with a frilled white shirt, white waistcoat, and white tie. She'd never seen him dressed in such finery—wouldn't have supposed he owned the like—and her thoughts literally splintered. Oh, it was not fair for him to come like this with no warning, no—

"Levi, how could you?" she whispered. "How could you?"

"I wired Joelle, and she thought it would be—"

"You wired—and you never thought to tell me that you could be playing piano on a concert stage in—in New York or somewhere?"

His dimple appeared then. "Well, you know we got the important things out of the way first. Like my talent for kissing."

She stamped her foot. "Stop that! I'm *angry* with you!"

"Really? Because for a minute there, you looked a little bit glad to see me. Which was the whole purpose for making Joelle keep my secret."

"Of course I'm glad to see you, but this is outrageous." She walked up to him, stepping around the piano stool. "Look at you in this—this—" She ran out of words again.

Levi looked down at himself, suddenly self-conscious. "Is it not all right? Beaumont said—"

"Don't be ridiculous. You are beautiful. And that is the point. On top of everything else, you made me believe you were a perfectly ordinary man, and I could never trust you not to—"

She had to stop, for he had seized her face in those big hands and begun to kiss her. In fact, he kept kissing her until she had to put her arms around his neck to keep from sliding to the floor.

"Oh, Selah," he said when he paused to breathe. "There are a lot of things I'm looking forward to letting you know about me. But let's begin with this. I love you. I've loved you from the minute I saw you through a train window. And I'm going to keep telling you that every day until you believe me. Here, let me show you something." He let her go—which she found dissatisfactory in the extreme—to reach into his pocket for a familiar leather-bound notebook. He paged through it, found what he was looking for, and turned it so that she could read his spiky handwriting. It said, "I have found the woman I'm going to marry," and it was dated February 25, 1870.

The day of the train wreck, when they had met.

Her eyes watered.

"Yes, I wrote that on the train before I ever talked to you." He pocketed the journal and gathered her close. "I didn't even know if you were married or not, but I liked the way you talked to Mrs. Norton, and I liked the way you bit your lip, and I could tell there was a light on behind your eyes. Maybe I didn't start out telling you everything—but trust has to be earned and learned. From here on out, I will never lie to you, even by omission. You're going to get tired of me telling you things and making you tell me things, because that's what friends do. I've watched my parents live that way all my life, and I want that. I need that. Now. I'm going to shut up and insist that you tell me I haven't made a complete fool of myself."

She kissed the crease flickering in his cheek. "You're doing really well. But at the risk of derailing everything, so to speak, I have to remind you that we are about to have a hundred people descend on us. I'm afraid we'll have to temporarily suspend this fascinating conversation." All but delirious with joy and relief, she pressed herself into Levi for another delicious moment and whispered in his ear. "I expect a waltz, sir, at the very least, before we discuss some very tricky questions."

He held her to him, the tension of his body communicating his frustration. At last he released her with a sigh and bowed. "I suppose I've waited this long, another hour won't kill me. Miss Daughtry, may I have the honor of the first waltz?"

Thirty-Two

As Selah flitted away to welcome guests at the door, Levi laid a hand over his aching shoulder, still bandaged under his shirt and coat. Perhaps the Rondo alla Turca might not have been the best choice for someone less than two weeks past a gunshot injury.

The orchestra members—who had discreetly tiptoed out of the parlor as Selah made her appearance—returned to pick up their instruments and resume their seats. As he went to a mirror to straighten his tie, Levi responded to James Spencer's questioning expression with a shrug.

With a shake of his head, the band director drew his baton from his pocket. "Some cases require a good deal of persistence. But those are generally the more satisfying when settled. Let me know if you need a little help."

Levi laughed and righted the piano stool. "Yes, sir. I will."

He spent the next thirty minutes greeting the family and staff as they gathered in the rotunda. He approached a little cluster composed of Joelle, Aurora, and their grandmother.

Joelle was dressed in a severely simple gown of deep coral silk that should have clashed with her hair but somehow made one think of sunsets, and Aurora wore a fluttery copper concoction just a shade darker than the curls bouncing about her shoulders.

Mrs. McGowan, in puce, gave Levi a disapproving frown belied by the twinkle in her eye. "It's about time you made an appearance, boy." With a sniff, she turned to stump off in the direction of the lemonade in the dining room.

Joelle flung her arms around Levi, then drew back when he grunted in pain. "Sorry, sorry! I forgot. You should at least be in a sling so people won't maul you. I suppose Selah made it worse." Blue eyes twinkling, she glanced at her sister, who was greeting the Whitmores. "What did she say?"

"About what you would expect," Levi hedged. "But I think there's hope."

Joelle huffed. "Of all the chuff-heads. You should be betrothed by now."

"Well, it's not for lack of trying!" Levi turned to Aurora. "I hear you have been leveraging the interest of the press. Are reservations coming in?"

Aurora dimpled. "Yes indeed! I'm quite pleased, and judging by the crowd tonight, we'll have to turn people away. Will you be staying here tonight? Wyatt begged me to make sure you know you're welcome to stay with him."

"I hope so. Where is the young rascal? I'll tell him thanks myself."

"Probably between house and barn. Mose has put him in charge of securing horses and equipages."

"Perfect. The busier he is, the less trouble he can get into."

"Exactly." Aurora waved at someone behind Levi. "Excuse

me, Schuyler seems to have created some crisis. I'd better go see what it is."

Joelle scowled. "I wish the man would just go about his merry way and leave us to run the hotel. Things would go a lot smoother if he'd stop interfering. It's his fault Wyatt went off into that electrical tailspin—"

"Joelle, far be it from me to disagree with such a dispassionate assessment of Beaumont's character, but remember that none of us would be here this evening without his family's money. Perhaps we should extend a bit of grace and kindness, and thereby direct his enthusiasm into . . . more appropriate channels. He really is a bright, goodhearted fellow."

"That's all you know," she muttered cryptically.

Before he could question her further, he heard the orchestra take up a lively tune to launch the party. Out of the corner of his eye, he saw Selah take the arm of an elderly gentleman in an outdated frock coat and accompany him gaily toward the parlor. Disappointed, but somehow proud of her for her choice in opening partners, he looked around and noticed ThomasAnne hovering a little apart from the crowd. She kept looking over her shoulder as if considering a route of escape.

Levi reached her before she could bolt up the stairs, and bowed. "Miss ThomasAnne, would you do me the honor of this dance? If your card isn't full already?"

"Oh, my goodness, if it isn't Mr. Riggins!" She extended her hand and blushed when he took it to his lips. "We're so happy to have you back with us. That is, are you back with us?"

He rose, smiling at her flustered pleasure at being noticed. "That, ma'am, depends on your cousin Selah's response to a certain question I plan to ask. I hope you'll put in a good word for me."

She tittered. "Of course I will! And I'd love to dance, if you're serious. I used to be quite the belle—when I was a young lady, I mean. Not that I'm *that* old, as some people like to claim." She cast a hurt glance at her aunt Winnie, just emerging from the dining room with a fluted glass of lemonade.

Since he could think of no tactful answer, Levi offered his arm with a smile. Carrying off his prize to the parlor, he found several couples already knocking about the room. The dancers seemed not to mind the awkward instrumentation of the orchestra crammed into a corner behind the piano. A couple of trumpets, a flute, and a clarinet, plus a rather wheezy violin and Spencer's tuba, managed to keep a creditably even tempo while straying out of tune only once or twice during that first song.

Finding ThomasAnne to be as good a dancer as she'd claimed, Levi enjoyed giving her an occasional twirl and watching her laugh. As the final notes sounded, her blue eyes sparkled, her freckled cheeks bloomed with color, and he realized she was a handsome woman, if not beautiful in the traditional sense. He couldn't help wondering what had happened to beat the light out of her sweet face.

As she rose from a graceful curtsey, Levi kissed her hand again and said with a grin, "That was great fun, my dear. Would you like to go again?"

"Oh, indeed I would!" She peeped up at him behind a flirtatious flick of her fan.

"Not fair, Riggins," interrupted a deep voice from behind Levi. "The rest of us would like a chance."

Levi turned to find Dr. Kidd presenting himself with a bow. "Good evening, Doctor," Levi said. "I see you've managed not to electrocute yourself since I last saw you."

"It's been a near run thing a couple of times," Kidd replied. "How's the shoulder?"

"I'll live." Levi couldn't help noting that the doctor's question masked an odd edge that he couldn't quite put his finger on. It almost seemed like jealousy. He glanced at Thomas-Anne. She had frozen, eyes downcast, one hand pleating her dark gray gown, the fan drooping in the other. "Miss McGowan, if you'd rather not dance, I'll fetch you a lemonade."

Her eyes flashed upward, wide with stark fear. "Oh, no, really, don't leave—"

"ThomasAnne, please dance with me." Kidd stared at her, hands clenched at his sides.

"I can't—"

"Yes, you can." Kidd took her hands, loosened the fingers clutching the fan, and kept her from running away by some unseen force of will.

The music started again and Levi watched, astonished, as the couple's awkward, almost combative movements relaxed into a dance of aching tenderness.

What an interesting development. He looked around for Selah, wondering if she'd noticed, but she'd disappeared from the room. The two of them seemed to be engaged in their own awkward pas de deux. Well, he wasn't going to chase her down. The waltz would arrive all in good time.

Lemonade. That would distract him for a few minutes. Tugging his waistcoat into place, he strolled from the crowded parlor into the even more crowded dining room. He snagged a tall flute of the icy beverage—apparently the ice house was back to its intended use after all the excitement of break-ins and explosives—and drifted toward a clump of guests who appeared to be engaged in a heated discussion.

Oliver Whitmore and his well-dressed wife stood in the center of the group, also composed of Schuyler Beaumont and two men and a woman Levi had not met before.

"It's unfortunately true," Whitmore said as Levi approached. "I don't wish any harm to these poor young ladies, who are only trying to hold on to their home, but if we don't stand our ground, those of us who built this town will find ourselves put out of business by an undesirable class who don't understand how to uphold decency and order."

Beaumont frowned. "Exactly what 'undesirable class' do you refer to, Whitmore? The Daughtry sisters are as educated and gentle of manners as anybody in this county!"

"Of course they are," Mrs. Whitmore said, looking sad. "Everybody knows they went to that school up in Holly Springs where a teacher was *fired* for her liberal social ideas. I'm sure that's no reflection on their home training. But I have heard a disturbing rumor that not a single white person was invited to apply for a supervisory position here. Bless her heart, Selah has elevated her personal slaves to those places without even opening the jobs up to anyone else. With so many returning soldiers out of work, that can hardly be considered a logical or fair business move."

As a murmur of agreement went up from people listening outside the central group, Whitmore patted his wife's hand. "My dear, we must be kind."

"I am being kind," Mrs. Whitmore said. "Kind enough to tell the truth. No one with any self-respect would stay in a place run by ex-slaves and loose women. I'm sure there's an explanation why none of these girls—or their poor old cousin—has married yet. You know what they say. Single for a season or single for a reason."

Levi set his drink on a table and shouldered through the crowd. "Good evening, Mr. Whitmore. I presume this is your wife whom you told me so much about on an earlier occasion." He bowed to the lady, who gave him what he considered a supercilious smirk. "Perhaps I could correct several of your misapprehensions regarding the founding and operation of Daughtry House, since I have been part of it from the beginning." He glanced at Schuyler, whose kindling expression indicated his own proximity to ignition point. "I'm sure Mr. Beaumont, one of Alabama and Mississippi society's leading bachelors and a full partner in the venture, will stand with me."

Schuyler eyed Levi obstinately for a moment, then gave a jerky nod.

Levi smiled and returned his attention to Whitmore's wife. "First of all, as a returning soldier myself, I will posit that those of us with any amount of gumption and drive have not waited five years to find ways to support ourselves and our families. We are assessing our skills and finding places in our states and communities that need them. The transportation market, for example, is exploding, and as people travel from one end of the nation to the other, more and more establishments such as Daughtry House will spring up along the railroads. You are also mistaken about the Daughtry sisters' willingness to hire their former slaves. At least four of them are more in the nature of partners, rather than employees. These people—the Lawrences and the Vincents—are not just available and willing to work cheaply. They are the most skilled and experienced managers I have encountered in all my travels across the Midwest and the mid-South. And I assure you that has been extensive. Charity has its place, certainly, but this is pure business savvy."

By now he was breathing hard, but realized he hadn't stammered once during that entire speech. He looked around to find that an even larger crowd had gathered. It appeared that he was making an impromptu speech to the entire party. Well, in for a penny, in for a pound.

"Furthermore," he said pleasantly, "I believe the public at large will find Daughtry House to be a comfortable, well-run lodging with a flair for food, entertainment, and luxury beyond compare—and word will spread to that effect. I am proud to be associated with these three beautiful sisters, one of whom I intend to marry—which completely negates your final assumption, ma'am." He bowed and stalked out of the room to stand in the empty rotunda.

He had not meant to add that last point.

Levi certainly had a carrying voice when he chose to use it. Standing in the breakfast room doorway with her sisters just behind her, Selah collapsed against the doorframe.

Aurora let out an unladylike whistle. "Well, that settles that," she said to Joelle. "I'm definitely not going back to Memphis now. I wouldn't miss the fireworks for anything!"

Joelle gave Selah a shove. "You'd better go check on him. He looks like he might lose his supper."

Selah turned her head to take in the sight of her champion and defender, standing in the full light of the chandelier with his face white as a bale of cotton. He did look a bit sick.

She took a deep breath. "Pray for me, girls." She approached Levi, vaguely aware of the buzz of conversation that had erupted after Levi left the dining room. Bees of another pesky sort, she thought. "Levi Riggins," she said quietly, "I heard what you said."

He looked at her, lips pressed together. "I'm not sorry," he said. "I'd do it again. And I'm going to keep asking until you say yes."

She laughed. "All right. I think I'll enjoy that. But I want to show you something first." Keeping a slight distance, she swayed a little while he watched, rapt. "You told me to hold on to my handkerchief until I was ready to give it back to you to keep." She reached into the front of her dress and pulled out a neatly folded scrap of fabric, then walked up to him, close enough to brush his waistcoat. "I'm ready."

"Selah," he breathed and reached for her.

"Oh, no, no, not yet." She stepped back. "Look here." She showed him the embroidered corner of the handkerchief, where she had repaired the damage to the colored thread of her initial and connected a new one to it.

"That's an *R*." His voice was low, hoarse.

"Yes. Do you know when I worked on this?"

He shook his head.

"The day after you returned it to me. When you went home to Chicago, I slept with it under my pillow every night, praying for you. Until last night. That's when I told God I wanted what he wanted for me and for you, no matter what."

"Did you?" He was smiling a little now, the color coming back into those sharp-bladed cheeks. "I told him the same thing, just a minute ago."

"Will you waltz with me, Levi?"

"I'll do better than that." He picked her up off the floor, whirled her around in a triple-meter step, and started humming the "Blue Danube." After a minute, he said, "Selah Daughtry, will you marry me? That way you won't have to take the R out of your handkerchief."

"Well, it's your handkerchief. You did want it back, didn't you?"

"How about if we share it? You have custody for a year, then it'll be my turn. And so on."

"All right. You always know the right thing to say."

"Which is a good thing, since you tend to make people angry." Levi whistled. "Mrs. Whitmore is quite the witch when she's insulted, isn't she?"

Selah laughed. "We don't have to let her stay here. It's our hotel."

"Yes . . ." He set her down, steadying her when she reeled a bit. "You do know that I have to keep my job, don't you?"

"And I have to stay with the hotel." She blinked, dizzy and in love. "We're going to figure that out. But right now I want to kiss you."

He let her.

READ ON FOR AN
EXCERPT OF *BOOK 2* IN THE

Daughtry House

Series!

One

THE WRITING WAS ON THE WALL: apparently she had been weighed in the balance and found wanting. Why else would Schuyler Beaumont have come to the opera tonight?

Joelle adjusted the focus of the opera glasses Grandmama had loaned her for the evening. The mahogany paneling, gilded gaslit chandeliers, and velvet draperies of the Green-law Opera House blurred into the background of Schuyler's laughing countenance. He was golden himself, drat him, like Dionysus come down to carouse with his mortal fraternity brothers. Clad with careless elegance in a well-tailored black suit and snowy linens, longish hair tumbling over his brow in burnished waves, he fairly glowed with *joie de vivre*.

"Joelle, are you not feeling well? Perhaps I could fetch you a lemonade."

Startled, she dropped the glasses to her lap and turned to find Gil Reese blinking at her with myopic concern. He was already halfway out of his seat.

She waved him down. "No, no, of course not. I'm perfectly

fine." She sucked in a calming breath and forced Schuyler out of her mind. Mostly. "I'm having a wonderful time."

"But you were growling. Or clearing your throat. I thought you might be about to—you know . . ." Gil's narrow, homely face flooded with color.

Joelle's older cousin ThomasAnne, seated to her left, patted her hand. "Oh, dear, I knew that fish at dinner looked suspect."

"There was nothing wrong with the fish." Amusement rescued Joelle from aggravation. "I'm not ill. I am merely surprised to find our business partner in the audience, after he assured me he'd rather be shot at dawn than—"

"—than watch a lot of fat ninnies caper about in tights, caterwauling in some foreign language." Dr. Ben Kidd, slouched in his seat on the other side of ThomasAnne, laughed. "Good line, that. As was yours that you could surely find someone to oblige him."

Joelle treated Ben to a frown. He was well aware that she'd invited Pastor Gil more or less to spite Schuyler—all three men had been present when the tickets arrived at Daughtry House three days ago by special courier. The satisfaction of watching Schuyler's lips tighten almost outweighed the discomfort of today's long train ride from Tupelo to Memphis, magnified tenfold by guilt over Gil's undying and equally unwanted adoration. It had been a great mistake to raise his hopes this way.

How many times over their lifelong acquaintance had Schuyler goaded her into some decision she'd come to regret?

"Where is he?" Gil grabbed the glasses and began to search the audience.

"Down front with that pack of loud young men." Joelle

attempted nonchalance. "The tall one in the middle with his cravat half untied."

"I don't know how you can tell that from the back." Gil handed the glasses back to her. "But I wouldn't be surprised. Beaumont is an undisciplined—" he stopped himself and glanced at ThomasAnne—"idiot."

Joelle felt no need to encourage Gil's incessant criticism of Schuyler, however justified it might be. "Shh. The lights are dimming."

"Oh, joy," muttered Dr. Ben.

The curtain opened, and Joelle was soon lost in musical euphoria. Tonight's program, Mozart's comic opera *Così fan tutte*, starred the celebrated Italian soprano Delfina Fabio as Fiordiligi. Other roles were filled by local talent, and the Memphis Symphony Orchestra accompanied with creditable style from an improvised pit at the foot of the stage.

Joelle might have her differences with her autocratic grandparent but could only be grateful for this unexpected gift of tickets to a performance she would never have been able to afford on her salary as associate manager of the Daughtry House Hotel in Tupelo, Mississippi. The lights came on for intermission, and she couldn't help glancing at her escort. The possessiveness in his expression made her jump to her feet. "I need some air."

"I'll go with you," Gil said, rising.

"No, I have to—I need to—" She circled a hand vaguely. Blushing, Gil dropped back into his seat. "Oh."

She'd just lied to a pastor, compounding her sins. But if you didn't say a thing out loud, was it really a lie? Before ThomasAnne could offer to come as well, she made her way to the aisle, stepping over people and muttering apologies.

She'd almost made it to the lobby when someone grabbed her by the arm. She whirled, set to clobber the drunk who had accosted her.

And faced the untied cravat and stubborn, slightly whiskery chin of Dionysus himself. She looked up and found Schuyler treating her to a disapproving glare.

"What are you doing out here by yourself?" he growled.

Gently bred single women didn't wander around alone. She knew that. But one didn't make it through a brutal civil war without some skill in self-defense. She should punch him after all. "That's none of your business."

"I respectfully disagree. If you are leaving, I'm going with you. I've had enough of—"

"I'm not leaving, you cretin. It's intermission. I'm doing what one does during intermission."

He eyed her suspiciously. "Women travel in packs. Where's ThomasAnne?"

"Schuyler, you are not my guardian. You are not my brother. Thank God, we are only remotely related. So what I do during intermission, and who I am with, is none of your business. But if we are being interfering and inquisitive, it occurs to me to wonder what brings you here, considering your violent disdain for the fine arts."

"Tit for tat, my lady bluestocking." Schuyler had drawn himself up so that he towered over her nearly six-foot height. "You will just have to remain in suspense."

"Well, if you're going to be childish, please excuse me while I conclude my business." She dipped a pert curtsey and turned.

"Wait—Joelle, don't go like that." He caught her hand, and she whirled.

"What, Schuyler?" she said through her teeth.

"I want you to meet my friends. These are important people who can wield great influence on the success of the hotel."

"Is that what this is? You need a pretty face to sweeten some deal you're working on?"

"No! I mean, of course you're pretty, but that's not what—" He looked at her in gratifying frustration. "How do you always contrive to twist my words to come out wrong?"

"You seem to manage that quite well without my help." When his face reddened but he somehow restrained a retort, she sighed. "I suppose I can spare a few minutes before we go home when the opera is over. Who are these important guests?"

"General Nathan Bedford Forrest, for one. He is interested in bringing his wife over to Tupelo to celebrate their wedding anniversary this summer."

She supposed she should be flattered. The general was one of the most celebrated Confederate officers to survive the Recent Unpleasantness. In fact, the man had come out smelling like the proverbial rose, retiring in seeming obscurity to his north Mississippi plantation, from whence he quietly directed the post-war recovery of the Southern ruling class.

Oh how she was going to enjoy making sure that never happened.

NOTE TO THE READER

Writing a novel set during the Reconstruction Era turned out to be an educational experience as well as an emotionally draining one. I'm not sure where the original idea came from, but somehow I thought I was going to write a light, romantic story about three sisters trying to run a luxury hotel in northeast Mississippi.

Um, for anyone who might be in doubt, five years past a bloody civil war in an economically and socially crushed culture is not exactly a lively setting.

Fortunately, though, the human spirit manages to find love, hope, and encouragement—and yes, even humor—in the darkest of times.

The elephant in the room, of course, is the complicated and emotionally charged subject of race relations. Some of what I read in the course of research made me cringe. Some of it brought me to tears. Some of it made me laugh. I tried, with the guidance of my early readers and my editor, to keep terminology both historically accurate and sensitive to the ears of modern readers. That is a really, really tricky thing to do, and if I missed the mark one way or the other, I hope the reader will forgive and put it down to "the author tried her best to tell a rip-roaring good story." I was more interested in low-level individual, family, and neighborly relationships, rather than the broader cultural impact on the nation—but that may change in later books. We'll see.

The reader may find some of the "technology" included in this story to be anachronistic or, at the very least, surprising. There was a real swimming pool at Ithaca (there was one at Waverley, on which Ithaca is based), the chandelier was lit by gas, and yes, there was indoor plumbing in some parts of the country at the time. Scientists were making great strides in experiments with electricity and magnetics, leading to the development of electric trains (though likely not by a fourteen-year-old genius).

There was a real Thompson House hotel in Oxford, Mississippi, which opened only a couple of months after the date of the events in this book. I hope that slight adjustment of fact won't ruin the story; I just couldn't resist including it. And the reader will probably be interested to know that the opening train wreck is based on a real-life tragedy (though it's doubtful it was caused by a saboteur!).

Most readers like to know which characters are "real people." Levi's wartime commander, Brigadier General Ben Grierson, was quite the Union hero. Several books and historical articles have been written about his cunning and courageous exploits during his raids through Mississippi (including his memoir, which I found particularly useful and fascinating). Except for Grierson and a few well-known Civil War historical figures like Lincoln, Lee, Grant, and Pinkerton, all other characters are my own. The renegade plantation raid during the Chickamauga Campaign was based on a real event, and the fact of Southern war criminals defecting to Mexico happened as mentioned in the story. The basic plot is my own, though I read several of Allan Pinkerton's detective stories to get a feel for how an agent would function undercover. Really entertaining stuff.

For details of daily life during this fascinating period, I recommend *A Lost Heroine of the Confederacy: The Diaries and Letters of Belle Edmondson*, edited by William and Loretta Gilbraith. Belle Edmondson lived in Memphis but traveled extensively through eastern Mississippi—as a Confederate spy!—and spent a good bit of time with the Snow family at Waverley. I can't recommend this book highly enough.

I hope you enjoyed Selah and Levi's story. Meanwhile, I'll be having fun settling Joelle and Schuyler's lifelong feud! As always, I welcome comments and questions through my website at www.bethwhite.net.

ACKNOWLEDGMENTS

THIS BOOK WOULD NEVER have seen the light of day without the intervention of the "usual suspects": my agent, Chip Mac-Gregor; my editors, Lonnie Hull Dupont and Barb Barnes; my husband, Scott; and my best friend, Tammy Thompson. My son, Ryan, was also embroiled in plot twists that I would never have thought up in a million years.

For the specifics of this story, I'm greatly indebted to the Snow family, who own Waverley Plantation Mansion in West Point, Mississippi. I spent a wonderful day at Waverley in the summer of 2015, looking around, asking questions, and taking notes about life on a plantation before, during, and after the Civil War. That same week I poked around for a few hours in the Oren Dunn City Museum in Tupelo, Mississippi. A bonus of that research trip came when I was able to share a meal in Tupelo with my dear friend and fellow high school band geek, Jimmy Spencer, and his sweet wife, Monica. The Spencers answered all kinds of weird questions about their city—known to the modern world as the birthplace of Elvis

Presley—and somehow managed to refrain from shouting "Hotty Toddy" even once (Go Dawgs).

I would like to thank my new friend John McWilliams, guru of antique firearms, for instantly answering questions that it would have taken me hours of research to track down. Also DW Lynd, who helped me sort out train wreck details. All mistakes are mine, though, I assure you.

Lastly, I mustn't fail to mention the people who faithfully prayed for me as I wrote and rewrote and started over and rewrote some more . . . especially Hannah, Mom, Robin, Katie, Kim, Emma, Jan, Kathy, LG, Cindy, Bobbi, Penny, Redemption orchestra folks, Redemption staff, and members of my Grow Group. And I'm grateful to my choir students at Davidson High School for understanding and forgiving when Mrs. White gets the book deadline crazies.

I hope you guys enjoyed the story.

Beth White's day job is teaching music at an inner-city high school in historic Mobile, Alabama. A native Mississippian, she writes historical romance with a Southern drawl and is the author of *The Pelican Bride*, *The Creole Princess*, and *The Magnolia Duchess*. Her novels have won the American Christian Fiction Writers Carol Award, the RT Book Club Reviewers' Choice Award, and the Inspirational Reader's Choice Award. Learn more at www.bethwhite.net.

GET TO KNOW

Beth White

Visit BethWhite.net to

• Discover More Books

• Sign Up for the Newsletter

• Connect with Beth on Social Media

WITH SPECTACULAR DETAIL BETH WHITE BRINGS THE CULTURAL GUMBO OF THE COLONIAL GULF COAST ALIVE.

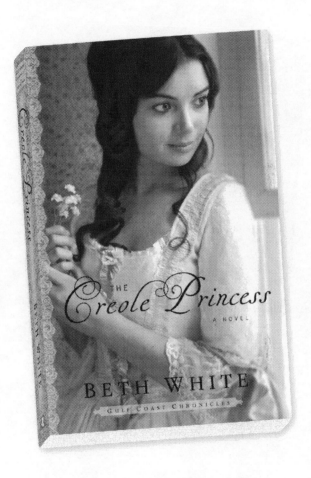

Torn between loyalties to family and flag,
one young woman is about to discover that her
most important allegiance is to her heart.

ANOTHER WAR RAGES IN FIONA LANIER'S HEART—ONE THAT THREATENS TO TEAR HER FAMILY APART.

As tensions rise during the War of 1812, Fiona Lanier must choose between protecting a handsome shipwrecked sailor and preventing her brother from becoming a casualty of war.

Printed in the United States
By Bookmasters